My Zombie Honeymoon

Love in the Age of Zombies Book One

James K. Evans

Copyright © 2015 James K. Evans
All rights reserved.
ISBN: 978-1500143459
ISBN-13: 1500143456

DEDICATION

For Gabriel and Gretchen,
my pride and my joy.

ACKNOWLEDGMENTS

Thanks to:

Vicki Connell, Stacie Court, Penny Overcash, and Adam Smith
for reading the first draft of this book and offering their advice and encouragement.

Gretchen
for her unwavering faith in me
and for technical advice on the characters' medical problems.

Stan Williams
a true friend who drove me around the back roads of Michigan.

And to the *Sure Happy It's Thursday Club:*
May your margarita pitcher never run dry.

September 19th

I went for a bike ride today. I haven't spent much time outdoors for the past couple of weeks because of all the work on the basement renovation and felt restless.

As I rode my bike through the streets, there was a strange tension in the air. The few people I saw seemed anxious to avoid me. I saw no dogs walking their people (hah!) no kids playing catch or riding skateboards. No joggers. Most houses had their blinds or curtains drawn, but even so I felt I was being watched. I couldn't help but wonder if something was going on.

I haven't watched or read the news in a long time. I'm sick of it. Sick of politics, tragedy, and especially sick of commercials. TV, radio, internet . . . it's all one big trick to manipulate me into thinking I need something I don't, or thinking that the way actresses look is the way women are *supposed* to look, when it's not. Actresses look unnatural, and the longer I go without watching TV, the less natural they look. The only problem is that when big events happen, I often don't hear about it until well after the fact. Had a big event happened? I pushed the thought away and rode on.

I headed northwest past Dexter, avoiding major roads. Out in the country, I saw a lot of stately older homes, once symbols of affluence, which have been neglected and are slowly falling apart. More than once I thought, *I'd love to restore that house to its original condition!* The detail work on those homes was fabulous despite the decline.

It was a typical fall day in Michigan. I heard crickets, although not as many as a month ago, and their call was winding down. I heard birds and an occasional dog barking. At one point I stopped where the trees had just begun turning, bright hues of red, gold, and yellow, mixing with the predominant green. They arched over the road, making it look like a tunnel. Resting on the shoulder of the leaf-strewn road a few minutes, I recalled the last time Tammy and I had gone for a bike ride out this way, before we knew she was sick. It was a day much like today, though a bit later in the season—crystal blue sky, brilliant fall foliage, cool air. The ride was exhilarating, and riding behind Tammy and watching her ass aroused me. On impulse, I pulled alongside her and said, "Follow me!"

I turned down the next side road, then down a two-track running between a field and a wooded area, and then into the woods. Tammy asked what I was doing, and I stopped my bike next to hers and kissed her passionately. We ended up making love right there in the woods, with the scent of fall around us and the slow shower of red and golden maple leaves. It was only a quickie, but it was great—until we heard the sound of a gunshot off in the distance and scrambled to get back on our bikes. We had a twinkle in our eyes the rest of the ride. It was a good time in our marriage. We were still best friends, still had a lively sex life, still gladly spent a lot of time together. It was a good day.

The memory filled me with joy and sorrow. Once again I missed her with such ferocity I could feel it in my skin. With a sigh I resumed my ride.

The traffic was horrible, even on the back roads. Many of the cars and trucks were packed as if for vacation, except families don't go on vacation in mid-September. The entire time I was competing for the road, not sharing it. On more than one occasion, horns startled me as cars impatiently accelerated past me. The traffic made me tense, and I wasn't able to commune with nature as I like. The traffic puzzled me – there wasn't a home football game, it wasn't a holiday. And yet the roads were unusually busy.

About twenty five miles into the ride, everything was shaken with the force of a huge explosion to the west-northwest. I had no idea how close or far it was. But it shook my bones and rattled my psyche.

Near Onandaga, just west of a branch of the Grand River, I stopped at a combination gas station, miniature convenient store, and pizzeria. It's one of my guilty pleasures—any time I ride out there, I stop to buy a beer. The store has the odd name of Clone's Country Store. When I asked about it the owner told me it was an old Welsh family name.

Inside, I noticed there were only three gallons of milk left, all skim. The beer cooler was almost empty as well. I grabbed the last bottle of Founder's Red's Rye and moved to the checkout. The two ladies behind the counter stopped what they were doing to stare at me.

An older woman, wearing a hair net and a somewhat dirty blue apron was making a pizza. She had a resigned, no-nonsense look about her. A younger woman with short cropped blonde hair, probably in her twenties, was slicing mushrooms. She, too, wore a hair net but instead of an apron she had on blue jeans and a white t-shirt with the blue image of a crown, and the caption

STAY CALM
and
RUN FASTER.
The bear's catching up.

    I said good morning, then asked why their shelves were so empty.
    The older lady said they hadn't had any deliveries in a couple days. Something about too many drivers calling in.
    They younger girl said with all the traffic they've been selling "more milk and stuff" in the past week.
    "That's 'cause the salmon are running on the Grand," the older lady responded. "We always sell out."
    The younger girl rang me up, but when she looked at me she raised one eyebrow. It made me think she wasn't buying the explanation her coworker offered. "Things are weird right now," she said under her breath. Something in her eyes gave me the impression she was on edge.
    "Jennie, get back here and finish slicing those mushrooms. We have five pizzas to make by noon," the older lady said.
    Jennie took my money and looked me in the eye. She didn't say another word and didn't need to. I got the message she was sending, and it gave me pause.
    "Did you hear that explosion earlier?" I asked.
    They nodded and the older lady said "One of our customers said something happened at the airport in Lansing." Good grief. The Lansing airport is probably twenty miles from here! Shaking my head sadly, I wished them both a better day and left.
    Stepping outside, I walked over to my bike, then stopped and took a long draught of the beer. While I was contemplating the sweetness of the bite, I noticed a young guy, maybe seventeen, gassing up his Jeep. On the roof rack were two classic wooden canoes, kept in marvelous condition but obviously well used. Inside the Jeep Wrangler I could see three other

guys about the same age, along with fishing and camping equipment.

I wheeled my bike over to him, taking another drink of the Founder's as I did so. "Going fishing?" I asked. Duh.

"Yeah, my friends and I have planned this for a while, and somehow this seems like a good time to go."

"Where are you headed?"

"About three hundred miles north, up into Ontario," he replied, topping off his tank.

"Getting kind of a late start, aren't you?" I asked. "It'll be dark by the time you get there."

"Yeah, it probably will be," he replied. "Looks like we'll be paddling in the dark. That's okay. It's strange," he said, "in all my years of fishing, I never considered what it must feel like to be the fish. I thought of ways to outsmart it, I tried to get in its head, I tried to figure out what it was hungry for. But I never wondered how it felt to *be* the fish . But now I think I do. I feel like a fifteen-inch brown trout during fishing season in the Platte, wary of things I don't understand, acting on pure instinct." He put the gas cap back on the tank, then stood up straight. "And right now my instincts tell me it's time to go fishing. But then again, anything's an excuse to go fishing."

He had a gentle, intelligent tone, and after another taste of my Founder's, I held out my hand. "My name's Kevin. Kevin Williams. Good luck to you and your friends. And good fishing!"

As he firmly shook my hand, he said "Thanks, Kevin. My name's Jerry. I wish you good fishing as well, whatever it is you're fishing for. Oh, and good choice in beer," he grinned, nodding toward the nearly empty bottle of Red's Rye I still held. He jumped into the Jeep and drove off. I heard country music drift out the windows, and one of the guys laughed. Inwardly I again wished them luck, and got the feeling he and his friends were walking backward into adulthood. This was their last look back on childhood, the last time seeing the world through a child's eyes. It made me sad and envious.

I got back on my bike and pedaled over the bridge toward home. I passed through Chelsea, where the actor Jeff Daniels grew up. Every time I pass near the city, I can't help but sing the Elvis Costello song "I don't want to go to Chelsea."

I saw the huge Jiffy cornbread factory silos, but the factory appeared to be closed—no tours today. As I was riding beneath and past the ornate clock tower in the center of town, the bells sounded, scaring the crap out of me. Again, there was little to no foot traffic but a lot of cars and people acting skittish. Having been on my bike for a good part of the day, I wondered if there was something on the news I missed. Otherwise, why was everyone so jumpy?

I was pedaling through a scenic back road east of the village and saw a huge maple tree in the middle of a field of hay. The upper leaves had already turned a brilliant golden-red, but most of the lower leaves were still green. It looked like it was on fire, silhouetted against a hunter green pine grove. The colors were mesmerizing. I slowed down to admire the view, then stopped as a huge shiver ran up my spine.

Standing under the maple tree was the silhouette of a man watching me. It gave me the willies but at the same time I felt silly for reacting that way.

Man up, I thought, *you're acting like a scaredy-cat.* Staring back at him, I thought *Take a picture, it'll last longer.*

I sat up straighter, went out of my way to slowly finish the bottle of beer, and began pedaling away. About a quarter mile down the road, I looked back. Whoever it was had come out of the shadows. He was still staring at me. As I watched, he began to move toward me across the field. His walk was unnatural, like he was deformed or injured.

I hurried on until I rounded a gentle curve and was out of sight, then slowed down and tried to enjoy the ride again. I figured I was just being paranoid. Even so, I was uneasy the rest of the ride, anxious and depressed. It was not the stress-relieving appreciation of nature I had hoped for. "Other than that, how was the play, Mrs. Lincoln?"

I was getting tired and ready to get back to my own sanctuary, where I, too, could sit with the curtains drawn, peering out suspiciously at people passing by. And watching the news.

I took my usual back route as I made my way home. *The fewer cars or people I see the better'* has always been my attitude. I don't ride my bike to see *people*. But I saw plenty of cars, and in the neighborhoods I saw people packing their cars, SUVs and trucks.

When I got to my street, I noticed it was locked up tight. Nearly every home had the blinds drawn and lights off except for flickering TVs. Some just felt empty. I imagined I was being watched as I rode up the driveway and secured my bike to Tammy's, then went inside and fixed a drink. Now it's time to figure out why everyone's so spooked.

September 21st

When I got back home a couple days ago I got online. The news was all about an unknown disease that has suddenly become a pandemic in Europe, Asia, and Africa. It spreads unusually fast. Details are scarce, but politicians are talking about closing the borders. A few governors have threatened to ban flights from infected countries from landing in their states. Naturally this is causing a *huge* controversy. Editorials suggest banning the flights is premature and politically motivated, while other editorials suggest *not* closing the borders shows a lack of foresight and leadership.

The World Health Association and the United Nations have supposedly had several closed door meetings to discuss the situation, but no one is talking. Having tight lipped politicians makes me nervous.

The White House released a statement offering moral support to the affected countries and is sending CDC experts to help determine the type of disease and best course of action.

Locally, the story isn't front page news yet. Hopefully it never will be.

Yesterday I met my new neighbor, Michelle. I was coming back from a short bike ride when I saw her struggling to unload a mattress from a rental truck into her garage. I called out, "Need some help?" and although at first she seemed reluctant, she ended up accepting my offer. "Welcome to the neighborhood!" I told her as I grabbed the end of the mattress. She grabbed the other end and led the way through the house into the bedroom, where the box springs was already leaning against the wall. I wondered how she'd managed to move it by herself.

Once we put the mattress down, she sighed and arched her back, stretching. Do women do that intentionally to make a guy look at their breasts, or do they honestly not realize the effect it has? Those women are either deliberately teasing men or they're signaling they're available and interested. Or else they're just naïve. But how can a guy know which it is?

I did take a quick glance at her spectacular rack (it took *a lot* of self-discipline not to stare), but did my best to look her in the eyes.

"My back is so sore from moving all these boxes!" she said, "I thought I was in better shape than this!"

As we walked back through her house, I asked if she needed help with the rest of her stuff. She said the mattress was practically the last thing on the truck. Her garage was full of boxes, and I told her I sympathized with her. Moving is such a pain. We made a bit of small talk—she's from Indiana, moving here to finish her nursing degree. I didn't ask about a husband or kids, as she wore no wedding ring and I saw no toys, sporting goods, or anything else to indicate she has a family. What if she's a lesbian? Not that it would bother me. But so many lesbians I've met are outright hostile to men, it would be a shame to feel uncomfortable with someone I share crabgrass with. Can't we all just get a lawn?

I helped her unload the few remaining boxes and one bookshelf, accepted a bottle of water from her, and again welcomed her to the neighborhood.

"It's a quiet street," I said, "several of the houses are owned by retirees. The house next door is owned by the Ericksons. They're a nice couple. He has a great garden every year. Grows hybrid tomatoes and always has plenty of squash and zucchini. The soil and climate are great for summer crops."

She glanced at her watch and said, "I'd love to chat, but I have to have the truck back to the dealer in twenty minutes. I never could have done it without your help! I owe you a big one!" Me, with my filthy mind, thought, *That should be easy—you have* two *big ones!*

Since she basically told me thanks but get lost, I said "No problem, I understand. If you need more help, just holler." I grabbed the bike and walked back to the house. I needed to work on the basement anyway.

September 28th
Much has happened in the past three weeks. I've had little time to write. I've spent nearly all my free time trying to finish the basement. Why do my projects always take five times longer to finish then I estimate and cost three times as much? Sheet rock, walls, carpet, painting—I even painted the bedroom walls with phosphorescent paint to make them seem less like a cave. It looks pretty cool. I may add a second coat so they glow brighter and longer.

I paid an electrician to wire the basement according to code. I bought a sofa and set up the grow room with tables and trays for my hydroponic garden. Once the lights come in, I'll be in business.

The disease I mentioned in my last entry is now front page news. It's been spreading across the world at an unbelievable rate, and the way it affects humans is, frankly, mind boggling. According to news reports, once you get the virus, you start running a fever which escalates rapidly to 105° or higher. This alone causes many people to die, but in addition people start vomiting and losing blood from every orifice. Antibiotics don't do a thing. Neither do antivirals. The fatality rate is 100%. But then things get very weird.

Although the media and the public (myself included) were understandably skeptical at first, reports insisted that a few hours after death, the bodies began moving again. No heartbeat, no breathing, and yet these people not only began to move around, but began to act aggressively toward any person near them. When I say "aggressively" I mean they attack any person—anyone, even former loved ones—and begin to bite them and actually ingest their flesh. Once anyone is bitten, they begin to show signs of infection within 48 hours, and the cycle continues.

The infected people do not attack other animals—dogs, cats, horses—just humans.

Scientists say the organism—virus, bacteria, whatever—takes over the central nervous system, including the brain, and suggest its singular goal was survival—continuation of the species.

While I'm just a layman, I can't help but wonder if the scientists aren't going after the wrong target. Perhaps a fungus is responsible for the disease, and merely exhibits virus-like tendencies. If this is true, antibiotics and antivirals are useless. After all, there's precedent in nature; one type of fungus grows into the brain of a particular species of ant, causing the ant to relocate to an environment deadly to it but beneficial to the fungus. When this happens they're called Zombie Ants.

Can you imagine? What if the crazy, supposedly reanimated people have had their brains taken over by a fungus? What if these infected people are releasing spores when they bite other people? Maybe that's the only way to reproduce, by biting uninfected people and turning them into the human equivalent of the Zombie Ant.

October 1st

There are now reports of the disease in the US—New York and Los Angeles were the first. Much of South America is also infected and some cities are overrun. Video clips on YouTube show huge groups of these reanimated people shuffling around. Many of them show signs of horrific injuries—blood all over them, broken bones sticking out—that sort of thing.

Several clips show them attacking uninfected people. They are not for the squeamish. The videos with sound are the worst, as you can hear the uninfected people screaming as they try to fight off their attacker. Usually they're unsuccessful.

The videos do not stay up long. YouTube removes them as fast as they're posted.

Until the scientists find a way to cure, prevent or contain the disease it's only a matter of time before it reaches Michigan. That's what the bloggers say. I hope to god it isn't true.

A lot of people—me included—are using vacation time to stay home from work. Some people have headed out of town for more remote areas. They seem to believe the disease is hiding in the shadows, ready to jump out at them.

I keep the news on in the background while I continue working. I'm not panicking; but it sure as hell keeps me motivated.

Of course, all the news channels are milking the story for all it's worth. One has regular updates of what they call *CRISIS: PANDEMIC*. Even in the face of a health crisis, they're worried about ratings.

While the public is nervous, it's mainly the survivalists who are taking any real action. By "real" I mean doing more than stocking up on beer and milk. According to the news, many web sites specializing in survivalist supplies have begun selling out.

October 5th

I purchased a gun today, a .22 caliber revolver. I think the .22 part refers to the size of the bullets but felt stupid asking. The guy behind the counter was friendly and eager to offer advice.

I told him I wanted a simple weapon for personal protection. He recommended a few in the mid-price range along with lots of technical information I didn't understand about barrel length and trigger pull.

I decided on a revolver, not a pistol. I didn't even know the difference when I walked in, but he explained how a revolver has the bullets stored in a revolving chamber so you don't have to reload between every shot. He seemed to approve of my choice, and made the comment "This isn't the best selection for protection gear, but hey, it's a start!"

I bought way more ammunition than I believe I'll ever need, but they had a special deal for customers buying guns. When deciding how much to get, I remembered when Jason was born. After we got home from the hospital I was sent out for supplies. I came home from the grocery store with a package of ninety-six diapers, and I said, "We won't need to buy any of these for a couple of months!" Only to buy just as many only two weeks later. So I figured it made sense to buy more than I thought I would ever need. Lord knows I hope I won't need it.

I went by the liquor store and purchased two cases each of Maker's Mark, vodka, and tequila. I tried to buy more, but they told me there was a two case limit for each customer. Even with the case discount they gave me, it set me back quite a bit. The store was very busy, and some people looked at me like I was crazy, buying so much, but I didn't care—and I wasn't the only one buying in bulk.

Come hell or high water, at least I'll have some good bourbon to drink. I also bought ten cases of soft drinks.

Most of the basement is finished, and the storeroom is nearly complete. I have maybe a hundred cases of nonperishable goods, bottled water, and rechargeable batteries with solar battery chargers. I have a decent first aid kit, boxes of used books and DVDs I bought in bulk, and an embarrassingly large collection of used porn which I also bought used in bulk from a guy on Craig's List. I hope the porn isn't god-awful. I know next to nothing about porn, and was too embarrassed to stand there scrutinizing the disks. Of course, there was no one I could call and ask—*Hey, this is Kevin. Can you help me pick out some good porn?*—so I just bought the whole case of DVDs. I haven't had time to look through them.

Deliveries are still coming in, but my Amazon Prime membership no longer guarantees two-day delivery. Now I'm afraid to order anything if it won't be delivered for a week or two, because I can't begin to predict what will be going on by then. Will everything be back to normal so I won't feel compelled to order (for example) the infrared, motion-sensing video system to see what's going on outside, or will I desperately wish I'd ordered it sooner?

October 7th

I've spent a little more time with my neighbor, Michelle. I had harvested a bunch of basil and had more than I can use, so I thought I'd offer some to her. As I stepped outside the house, I saw her sweeping her back deck. She waved and we chatted over her privacy fence. She seemed delighted to get the basil—fresh organic homegrown basil in October!

It was a warm afternoon, and she offered me a beer. I hesitated for a moment, then thought *why not!* She opened the gate of the fence and as we walked toward her deck she put the basil to her nose and breathed in deeply. She said she loves the smell of fresh basil.

She went inside with the basil and returned with a bottle of Bud Light. She was drinking wine from a stemmed glass. I took a long draught of the beer and was surprised to relearn how refreshing an American pilsner can be on an sunny afternoon.

When she asked how I was able to grow basil this time of year, I told her I grow it hydroponically. She seemed quite impressed, and I ended up going back home and grabbing some lettuce to give her as well, even though I'd been saving it for myself. She asked if my wife minded giving up all the basil and lettuce, and I explained that Tammy died ten years ago. We made some slightly strained small talk for a few minutes. I felt a little awkward, but at the same time couldn't help but notice how pretty she is. And how nicely the late afternoon sun fell on her body, accentuating her curves and bringing out the texture of the sweater she wore.

I still had a lot to do, so I finished the beer and told her I had to get going and came back home.

I wonder why she asked about my wife? Surely she could tell no woman lives in this house. Then again, I do still wear my wedding ring.

I miss you, Tammy. I wish you were here with me.

October 9th
I saw Michelle's naked breasts last night.

It was a happy accident, I swear. After I finished writing, I went upstairs and walked through all the rooms, looking out the windows to see if anything was going on. When I looked out the window facing Michelle's house, she was in her bedroom, taking off her sweatshirt. The room was well lit. She wasn't wearing a bra.

She had marvelously full breasts, riding high despite her age. Areolas the size of silver dollars, a wonderful dusty rose color, not dramatically darker than her skin. Her nipples were even erect. Her auburn hair cascaded over her shoulders. As she walked across the room, her breasts swayed. She looked mighty fine, let me tell you. She never looked out the window, and if she had, I doubt she would have seen me. She put on a bathrobe and turned off the light as she left the room. I breathed out a sigh—I hadn't even realized I was holding my breath—and went to bed. Like the old Tom Waits song says, I felt like I was "sharing this apartment with a telephone pole!"

I was tempted to watch some porn, but honestly I didn't have it in me. I was just too tired. My dreams were, predictably, of a sexual nature.

I can't drum up the energy to feel guilty. I wasn't spying. I didn't do it on purpose. She's the one who left her shades open and lights on. I can't help but wonder if she did it intentionally. Or, to rephrase that, I can't help but wish she did it on purpose, although I know a beautiful, big breasted woman like her has no reason to want to titillate an old geezer like me. If she knew I'd seen her, she'd probably call me a *dirty* old geezer.

Now it's time to get up, no pun intended, and face another day. I need to turn the news on and see what's happening.

Later—

While I was in the midst of my hot blooded sexual reverie, the world was falling apart.

The virus is now being reported in nearly every major metropolitan area. Atlanta. Phoenix. Miami. Chicago. New Orleans. Los Angeles. Overnight, the federal government shut down all the airports. Most of the major cities—and some minor ones—have declared martial law. No one is allowed outside after dark—and this time of year, dark comes pretty early. Blockades are being set up across major interstates, to stop people from traveling.

The President came on TV and did the usual effing political BS about staying calm, order will be restored, sacrifices have to be made, the situation is being dealt with, we will prevail, be patient, etc. I call bullshit.

The media is doing the usual share of reporting based on emotion. Rather than spending time interviewing scientists and doctors, they're focusing on the *'matters of the heart'* aspect: interviewing sobbing mothers separated from their children, wives who can't reach their husbands, that sort of reporting. Emotional drivel that doesn't help *anyone*.

People are attempting to bypass the blockades by taking back roads. Little-used country roads are sometimes bumper to bumper. And to make it worse, most of the gas stations are closed—the gas tankers have quit delivering. I wonder if Clone's is still open.

October 10th
I don't trust the TV stations. They don't sound the same. And there are a lot fewer commercials. Like many, I'm convinced they're under government control. The news outlets are all basically giving the same

message: do not panic, stay inside and the government will get everything under control in a jiffy. But a cursory surf of the net shows otherwise. Facebook was either shut down a few hours ago, or their servers couldn't handle the traffic. On YouTube people had been posting photos and videos of the traffic gridlock and footage of zombie attacks. That's what everyone calls them. It was funny the first couple of times. It's not so funny now.

Detroit is infected. Detroit!—less than fifty miles from here. People are starting to panic, and the grocery stores are a madhouse but shelves are nearly empty. I'm glad I'm already stocked up.

For years I've been spent reading dark, frightening and sometimes apocalyptic books. Books like *Thirty Seconds Later, the Hot Zone* (all the more frightening because it was non-fiction), *the Doomsday Book, The Road, No Country for Old Men.* Even though it was sometimes grisly reading, it caused me to evaluate my living situation and to ponder what I should do to prepare—just in case. Perhaps I was only looking for something to distract me from my grief, but if I hadn't prepared, I'd be a whole lot more worried than I am. Without those books and my own depressed and pessimistic view of the world, I wouldn't have spent the money on the solar panels, supplying the storeroom, turning this basement into a survival bunker or *bomb shelter* as they used to call them back during the Cold War. I had no idea anything was going to happen, and can't believe how lucky I am to have gotten as much done as I did before the bottom dropped out. The one thing I didn't do was make this place radiation proof—funny how it's not much of a worry these days.

I saw the Harvey family across the street pack up their SUV and screech out of their driveway. I don't know where they're headed, maybe to their lake house at Boyne Falls. Maybe somewhere even more remote. Maybe they have connections with a survivalist's camp where they hope to be safe.

About a half hour ago, a patrol car cruised slowly down the street. First one I've seen today. No one in the neighborhood is outside. I occasionally see slight movement of a curtain or a blind as someone looks out. For all I know, they see my curtain move when I look out. It'll be dark in another hour or so and I think people are afraid something bad might happen. I know it entered my mind.

I'm going through the house, sealing off the windows with black plastic, hoping to prevent any light from leaking out. Using black makes the window look dark; using foil calls attention to the fact that you blocked out your windows. I have a moveable flap of overlapping plastic a couple inches wide on each window so I can (hopefully) go unnoticed as I peek outside to watch the neighborhood.

I unplugged all the lamps just to make sure I don't accidentally turn any lights on. I don't watch the TV up here, I only watch it downstairs. I don't want anyone to know I'm here. If the wrong people had any idea about the food and booze I have, they'd try to take it by force. Hell, I've watched *Twilight Zone*, I know how formerly good neighbors can suddenly turn into *the wrong people.* Now I understand the need for weapons. Not to attack, but to defend.

I've scrutinzed the trap door into the basement. Unless you know *exactly* where to look, you would never suspect it's there. And I was very smart when I left the original entrance to the unfinished basement intact—anyone looking for a basement would go downstairs, only to find it cluttered and unfinished with an old, rusty washer and an empty chest freezer that's not plugged in.

I'm moving the last of my things into the basement. With the windows blacked out I can still come up into the house whenever I want, but once I start living there I'll need to restrict how often I come up. I need to quit writing now so I can get more done. If my intuition is right, I'll have plenty of time to write before long.

October 13th

Nearly all the stuff has been moved into the basement. I've checked and rechecked everything—the power, the gas, the composting toilet and water. It's quiet, a bit too quiet, but the fan in the grow room provides white noise so I should sleep okay.

I watched the street from upstairs for a while. I've seen cars driving by, sometimes filled with people just gawking, like they're hoping to see something horrible.

I saw an SUV stop about a half-block up yesterday. Three guys got out and went into a deserted house (I think it's deserted). A few minutes later they came back out, carrying stuff they loaded into the car. One guy wrestled a big TV into the trunk. What good is a TV when the power goes out?

My first reaction was to pick up the phone and call the police, but the land line quit working a couple days ago and I'm no longer getting any signal on my cell. Where are the cops? Where is the National Guard?

My second reaction was to head downstairs. It already feels safer.

A few hours ago I saw a small knot of men walking down the street. I got the impression they were looking for trouble. One guy carried a rifle. I stayed out of sight, although I do have my .22 in its holster, strapped to my hip. I feel stupid wearing it, like I'm nothing but a poser, which I guess I am. I don't know if I could hold it steady enough to even aim. Were those guys looking for someone to mess with? Were they an ad hoc neighborhood watch?

October 16th

The leaves are rustling in the trees and falling in a colorful shower, the air is cool, the moon is three-quarters and waxing. By all rights, this should be a beautiful day for fudgies to drive north for color tours. But this year there are no fudgies, no art- or harvest-festivals, no color tours, no wine tastings.

Perhaps the only upside is not having to endure political campaign commercials and mailings and ads stuck in my front door. Politics likely got us into this mess; it sure as hell didn't get us out. To hear empty promises and spurious finger-pointing would be more than I could stomach.

I haven't made downstairs my permanent home yet. I slept down there a couple of nights, but I usually sleep in my bed. The nights I spent weren't very restful—just being in a room with different acoustics is enough to throw off my sleep patterns.

I think it might be time to make it a habit though. Things aren't improving. It's impossible to say when order will be restored, and when it will be safe to go out again.

I'm upstairs. Satellite TV is out. The local broadcast channels are out as well. The internet is down. It feels very strange. I feel absolutely cut off. I was smart enough to start DVRing the news, so when I have time I'll be able to see what the last few hours of news broadcasts were like. But current news is gone—no TV broadcasts, no ability to Youtube or Google—it's only a mystery what's happening across the world, much less in Ann Arbor. The only signals I pick up on the radio are looped broadcasts warning everyone to stay indoors, martial law is in effect, violators will be arrested, looters will be shot. Stay inside and wait for the authorities to restore order. I think if someone isn't set up like I am, following that advice is lunacy. Doing nothing is what cows do on their way to the slaughter house. You'd be waiting to starve to death, or find a stranger pointing a gun at your head while he steals your food or rapes your wife or daughter. Or you.

Something's going on near Michelle's house. I heard what sounded like screams and gunshots. I'm going to check it out.

Later—

I checked the window facing her house. It looked like a house was burning a few blocks over. Smoke filled the sky and washed over the neighborhood, but I heard no sirens and saw no fire engines go by. While I was watching, the electricity went out.

I didn't see any activity in or around Michelle's house, so I did what may have been a stupid thing—I got a piece of paper and wrote ARE YOU OKAY?, then taped it on the window under the plastic so she might see it. I prowled around the house, peeking out other windows, and every few minutes checked back. After about thirty minutes, I could see her pacing back and forth in her bedroom, and when she glanced toward my window I took down some of the paper and waved to her.

She looked very upset, like she was barely holding it together. I thought for a couple of seconds and made a decision I hope I don't come to regret. I wrote MY SIDE DOOR on another piece of paper and held it up. Then I pantomimed pointing at my watch and held up two fingers. I pointed down the gate in her fence between our yards. From her door to mine it's only forty feet or so. She made the okay sign with her thumb and fingers. I waved and blocked the window again.

It's 1:50 now. I hope she's smart enough to make sure no one's around when she runs between our houses. I don't know what I'll be able to do for her. I don't know why she's so agitated. I don't know what she needs. I don't know anything. I'm tense, and I'm entering uncharted waters. Heaven help me, I pray I haven't made a huge mistake by reaching out to her. When will I learn not to be a rescuer?

October 17th
She's here now, uneasily sleeping in my bed. She keeps tossing and turning. I'm trying to stay awake in case she has a nightmare or sleep walks or something. How should I know what her sleeping habits are?

Yesterday ended up being quite an ordeal. I had initially figured someone tried to break into her house, or maybe she'd seen the house next door get broken into and was freaking out. But it turned out to be much worse. At 2:00, just as planned, I went to the side door and unbolted it. I then looked out the peep hole. Within about thirty seconds, I saw her fence gate open and she sprinted to my door. By the time I got it open, she was in a state of near panic.

She looked at me, her face pale, eyes wide. She lunged into the room and immediately began to whisper hoarsely *"Close the door! Close it!!"* While I was doing just that, she threw her body against it, causing it to slam shut. She even drew the bottom deadbolt while I locked the upper ones.

"It's okay, Michelle, you're safe now. They can't get to you," I said, still thinking she'd been threatened by an armed group of thugs.

"Did you see them too?!"

I didn't know what she was talking about.

"I saw the guys break into a house down the street and I saw a group of guys walk by," I said, holding on to my naiveté for an extra moment.

She was breathing so hard and fast I thought she was going to hyperventilate. She stared at me as if she didn't know how to respond. Then she shook her head as if trying to clear it and said, "Please, we have to get away from the door! I don't want them to hear us! We have to hide!" I still had no idea what was going on, but agreed it was a good idea to get downstairs where it was safe. I raised the trap door and she scooted under my arm and practically ran down the steps. *"Hurry! Hurry up!"* she pleaded. I closed and locked the door behind me, then hurried down the stairs.

She's the first person to see my basement since I finished it, and I don't think she even knew where she was. She sat in one of the arm chairs, nearly in a fetal position, her hands over her face, her whole body shaking. It looked and sounded like she was having a panic attack.

"Michelle. *Michelle!*" I said. She was unresponsive to me. It crossed my mind that she might be in shock. I went into the storeroom, opened one of the bottles of bourbon, poured a small glass and, bottle in hand, went back into the living room. She hadn't moved, and but had started whispering what sounded like "I don't . . ." over and over.

"Here Michelle, drink this!" I said, gently prying her hands away from her face. She took the glass from me without looking at it and swallowed a huge gulp, then immediately started choking and coughing. "What . . . what . . ." she gasped.

"It's bourbon," I said, "I thought you could use a drink. Would you rather have some water?"

She looked at the glass as if trying to comprehend what bourbon was, then choked down the rest. I took the glass from her and half filled it with more bourbon. She took the glass and emptied it, then looked up at me.

Her eyes had that shattered look I've only seen a couple of times before, once at the scene of a car wreck, and once at the funeral home when a friend's husband died. Michelle had the same look in her eyes, the look of fear, the look of *I've completely lost my moorings and don't even know who I am.*

I took the glass from her and filled it with water. While I was doing that, she started pacing back and forth. When I handed her the glass, touching her on the shoulder, she jumped as if she hadn't even known I was there. I could see the light come into her eyes when she came back from the dark place her mind had taken her. She ignored the glass of water, and instead fell into my arms. I know it sounds cliché, but it's true—I could feel her whole body shaking.

I could smell the bourbon on her breath, too. Normally I like the smell of bourbon on a woman's breath, but in this case the smell was mixed with another scent, perhaps fear. It seemed to emanate from her very pores. When she fell against me, I dropped the glass, water splattering against my jeans.

Michelle continued to cry while I held her, and in the back of my mind I thought *I can feel her breasts!* I ignored this and started trying to comfort her, stroking her hair while I led her back to the chair she'd been sitting in, softly saying, "It's okay, you're safe. You're safe, it's okay . . ." I sat her down in the chair, kneeling beside her while she still had her arms wrapped around me. "Take deep breaths," I told her, wondering if maybe she was a little crazy. She completely filled her lungs, her breasts pushing against me even more, then another deep breath and another.

I could feel her muscles begin to relax as more of the bourbon entered her blood stream. I sat there with her for I don't know how long—a few minutes? ten? anxiously wondering what was wrong with her, what I was going to do with her, and what had terrified her. She was physically okay—what was going on?

"Michelle, talk to me," I said softly into her ear.

She took another deep breath, and stared at a spot on the carpet. Then she started talking.

"I was in my house, trying to keep quiet and keeping an eye on the street through a corner of the closed blinds. I'd seen some guys pass by earlier and it scared me. Groups of riled up guys are something women should avoid. They passed by, but I knew if they came back I could be in trouble. But they didn't come back. Instead I saw . . ." She stopped again, then looked back into my eyes, the shattered look starting to return.

"What did you see? You can tell me. It's okay. You're safe inside. With me." I said, trying to reassure her.

"I saw two of *them* walking down the street," she whispered. I wasn't sure who she meant. "They acted kind of strange, walking slow and shuffling. One had a bunch of blood on his sweatshirt. The other guy was dressed nice, but he had a huge rip in his slacks, and blood had soaked into the material. One of his shoes was gone. They were still about a half block away. I thought they were sick or in shock."

"Mrs. Erickson opened her door and quietly called out *are you okay?*

Do you need help? Should I call the police? As soon as they heard her they turned and began stumbling toward her. *I don't have any money, but I can feed you if you're hungry . . . '* she said as the first guy got close to her. Suddenly I saw him lunge at her, and before she could close the door, he grabbed her hair, and then . . ."

She stopped again. I pulled away, picked up the fallen glass, and refilled it with water. She never took her eyes off me, as if she was afraid I'd disappear. When I handed her the glass, she was shaking so badly some of the water spilled out before it reached her lips.

"I saw the other guy grab her too. Then he fell on her with his mouth open. He was making this horrible sound, like he was a rabid dog or something. One guy was biting her arm and the other guy was biting the back of her neck as she fought them, screaming the whole time. Mr. Erickson must have been in the other room, because he suddenly appeared with a shot gun. He shot the man! Right in the chest! It didn't even slow him down. He kept on biting her as Mr. Erickson tried to pull her away. The guys' faces were covered in blood and they just kept biting and biting!

"Mrs. Erickson was still moving, but that . . . *thing* must have torn her throat out, because there was so much blood everywhere, and she wasn't screaming anymore. I've never seen so much blood!"

And she's a nursing student! I thought.

By now Michelle was talking in a monotone and her eyes were glazed over— another sign of shock. Good God, what am I supposed to do with a woman in shock? It crossed my mind she might be crazy—but I'd heard the news over the past few days and had seen the videos. What she described matched exactly the reports and videos of zombie attacks.

Zombies? Here? No way, I thought.

She paused to finish the glass of water. Even when the glass empty, she held on to it very tightly, her knuckles white.

"She was barely moving when Mr. Erickson finally pulled one of the guys off her and shot him point-blank in the head. He fell over and didn't move. Then he shot the other guy in the chest—*again!* The force of the gunshot made Mr. Erickson stumble back, and then he slipped on all of the blood and fell down on top of Mrs. Erickson. The guy he'd just shot grabbed him by the foot, stretched his neck out and started biting his leg!

"Mr. Erickson was shouting, *Leave me alone! Get off me!!* Then he started screaming. No matter how hard he tried he couldn't get away from the guy. I saw that . . . *man* . . . keep biting—tearing huge stringy chunks of flesh then chewing and swallowing! *He was actually eating Mr. Erickson!* Then he must have hit the fibular artery because I saw a lot of blood come pouring out of the man's mouth and spray their front door. He was still making that horrible noise, and he didn't stop. Kevin, *that thing didn't even slow down! It was like an animal!*

"I saw Mr. Erickson try to get up again but fall, and then the man started eating his midsection. Mr. Erickson started screaming again, then suddenly stopped. I don't know what happened because I'd dropped away from the window and was hiding against the wall. I don't know how long I stayed there. I might have fainted or something. When I peeked out the window, the guy who was shot in the head was still there, and Mr. and Mrs. Erickson were lying there, dead in their own blood. The other guy was gone. It looked like the man kept eating them even after they were dead. Blood dripped down the steps and onto the sidewalk. There was even a bloody handprint on the front door under the splash of blood. It was bloody and smeared. I saw bloody footprints in the grass, leading toward my house.

"I was afraid that crazy man might be somewhere outside my house, so I went around on tiptoe, peeking out. That's when I saw your sign in the window." She paused and looked down into her hands, which were holding the empty glass so tight I thought she might break it. Thank God it's plastic! I didn't know what to say, so I just reached out and touched her hand. She dropped the glass, grabbed me and squeezed my hand with both of hers so tight it still hurts. We sat there for a minute before she took a deep breath and said, "I read your sign and waited to come over. Kevin, tell me I'm not crazy! No, I take it back, tell me I *am* crazy and imagined it all! Those guys weren't acting human! Are those the zombies they talked about on the news? What are we going to do?!"

We talked things over for a few hours. She told me the story over and over. I continued to give her water and bourbon. By early evening I knew she'd had enough to make *me* drunk, so I knew she must be very intoxicated, as if her slurred words weren't enough to tell me. Her eyes had lost their shattered look, but now were kind of unfocused. Even so, she seemed tipsy, not drunk.

After that much bourbon?!

"Look," I said to her, "why don't you take it easy for a few minutes? I promise I won't go anywhere. We'll figure out what to do." I'm not sure if she heard me, but when I stood up, I pulled her up too. She was mumbling by now, something about Mrs. Erickson's floor getting stained with all the blood, and I led her into the bedroom. I don't think she knew where she was at this point. I took her shoulders and gently pushed her down onto the bed, and then onto her back. I took off her shoes and pulled a blanket over her. I pulled up the wooden chair and sat next to the bed. She had been asleep for a couple of hours when she jerked upright and whispered *"Kevin! Where are you!"*

"I'm right here," I said, touching her on the arm. I had turned the lights off, but the glowing walls still allowed me to dimly see her.

In the middle of the night she mumbled "'ts'hot in here!" and pulled her blouse up over her head then dropped it onto the floor. She lay back down and closed her eyes. I gently pulled the blanket up over her again, pausing to admire her breasts in the dim light. They were in a pretty bra— blue or black—with lace on top. I could just make out her nipples.

I wished I'd put a second coat of phosphorescent paint on the walls.

So now she sleeps. I'm wondering what to make of her story. Part of me thinks she must have seen a couple of zombies, but the skeptic in me simply won't believe it. I hadn't heard reports of the disease in Ann Arbor. Detroit, yeah, but Ann Arbor? Nah. Zombies are just in the big cities, if they're really zombies.

I'm tempted to sneak outside and go over to the Erickson's house, but it's already dark outside and I'm no fool. Besides, she might wake up. I don't know how she'd react if she woke up and couldn't find me.

October 18th

Michelle slept through the night, although she woke up twice and I had to calm her down. I slept on the sofa when I wasn't sitting in the chair, thinking and writing.

This morning I took her some coffee. It's strange to be living in a world without any visual clues about time other than the clock. No dawn light creeping through the blinds, no sound of birds or traffic.

Anyway, I took Michelle some coffee. She awoke with a start.

"Good morning," I said. "How do you feel?"

"Ohh, my head hurts . . . what am I doing here?" she asked, sitting up.

"You were pretty upset last night. I gave you some bourbon to calm you down. You drank quite a bit and got pretty tipsy. I would have taken you home, but, well, all things considered . . ."

She looked blank for a minute before her eyes opened wide and a look of horror dawned upon her face. "The Ericksons! Oh, my god . . ."

"I made you some coffee," I said, handing her the mug. "Hope you like it black. And here's some ibuprofen."

As she took the cup from me, she said "You have coffee?! God bless you!" After she swallowed the ibuprofen she started sipping her mug, gazing at nothing. She hadn't noticed the blankets had fallen away from her, revealing a substantial—and lovely—bosom. Ample cleavage. I could smell a distinctly feminine scent coming from her, too. I love the smell of cleavage in the morning. It smells like . . . victory.

"Did I . . . I mean, was . . . do you think I saw a zombie? Do you think I made it up?"

"Well, to be honest, I was hoping you made it up as a clever excuse to get into my bed," I told her, trying to keep things light. Evidently she didn't care for my humor because she gave me one of those stares women are so good at. Or at least they're good at with me. "Seriously, though, I don't know what you saw. But I know you were extremely shaken up. And in case you're wondering, I slept on the sofa last night." I saw her glance down, then chastely pull the blanket high enough to cover her cleavage. Damn. "In the middle of the night, I heard you say it was hot and I guess you took your blouse off. It was dark." I said, feeling sheepish. She glanced at me and I'm sure she noticed my blushing. I'm glad she didn't take her jeans off too, or she might have thought I'd assaulted her.

She cleared her throat and said, "You slept on the couch?"

"Look at the other side of the bed. It's still made."

She glanced over, then took another sip of coffee, and when she looked up at me again I saw a different look in her eyes. It was indecipherable, but it wasn't a defensive or accusatory look. Maybe less guarded?

"Do you think it's safe for me to go back home?" she finally asked.

"We'll have to check. How secure is your house?"

"Every door has deadbolts and I've locked the garage door. It's very heavy, I doubt anyone could open it alone."

"Are you sure all the doors are locked?"

"I checked them yesterday."

"How about the windows?"

"I keep the windows locked everywhere I live, ever since I had a break in about ten years ago."

"In that case, if there's no one outside watching us . . . no one or no *thing*, we could check the doors and windows to make sure they're all still secure. If none of the windows are broken and the doors haven't been forced, we'll know no one's been in your house."

"But what if someone has broken in? What if they're still inside?"

"If we see a door or window has been forced, we'll come back here and figure out what to do. I don't want to start speculating. First we need facts." I said.

Now that we had a plan, she acted more stable. "Listen, why don't you take a few minutes to finish your coffee? I have some plant work I have to take care of, " I told her, "I have to check the water level of my hydroponic system, check the pH, look for pests, blah blah blah. It shouldn't take me long; I don't have any serious work to do. I should be ready in about 15 minutes."

She nodded her assent and I left her sitting up, sipping her coffee. As I worked in the grow room, I heard her get out of bed and perhaps just imagined hearing her pull her blouse back on. Even if it was just my imagination, I liked the images it brought to mind.

After I'd finished my chores, I came back to find her in the living room, blouse on, kneeling down and looking into one of the boxes I'd left unpacked—mainly boxes of books and DVDs.

"Feeling better?"

"I don't feel great but the headache isn't as bad," she said and then paused. "I don't mean to get personal," said the lady who twenty minutes ago was sleeping in my bed, "but are you into . . . I mean, you seem to have some strange . . . tastes." I had no idea what she was talking about until I noticed she was looking through the porn DVDs. I never got the chance to go through them.

I could feel myself blushing as I told her "No, no, I'm not some creep! I don't have any weird fetishes or anything. I'll be honest with you, when I began to suspect I was going to be holed up in here—alone—I bought a that box of used porn."

"You bought *used porn?!*" she asked incredulously.

I ignored her. "I don't even know what's in the box, honestly! I haven't had time to look through it! I'm pretty much just a guy who likes . . . well, who's normal!"

"Whatever normal is," she said, "After reading *Fifty Shades of Gray*, I'm not sure anymore," she blurted out. Then it was her turn to blush.

She read Fifty Shades of Gray? I thought. "Yeah, I knew the book had gone mainstream when I saw it for sale at Sam's Club," I answered. "But really, I don't know what kind of stuff is in the box. I'm hoping it's not all disgusting, cheap trash. I don't know much about porn—hell, you couldn't even buy it around here not too many years ago. I know there's good porn and bad porn, but I'm not sure how to tell."

She went back to rooting through the box. "Here's one," she said, pulling a case out of the box, "it's called *She's a Milker*. She turned the case so I could see it—it showed a topless, lactating woman with milk squirting out of her nipple. Michelle had a funny smile on her face, but I could tell she was watching to see how I'd react.

"Okay, okay, I get the point," I said. "Why would anyone find that a turn on? Please, put it back, you're embarrassing me. We have things to take care of," I practically begged.

I swear, she had a smirk on her face. In the middle of all this she was somehow *playing* me?!

"If you're ready, let's sneak upstairs to see what's going on." She agreed, and we quietly made our way upstairs. Before opening the trap door, we stopped and listened. We heard no sounds, so we climbed out of the basement into the kitchen.

"All the windows are blocked, but a window on every side of the house has a small peep hole," I explained to her. "I'll check this side of the house, you check the back yard and side yard." I wanted to make sure I was the one to check the street, not knowing how she'd react if she saw something gross. I didn't see anything when I first looked out, but then farther up the block on the other side of the street I saw what looked like an injured woman shuffling off in the opposite direction from my house. I didn't know if she was a zombie or not and frankly, I wasn't going to find out. I also saw a dog nosing around a few houses in front of her, but he ran off in a hurry when he heard her.

When I was sure there was no other movement anywhere, I went and found Michelle. She was still peering outside. "Do you see anything?" I asked her.

"I see a lot of smoke in the neighborhood, but that's about it," she said, "no people or anything. How about you?"

That must have been smoke from the house fire I saw yesterday.

"There's a woman walking down the street, but she didn't seem right. She should be out of sight by now. Let's take a minute and plan the best way to do this. You have your keys, right?" I asked. She nodded and pulled them out of her pocket. "How about you go through the gate into the back yard and check the door and windows there, and I'll check the front of the house," I suggested. She nodded her head in agreement.

"Then, assuming I don't see anything to be concerned about, we can get inside through the back door. Then we'll go through the house—together—and make sure it's safe. Oh! I almost forgot!" I said. "I'll be right back!" I ran back down into the basement and found my gun. I nearly forgot to get the ammunition for it. I had an instant image of me as Barney Fife.

"You have a gun?!" She exclaimed with a skeptical look in her eyes. "Do you know how to use it? You don't exactly look like the gun type"

"What does the *'gun type'* look like?"

"For one thing, he looks like he knows how to handle a gun," she said,

"Right now it's pointed at me. Is it loaded?"

I pointed the pistol at the floor. "No, it's not loaded. To tell the truth, I've never even shot it," I admitted.

"You mean *fired it*. You don't shoot a gun, you shoot bullets. You fire a gun. Maybe you should give it to me. I used to go hunting with my dad all the time," she said. I handed it over, feeling like I'd symbolically just handed her my testicles. The *guy* is supposed to carry the gun. But this was not the time to slip into some gender identity role that no longer mattered. I shrugged it off. I'm comfortable with my manhood.

"Okay, let's go. Remember, be as quiet as possible. If those things are out there, we don't want them to hear us," I reminded her. I quietly undid the three deadbolts and we poked our heads out, checking all around. Seeing the coast was clear, we stepped out. I almost forgot to close the door behind me, reminding me I wasn't very good at this security and stealth kind of thing.

By the time I turned around, she was nearly at the gate to her back yard. I saw her open the gate quietly and creep inside, the gun cradled against her shoulder. *Reminds me of agent Scully,* I thought, *Except Michelle has much nicer breasts!* I mentally smacked myself on the head as soon as the thought passed through my mind. *Focus, you idiot!*

I checked all the windows, the front door and the garage door as quickly as I could. I was trying to be stealthy and not attract any attention. Everything was secure. I took a glance at the Erickson's house, then abruptly stood up, staring. There was a dead body lying in the grass with most of his head splattered around him. There was an arc of dark red dripping down the front door, along with a smeared handprint. I saw a lot of blood but no other bodies. *Strange,* I thought, *where are the bodies?* I hurried around the back. She was standing on her deck, looking around. "Everything's fine back here," she said, "except for all the smoke. That's probably not a good sign, is it? And notice how quiet it is?"

She was right. I hadn't noticed, but there were none of the usual suburban sounds I'd come to expect. No sounds of traffic. No lawn mowers. No sirens. Looking up into the sky, I didn't see a single jet trail. Usually I could see several at any given time, Ann Arbor being situated in the flight path between Chicago and Detroit.

Not waiting or needing a response from me, she unlocked the door and we quickly stepped inside. It was dimly lit and as quiet as a graveyard. Ooh, bad metaphor. Together we checked every room—every closet, every alcove, behind furniture. It was exhausting. Not only was I having to peer into dark rooms where zombies could be lurking, I also had to act like I wasn't scared out of my fucking mind. Inwardly I cringed at practically every step. All of my senses were on full alert, and I didn't like the feeling. She'll never know how relieved I was when we agreed the house was empty and safe.

She had a decent amount of food in her pantry, and her deadbolts looked pretty substantial. Her décor was a bit too decorative for my tastes—you could tell a woman lived here without a man—but she had good taste. Some of her framed art looked to be originals. She leaned toward art deco.

We stood in the living room, still looking around. "Seems secure," she said, "what do you think?"

"I think you're good. You have food to last a while. The water still works. How are you set for heat?"

"I have a natural gas stove and a fireplace."

"You're using a *fireplace*?!" I said. I suppose I sounded almost accusatory. "You can't—"

She interrupted me, saying, "Kevin, do you see any blonde roots in my hair? Give me some credit, willya? I'm not stupid. I'm not talking about a wood fire. People would see the smoke coming from my chimney and know someone was inside. Duh. I have natural gas logs. I'll keep plenty warm."

"Sorry, I didn't mean to imply that you were stupid. Although you might look nice as a blonde," I said, tilting my head and squinting my eyes as if mentally replacing her auburn hair with blonde hair.

"Yeah, you too, if you actually *had* any hair," she shot back. "I think you can go back home. I've had a very rough day, my head still hurts, and I have to pee."

"Okay, but make sure you lock the door behind me," I said as I headed toward the door. I saw her roll her eyes, as if to say, *There he goes again. I'm not an idiot.*

With the door cracked, I took a look around to make sure it was safe. While I was doing so, I heard her say behind me, "Thanks for everything. You really helped me out, and I appreciate everything you did, being so neighborly and all. Hopefully I can return the favor sometime."

"Hopefully you'll never need to," I responded, then quickly crossed the distance between my house and her house. As I opened the door I glanced back. She gave a weak wave as I nodded my head and went inside.

So now I'm sitting here, processing the last twenty four hours. She says she saw a zombie. I saw a woman in the street who looked and acted weird, and she sure scared the dog away. I saw a dead body in the Erickson's front yard, and a lot of blood.

I also had a woman sleep in my bed. I can't recall the last time that happened. I'm in bed now, having spent the rest of the day taking care of things around here—working with the plants and unpacking those damn porn DVDs she happened to find. How embarrassing. She was right, there were some very strange titles in there, but there were also some that looked, um, entertaining. Even when living in the land of zombies, a guy has urges. I started to put the box of DVDs in closet, but then thought, *Hell, there's no one going to be dropping in. I might as well put them with my other DVDs*. So I added a bunch of them to my movie collection. I only wish I'd unpacked the box before she was here. And wouldn't you know, she'd pick out one of the stranger fetish DVDs. She probably really does think I'm a pervert.

I don't know if she wears perfume. I have no idea what kind of soap or laundry detergent she uses. But somehow I still catch a whiff of feminine scent in my bed. Maybe it's just pheromones.

It sure was weird having a practical stranger spend the night at my house. Neighborly, she called it. Hmm.

October 19th

We had frost last night. The first of the season. It made me wonder: what happens to zombies when it gets seriously cold . . . ? Do they freeze? Do they stop moving and never move again? Do they just move slower? I'll know within the next two months.

October 20th

I saw one. One of them. There is no doubt. I was standing in the side door, taking a look around. The trees are at their peak. The maple in Michelle's yard has leaves of golden red on the outside, but the inner leaves are greenish-gold. It's a gorgeous layered effect. The poison ivy on the back fence is brilliant vermillion. It's beautiful. Reminds me of some women I've known.

The air is getting cooler by the day. Looking around, I began to wonder if Lake Michigan was still warm enough to wade in. It's probably too cold for swimming unless you're a polar bear.

In years past, September and October have been my favorite times to go to the beach. The fudgies are gone, the kids are back in school. I've had extremely warm and pleasant days when I had the beach to myself. Once or twice, the water was warm enough in early October for me to skinny dip. I've also found some of my best Petoskey stones in October.

It's a whole different experience, looking for beach stones in the fall. Heading north, the view north to Frankfort is spectacular. The slant of light is different than during summer, and at their peak the trees on the dunes are radiant, especially close to sunset when surrounded by darker evergreens and pines. Offshore, the color of the water is darker, and few recreational watercraft dot the surface. No paragliding this time of year. And maybe it's just my imagination, but the water *sounds* like fall. Less celebratory, more resigned.

It's almost sacred, being surrounded by such transient beauty while getting distracted by the search for pretty fossils of coral that lived millions of years ago. The brief and the seemingly eternal both impressing themselves upon my consciousness.

So I was daydreaming about the Lake when I heard a scraping/crunching sound. It took me a minute to place it—it was the sound of fallen leaves being walked on. I couldn't tell exactly where it came from, so I quietly crept to the front corner of the house to look around, being careful not to step on any leaves myself. As I peered around the corner, I saw a man. Or what used to be a man. He was sort of staggering around, aimlessly walking through my yard just shy of the street. I kept out of sight and watched him.

He looked to be in his late fifties, but that's just a guess. It was hard to tell. He wore what used to be a white V-neck t-shirt. Only now it was filthy, ripped, and stained with dried blood. The whole left side of his face was a dried up, unhealed wound. I could even see some of his sinus cavities. It looked like most of his hair on the other side had been burnt off. Gore had dripped down onto his shoulder, and the left arm hung limply at a strange angle.

It moved forward down the street, occasionally jerking its head this way and that. I can only guess it was looking for flesh. I crept back inside and locked the door, then watched it until it was out of sight. I was nauseated and shaking. What used to be simply a concept for me has now become a reality. I've seen a zombie. They are real.

"We have met the enemy and he is us." —*Walt Kelly (Pogo)*

November 1st

The last ten days have been pretty quiet, if you call hiding in the basement of my house while more and more zombies mill about *quiet*. After my last entry, I started to see one or two a day, then I started seeing more . . . four or five, sometimes six. Sometimes two or three at a time. Yesterday I counted 12.

It feels strange to lurk around my house, listening to the silence. Except for them. Everywhere they go, they make that snarling, rasping noise. When several of them get together, it sounds like a horrible, monstrous choir.

I saw Michelle yesterday. I happened to be upstairs, peeking out the window (no, not toward her bedroom) when a huge explosion rocked the house. If I have my bearings straight, I think it came from the airport. But who knows, surely it wasn't the Marathon refinery—it's over twenty miles from here! Wherever it was, the explosion was huge, and like I said, it shook the house. It didn't seem to frighten the zombies, but they all turned and started gravitating toward the sound. Evidently sound attracts them—which is good to know. Soon most of them were out of sight. I unbolted the side door and sprinted to Michelle's house. I knocked quietly on the door, nervously looking around. She immediately opened the door and motioned me in. As soon as she closed and bolted the door behind me, she said, "Holy crap, Kevin, you scared the bejesus out of me!"

"Sorry," I said, "but I wanted to check on you. What do you think that explosion was?"

"I was wondering the same thing. It might have been a gas station. It wasn't the gas lines—I checked and the natural gas is still on," she said.

"You holding up okay over here?"

"I'm not fishing for an invitation, but being alone is wearing on me. I feel like I'm in solitary or something. Don't take that as a hint—I know it's not safe to go traipsing back and forth between your place and mine. Have you noticed there are more and more of those things out there?!"

"I had noticed. I guess they're coming from downtown or the university. Who knows, maybe even Detroit. How are you on food and water?"

"To be honest with you, I'll be glad when this is over. I try to keep a stocked pantry, but I never planned on being stuck inside for weeks at a time. I sure hope things get back to normal soon," she said ruefully.

I thought, *Back to normal? I'm afraid this is normal. The old normal may be gone forever.* I also wondered who she thought would get control soon—the police? From what I saw on the net before it went down, the chain of command had fallen apart. There are no more police, or none on duty. I haven't seen a patrol car in weeks.

But I didn't say it—instead, all I said was "Okay, I just wanted to check on you. Being neighborly and all that." Parroting her earlier words, of course.

"You don't have to leave! I could use some company. And we should at least check the, shall we say, traffic before you open the door."

"True, I need to start remembering that." I noticed she'd covered her windows with aluminum foil. "You have foil on all your windows?" I said.

"Yep, every window is sealed tight. I did leave a small gap at the top of each window to let light in, otherwise it would be nearly dark in here"

"Nearly?"

"I have a skylight in the kitchen. I spend most of my time either there or by the fireplace, since it gives off light when the fire is lit. Who knows how long the gas will stay on. C'mon, I'll show you the kitchen."

She led me through the dim light into the kitchen, which was indeed much brighter.

"How do you see to get around at night? I've learned my lesson—I know you're not an idiot and didn't walk around with a flashlight or anything that could be seen," I said, hoping to regain some ground I lost by implying she wasn't very bright.

"I mostly feel my way around once it gets dark. Now I know how blind people do it. I know where everything is even when I can't see it. I'm also going to bed earlier, since there's nothing else to do. Can't read, can't make a fire, can't cook . . . it's miserable really."

"Too bad it's not safe for you to come visit me now and then," I said, "I have lights on 18 hours a day. No way any light can possibly leak out. I can cook, and I can watch DVDs, I can even read at night."

"How can you do all that? The electricity's been out for weeks!" she asked me.

"I started reading a bunch of end-of-the-world books. I was in an apocalyptic mood. I also read books about tough characters in rough situations. I even went back and read Jack London's books. It was fascinating to see what the characters would do to survive. A lot of the current books involve survivalists. I took a look around and realized how fragile my lifestyle was. One catastrophe—a pandemic, an electromagnetic pulse bomb, a terrorist attack, a severe climate disruption a hundred times worse than global warming—and I could lose everything and die a horrible death. If the grid went down, life as I knew it would disappear . . . it scared the hell out of me. I started stocking up on food and water, but the more I thought about it, the more I realized food and water wouldn't do any good if I wasn't safe and warm. On my roof are several banks of solar panels which charge the batteries downstairs, enough for me to run my LED lights for the plants and keep myself mildly entertained. I have a pretty good set up. I never dreamed I'd have to rely on it this soon."

I admit it—I was bragging. But I hadn't been able to brag to anyone else about it, and I am proud of what I accomplished. "I also had professionals come in and renovate the unfinished basement. Took a huge chunk of change, but I had money left from Tammy's life insurance, plus my 401k. Hah, my 401k. I guess that's gone forever. Wish I'd spent it all! Everything is VERY energy efficient. What with the hydroponics, the stored goods, the liquor, and the books—"

"And the porn!" She interrupted with the flash of a grin.

"- and the *DVDs*, I'm set for quite a while. I don't *just* have porn, you know. I have a huge movie collection."

We started talking about movies. It was refreshing to talk with someone, *anyone*, and I completely enjoyed it. I don't know if it was just because I was starved for company or if I would have enjoyed her conversation just as much in different circumstances, but it was great.

At one point she said something funny—I think she was talking about a scene from *Date Night*—and I started laughing my head off. "*Shhhh*!!" she shushed me with a look of alarm in her eyes, "you're being too loud! They'll hear you!!"

We heard a noise out front. We jumped up from her kitchen table—we'd been there for a while—and bolted to the living room window. Apparently she was right—there was a zombie scratching at her front door, and several zombies ambling toward her house.

"*Shit!*" she whispered.

I immediately felt guilty and a little scared. "I'm sorry," I whispered back, "I wasn't thinking."

"It wasn't your fault. I was having a good time, too," she said, touching me on the arm. "I think we're safe. No way they can get in, and if we're quiet, maybe they'll go away."

I didn't feel safe, not like I would in my own home. Knowing they were just outside was quite unnerving.

We sat down on the carpet near the window so we could keep an eye on them. Between it being so dim and us having to talk in near whispers, I felt like a kid again, staying up late at a friend's house. I even said something about it. She agreed and said it felt like we were sneaking around.

"Don't worry, my parents aren't expected home for a long time," I said. "We can do whatever we want. Except make noise. Or build a fire. Or go outside. Or order a pizza. Or watch a movie."

As we fell silent, a fantasy leapt to my mind of her responding *Or watch porn . . . but wait, we can! Or you can. So far I haven't been invited to the party,* with a pouting come-hither look. *Now stop it!* another part of me said, *You know you don't want to go there. There be dragons.* I tried to refocus.

We started quietly talking again. Compared notes on how this came about. Wondering about our friends. Wondering what was going to happen next. Soon we were having an intimate conversation about how we were responding to the horrible mess. She confessed she was stressed out and depressed. I admitted I sometimes wondered what the point was of trying so hard to survive when things were so grim. I admitted it made me miss my wife, and life hadn't been so great since she died. We fell silent again. And yet, it was a companionable silence. Better than solitary silence.

Eventually the zombies wandered off, since there wasn't anything else to see or hear. I decided it was time to leave while the coast was clear, and told her so. As I headed for the door, a thought struck me: I had two sets of wireless baby monitors. I planned to keep one upstairs as a cheap security system, so if someone tried to break in, I'd hear them. The other set was a backup in case the first one quit working.

The monitors have two components—a transmitter and a receiver. The part you leave in the baby's room transmits but doesn't receive and the one you keep with you receives but doesn't transmit. Since I had two sets, I could give Michelle the receiver from one kit and the transmitter from the other kit, and we could keep in touch with each other. Since the sets are on different frequencies, anyone listening in would only hear one side of the conversation.

Is it possible anyone's listening? Or should I say, is it *probable?*

Michelle thought the idea was great. I think she's been much lonelier than she lets on, and I can tell she's losing weight. She's still a big girl, but her clothes are looser. I hope she doesn't lose weight up top.

She's looking pale. She must be trying to conserve food. At least if we had someone to talk to we wouldn't go quite as stir crazy, and it adds another layer of security as well. She can watch my back. I can watch her front. Heh.

She even suggested we set up checkers or backgammon, and play over the radio. That sounds like fun, but we'd have to have the honor system for rolling dice.

Tomorrow if the coast is clear, I'll take the radios over. I have fresh batteries and they should last a couple of weeks before they need to be recharged, which is no problem with my solar battery chargers.

November 3rd

The plans for yesterday didn't work out for a couple of reasons, the biggest one being the number of zombies milling around. I don't know if they somehow smell live humans, or sense us in some other way, or if there's some residual memory of hearing us yesterday, but there are definitely more wandering around today than there were a couple of days ago. Even though they're pretty slow, I didn't dare try to take the radios over. I'll try again tomorrow.

I finally bottled the beer I've been neglecting in the carboy. Actually I bottled half of it, and kegged the other half. I sampled it, and even though it was warm and uncarbonated, I could tell it turned out mighty fine. I can pretty much guarantee it's the best fresh homebrew in town. Tomorrow or the next day it should be ready to drink. I wonder if Michelle likes beer? Maybe she's more of a wine kind of gal.

I wonder what it's like at the Jolly Pumpkin brewpub downtown. Probably not so jolly.

November 5th

Another day with lots of zombies. But I learned something interesting last night. My camera has a nightshot mode which essentially is infrared—meaning you can see in the dark. Looking through the viewfinder, I could see well enough to spot zombies. Apparently they either can't see in the dark, or somehow they respond to the light/dark cycle, because all of the ones I saw were just standing there, barely moving. I say barely, because they weren't completely still, and now and then one would walk few random steps. I think if they had sensed me they would have moved my way.

Of course, I was watching them through the window. Perhaps if I had been outside, things would have been different.

At one point they must have heard a deer or dog across the street, because they all slowly turned their heads the same direction. No effort was made to move toward the sound, however.

I'm thinking if the need arises for me to visit Michelle, I should do it at night when it's safer.

I'm going to write a note and stick it on the window to let her know I'll try to go over at 10 p.m. She doesn't know my camera lets me see in the dark, so it might make her worry some, but I'm anxious to get this communication setup up and running.

I won't admit it to her, but I'm scared shitless about going outside tonight, even if it's just to run to her house.

November 7th

The last two days have been a roller coaster. Two nights ago, my plan worked, but it nearly cost me my life.

At 10 p.m., conditions were perfect. It was completely dark and raining. I figured the noise would help cover any sound I made.

Just before 10:00 I put the radios and a bar of dark chocolate (yes, I stocked up on it too) in my backpack, grabbed my camera and went upstairs. I quietly unbolted and opened the door. I had already checked—the side of the house was free of zombies.

I made my way to Michelle's back deck and didn't have to knock on the door before she opened it. She didn't say "Come in!" of course—that would be foolish—but as soon as I was in, she quietly closed the door, then squared her shoulders and told me either I was crazy, had a death wish, or both. She was actually angry!

The room was completely dark. Not dark like it is in the city—I mean pitch black dark. I kind of laughed, then turned the camera around and showed her how it helped me see in the dark. I also told her about the zombies and noise. She seemed to accept my behavior as perhaps not being quite as foolhardy as she'd thought.

It was strange, standing in the dark, talking to her so quietly. I felt sure the rain would completely muffle the sound of our voices, but even so, we were both practically whispering.

As it got late, I didn't want to overstay my welcome and said I'd better get home.

"Why don't you stay?" she said.

Did she mean for a while longer or overnight?!

Between my having been outside among zombies and it being completely dark inside, I was a bit unnerved.

I told her, "Thanks for the offer, but to tell you the truth, I'm not used to the darkness like you are. And I'm sure I'll bump into things and make a fool of myself. I think it's safer if I go home."

I held out the plastic bag. "I'm holding out my arm," I said, "I have a plastic bag with the radios inside."

She reached out and found my hand. But before she took the bag, she just stood there holding my hand. For a long moment.

I don't know why she did that—I guess she needed a human touch.

When I cleared my throat she shook herself and said, "Sorry, I was lost in thought for a second," and then took the bag from me.

"Lost in thought?" I asked her.

"I was thinking about my first boyfriend. I was remembering the first time he held my hand. For some reason I was just now reminded of that night. Maybe it's the rain. I remember my heart was pounding so hard I was afraid he could hear it. Just remembering it made my heart start racing! Here, feel!"

As she said this, she placed my hand—I kid you not—on her breast, over her heart. Not on the nipple, but closer to her collar bone. But even so—my hand was touching her breast!

Damn.

Her heart definitely *was* racing, and mine was too. As if I was eighteen again, I felt myself getting a woodie.

I swallowed—loud enough for her to hear—and said, "Wow, it is beating hard!" Immediately I regretted my choice of words. "It must have been some night!" Actually, I tried saying it once and found my throat was all closed up, so I cleared my throat and started over.

If I were a more aggressive guy, I might have lowered my hand and given her breast a squeeze, but like it or not, I'm just not that kind of guy. Most guys would say she was practically *begging* me to make the next move, but how could I know for sure? I didn't want to make an assumption, act on it, and her mad, or be accused of assault, for god's sake. I liked her; I didn't want to ruin a potentially good friendship.

And even though I'm nobody's fool, I feel pretty sure she was, indeed, flirting with me. I was glad it was dark—otherwise she'd have seen me blushing and would probably have noticed my hard-on.

I stood there, my hand still on her breast, enjoying the feel of it and feeling her heartbeat, when I suddenly became quite self-conscious. I practically jerked my hand back.

She answered my question with a sigh (what did I ask? Oh yeah, *must have been some night!*), and said, "Yes, it was. It was sweet. We were both so naive. We ended up making out—my first French kiss, too. It was disappointing, but to be honest, I've gotten used to disappointment with guys." Was she talking about that night with her first boyfriend, or about tonight?!

"Let's turn the radios on at, what, 9:00 tomorrow morning?" I suggested. She liked the idea, and I said I'd better get back home. I opened the door, then turned my camera back on (it had timed out) and whispered, "Talk to you tomorrow!"

"I'm *really* looking forward to it," she whispered, "thank you *so* much!" Then I took off.

One thing I hadn't thought of was this: Yes, it was dark. Yes, my camera was infrared capable so I could see. But the camera LCD screen emitted plain old visible light, so it must have lit my face up earlier.

When I went through her gate, a zombie was just on the other side of the fence. The stench hit me first—it's a dead animal smell, mixed in with something else, something I can't quite place. Sort of like rotted garlic.

Before I could react, it grabbed me, snarling. I tried to lunge away, but its grip on me was very tight. Without my camera to help me see (I'd almost dropped it, but managed to hold on to the strap) I was blind and nearly gagging from the foul odor. I couldn't tell where its face or mouth was, and when I tried to wrench my arm away, I slipped on the wet grass and fell to the ground. I involuntarily let out a series of shouts, which was a mistake. Immediately the zombie was on top of me, still snarling, bits of wet rotted flesh falling off its arms and landing on me. I could hear the sound of other zombies not too far away.

Apparently light affects them like sound. They gravitate toward it. And when motivated, they do move at night.

Without thinking—panicking, really—I swung the camera with all my might in the darkness. I connected with something—head? shoulder?—hard enough for the zombie to lose its hold on me. I jumped to my feet and ran in the direction I hoped was my house. I misjudged the distance, though, and ran smack into the side of my house and let out a shout of pain.

Between the impact of my head and body hitting the side of the house and my shout, I'd made more noise. I could hear the zombie behind me, moving closer. I heard other snarling sounds much closer than they had been. I didn't know it at the time, but I'd also done a number on my nose and was bleeding profusely. This was my first clue that zombies somehow sense fresh human blood and get excited, because the volume and intensity of the snarling was increasing. Stunned, I groped my way to the door.

Just as I started to open it, either the same zombie or a different one grabbed my shoulder. The fingers were half rotten, and even with my nose messed up, the stench was overwhelming; I could even taste it.

This time I lunged forward with all my might, got through the door, and tried to slam it shut. The zombie still held onto my shirt. I couldn't close the door. I shoved with all my strength, pinning the arm inside. Keeping my weight on the door, I stripped off my shirt, grabbed the half rotten arm, and managed to force it out, still clutching my shirt. Bits of dark, congealed and rotted flesh were smeared all over my hands.

I finally got the door locked and bolted, but my shirt was now half in, half out of the door. I had a severe case of the willies, so I fled down a couple of steps, then hurriedly closed and bolted the trap door before heading downstairs.

Once I got in the light, I saw blood dripping on my chest. I was afraid I'd been bitten, so I grabbed a lantern and headed into the bathroom. Looking in the mirror, I could see blood streaming from my nose. I gave myself a quick examination to check for bite wounds (thank god there were none!) then grabbed a towel and pressed it to my nose. Ouch.

I started the shower and jumped in. I tipped my head back, letting the water rush over me. I held my hands in the stream to clean them. When I saw my hands were free of zombie flesh, I let the soaked towel drop to the floor, then reached up and pinched my nostrils shut. My heart was still pounding furiously. With my system so amped up with adrenalin, I probably bled even harder. But eventually, my heart slowed and I was able to let go of my nose without it bleeding again. By that time my breathing had slowed as well. I allowed myself the luxury of staying in the shower for a few minutes, trying to stop shaking.

I finally got out, dried off with a fresh towel, then went for the bottle of bourbon I'd opened when I gave Michelle a drink. I poured myself a stiff one.

My hands were still shaking very badly. I downed the drink and had another. Even swallowing hurt. That's how much my face was swelling. I sat there, dazed, a myriad of thoughts swirling around my head. The zombie. It had almost bitten me. My hand on Michelle's breast. The zombie. The stench. Her voice. My hard-on. My camera. *My camera!*

I got up and retrieved it from the floor where I'd practically dropped it. The lens was ruined. But the power came on. So maybe only the lens was trashed. I have other lenses, but damnit, it was my favorite. What an idiot I was. The zombies . . . now there are a bunch of them out there, and they know I'm in here. They smelled or sensed my blood.

All these thoughts were running around, getting mixed up, repeating themselves . . . After I felt some of the bourbon kick in, I quietly went back upstairs. My heart was pounding again.

I stood there in the dark, listening. Not only did I hear the sound of the rain, but I also heard the sounds of zombies. A lot of zombies. It sounded like twenty or more. They were scrabbling at the door, pawing at it, scratching at it . . . many were rasping and snarling.

As I stood there, they pulled my shirt the rest of the way through the door. For a moment the rasping increased, but when they realized they hadn't found food, it died down again. Even when they weren't as loud, it sounded horrific.

It scared the shit out of me, too, so I went back downstairs and locked up tight. I had a few more drinks and some melatonin, and eventually dozed off (or passed out).

When I woke up this morning, I had a pounding headache. The lights were on in the grow room, so I knew it was morning. When I looked at my watch, it said 9:23. 9:23? *Shit!* I got the radios and turned them on.

"Bichelle?" I said. I couldn't breathe through my bruised and swollen nose and my voice sounded funny.

I heard an electronic crackle, and then "Kevin?!" she cried, "I thought you were dead!!"

"Whad are you dalking about?" I asked.

I heard Michelle sniff *(Is she crying?!)*, and with a lot of raw emotion in her voice, she said "Right after you left, I heard something happen outside. I heard zombies making all kinds of noise and I heard you yell. Then I heard more strange sounds, and then I heard *a lot* of zombies. It sounded like there were a thousand of them! Then this morning I saw one chewing a shirt that looked like the one you we wearing. It was bloody. I thought I'd never see you again, and when you didn't come on at 9:00 like you said you would, I was *sure* you were dead." She started sniffing more and I was sure she was crying. It made me feel bad.

"I'b so sorry," I said, "you were close, but dankfully not quite--."

"What's wrong with your voice?" she interrupted.

"I'b dryink do dell you. A sombie god me righd oudside your kade. I god away, but dhen ran indo my house. I don'd mead I ran idside—I mead I collided with the side of the house. I mighd hab broke my nose. It's all swolled and I cad't breath. I god idside bud by shirt got ripped off."

"I was pretty udset. I dradk sode bourbon . . . a *lod* of bourbon—to cald dowd, and fell asleep on the coudch. I djust woke up. I'b sorry, I did't bead do scare you."

"Did you get bit?" she asked me.

"No, but it was close. Add I'd afraid I adracted a butch dore of thed. They dnow I'd here."

"You got that right. It looks like there are about forty of them out there! You jerk! Don't scare me like that!"

"You dink *you* were scared . . ." I said.

"Can't you hear them?" she asked me.

"Dot dowd here," I said.

"Listen . . ." she said. I guess she held the radio close to the window, because I could hear rasping sounds in the background. "Now I have to listen to that creepy sound! It's driving me crazy!" she said. "I didn't sleep a wink last night I was so worried! Oh, and I'm cold. The gas quit working. I'm cold, I'm hungry, I'm exhausted, I'm scared shitless, those things are making all that noise, and I'm alone. Thanks, Kevin, "she said sarcastically, "you're quite a guy."

She must have turned off her radio, because that's all I heard from her.

I had all day to think about our conversation as well as the events of the night before. I also had all day to obsess on my nose and whether it's broken. I don't think it is, but it's all black and blue and very swollen.

I did my usual work with the plants, started a new batch of lettuce, and generally moped around. Every time I leaned over, I could feel the pressure in my face increase from the swelling. It hurt like hell. I kept wanting to look at it in the mirror.

I was feeling quite a stew of emotions. I was still freaked out by my close encounter of the zombie kind, still trying to convince myself she was coming on to me, and feeling guilty over scaring her half to death. I wondered if she was washing her hands of me, which I found depressing, but also had momentary spells of pride. After all, I'd found a clever way for us to communicate, she seems to really like me, and she was *obviously* coming on to me. But within minutes of thinking that, I'd start second guessing myself and trying not to let myself get overly hopeful.

I left the radio on all day in case she relented. She never did. Around dusk I went back upstairs briefly. She was right. The number of zombies had grown. It's now a zombie mob. Most of them are around the side of the house, where they can still smell any blood that hasn't washed away. But they're also in front of both of our houses and meandering up and down the street.

So I had figured out a clever way for us to communicate. But now she won't speak to me. Plus I drew zombies to us. Brilliant. Another gold star day.

November 8th

I didn't sleep well last night. When I tried to sleep on my side, my face touching the pillow hurt. So I lay on my back, watching the glow in the dark paint slowly fade. Around two o'clock I got up and downed a couple shots of bourbon and some melatonin. Fell asleep a half hour or so later. But at some point before I fell asleep, my emotions began to change. I went from feeling bad and guilty to feeling pissed off. Royally pissed off.

I risked my damn life doing her a favor, being neighborly and all that. I nearly lost my life in the process. I smashed up and maybe broke my nose. My face hurts. I can still smell zombie on my skin, no matter how much I wash or what I do. And instead of being concerned about how badly I'm hurt, instead of expressing concern or gratitude or whatever, she gets pissed at me? Where does she get off?

Now I remember why I haven't dated since Tammy died. Women are emotionally unreliable. I never know how they're going to feel or what kind of mood they're going to be in, and no matter what they're feeling—especially if it's bad—somehow it's my fault.

If Michelle wants to get mad at me for facing the zombies alone, for trying to make her life easier, for risking my life and nearly dying, let her be mad. I don't need it. I have my books, my DVDs, my plants, my food and booze. I'm self-sufficient. I have electricity, water, and light. She has a dwindling supply of food, very little light, no electricity, no heat, and probably no water. We could have been good friends or more. But she chose to be a bitch. So let her suffer the consequences of her choice.

I've turned off the radio. I don't want to talk to her.

November 9th

Happy Halloween three weeks early. I look like I'm wearing a mask. Much of my face various shades of blue and a gross looking yellow from the bruises. But at least the swelling's gone down.

I'm not so mad any more. If anything, I'm pretty sad. Michelle's the only person I know who's alive. I truly enjoy her company, and it's not just because she's so attractive and has a great rack. She's smart and funny. Intelligence combined with humor (and a great rack) is such a turn on. I don't want her to suffer and I don't want her to go anywhere.

I turned the radio back on a few minutes ago. Maybe I'll even try to reach her later.

Meanwhile, some of my lettuce is ready for a partial harvest, along with some cherry tomatoes. The beer I bottled has conditioned enough to start drinking. I'm going to have a nice salad and a beer for dinner, then try to get some exercise and maybe watch a movie. After the problem with Michelle, I wasn't in the mood to watch any relationship movies or even any porn—instead I watched *the Godfather*. Maybe when she thanked me for bringing the radios over, I should have said *"Some day, and that day may never come, I will call upon you to do a service for me."* I can think of many ways she could service me.

Now that I've simmered down, I feel restless. I wish I could go for a bike ride. But it's not safe. Maybe I'll go through the porn and see if I can find something halfway decent. Or decently indecent.

Later--

I heard another explosion a bit ago. I'm not sure where it came from, the sound down here makes it hard to tell. Maybe I should go upstairs and check around.

Even later--

When I went upstairs, it was already dark. From the east windows I could see a glow on the horizon. It wasn't super bright, so I really have no idea what it was or how big a fire it was. After all this time, it was strange to see something besides the moon and stars in the sky. I could very faintly see one or two zombies facing the light, slowly making their way in that direction, whether because of the light or the earlier sound of the explosion, who knows?

November 11th
What a day. Early this afternoon I heard Michelle on the radio. "Kevin are you there? Please answer. Hello? Kevin?"

I stood there for a minute, debating. Did I want to answer? Maybe get back into the same cycle, where I start having feelings for someone, with possible hopes for something more, only to have her stomp on my heart with a hobnailed boot? Would it be better to turn off the radio and mind my own business? Or should I just get over it and move on, still being friends?

I'll admit it, hope surged in my heart. She wanted to talk! She didn't sound mad!

In the end, I caved. Or came to my senses, depending on how you look at it—or how things turn out. I picked up the radio and hit the transmit button, relieved to hear my voice was back to normal.

"Hey," I said, "what's up? Everything okay?"

"If it's okay I'm coming over. Be there in ten minutes. If that's okay," she said.

"Don't be a fool! It's not safe!" I warned her.

"Most of them are gone," she said, "go see for yourself. Meanwhile, is it okay if I come over? You never answered me."

"Sure, I'll be at the door in ten minutes," I replied. My heart was beating fast, and any lingering resentment evaporated. Feeling hope was kind of refreshing—it's been a while since I had hope, especially when it involves women.

I quickly went into the bathroom and checked myself in the mirror. In my haste I forgot to grab a lantern, so I couldn't see much. The only light was from the grow room LEDs so my face looked purple, and not just from the bruises. I tried to comb my sparse hair, but it was no use. There was no way I was going to make myself look good.

I gave up trying, climbed the stairs, and opened the trap door. I quickly walked through the house, checking the peep holes in the windows. She was right. I didn't see any zombies on the side of the house, and only a few in the street.

After a few minutes, I went and stood by the door. I was thinking: *why does she want to come over? Is something wrong? Does she need food? Does she have some kind of news? Or does she just want to tell me off in person?*

When she finally knocked on the door—quietly—I opened it and motioned for her to come in. After she stepped in I took a quick look outside—no zombies in sight. In the grass about ten feet away lay part of my shirt. It was stained with blood and ripped apart.

I closed the door, set the bolts, then turned around to look at her. Since all the windows are sealed up, the only light was from the stairway into the basement. But I could see enough to tell she wasn't smiling. In fact, her whole demeanor seemed kind of tense.

"What's a nice girl like you doing in a place like this?"

"Oh my god! Your face looks horrible!" she said, her eyes darting back and forth over my bruises. Even in the dimly reflected light from downstairs she tell I'd been hurt.

"Like I haven't heard *that* from a woman before," I mumbled.

She paused for a moment and said, "I want to apologize to you. I completely overreacted. It wasn't fair to you, especially since you were doing something nice for me. I'm sorry, and I hope we can be friends again." She held out her hand, which I willingly shook. She kept talking. We kept holding hands. "When I thought you were dead, I guess it touched on a nerve. I've had people abandon me before, and it dredged up a lot of baggage that doesn't belong to you."

"Let's not talk up here," I said, "let's head downstairs." I let her lead the way and closed the trap door behind me.

Once we got downstairs, she took a quick look around. "Kevin, this is great! I didn't really notice before! It's warm, comfortable, it's well lit, and it feels pretty . . . homey! My place is cold and dark!"

"Thanks," I said, "I tried to think long-term and tried to have everything I'd need to be comfortable." I told her about having the walls insulated, and the composting toilet, and the tankless water heater.

At one point she took me by the hand. I was startled, but then she led me into the grow room.

"I want to have a look at your nose," she said, pulling me into the light. She examined me closely and used both hands to gently prod the area around my nose. Her fingers were warm, but I winced at the pain. "It's obvious zombies don't have a sense of humor," she said with a smile, "otherwise they'd have laughed when they saw you run into the wall! I know it's not funny, but . . . actually it *is* kind of funny." She was smiling.

She continued examining me and poking. I kind of liked the attention.

And I liked her standing so close to me. But it still hurt.

Finally she seemed satisfied I was going to live. "You didn't break it, so that's a good thing. It'll heal up just fine. A few weeks from now you won't even be able to tell." She looked around at the plants. "Holy crap, Kevin! Your plants look great!" It had been a month or so since she was last here—a month is a long time when you're growing lettuce, herbs, and tomatoes.

I bragged to her about having fresh salad for weeks, and offered to give her some to take home. She said she'd rather eat it here, because my place is warmer and brighter than hers. I asked her if she was hungry, and she said that even if she wasn't, she'd be crazy to turn down fresh salad.

I told her she was welcome to stay for dinner, but she'd have to earn it first. She looked at me suspiciously, like I was going to ask her to do something unsavory, and I told her I was going to make her pick her own lettuce. We went back into the grow room and I handed her a pair of scissors. I told her to cut off a few of the older, outside leaves from each plant. The plants continue to grow, and if you're careful, you have a constant crop until the lettuce starts to bolt.

As I was telling her this, she was tenuously cutting leaves. A few cherry tomatoes were ripe, so we picked them as well. None of the peppers were ready yet, but I doubt she would have wanted them anyway—they're really only for chili hot heads.

When we had a large bowl filled with lettuce, we went into the kitchen where I started tearing them into tinier pieces. She asked me why I wasn't washing them first, and I explained to her there was no need—they were never exposed to any pesticides, there were no bugs to worry about, no dirt to wash off . . .

We'd picked plenty, and I added some raisins, sunflower seeds and croutons, then added some oil and vinegar (no refrigeration required) and we went into the living room to eat. I don't have any kind of table.

We ended up watching a movie, comfortably sitting side by side on the sofa. It wasn't a *movie* movie, more like a long music video. It was called *Koyanisqaatsi* and shows a lot of time lapse video showing the serenity of nature contrasting with the hyperactivity of man. Phillip Glass did the sound track, and the music and visuals are perfect for each other.

I didn't know how she'd react—I've tried to watch this with other folks and have gotten a very lukewarm response. Most women want to watch a chick-flick, or at least a movie with a plot and dialog. This had neither. So I was pleasantly surprised when she told me how she liked it!

By now it was getting late—not that it mattered—and we were both yawning. She said she should get going, so I bagged up the rest of the salad for her.

She joked on the way up the stairs that it felt like I was walking her home after a date, and it did feel that way. I used my camera's night mode to make sure the coast was clear, then opened the door for her. She thanked me for being so gracious about her being a bitch, and as she said goodnight she leaned in and gave me a kiss on the cheek. Imagine that. A kiss!

I closed the door behind her after telling her to call me on the radio when she was safely inside, then headed downstairs. Immediately she transmitted and once again thanked me for everything. I told her it was my pleasure, and I hoped to talk to her again soon.

Since this is my journal, and my mother won't be reading it (or my daughter, since I have none) I can go ahead and admit it: After we finished talking I looked through the porn DVDs until I found one featuring big-busted women, and I watched it for a while then went to bed.

Based on how the day started—with us not talking—I never would have dreamed the day would finish with a happy ending. Heh.

November 15th

Michelle and I have been talking on the radio a lot. By a lot, I mean sometimes for an hour at a time. It's been fun getting to know her. I love her laugh and she has a great sense of humor. She hasn't been back over to my place—and I haven't been to hers—but maybe soon we can visit.

We've been playing backgammon as well. We tried playing checkers, but it was too difficult to explain which piece we were moving. I usually win.

In some ways, I feel sorry for her. She's in her place, sitting in semi-darkness, with nothing but me to entertain her. Especially at night. While

I can (and do) listen to music and watch DVDs, she has nothing. She can't even read a book after dark. If I had something to loan her, I would, but I suppose it wouldn't be very safe in the long run. Any light or sound escaping her house would only draw zombies.

Earlier today I was watching my Looney Tunes cartoon collection, and when she came on the radio she asked me to let her listen in. Even though she couldn't see Bugs Bunny or Daffy Duck, she laughed out loud as Bugs and Daffy were arguing: "Duck season!" "Rabbit Season!"

We have a long Michigan winter ahead of us—what will she do when it gets brutally cold? How will she stay warm? I'll have to ask what her plan is. If she has one.

November 19th

It's gotten very cold out. I saw a few snow flurries earlier, although it didn't stick.

Days are blurring together. With no schedule, no deadlines, no frame of reference, I sometimes can't recall what day of the week it is. I guess it doesn't matter.

I have three ways to judge the passing of time. One is by the growth of my plants. Another is my facial hair and how fast *it* grows. The final way is by watching the bruises on my face slowly fade. Otherwise, it's just another day.

Except for Michelle. I must admit, she's the bright part of my day, and I always look forward to talking to her. Truth be told, I'm kind of sweet on her. But now I have to make a decision.

This morning she called me on the radio. She said it was quiet outside and wondered if she could come over. I was glad to say yes, and when the coast was clear, I met her at the door.

She was wearing a cardigan sweater, a color of brown which matched her eyes. She gave me a big hug and told me it was good to see me again. I felt the same. I also felt her marvelous breasts as they pressed against me. Have mercy, does she have a rack.

We made some small talk as we headed downstairs—she was asking me something about the music I have. When we were in the living room, she handed me a small bag I hadn't noticed she was carrying and said, "I made you a little thank you gift."

Inside were some chocolate cookies—the no-bake kind made with oatmeal. I immediately ate one, and it was delicious. I didn't stock up on many sweets (except dark chocolate), so it was a real treat. And I commented on how smart she was to come up with something that didn't require cooking!

She started looking a little bit nervous, and said, "There's something I'd like to talk about." Statements like that always make me wary. "I have a proposal to make." I was feeling a bit jumpy, and to stall for time I offered to make some coffee. "Oh my God yes! I haven't had coffee since . . ." her words faded off. The last time she had coffee was when she was over here, upset because she saw the zombies attack and kill the Ericksons.

When I asked her how she wanted it, she said black as sin. She definitely had a twinkle in her eye. I didn't know if it was because of the hot coffee or the sin.

I went into the kitchen and ground some beans with the hand grinder. I poured the grounds in the French press, then heated up some water. After it came to a boil, I poured it on top of the grounds and carried the pot and two mugs into the living room. "We'll let it steep for a few minutes," I said. "Meanwhile, what's your proposal?"

"I'm living in a dark house with no light, no heat, and no diversions other than you. Looking out the window and seeing zombies freaks me out, so I don't do that. You've helped me keep my sanity. Just knowing you're over here has really helped me. I was thinking back to when you brought the radio over and got attacked, and how I reacted so strongly. To be honest with you, I was pissed at myself for letting you become a friend. I don't do well with men. I have some baggage. So when I thought you were dead, that I might see you out there shuffling along with the rest of the zombies, it really messed with my head. I freaked out. So again, I apologize," she said, looking into my eyes. It was a bit unnerving, and I was the one who looked away first.

"Please, that's all water under the bridge," I replied.

"I tried to reach you on the radio the next day, but you wouldn't answer. Part of me was afraid you'd gotten infected and had turned into one of them, and it made me feel desperate. But part of me thought you had written me off, and you'd never talk to me again. That night I drank a lot of wine and woke up with a hangover."

In turn, I admitted to having gotten angry with her for yelling at me. I felt it was unjustified. I'd risked my ass to take her the radio, and felt like I deserved better treatment. I told her the anger didn't last long.

"You were right," she said, "it was unjustified, and you deserved better. But since then we've had a fresh start."

"Agreed."

"So back to my proposal. I'll be straight-up with you. I'd like to move in. Strictly platonic. I could sleep on the couch or wherever is best. But I think two people living in one place are safer than two people living in two places. I was reading my Bible yesterday," she went on.

She reads the Bible? I thought

"... and I came across the verses in Ecclesiastes—you know the ones that say:

Two are better than one, because they have a good return on their labor: if either of them falls down, one can help the other stand up.

"I felt like it was sort of a sign. And to lay all of my cards on the table, I don't have much food left. I'm cold, I'm lonely, and I'm depressed. Except when I'm with you."

"So what's in it for me?" I asked.

Before she answered my question, she stood up. "Hold that thought," she said. "Your place is much warmer than mine. This sweater is making me hot." As I watched, she unbuttoned the sweater and took it off, revealing a pretty teal blouse, conservatively cut and yet still showing more than a hint of ample cleavage. I suppose with breasts as large as hers, cleavage nearly always shows. She sat down, holding the sweater in her lap. I suspected it was a blatant attempt at manipulation but in this case, I didn't mind being manipulated. "I could help out around here. I could help keep the place picked up. It looks like you could use some help in that area," she said, looking around the room which had admittedly gotten pretty cluttered. The floor needed sweeping, there were a few dirty glasses here and there along with empty beer bottles and DVDs in and out of their cases. Thank god I didn't have any porn DVDs lying around! "I also have nursing school experience. If you get sick or hurt, I can help you. And I have one trick up my sleeve you don't know about," she hinted.

It's not what's up your sleeve that I'm interested in! I thought, glancing at her exposed cleavage. I dismissed the thought. "You have a trick up your sleeve?"

"Yes." She paused, keeping me in suspense.

" . . . I have . . . in my garage . . . a shortwave radio!" She said. A shortwave! Why didn't I think to get one of those?! Damn!

"You have a shortwave? Does it work?!"

"Yes, I have one, but I don't know if it works—I don't have power, you dufus! So that's my proposal. I don't want to be alone anymore. I know we barely know each other, and you don't owe me anything, but we're both alive. Let's be roommates, if we can't be friends. I won't give you a hard time about any of your, um, habits," she said, glancing over to my movie collection. "I'll help out with whatever needs to be done around here, and I'll keep you company."

"What makes you think I have enough food for both of us?" I asked her.

"I don't know if you do. But I could bring over the food I have, and if the zombies stay away, maybe we can go scavenging in the empty houses." I sat there, thinking. I had plenty of supplies to last one person a year or so. I had my hydroponics. I had enough food to last two people a long time. And she was right—there's safety in numbers. I could watch her back *(or front!),* she could watch mine. As I was thinking, she continued to talk. "So, here specifically is what I'm proposing. I propose we bring my shortwave radio over here and anything else you think you could use. I propose I stay here on a trial basis. If we hate each other after two weeks, I'll move back to my house and figure out how to survive. But if we don't hate each other, we'll agree to extend the trial period. "I had roommates in college," she said, "I know how they can start out being fun, but after a while you end up despising them. So I know it could happen. But you're a nice guy, and I'm usually a pretty nice person, so if you accept my proposal maybe we can make it work. I don't expect you to answer me right now. But could you at least think about it before you say no? Please?"

I poured the coffee, lost in thought. I offered her a cup and as she took it from me our hands touched. She sipped her coffee and waited through my silence. In the end, I told her I'd sleep on it and let her know tomorrow. She seemed a bit deflated that I didn't give her an answer right away, but I don't rush into things. I do want to think it over. I want to think about the pros and cons of having a near-stranger—and a woman at that—living with me in my basement. A beautiful woman. Using my supplies and electricity. Potentially making me miserable. Or very happy.

"Thanks, Kevin. And if you decide it won't work, I hope we can stay friends and keep each other sane," she said.

I lifted an eyebrow and said, "You think you're sane?"

"As sane as you are," she teased back. We sat there drinking our coffee and talking, and time passed quickly. Around lunch time I was hungry, so we opened some canned chili and heated it in the microwave. She asked if she could make us more coffee.

"You only love me for my coffee," I said with a smile.

She gave me a sultry look, slowly licked her lips, and with a husky voice said, "I'd do just about *anything* for a cup of hot coffee!" She then laughed out loud, long and hard. She has a wonderful, vivacious laugh. I couldn't help but laugh along with her, even as I felt my manhood stir in response to what her words conjured up.

She opted to have hot coffee with hot chili. A combination that doesn't appeal to me, but then again I've enjoyed hot food all along.

After lunch, she said she was going home to give me time to think. I walked her up the stairs and we checked the windows. There were still a couple of zombies on the street, but they weren't moving much, and were too far away to possibly see her run between our houses.

As we stood by the door, she began to put her sweater back on, giving me a cheap thrill when she had to arch her back to get both arms in their sleeves. Even in the dim light she looks good.

When we were both sure the coast was clear, I unbolted and opened the side door a crack. Michelle gave me another big hug (complete with her big breasts) and said, "Thanks, Kevin. Thanks for hearing me out. I'm glad we're friends and neighbors." I was hoping she'd give me another quick kiss, but she didn't. She scooted out the door and I watched her scramble through her gate. When I heard the door to her house open and close, I closed and bolted mine as well.

After she left I was curious, so I looked up the Bible verses she quoted. It took me awhile to find them, but I remembered her saying they were in Ecclesiastes (which took a while to find too). I was mildly surprised when I found them:

Two are better than one, because they have a good return on their labor: If either of them falls down, one can help the other stand up. But pity anyone who falls and has no one to help them up.

Here's the part I was surprised by, the part she intentionally or unintentionally left she left out:

Also, if two lie down together, they will keep warm. But how can one keep warm alone?

Damn this libido! It's so distracting.

November 20th

I've been thinking it over. I made a list of pros and cons. For the pros, I had things like: *having someone with medical training around would be good, she has a shortwave, two really are safer than one, she has large breasts, she's good company.* For the cons I listed other things, like: *supplies would go twice as fast, one quarter of the time she'll be in PMS, she has large breasts but they're off-limits which keeps me constantly aroused and frustrated.*

I'm sure I could think of more things.

I like Michelle—she and I have the same tastes in music, movies and humor, she seems intelligent and I really *enjoy* talking to her. I don't know her politics or her sexual proclivities—if she has any. I don't really know much about her at all.

But I remembered back in college when I moved in with Steve. We became good friends and kept in touch over the years. I always looked up to him. I hope he found a way to survive.

I think I'll be able to handle having her as a roommate. And like she said, if it's not working out, we'll both know.

I wish I had more time to think about it, but I told her I'd tell her today. It wouldn't be fair to make her wait longer.

I still have some reservations. I know from past experience how a woman can make me fly high or sink low. I know getting close to someone, especially now, is asking for heartache. And if things get really bad, I don't know if she'll be an asset or a hindrance.

Bottom line: I want it more than I don't want it. Just like her, I'm lonely. I think if I had to stay here alone until spring, I'd probably go nuts.

If it works out, it could work out great. We could both be happy. Being happy and making someone else happy is worth the risk.

I'm going to get on the radio and let her know.

November 22nd

I talked to Michelle over the radio a couple days ago. "I'd like to formally invite you to move into my place," I said. I heard a big sigh of relief.

"That's great news. I think it's a win-win," she said. Then she got quiet for a few moments. I think she was so relieved she was crying. She spent a few minutes assuring me I wouldn't regret it, and towards the end she was practically gushing with excitement. I'll admit, part of me was rolling my eyes, but it made me feel good, too.

We spent about a half hour going over what she could bring and what things I didn't need or didn't have room for. Her furniture wouldn't fit, for example. And heavy bulky stuff would be too risky to attempt to move—we would be outside far too long. I'm glad she has a blow-up mattress, so she can sleep on the floor and I won't feel guilty. It'll make the living room cramped when it's inflated, but we won't be using the living room and the mattress at the same time. It'll be deflated and put away during the day, and we'll only get it out when she's ready for bed.

I started doing what I could to make room for her—I cleaned out one closet for her clothes. Neither of us really need a lot of clothes—it's not like I'll ever have a reason to wear my tux again or even a neck tie. And we have the closets upstairs to use if we have to.

I also ended up feeling kind of guilty about the porn, so I went through my movies and selected the ones with the most egregious titles and put them in a box in the closet. I really have no interest in watching *Masturbation Mayhem #3* or *Full Bush Amateurs* or *Buttman 11: Anal Cherries*. And with her here, I'd be embarrassed to play the ones I might like. Fortunately for me, I do have a set of earbuds so I can discreetly watch some on my laptop in private.

A select few that didn't look so bad stayed in my collection. And I admit it—all things considered, I decided to leave "Night of the Giving Head" and "I Can't Believe I Fucked a Zombie" on the shelf.

It's my sense of humor. She'll have to get used to it.

Yesterday it rained, and I mean hard, so we agreed to hold off moving until the sky cleared. We don't want her stuff to get wet, don't want to slip on the wet grass and drop anything.

It was peculiar, looking out toward the street. Zombies slowly wandered aimlessly around, their rotting faces void of expression. Some had suffered horrible injuries but were oblivious. One of the zombies was a topless woman who had evidently had a partial mastectomy.

I watched the cold November rain pour down from the gray sky upon the lifeless yet animated corpses of human beings, obviously not alive and yet not quite dead. They shuffled around, their clothes sopping wet, water dripping off their hair. They were pitiful.

All my life I've dealt with depression. Years ago I realized depression was my oldest companion, practically a friend, as familiar as an old worn sweater.

But seeing the zombies slowly shuffling around in their sodden clothes on this dreary and rainy Michigan November day, I let go of some my depressive, *always a slacker* feeling. No matter what's going on, I'm not one of them, a lifeless horror whose only desire is to eat live human flesh. I still have life, and hope, and feelings. I can think. I can laugh and cry. I'm still a *man*.

Those thoughts made me glad to be alive.

I can't get a grasp on what, if any, intelligence they have. Even dogs know to come out of the rain. But zombies don't seem to care about the weather. I've noticed they move slower as the days get colder—what will happen when we have a deep freeze?

I feel like I have a day of reprieve, one last day to be a confirmed bachelor without having to explain anything I do. I can fart as loud and often as I want, I can belch, I can pick my nose or scratch my butt, and no one will care. I can watch porn and spend time trying to satisfy myself. This may be my last chance to be lonely.

That reminded me of a couple lines from a William Carlos Williams poem:

> *I am lonely, lonely.*
> *I was born to be lonely,*
> *I am best so!*

And yet I'm giving up my loneliness.

Tonight I'm going to have another salad, and will splurge with a bourbon and Coke. I put two cans of Coke in the root cellar to chill. I'm not going to be stingy with the bourbon when she's here, but I'm also not going to offer it to her every freaking day. I do have a limited supply.

I'm going to enjoy myself and do whatever I feel like tonight and live to excess without guilt. Starting tomorrow, I'll have to be a nice guy for who knows how long.

I figure at times I'll regret my decision. My only question is: how long before the thought runs through my mind, *What was I thinking?!*

November 23rd

Another day that may prove pivotal in many ways. Michelle moved in, I shot a zombie in the head (now they're swarming again), and Michelle got frisky.

I woke up with a headache. Not bad enough to incapacitate me, but bad enough for me to regret that last bourbon . . . or two. Sometimes I don't mind mild hangovers; they prove I can let go of the leash now and then. I believe in moderation—in moderation.

After I made some coffee—still relishing my last few moments of bachelorhood—I went upstairs and had a look around. Things hadn't changed much—there were still only a few zombies in the street and front yards. A warm front must have brought the rain, as they seem to be moving faster than yesterday. I suppose they're in the back yards, too. I didn't see *many* zombies, but truth be told, for all I know they're like roaches: if you see one, you know there are a hundred more close by. Or a thousand.

The few I saw were mostly headed from the direction of the explosion we heard. I wonder if it means they gravitate toward light and sound, but eventually gravitate back to an area. Their home stompin' ground.

If that's the case, I thought, *we may not have much time to move Michelle and her stuff before too many come back.*

That was enough to motivate me. I went back downstairs and got on the radio. "Michelle!" I said. It took a few seconds for her to answer. "Hey, Kevin. What's up?"

"Have you noticed anything outside?"

"You mean the zombies coming back? Yes. As soon as I noticed it I started moving my stuff over to the door. I don't have much, but I'm ready to get this done when you are."

"Gotcha. I'm going to get my gun and head on over. How much more time do you need?"

"Give me until ten o'clock, okay? I've gathered all the really important stuff, now I'm having to decide on some luxury items."

"Luxury items?"

"A few favorite books. And some DVDs. Not the kind *you* like, though, chick flicks," she said mockingly. "I know this may be temporary, but I don't know when it'll be safe to come back. It feels weird to leave most of my possessions behind. I feel like I'm closing a door on my past life."

"Michele, my dear, I'm afraid anyone who's left alive has had the door closed to their past life. But feel free to bring whatever you'd like. I have the room and I don't want you to feel like this is a prison."

"Okay, I'll see you at ten. Thanks, Kevin." Why was it every time she says my name, I feel a little thrill in the pit of my stomach? Is it just because she's a woman? Or is it something more?

Maybe I just like to hear my name.

I busied myself for most of an hour, combining a few half-empty boxes in order to make more space, then I made the bed. When it was about five minutes till ten, I headed upstairs, securing the trap door behind me. I checked outside again, paying particular attention to the side yard. The number of zombies seems to be increasing—I could easily count six—but none were close to our houses and definitely none were in the side yard.

I went to the door, braced myself, and quietly opened it. No zombies in sight. I held my gun out with arms locked like I've seen on TV, and quickly made my way through her gate and onto her back deck. Michelle opened the door as soon as I got there.

"Why are you holding your gun like that?!" she asked me.

"Isn't it the way you're supposed to hold it?"

"Only if you have a script. Mind if I take a look?"

Script? I thought. Oh. Script. Like for a TV show or a movie. I handed it over to her.

She checked to see if it was loaded (it was) and said, "How about I carry the gun? I'd feel a bit more secure, knowing I could actually hit a target and knowing I won't accidently get shot by friendly fire." She poked me in the ribs with her forefinger, and once again I had this fleeting image of Barney Fife. At least I didn't carry a bullet in my pocket.

"Here's the ammo," I said, pulling the box from my pocket.

"Lord, did you really think we'd need this much? I'm hoping we don't need any!" she said, taking the box from me.

"I wasn't really thinking anything except that I didn't want to run out," I said, defending myself. "If I'd come over here without any extra ammunition, you'd probably have given me a hard time about that, too!"

"Somebody has to give somebody a hard time around here," she said. The innuendo did *not* escape me.

I looked around at the items placed near the door. There was more than I thought there'd be. This would easily take four or five trips, even more if she didn't carry anything but the gun.

"I know it looks like a lot, but it's mostly clothes, food, medicine, and first aid supplies," she said, "I didn't know what all you have, and I'd rather have too much than not enough. Especially in an emergency."

"What kind of meds?" I asked.

"I have some antibiotics, some anti-anxiety, some prescription painkillers, and some allergy meds. The basics. For all we know, I may be allergic to something in your place."

"Where did you get all that stuff?" I asked.

"My father was a doctor. He made sure I always had the essentials. Some of it's expired, but that just means it's not quite as effective."

I didn't have much in the way of medicine—just some ibuprofen and some cold medicine, since I seem to get those a few times a year. And even if I had had the time, I wouldn't have been able to get prescription medicines.

"I'm impressed!" I said. "So you're bringing more to the table than just your blow-up doll and short-wave radio!"

"Did you just say *'your blow-up doll'*?"

"What?! No, of course not. I said your blow up mattress and short wave radio."

She looked at me askance then said "That's right, all this *and* my good looks *and* my charming personality! I should be charging you!"

"As long as you give me my money's worth," I said, immediately realizing it could be taken the wrong way. I could feel my cheeks blushing as I quickly said, "Let's get this underway. I don't how long it'll be safe."

When I glanced up, Michele was smiling at me. She'd obviously noticed my blush. Which, of course, made me blush more. I hate blushing.

"Ready when you are," she said through her smile, arching one eyebrow.

I turned my head to hide any further blushing. "Which is the heaviest?" I asked, picking up a few to test their weight.

"Probably the inflatable mattress. It's over thirty pounds," she said pointing out the box. It was a queen sized mattress with a self-activating pump, the box said. Sounded comfortable. I bent at the knees and grabbed the box, straightening out as I lifted. "Ready to get the door?"

"Set the box on the counter, I want to make one more check outside," she said, moving into the living room. I did as she suggested, waiting until she got back before I hefted the box again.

"You do that so easy!" she said, "I had to drag it across the floor! The coast is clear, but will you be able to carry it all the way?"

The box really wasn't *that* heavy. I wondered if she was flattering me on purpose.

"Sure, no problem. I'll let you open the gate, close it behind me, then scoot ahead and open the door to my house."

"Sounds like a plan," she said, grabbing what looked like an overnight bag. "Ready?"

As I nodded, she cracked open the door, took a quick look around, then opened it all the way.

"It's show time!"

I headed out the door and toward the gate. Behind me Michelle quietly closed the door then sprinted in front of me. She opened the gate, again looking around, then opened it wide enough for me to get through.

Smart girl, I thought, *Quiet as a mouse!*

As I went through the gate, I took a look toward the street. No zombies in sight. That was a relief.

Michelle closed the gate behind us, then quickly headed to my house and held the door open for me. She bolted it behind us as I headed toward the hidden trap door.

"Where's the trap door?" she asked me. "I can't see it!"

I put the mattress down, then walked over and placed my weight strategically on one board. It looks like the board has an uneven crack in it, but it's actually weighted so one end lifts up if you step on it just right. When the end lifts up, you can see a ring to grab. Michelle grabbed the ring and pulled. The trapdoor opened, the wood plank ends staggered so there was no obvious seam in the floor.

"Very nice!" Michelle said. As she continued lifting the door, she said, "Why is the door so light? I expected it to be heavy!"

"It has a counter weight," I explained, "that's what makes it so easy to lift."

"Sweet!" she said. We grabbed her stuff and went down the stairs where we placed them in an empty corner of the room.

When we went back upstairs, I said, "Let's leave the trap door open.

I just wanted to show you how it works."

It still looked safe outside, and Michelle looked pretty awesome in the dim light with my gun sticking out of her belt. I'm sure it looked better on her than it did on me. We made three more uneventful trips. After the fourth trip, there was barely anything left. "Do you want to take a last look around?" I asked.

"No, this hasn't been my home for long," she said, "it's really just a house. The stuff in the house matters to me, but that's it. I don't have an emotional connection to the place."

What happened next was a combination of mistakes. First, in our haste to finish, we didn't check outside for zombies. Next, when she opened the gate for me, she glanced toward the street—but not behind the gate. As I hurried toward my house I heard Michelle scream.

I turned around and saw a zombie attacking her. It had been hidden behind the gate. It was a female zombie—or used to be a female. The clothes were soiled, and in tatters. Her blouse was nearly torn off, exposing a gaping wound in her side. One shrunken breast flopped around as she tried to grab Michelle, her desiccated nipple the color of a dark bruise. The bra hung limply around her waist.

Michelle stumbled, the gun falling out of her belt.

She had the box between her and the zombie. It went into a craze, smelling her blood I guess, and began making the loud snarling, rasping sound. It was desperately reaching out, trying to get her, snapping its teeth and clawing her.

Despite the zombie's advanced stage of composition, it still had a lot of weight and strength, knocking Michelle backwards onto the ground. The box and the zombie fell with her. As they hit the ground, the box crumpled and with her claws the zombie grabbed hold of Michelle's hair, stretching her head and neck to try and take a bite.

"*Kevin! Help me!!*" she shrieked. I was already in motion, having dropped my box, and was going for the gun she'd dropped. I picked it up, pointed it at the zombie and pulled the trigger. The gun went off, making a not-so-neat hole in the fence, just a few inches above Michelle's head. Michelle's eyes went even wider as she yelled "*Shoot IT! Shoot IT!! NOT ME!!*"

This time I fired at the zombie's back. The impact of the bullet caused the zombie to lurch, but it continued grasping for Michelle's neck. I aimed again, this time for the head, making sure Michelle was not behind it. I pulled the trigger, and instantly half of the zombie's head exploded, showering Michelle in dead tissue, brains, and bits of bone. The zombie collapsed, no longer moving. Michelle pushed zombie off her, then scrambled to her feet, screaming, *"Kevin! Behind you!!"*

Turning around, I saw two zombies about fifteen feet away, stumbling toward us. They had smelled us. Or heard us. Probably both.

I shot at the first one but missed. "Kevin! Wait!" Michelle shouted. Next thing I knew she was peeling the gun from my hands, making it look easy as she shot the first zombie in the head. As the zombie fell, she shot the other one.

The sound of the shots echoed around the neighborhood, and we heard a small ensemble of rasps in response. Just then, a very tall zombie came around the corner of the house. He was wearing a t-shirt and no underwear. The zombie's pecker was shrunken and nearly black.

"Grab your stuff! Let's go!!" I shouted, picking up my box. Michelle shoved the inert zombie off her, then picked up her crumpled box, smearing herself with more zombie detritus. As she and I ran for the door, the zombie moved closer. It was only about ten feet away, with another half-dozen more a few feet behind it.

We made it through the door, slammed it closed, and bolted it. As the zombies began to pound and scrape at the door, trying to get at the fresh meat and blood they smelled (or sensed), we leaned back against the wall. We were both breathing heavily, both of us under an adrenalin rush.

"Let's get downstairs and get you cleaned up," I said, "maybe they'll lose interest and wander off."

We headed down the stairs, closing the trap door behind us. Even with the trap door closed, I could hear them pounding and scraping at the door.

Michelle looked at me with a wildly desperate look in her eyes. "Kevin," she pleaded, "I'm covered in zombie guts! I've got to get cleaned up!" Her hair was matted with zombie brains. Her face and neck were splattered. In fact, she was nothing but a mess. "Ugh, it stinks!"

"Don't worry about how you look or smell," I said, "at least you didn't get bit!"

"I don't give a damn how I *look*! I have zombie guts on me, Kevin! I could get infected!!"

I hadn't thought of that. I quickly headed toward the bathroom and started the shower.

"In here!" I shouted over my shoulder. "I have a shower!"

When I turned around, Michelle was trying to take off her blouse. I said "Wait, let me do that. Raise your arms." I grabbed the bottom hem of her shirt and carefully pulled it up, turning it inside out in the process so all the dead tissue remained with the blouse instead of getting all over her. Examining her body (and I must admit I enjoyed this part), I couldn't see any sign of cut, bite, or injury.

She had a lovely body, at least from the neck down. Not the fake, plastic, flat-bellied model kind of beauty, but the all-American, healthy *curvy* kind of beauty. She was voluptuous. The kind of woman who felt soft in your arms, not hard and bony.

After I peeled her blouse off, she was standing in front of me wearing only jeans and her bra. And zombie guts.

I noticed it was a pretty purple bra. Pretty, purple, and *big*. She reached back and unhooked it, turning her back to me as her breasts spilled out.

Despite everything, I could feel myself getting hard. Not having sex for ten years will do that to a guy.

"I'll get a garbage bag for these clothes," I said as she unbuttoned her jeans. I glanced back as I left the room and saw her pulling them down and stepping out of them, wearing only a pair of purple panties with little ribbons interwoven into the elastic. They matched the bra.

She closed the door behind her, then shouted as the room grew dark. She hadn't realized there were no lights in the room. She opened the door a crack as I said, "I'll get a trash bag and a lantern."

I heard her open the shower door and get in, despite the darkness. I got a trash bag and the LED lantern, then went back into the room. Between the relative darkness and the opacity of the shower door, I could barely make out her figure in the shower. I picked up her blouse and jeans, making sure the part I touched was clean of zombie, and dropped them into the trash bag.

I thought I heard the sound of sobbing. "Hey, are you okay in there?" I asked.

"I'll be okay. I'm just freaked out. And I stink like zombie," she said through her tears. I remembered what I felt like when I'd had my close encounter of the zombie kind.

"Listen, you're okay. We're both okay. You take a nice hot shower and get yourself cleaned up. I'll have a drink waiting for you to help calm you down," I said, "unless you'd rather have a pharmaceutical."

"I could really use a Xanax," she said. "I'm shaking like a leaf! And I think I might . . ."

I heard retching sounds, and quickly left the room figuring she'd rather puke in private. At least she was in the shower and I wouldn't have a mess to clean up.

I went back to the first aid box and rooted through it until I found the Xanax. 1 mg. Not a strong dose. I shook one out of the bottle, grabbed a glass of water and went back into the bathroom. Michelle seemed to be done puking.

"Here's some water," I said, "and the Xanax." She opened the door and stuck her hand out, taking the tablet and then the water. Without saying a word, she closed the door, and I vaguely saw her take the pill and drink the water. Then I guess she started scrubbing and shampooing again. I would have liked to stay and watch, but decided to use discretion and left the room.

I didn't know what to do with the bag of soiled clothes. Eventually I took them upstairs—all the way to the second floor, where I put them in an empty closet. Maybe at some point I can burn them. I left the bra in the bathroom since it had no zombie guts on it.

Eventually I had to knock on the door and tell her she needed to get out, the hot water heater was draining the batteries. As she turned the water off, she asked me to get her bathrobe out of one of the boxes. Once I found it, I opened the door a crack and hung it on the hook mounted on the inside of the door.

I was sitting in the living room when Michelle came out of the bathroom, wearing her bathrobe. She came in and sat on the sofa.

"So . . . how are you doing?" I asked. When she looked up at me she was a bit glassy-eyed, and I knew the Xanax was kicking in.

"I'm okay," she said, "I'm trying to shake it off."

As we sat there talking, the steamy, soapy, clean smell of a hot shower wafted into the room. I hadn't smelled that in years. I don't notice it when I'm in the shower. But when someone else takes a shower, sometimes I become aware of the comforting smell as it wafts over me. I found it evocative.

It reminded me of Tammy. Many times she'd be in the shower and would call for me to join her. We liked to take showers together. I wondered if Michelle was a shower-sharer.

It hit me then—I was mentally disturbed. Probably all of my family and friends were dead. Outside my house were half-rotten *creatures* who used to be living, breathing friends, neighbors, and strangers. Now they were monsters who wanted to attack me, eat me, to infect me. I was hiding out in my basement. There were no police, no law, no doctors. I had limited food, limited fuel, and limited luck. The odds were stacked against my surviving.

And in the middle of this maelstrom of horror, pain, misery, and death, I was getting a hard-on, looking at a pretty woman in front of me, naked beneath her bathrobe, skin warm and flushed from a hot shower. I kept wishing the bathrobe would fall open.

Just then Michelle said, "Kevin, I think I'm going to . . ." Before she could finish, she got a strange look on her face, one of alarm and disgust, and quickly capped her hand over her mouth as she began to gag. She sat down for a minute before she removed her hand from her mouth.

"Ugh," she said, "that smell came back into my head for a second. I scrubbed and scrubbed, but I can still smell it."

There's nothing quite like a beautiful, sexy woman gagging in your face to break the mood. I went and got one of the small buckets, which I placed at her feet. Just in case.

"I never even saw it coming," she said. "I didn't know it was there."

"She," I said.

"She?"

"It was a woman. She had long hair and breasts. She sort of had on a bra."

"Kevin. They're zombies. They aren't men and women any more. Not male or female. They're just zombies."

She was right. Suddenly she burst out laughing.

"You should have seen yourself holding the revolver," she laughed, "you had this uncomfortable look on your face, like you were holding a tampon."

I started laughing as well. "That's how it felt! Like it was something I had no business holding!" We were both laughing now. "But what did you expect? The last trigger I pulled was on a squirt gun!"

At my use of the words *'squirt guns'* she started laughing even harder.

"You should have seen the look on *your* face!" I laughed, turning the tables on her. "You looked so mad I think you would have shot *me* instead of the zombie if I'd given you the gun! And when I finally shot her—I mean *it*—and the zombie splattered all over you, you looked so disgusted I thought you were going to hurl right then and there! It was like a guy giving a girl an unexpected and unwelcomed facial!"

I was still laughing, thinking my analogy was clever, when Michelle got a funny look on her face, then quickly grabbed the bucket and gagged into it. I got her glass and filled it with fresh water.

When I handed it back to her, she glared at me, her head still poised above the bucket, and said, "That was not funny. It was rude. I can't believe you even *said* that." But moments later, she started laughing again. "Truth be told, I'd rather have that kind of facial than a zombie facial."

I started laughing again, mainly out of relief that she didn't stay pissed for long. But of course, even in the midst of laughing, I had an interesting visual of her getting a facial.

"Oh my," she said, wiping tears from her eyes, "that was so disgusting . . . I'll never forget how it felt when it splattered all over my face . . ."

"That's what *she* said," I added.

Michelle suppressed a giggle, then said, "We are two of a kind, Kevin. Just a while ago we were grappling with a zombie and having guts splattered all over us, and now we're laughing about it."

"It's pure stress relief," I said, "it's how our bodies purge those *fight or flight'* chemicals."

"I'm feeling a bit loopy right now," she said, "do you mind if I just sit for a few minutes?" As she said this, I noticed her robe had loosened, and a bit more cleavage was showing. It must have been all the laughter that did it.

I tore my eyes away. "You sit here as long as you want," I said.

We sat there for a few minutes, going over what happened and how close we came to calamity. Then her face scrunched up.

"Kevin," she said tensely, "do you think I'm infected?"

"I have no idea. I doubt it, but I'm not sure. When the TV and internet still worked, the reports were all about getting infected by zombie *bites*. You didn't get bit. You don't have any open sores or anything. I'm pretty sure you're okay. Let's try not to obsess about it. I know I'm not going to—I think you're fine. Let's think about something else. Come help me with the plants."

I left the living room and went into the grow room. My spinach seeds had sprouted, so I transferred the peat pellets into neti pots, then added them to a raft in my seedling reservoir. I had been working for about ten minutes, and was about halfway done, when I saw Michelle standing in the doorway, sipping her glass of water.

"So how does all this work? Don't you need dirt?"

I finished putting the sprout I was handling into the raft, then went to stand near her.

"See the tub of water I put the plant? I use a floating raft technique, where a sheet of foam floats on top of the water. The plants sit in holes in the foam. I've added fertilizer to the water and an air pump puts oxygen in the water—like in a fish tank. The plant gets everything it needs – water, light, and nutrients. It's an easy way to grow simple crops like lettuce and herbs."

"So why do you have so many different containers? Why not just one big one?" She asked.

"The table closest to us is for seedlings. See how close the lights are to the baby plants? The water has a very weak solution of fertilizer—it's for the youngest plants. Once the seedlings have matured, they go onto the second table, which contains a stronger nutrient solution and uses LED lights instead of fluorescent. See those red and blue lights above the plants on the second table? Those are LED lights. The plants stay there the longest. When they're about ready to harvest, I put them on the third table, which is mainly water and a few 'sweetening' agents. The water flushes any remaining nutrients out of the plants, because those nutrients don't taste good. And the sweetening agents help improve the taste as well." I was deliberately giving her ample information to distract her from her worries.

"So the plants actually grow under those red and blue lights?" she asked. "They don't seem bright enough."

"The light they emit is custom designed for plants. The light spectrum is just what the plants need. A lot of the visible light we see isn't used by plants. LED lights are extremely energy efficient, last a long time, and put out *very* little heat. Heat equals wasted energy. I wouldn't be able to grow nearly as many plants if I just used fluorescent, or if I used a 400 watt or 1000 watt metal halide light. Those blue lights are especially made for plants you don't want to flower—like lettuce and spinach. See the one with a mix of red and blue? It's over the tomato plants and peppers. See the little cherry tomatoes? That's because the red lights encourage flowering, which you need for fruiting plants like tomatoes and peppers."

"And your solar panels provide enough power for all this?"

"This, plus the coffee maker, the water heater and everything else." I said.

"Where is the water heater? I didn't see a tank," Michelle asked.

"I use a tankless heater. It only heats the water you need, not a whole tank full. That's why I had to tell you to get out of the shower. You were using enough hot water to drain the batteries. The solar panels charge the batteries during the day, so at night I can still have power. All the electronics I have are very energy efficient. Oh, and get this," I said, going into the bedroom to get the fluorescent lantern I'd placed in there. "Come in here, I want to show you something."

Michelle smirked. "Like I haven't heard that line before." She joined me despite her protests.

I showed her the bedroom—the full sized bed, the dresser, the closet. Nothing special. I held up the fluorescent lantern so she could see the whole room.

"Now watch!" I said, and I turned off the lantern. With the lights off, she could see the walls were glowing. Not a lot—they hadn't had much time to charge—but enough for her to get the idea.

"I painted the walls with phosphorescent paint, so if I read before I turn the lights off, the walls glow for a while. The glow slowly fades out, just like a sunset. In fact, with this paint, the walls never go completely dark. I used a new kind of glow in the dark paint that lasts much longer than the old stuff."

"Kevin, this is *so* cool!" Michelle exclaimed. "What a smart thing to do! In a really geeky kind of way. And I'd have never known it by the color, although I must admit I thought it was a bit drab."

"Let me show you something," I said, "Go stand against the wall with your arms held out." Michelle did as I asked. "Now stay there for about thirty seconds," I said, turning the lantern back on. She stood still as I counted out loud. When I reached thirty, I turned off the lantern. "Now look!"

Michelle looked back and gasped. Where she had been standing, the light had cast a shadow on the wall. When she moved away, the entire wall glowed except where she'd been standing. You could see a dark silhouette where she had been. The detail was amazing.

"Now that's pretty neat, I must admit," she said. "I'll bet it could be romantic, too, in the right circumstances." I'd never thought of it like that.

"Hmm . . ." I said. "I guess so. I did it as another way to save energy, and to make this place seem less like a dark, dingy cave. I haven't done the other rooms, but I have plenty of paint if we decide to. But for now, it's starting to get late. How about a beer while I make dinner? Then we should probably call it an early night. It's been a rough day."

Michelle nodded her head in agreement, and I led her back into the living room. "Do you really have beer?" she asked.

"Yes, I brew my own. I couldn't imagine going without beer for months at a time. Why, do you like beer?"

"I like some beer. I'm not crazy about it or anything though," she said.

"I prefer wine."

"You're out of luck as far as wine goes. I don't have a single bottle."

"I have a case of wine in my garage," she said, "I didn't think to grab it. Maybe if things settle down outside we can go get it. In the meantime, I'll try one of your beers."

I poured us both a pint from the kegerator, handed it to her, and busied myself in the kitchen. I was cutting up lettuce, spinach and cilantro, adding some croutons and cashews. Michelle slowly sipped the beer.

"This beer is pretty good," she said. "It has a lot of flavor. Kind of bitter, but in a good way."

"That's the hops," I explained. "Some people say it helps stop the beer from going bad. It also adds aroma and flavor."

I opened a can of tuna and added it to the salad and we sat down to eat in the living room. I noticed Michelle kind of picked at her tuna salad.

"Four hours ago I would have been thrilled to have a fresh salad," she said, "but now I've lost my appetite. I'm still freaked out and I'm trying not to let myself dwell on whether or not I'm infected."

I repeated that I didn't think it was likely as all the news reports I'd seen and read said a zombie bite is what infects you. She didn't have any open wounds either, and she'd scrubbed herself, so I told her I thought she was safe. That seemed to make her feel better. She started eating the salad.

"This is delicious!" She said, "And you're right! The lettuce is *so* sweet!"

"When's the last time you ate?" I asked.

"I had some peanuts yesterday," she said, "I was trying to conserve my food. I didn't know how long I'd have to make it last." She finished her beer and asked if she could have another.

"Sure!" I said, pleased she liked it. I poured her another and topped off mine, and sat down to finish my salad.

"Daughter of a doctor, eh?" I said, "So I guess you grew up pretty well-off."

Michelle told me a bit about her family and about growing up in Indiana. She continued to drink her beer, and the longer she talked the more I noticed her words getting slurred. *From two beers?!* I thought. Then I realized she'd had the Xanax as well. I suspected the combination would put her to sleep in no time. I finished up my salad, put the dirty dishes in the sink, and suggested we set up the inflatable mattress.

"Don't you mean *inflatable doll?*" she smirked. "I guess I am a bit tired. And tipsy! Those beers are strong!"

As I got the mattress out of the box, I reminded her about the Xanax. She hit herself on the forehead with the heel of her hand. "I should have thought of that!" she said, "Xanax and alcohol don't mix!"

I spread the mattress out near the sofa, then started the pump. Within a couple of minutes, the mattress was inflated and firm enough to sleep on. While I was getting it situated, Michelle helped herself to another beer and then found some sheets and a blanket among the things she'd brought over. Together we made the bed.

As we finished she said, "I'm gonna get in my pajamas," pulling out some pink camouflage flannel pajamas from her things. She went into the bathroom and quickly changed.

When she came back, I had a hard time not staring. The pj's were not the least bit provocative—they were flannel after all—but she filled them out very nicely. The top framed her breasts wonderfully, accentuating their fullness. The top two buttons were undone, giving me more than a glimpse of The Great Divide. Have I mentioned how nice and large her breasts are? I could see she didn't have a bra on, either, as her nipples were slightly poking out. Come to think of it, I guess women don't wear bras to bed. Do they?

The bottoms were not tight, but they made her ass look great. With an ass like hers, I could easily switch from a boob man to an ass man. I could feel myself getting hard again.

"Wow, those beers are really hitting me," she said, raising her arms and running her fingers through her pretty auburn hair. The effect, of course, was to lift her breasts even higher, and her nipples poked out even more. I couldn't help but look. They were wonderful. When I glanced up she was looking at me.

"What're you looking at, Kevin?" she asked slyly.

"Your pj's," I ad-libbed. "I've never seen pink camo before."

Michelle dropped her arms to her sides with a sigh then giggled. I could tell she was feeling pretty woozy. "Says the guy whose radio has yellow bunnies and pink kitties on it,"

"Hey, those are baby monitors! I didn't choose how they looked!"

She was a tad unsteady on her feet as she walked over to me. "I'm gonna get in bed, but would you stay here an' talk t'me for a few minutes?" As she said this, she sidled up next to me and put her arm around me, pressing her breasts against me. "I don't wanna have bad dreams tonight. I wanna have sweet dreams." Her voice now a whisper, she raised up on her tiptoes and brushed her lips against my cheek.

"Michelle . . ." I said, trying my best to protest.

Ignoring me, Michelle whispered, "I wanna dream 'bout *you*." She put her finger tips on my chin and turned my head to face her. Her lips met mine. I gave in. Our lips parted and I felt her tongue slip in. Hesitatingly, my tongue met hers. I pulled her body close to mine, relishing the feeling of her breasts and hard nipples, holding her abdomen against mine. My hardness pressed against her body. We kissed for a few seconds before she abruptly pulled away.

"I'm sorry, Kevin," she said drunkenly. "Sometimes alcohol make s'me forget my social grazes." She was making an attempt to articulate, but it was obvious she was struggling.

She giggled and ungraciously plunked down on the air mattress. "Whoopsie! I lost my balance!" I helped her as she tried to get under the sheet and blanket, then pulled them over her. Essentially, I tucked her in. Her eyes were drooping. She was fading fast.

"Thanks, Kev-Kev," she mumbled, "I think you are so . . . so . . ." And that was the end of that. She was fast asleep.

It was still somewhat early, probably about 9:00, but I decided to call it a night. I went into the bedroom, turned off the light, and in the newly-discovered romantic glow of the bedroom walls, lay miserably frustrated, staring at the ceiling while the walls slowly faded.

November 25th

It's been a couple of days since she moved in. I woke up early the next morning and just lay there in the dark, puzzling over what had happened.

I know she was intoxicated, but even so, she came on to me big time. I get the feeling that had I wanted to (and she hadn't fallen asleep), I could have had sex with her. Obviously I don't have much resistance. Who would? She's a beautiful, smart, engaging woman with large breasts. If she had gone so far as to undo one more button on her pajama top, I would have been unable to resist.

But as I lay there, staring at the ceiling I couldn't see and the very faintly glowing walls, the events of the night started to bother me. I agreed she could move in as a way to ensure security for both of us and as a helper for me. I didn't sign up to have a girlfriend, or even a friend with benefits. I've been around long enough to know that sex usually creates more problems than it solves. Lovers break up. Lovers have huge fights. Lovers don't last. Friends do. If I were to allow myself to get into a casual sexual relationship with her, it could ruin everything. It would certainly *change* everything. Even if she said, *Hey, no strings attached, room-mates with benefits, you know?!* I don't think I'd believe her. I've been in that situation before. *You have needs, I have needs . . . let's meet each other's needs. We don't need to be in love.* That's what they say. But in no time, it turns into *Why don't you ever say you love me?* Ugh. The whole situation brings up bad memories of inadvisable decisions.

Those were my thoughts as I lay there, wondering how to proceed. I must have dozed off, because I awoke to the sound of dishes rattling in the kitchen. I got dressed and went into the living room. Michelle must have been up for a while—the inflatable bed was already deflated and I could smell fresh coffee. The dishes were washed and in the drying rack. As I walked into the kitchen, she looked up with a big sunny smile.

"Good morning! I hope you don't mind me making coffee!"

"Absolutely not! I'm just glad to see you're none the worse for wear! The combo of Xanax and beer really did a number on you!" I said, making every attempt to keep my eyes above her neck. She was still wearing the pink camo pj's, and the top two buttons were still undone.

"I can't believe I took Xanax and drank beer! Normally I would have known better, but yesterday I wasn't thinking straight. I still can't believe I was stupid enough to get attacked. If not for you, I'd be dead!" she said, "or worse!"

"So-o-o . . . tell me . . . how much of last night do you remember? After we got inside, I mean." If she remembered getting tipsy and coming on to me, but pretended not to, it meant she regretted it. If she didn't remember, all the better.

"I remember you made us dinner, and I drank a few beers, and you showed me how your plant stuff works," she said, "things get kind of fuzzy after that. I hope I didn't do anything stupid!"

"We made wild, passionate love until the cock crowed," I lied.

Her eyes grew wide with mock astonishment. "It *crows*?! Wow!"

"As in *cock-a-doodle-doo*," I said.

"Oh, that's too bad, I've never seen a cock *crow*," she teased. "You know, where I'm from, once a man has sex with a woman, she's considered his wife, my dear new hubby!" she said, as she wiped off the counter.

"Well, isn't that interesting!" I said, "Up here in Michigan, if a woman willingly has sex with a man she's not married to, she becomes his slave. Now get me a cup of coffee," I said, snapping my fingers.

"Yes, master," Michelle said demurely, pouring me a cup of coffee. "I don't know how you like it—strong or weak, cream or sugar. I like it on the strong side and black as sin."

I took a sip. It was good. It was especially good because I didn't make it.

"Seriously," she said, "I really am fuzzy about last night. Sometimes alcohol lowers my inhibitions, so if I said or did anything that made you uncomfortable, I'm sorry." As she said this, her eyes were downcast and there was a beautiful blush of pink on her pretty cheeks. "And I don't think I ever told you last night how wonderful it felt to take a hot shower. Despite the zombie guts. Ugh. All I've had for weeks is cold water. Given the circumstances, I think it really helped me feel human again to wash it all off and start to get re-centered."

I still wasn't sure if she remembered what happened or not, but I decided it didn't matter. It was a one-time accident. Hell, sometimes male and female friends slip up and have sex when they shouldn't. It doesn't have to ruin everything.

"No problem. The next time I want to make wild, passionate love to you all night I'll just have to remember to slip you a Xanax and a couple of beers. But I'm kind of insulted you don't remember how good I was," I joked. "In the meantime, I'd like your help in the plant room today."

"Do you have anything we can eat for breakfast first?" she asked.

"Sure," I said, and handed her a protein bar. "Enjoy it. I could make you some instant eggs, but they're not very good and I'm trying to save them. Otherwise, you could have dry cereal with instant milk. Or I could make some oatmeal. Unless you want canned vegetables."

She looked at the protein bar and sighed. "I guess the days of bacon, eggs sunny-side up and toast are gone."

"Like my dad used to say, if we had some bacon, we could have some bacon and eggs, if we had some eggs!"

"Maybe I'd like these protein bars better if they tasted like bacon and eggs. Or like toast and jelly. But having fake chocolate and caramel for breakfast just doesn't cut it," she said. "not that I'm complaining—I'll take what I can get. Except oatmeal. I never have liked it. But I do miss a hot breakfast. And the stars. I miss lying on my back and staring up at the stars. Seeing an occasional meteor. I miss the night sky."

"There's so much we miss we haven't even thought of yet," I said. "You know what I really miss?"

"Having wild passionate sex all night?" She said, chewing another bite of her protein bar.

"No, we had that last night, remember?"

"Damn. No, I don't remember. I wish I did. I hate to have missed all the fun."

"You won't believe me, but I miss cutting the grass. To spend an hour walking around in circles, pushing a mower. The smell of fresh cut grass mixed with the smell of lawnmower exhaust. I really miss that.

"All of the mundane things we took for granted but now long for. But I don't miss shoveling the sidewalk."

"I miss laying out in the back yard, topless, a cooler of beer at my side and a good, sexy novel lying next to me as I doze off in the sun."

"Seriously?" I asked.

"Absolutely. There's nothing better than feeling the sun baking your skin a golden brown. And a cold beer to take the edge off whatever you're trying not to think about."

I sat in silence, trying unsuccessfully to stop focusing on the image she planted in my brain. Of her laying out topless in the sun, her breasts tanning and her areola turning a dun shade of brown right outside my upper bedroom window. She was a girl after my own heart. I forced my imagination back to the here and now. "Now that you've finished your breakfast buffet, bring your cup of coffee into the growing room and we'll get started."

"Yes, master," she quipped. Then she asked what we were going to do. I explained how I needed to set up another tray and lights. The germination rate of the kale and lettuce seeds was higher than I expected, and I wanted to get another crop going. I'm not wild about kale, but it's much higher in nutritional content than lettuce. It has a good amount of zinc, niacin, potassium, protein, and fiber. I placed three twenty gallon reservoirs on the table. "What all *do* you have to eat?" she asked.

"Everything we could want short term. Canned meat, tuna, canned vegetables and soups, dried fruits and nuts, crackers, peanut butter, powdered milk, protein powder . . . instant mashed potatoes, spaghetti sauce and noodles, MREs, boxed meals, ramen noodles . . . I even have some yeast if I want to make some bread."

"All the comforts of home," she said, "but what I really miss is a fresh, hot pizza, delivered to my door. A pizza with the works."

"With plenty of hot sauce . . ." I added. My mouth was watering.

I made a few trips for water and started filling the tubs. "I think we should limit our talk of food we miss. It's only going to make us miss it more. Although I could go for some triple-chocolate ice-cream."

"With caramel topping," she sighed. "Ah well. I'm very grateful for what you have, Kevin. You really planned well. I'm impressed. You're not as dumb as you look."

"I couldn't be and live," I added. We both laughed at my lame joke. I finished adding water to the tubs but left the third one empty, as I wouldn't need it for at least a month. "See those sheets of foam with holes in them? Would you put one each in these tubs?"

"Yes, master," she joked as she grabbed the foam sheets. Once the rafts were sitting on top of the water, I arranged the containers of fertilizer and the measuring cups.

"Now here's what we do. This first tray gets a quarter cup each of these two bottles. It's two-stage fertilizer. Then add a tablespoon of this little bottle—it's root stimulant. We add the airstone, allow it to settle down for a few hours, then we check the pH. Plants like their pH to be just right."

"I'll take your word for it. I don't need to know what I'm doing, I just do what I'm told," she said

"I noticed that last night," I joked.

"Hey! No fair! I can't defend myself if I don't know what I did or didn't do!"

"You made me promise last night not to talk about it," I offered.

"You're making that up! Besides, I know you're joking because when I woke up I was still wearing my pajamas. I doubt I'd have them on if we'd gotten wild like you claim."

"Ah, but if you look close, you'll notice you put them back on inside out!"

She looked at me skeptically then took a quick glance at her pajama bottoms. Then she came over and slugged me on the shoulder. "You jerk! You almost had me believing you," she said as I laughed hard. She couldn't help but smile herself. I attached the hose to the bubbler and airstone and placed it in the tub. It immediately started bubbling with the hissing sound I've come to know so well.

"Let's finish up putting those sprouts in the neti pots, and put the neti pots in the holes in the raft," I directed. We spent about a half hour taking care of the plants, and then I showed her how to check the mature plants to make sure there weren't any dead leaves to trim.

"You have to keep the dead leaves trimmed, or they can start to rot and spread diseases." I told her. We checked all the plants, even though I'd just done it yesterday.

By the time we finished, it was well into the afternoon. I pointed out that she was still in her pajamas. I hadn't gone out of my way to tell her earlier, as she looked so damn cute and sexy in them. Every opportunity I had, I took a quick glance at her bust and her ass. She caught me looking a few times but didn't say anything, thank goodness.

When I pointed out that she was still wearing jammies in the afternoon, she smiled and said, "I thought you'd never notice!" She hurried into the living room and pulled some clothes out of her boxes, then disappeared into the bathroom after asking if she could take a shower. We haven't had much sun over the past few days, and the batteries are getting low, so I told her of course she could, and she didn't need to ask, but to make it a short one.

"Yes, master," she smirked, "but I prefer long ones."

I stood there, a neti pot in my hand, trying unsuccessfully to think of a witty comeback, but failed. She grabbed the lantern and went into the bathroom. I heard her clothes rustle and the water come on, and still stood there, my imagination once again distracting me.

Double damn this libido.

When she came out of the bathroom, she'd already changed into jeans and a University of Michigan football shirt. Once again the clean smell of a hot shower wafted through the room.

She looked and smelled delightful. Sometimes there's nothing better than a beautiful woman, freshly showered, her skin rosy from the hot water and her hair still wet.

For the hundredth time, I had to force myself to ignore my baser instinct.

"I was thinking—" I said.

"I thought I smelled something burning," she quipped.

"—that we should take one of the baby monitors upstairs and keep it on. So we can tell if anyone—or any *thing*—gets into the house."

Michelle agreed it was a good plan, so we headed upstairs. It was pretty chilly in the house, and I was once again thankful I'd gotten the gas heater. We quietly prowled around the house, peering out the windows. The zombies were still out there, at least as many as had been there the day before. They appeared to still be agitated, congregating more around my house than any other. Their rasping sounds were disheartening.

I don't know whether it's some kind of residual memory from yesterday or if they somehow actually know we're in here. Even from behind the window, looking at them in the state of decay—one had an eye hanging out of the socket, many of them had obvious broken bones—I could almost smell them. Michelle took one look and did an about-face—I don't think she'll be ready to see a zombie for a while.

Michele looked around the house. I think she was snooping as much as anything. Looking in all the rooms, checking out my place. "I'm sorry to ask this, but how long ago did you say your wife died?" she asked quietly. We spoke in near whispers the entire time we were upstairs.

"It was ten years ago this July," I said. "Why do you ask?"

"Well, no offense, but you haven't updated the house since then, have you?"

"No, I didn't see any reason to. This furniture is in good shape, and besides, she did the decorating. It made me feel like she was still here in some way. I didn't have the heart to change things. "We had a great marriage. She wasn't just my wife—she was my best friend with benefits, my partner in crime, my sister, my mother, my daughter, and my drinking buddy."

"Partner in crime?" she whispered. We were standing close together in the upstairs hallway.

"When she was getting chemotherapy, we treated the nausea with homegrown medical marijuana. That's how I got interested in hydroponics."

"Was it legal back then?" she asked me.

"No. But I didn't care. We were very discreet and were only using it for medicinal reasons. Or at least she was. I found it very relaxing and it helped to ease the emotional pain I was going through when I realized she might not make it."

"Do you think it should be legal?" she asked. I just stared at her, waiting for her to think through what she just asked. "Oh. Right. I guess it doesn't matter if it was or wasn't legal before—there are no laws now. But when your wife smoked it, did it help?"

"It helped us both. I mean, we think it slowed the rate of cancer, and it helped her tolerate the pain and nausea. It increased her quality of life. I was truly grateful. None of the prescription drugs were nearly as good, and they all had much worse side effects. After she died, I put the rest of the pot in a closet and haven't touched it since."

"What makes you think it slowed the rate of cancer?"

"She lived longer than most of the other patients at the cancer center. I doubt many of them were smoking. I know it's only anecdotal, but still . . . Have you ever smoked pot?"

"I used to smoke when I was in college if someone brought some out at a party. I never bought any myself. Back then it was an urban legend that getting a woman high made her horny, so guys always had some at parties," she said with a faraway look on her face. "Since then, I've heard about all the ways patients use it. I've read some fascinating studies about using it medicinally. Seems like it might be good to grow some."

"I'll keep it in mind, but I doubt the seeds I have are still viable. Maybe once the dust settles, we'll think about it. Does it really make women horny?" I asked before I could stop myself.

"Maybe one day you'll find out," she said conspiratorially, "maybe we'll mix it with Xanax and alcohol.

"Okay, fine," I whispered, watching her grin. "I made it up. We didn't really have wild sex all night."

"As if I didn't know."

"We only had wild sex for a couple of hours. Then you fell asleep, exhausted but happy, after telling me how incredible I was."

"Mmm-hmmm. I'm sure I said that. Just like I'm sure you have a ten inch penis."

"Ah-*hah!* So you *do* remember!" I crowed.

She rolled her eyes and said, "I surrender."

"I love it when a woman says that," I said dreamily.

Looking around the kitchen, at my outdated appliances and countertops, she whispered back, "Haven't heard it much in the past decade, have you?" Ouch. That one hit a bit too close to home, and I had no comeback. I placed the radio on the kitchen counter and turned it on. We headed downstairs, secured the trap door, and Michelle offered to fix us some dinner. While she was doing this, I played some CDs I'd grabbed while I was upstairs. That was probably a bad idea—the music reminded me of Tammy.

We made small talk while we ate, but my thoughts kept drifting back to Tammy. I was reminiscing, and sadness seeped into me. Michelle apparently sensed this or might have been feeling the same thing, because she kept to herself as well. After dinner, I let her pick out a DVD for us to watch. She picked out a movie she'd brought over, *Love Actually*, which was very good, but in some ways made me feel worse.

All in all, especially when compared to the night before, it was a very subdued evening. When the movie was over, I told her I was tired and was going to bed.

As she said goodnight, I headed for the bedroom. Just before I got there she said, "Oh, and Kevin, just so you know: I was only joking this morning when I said I liked to sunbathe topless. I was getting even with for you claiming we had wild sex all night." Her voice dropped down to a near whisper. "What I really do is sunbathe completely nude!" She then smiled at me and winked.

I couldn't tell if she was kidding or not. I stared at her for a second then closed the bedroom door.

I don't know how late she stayed up—the grow room lights are on a timer, so she didn't have to turn any lights off. Before I dozed off I heard the sound of the air mattress inflating. I fell asleep, wishing she was Tammy. Wishing I could smell Tammy's scent just one more time. Wishing I could tell her one more time how much I love her, and how much I miss her.

I shed a few tears, lying there alone in the dark. It's been awhile since I've cried about Tammy—or anything else.

Brittle

brit·tle: *adjective. Easily damaged or destroyed; fragile; frail:*

My heart is brittle.
One errant thought of you
and I will be undone

I have to believe
that part of you still exists
can you hear my voice?
can you feel my thoughts?
has everything that was you
disappeared?

"In Flander's Field the poppies grow"
those blooms and those words
are all that is remembered
of the men who fell that day.

But there are no poppies for you.
No words or poems
to remember you by
no one to recall unwritten words.

my recollection of you
is all that prevents you
from being unwritten.

My heart is brittle.
you are nearly unwritten
and again
I am undone

And again.

November 26th

I woke up this morning still feeling blue. I couldn't recall my dreams, but I felt a strong sense of loss. When I smelled the coffee brewing, I knew Michelle was awake, and somehow my heart was eased. I dressed and went out to see what she was up to.

Michelle was already out of her pajamas (by that I mean she was wearing jeans and a sweater), sitting on the sofa drinking a cup of coffee. The inflatable mattress was deflated and pushed under the sofa.

"Good morning," I said. "Sleep well?"

"Did I ever!" she said, putting the coffee cup down. As I poured myself a cup of coffee she had a huge yawn, and stretched her body in such a way that her breasts were pushed out, stretching the sweater in a wonderful way. Her arms were bent and were up around her head. I had ample time to once again ogle her body. I felt a kind of hunger grow inside me, and it wasn't for corn flakes.

"Sleeping on the air mattress, in a secure, warm basement, with a full stomach, a freshly showered body, a big strong man sleeping in the next room, and knowing in the morning I'd have hot coffee . . ." She paused as if trying to find the right words. "I haven't been this comfortable since before the end. I haven't been this *happy* in an even longer time. I know it doesn't make sense. Those *things* are just outside your house. But this morning I'm sitting in a room lit with electric lights, drinking a hot cup of coffee, and talking with an attractive older man I'm growing quite fond of."

"Older man? Like, what, I'm your dad's age?" I protested, unsure of how to take it.

Michelle looked at me. "Kevin, how old are you?"

"I turned fifty-one on August 3rd."

"Kevin, I'm not quite forty. You're eleven years older than me. You're an older man. I like older men. It's a compliment. So," she said, changing the subject, "what's on the list today?"

I told her that I'd show her how to check for pests. She gave me an appraising look which changed to an *I know a pest when I see one* look. I chose to ignore her.

There's always a risk some bug will find its way inside. Aphids and spider mites in particular. But since we rarely go outside and there are no plants in the house, odds are slim that we would introduce a pest who hitchhiked in on our clothes. Otherwise, the system is pretty easy to maintain. So checking and rechecking is part of our daily chores. If we're diligent and careful, we should have fresh herbs and a few vegetables until spring.

She was leaning back on the sofa, her right arm bent at the elbow, holding the blue cup of coffee near her chin. The light from the plant room illuminated her face. One side was lit with soft lavender light, the other side was dimly lit with the light reflected off the walls and ceiling. Her eyes were mostly in shadow. There were highlights in her hair from the LEDs, giving her auburn hair a purplish tinge. The light brought out the textures of her skin, I noticed, as I let my eyes wander down her face to her neck, and then below. She was wearing a blue sweater; it was fuzzy and looked like cashmere, softly conforming to the shape of her breasts. The light accentuated their fullness, and as I gazed at them, I realized she was watching me. I felt bold, and decided to keep gazing at her body. As I looked, my eyes moving over and around her breasts, around her full tummy, down toward her hips and crotch, I noticed her nipples hardening. I felt like that was a good sign.

"What are you looking at, Kevin?" Michelle asked quietly, repeating the question she'd asked the other night when she was tipsy.

"I'm admiring the way the light is falling on you. You look lovely. And the way your breasts look in particular, with the soft light on your sweater . . . they look absolutely wonderful. I'm tempted to get my camera. In fact—do you mind?"

"What, if you take photos of my breasts? I don't think I'm comfortable with that."

"Not of your breasts, dingbat! Of you!"

"Hmm . . . well, I guess in that case I don't mind. But no nudes. You'd probably post them on Flickr."

I haven't taken any portrait photos in a very long time. I haven't been inspired. I've taken plenty of landscape photos over the years— Michigan is nothing if not picturesque—but no people photos. It felt good to want to take her picture.

I grabbed my camera bag and went back into the living room. She hadn't moved. I attached the camera to the tripod and moved to where I felt the view was most flattering. I didn't want to use a flash; it would destroy the effect of the lighting I was so entranced with.

"This is going to be a long exposure, about half a second, so when I tell you, try to be still."

Michelle didn't respond. I looked through the viewfinder, made sure everything looked right—the composition, the lighting, how zoomed in I was. I set the timer for two seconds delay, hit the button, and audibly counted down: "Two . . . One . . ." The shutter clicked open and shut. I then looked through the viewfinder and zoomed in closer, highlighting her breasts. God, how beautiful they would look in this light without her sweater! Even so, they looked luscious.

I hit the button again and counted down like I did before. Then I moved the camera a few feet to the left to get more of a three-quarter profile of her face and breasts. I took a few close-ups, noticing her watching me intently. Her eyes were dark and dilated in the dim light. I tilted the camera to get a couple shots of her eyes. I knew from checking the images in the viewfinder that with a little editing to tweak the levels and saturation, the photos would look great. I nodded with satisfaction and turned the camera off.

"Don't I get to look at them?"

"Sure, but not right now. I promise I'll show them to you after I edit them. I have a rule; I delete any photo I take of someone if they don't like it. It helps people to relax, knowing I'll delete every photo of them if they want. Next time, I want to get a reflector and put it over there," I pointed to the far side of the sofa, "to add a little fill light. It'll make the photo really pop."

Of course, part of the reason I didn't want to show her the photos was because I didn't want her to think I'm obsessed with her breasts. Even if I am. I figured I'd show her when she's gotten to know me better and wouldn't think I was a pervert. Unless I learned she liked perverts.

"I didn't know you were into photography," Michelle said, "You're full of surprises." Taking her photos—*enjoying* taking her photos—made me feel more like the old me. I feel most myself when I'm being creative and responding to the muse. It came to mind that Tammy was the same way. While the sadness I'd felt upon awakening had lessened, it now came washing back over me. "I just gave you a compliment," Michelle said, "And it made you look sad! What's up with you?"

"I hope this doesn't insult you," I said, hesitatingly, "but having you here somehow makes me think of my Tammy."

"Tammy . . ." she said, weighing the name on her tongue. "I'm going to choose to take that as a compliment. I know you loved her. I'm sorry if I put you in a tailspin."

"Five years ago, I might have gone into a tailspin. You know what they say about time heals all wounds? It's true. But the past day or so, I've really been missing Tammy. Watching my best friend slowly die was a tough time, but I had to be strong for her, I couldn't let her see how devastated I was." I turned my head so she couldn't see my eyes misting. "But don't get me wrong, these thoughts or feelings or whatever, they hurt, but it's a sweet pain. Does that make sense?"

Michelle nodded, but I don't know if she really understood. I don't know what she's been through. I told her about Tammy practically the first time we talked; she hasn't said anything about her love life, and surely an attractive, intelligent, big-breasted woman like her plenty of offers.

"Tammy and I had a wonderful marriage. You know how a lot of times the husband and wife end up barely tolerating each other? It wasn't that way with us. We never fought. We disagreed sometimes, but even that was rare. We got along so well, it was simply astounding. The longer we were together, the better friends we were. I was constantly surprised—how can something this good just get better and better, I used to ask myself, but then a year later I'd realize things were even better than they had been."

"How long were you married?"

"We had seventeen years of marriage. Most couples are lucky to have one good year. We had seventeen. And I don't want to be crass, but you know, even the sex kept getting better. Sure, maybe the frequency went down, but the quality just kept going up. There were times we'd make love, and it'd be a spiritual experience, like our souls were melding . . . so when I think of her, my thoughts are incredibly happy thoughts and memories. I'll miss her for the rest of my life. But I don't regret these thoughts. Sometimes good memories make me feel sad, but I'd rather have the memories and be sad than to not have the memories at all."

I looked at Michele, my eyes still a bit moist. She was looking at me with a look I couldn't decipher. Her eyes were beautiful, and I noticed how lovely her lips are. "So what is it about me being here that makes you think of her?" she asked.

"Michelle, I'm afraid to say it. I don't want to jinx it. But how I feel when I'm with you reminds me of how she and I got along when we first met. I don't know how much of it's situational. We were thrown together; if this hadn't happened, would we have developed a strong friendship? You said you wondered when things will get back to normal. Truth be told, I think this is the *new* normal. But I'm talking about the way we fit together. Being with you makes me feel good. Look, I'm not coming on to you, this isn't some bullshit line I'm using to get in your pants," I said.

"Damn." she said.

"I just feel something for you I haven't felt in a long time. I like being around you. You make me feel better about the future somehow. Despite having creatures twenty feet away who want to eat us."

"Maybe without each other, those things outside would drive us to madness," she suggested.

"I don't know, maybe so. But I'm glad you're here, especially this morning. I'm glad you moved next door, and I'm glad you moved in."

"That's just because I have big boobs," she said, half mockingly.

"That's just frosting on the cake," I suggested.

"Frosting . . . there are so many interesting possibilities . . ." she said wistfully. Suddenly she got up off the sofa and said, "Let's take care of our chores and then figure out something to do."

I had an instant idea of what I'd like to do with her—or even to her. I was taken aback to discover I had an erection. "Something to do?!" I asked.

"We can play backgammon. Or we can talk. I like talking to you. You're smart, you're educated, you've lived a full life. I could learn a lot from a guy like you."

"That depends on what you're wanting me to teach."

"Like, about making things grow, getting them big . . . liquid fertilizer . . . keeping the roots nice and wet . . ."

I decided to ignore any possible implications of her words. "Let's check the pH of the water," I said. "You never know, those plants could save us."

"I've never understood the whole pH thing," she said. "When it's written, why is the 'p' little and the 'H' big?"

"pH is an abbreviation for "power of hydrogen" where "p" is short for the German word for power, and H is the symbol for hydrogen. Low pH is called acid, high pH is called alkaline. The H is capitalized because it's standard practice to capitalize element symbols. Like with H_2O, the H and the O are always capitalized."

"You are such a geek," she said, "how do you know that?"

"I took the pains to memorize it a while back. To impress all those girls who are attracted to geeks."

She rolled her eyes. "I think I should unpack my stuff while you do whatever you need to. I would like to see how you check the 'power of hydrogen' so we can keep having your delicious salads. I think we should go upstairs to check the herd and maybe see survivors, I think we should turn on the radio and see if we can find any broadcasts, I think we should make dinner and have a few drinks and then I think we should either play games or make out."

My mind had been drifting. She was still standing before me, and I was still obsessing about her gorgeous rack. But my mind suddenly focused on her last words. Make out? I was taken aback. "What did you say? Did you say *'make out'*? Are you serious?"

Her face lit up as she broke into a smile. "Ha-ha, now it's my turn to get you! I just wanted to see if you were paying attention. Too bad I didn't have the camera. The look on your face was priceless." She paused. "I like you, Kevin, you're smart and funny and you make me feel good about myself. The combination of those things makes you . . . interesting. And just so you know, I think you're handsome and sexy as hell, but in a really comfortable geeky way. Like that April Barrows song says:

I want a guy who's like an old stuffed sofa, someone who'd be nice to come home to. And when the world outside was frightnin', he'd be soft and so invitin'.

Just when I was starting to think she was flirting with me, leaving the door open for me to make a move, she says I'm like an old stuffed sofa. Great. Not only that, but now I had reason to believe she was playing me. Or delusional. Me, sexy? *I'm an older man* as she kindly put it. Much of my hair is gone. I have a paunch. The notion that someone could find me sexy is ludicrous bordering on crazy. But I wasn't really in the mood to point those things out to her. "Is that why you pressured me into letting you move in? Because you wanted an old stuffed sofa?"

She took exception to my remark. "Pressured you?! *Pressured you?!* I made a business proposal. You accepted it. There was no pressure! Don't you dare go making me out to be some freeloading vixen!" she exclaimed. The flashing of her eyes only made her even more attractive.

I burst out laughing. Michelle's eyes were hard with anger, but as I continued to laugh, they softened up and she began to smile. "What are you laughing at?" she asked.

"I got you again! I *invited* you to move in. You didn't pressure me. I do wonder though, how many newly-shacked up college couples have had this same conversation. *'You pressured me into moving in, I didn't really want to!' 'That's not true! It was your idea!'*" I continued to laugh and this time she joined in. "Michelle, I don't think of you as a freeloading vixen. I think of you as a freeloading vixen with a great rack and a shortwave radio," I said, feeling bold enough to reference her beautiful breasts. I wonder if she knows I'm a breast man? "Speaking of the shortwave radio, could I have a look?"

"There you go again, changing the subject," she said, "but fine, let's take a look at it." She rustled around in her stuff and pulled out a small box.

"This is a shortwave radio? It's so small!"

"What did you expect?"

"The last time I saw a shortwave radio was when I was about five years old," I explained. "My grandfather had one. It was about the size of a small microwave, with tubes and knobs . . ."

"Geez, Kevin, welcome to the 21st century!"

I realized how dumb I must have sounded, talking about huge radios and tubes. I should have known shortwave radios had gone digital and compact just like every other electronic device.

"Have you used this?" I asked her.

"No, I never really had a reason to. It used to belong to my boyfriend, but he left it behind when we broke up. I've never even taken it out of the box."

I read the information on the box—it had features that hadn't even been dreamed of when my Grandfather was alive. I took it out and looked it over. It had over twenty buttons, a digital display, a hand-held microphone, and a small speaker. The antenna didn't look like much, but I knew I could rig up a better one if I had to without much trouble. I plugged it in and began fiddling with it. First I set it on scan.

Within a minute or two, I heard the sound of someone talking and excitedly called Michelle over. We both looked at the radio as a calm woman said "We interrupt this program. This is a national emergency. The President of the United States or his designated representative will make an announcement over the Emergency Broadcast Network at 1200 hours GMT, 0700 hours Eastern Standard time." After a brief pause, I heard that weird sound I've only heard when they're testing the system; that attention-getting signal. Then her voice repeated the message. It was obviously a looped recording. I felt a cold lump in my stomach. I thought we'd heard a survivor.

Seven o'clock tomorrow morning I might finally learn something. Maybe the President will tell us what was going on. Maybe things aren't as bad as I fear. Maybe order is being restored, but it just hasn't made it to my neighborhood yet. Of course I will be up at seven o'clock to listen to the broadcast.

In the meantime, I had work to do and Michelle was sitting there waiting for me. I really wanted to surf the airwaves more, but decided it could wait. Survival here was the most important, and for now that meant taking care of business.

I needed some time to think as well—Michelle said I was "sexy as hell." But "like an old stuffed sofa." She also said she thought we should make out. She said she was joking, but behind every joke there's a kernel of truth. I wonder how she'd respond if I took her in my arms and kissed her? Do I have the nerve?

I couldn't believe I was struggling with this. I am a fifty-year-old man. I've had my share of lovers. I've been married and fathered a child. But it was all so very long ago . . . the very idea of making out made me giddy and nervous.

"Let's go check the pH," I said, "and then we'll check on what you called 'the herd'."

"And then?" she asked.

"I'm sure we'll figure something out." I responded. We checked the pH of not only the new reservoir, but the other six, as well. I explained to her how pH can fluctuate over time, sometimes simply by the plants absorbing the nutrients and changing the composition of the water. She was surprised to see how much the sprouts have grown in the past couple days.

I told her one advantage of a hydroponic system is that you're giving the plants exactly the nutrients they need to do their best, and in my climate controlled grow room they don't suffer any effects from high or low air temperatures. She appeared to be fascinated, and seemed to be taking to the idea quite well. I may turn her thumb from brown to green yet!

Once we were finished, we went upstairs to check on the herd. Initially when I looked out the window toward the street, everything looked about the same. Zombies were milling about, seeming to congregate more around my house than anywhere else, and I could see a few of them wandering up and down the street. But something didn't look right. It took me a minute to notice that some of the zombies were on the ground. They looked freshly injured—broken legs and even broken spines prevented them from getting up. The few that were immobile had horrific head injuries. They looked as though they'd been attacked. *What the hell?* I thought. And I realized: zombies don't attack each other. And other animals don't attack them either.

Only people attack zombies. This means we're not the only two people left alive in Ann Arbor! My first spontaneous reaction was one of elation—maybe the authorities *were* getting things under control.

But my second reaction was one of fear and caution. Someone was out there. There was no way to know if he or she was a friend or foe, but if it was someone struggling to survive, and if they found out I had food, booze, drugs, electricity, and a woman—they could them from me. And the simplest way to do that would be to kill me. Once I was incapacitated, they could do what they wanted with Michelle. The idea of someone breaking into my house, killing me, and raping or killing Michelle was horrifying.

Michelle had been looking through the other windows, but when she glanced at me she could tell something was wrong. "Kevin, what's going on? You look like you've seen a ghost!"

"I'd rather see a ghost, to tell you the truth!" I said. I showed her the zombies on the ground and how it looked like they'd been attacked.

"So someone is out there killing zombies in the street. Good for them. Maybe it's the authorities. What's the problem?" she asked.

"Let's go downstairs and talk." Suddenly I didn't feel safe. As we headed downstairs I thought about what she said and decided it was unlikely for any authorities to have caused the damage I saw, and I told her so when were safely in the living room with the trap door closed behind us. "If it was the authorities, they wouldn't kill or injure a few and quietly move on. They'd be knocking on houses, looking for survivors. Whoever it is, I doubt they're going around killing zombies just for fun. It's not a sport, and it's far too dangerous to do on a lark. The only sane reason would be for survival, maybe to get the zombies out of the way so they could scavenge some food. I wouldn't be surprised if they're systematically breaking into all the houses on this street and taking anything they can use. And think about it, Michelle—what would happen if they went into a house and found living people?"

"I suppose they'd try to take their stuff, no matter how. Survival of the fittest and all that."

"Exactly. And if these aren't good guys but are bad guys, what do you think they *might* do if they found a woman?"

Michelle's eyes grew dark. "I hadn't thought about that."

"Well I had. The thought of someone figuring out we're in here, then breaking in and either stealing our stuff or finding you . . . I can't allow that to happen."

"So you're worried about me and want to protect me, is that what you're saying? Like I'm some poor defenseless woman, a member of the weaker sex?"

"I know better. You're a hell of a lot better with a gun than I am, and I suspect you can take care of yourself just fine. But we're a team now. We watch each other's back. I watch your back, you watch mine. We're partners. I hope you feel the same. And of course I'm concerned about protecting you. I admit it. You're the only friend I have in the whole world. If something happened to you . . . I don't know what I'd do. Let's just say I've grown accustomed to your face."

Michelle stood there, thinking about it. Even in the midst of this new concern, I couldn't help but notice again how lovely she was in the light coming from the grow room.

We talked it over and agreed that there wasn't much we could do—we were already being very careful. But we did decide to keep the gun close at hand so either of us could get to it almost immediately. We also decided we should take turns watching the street through the window for a few days to see if we could ascertain who was out there.

"Do we have to do it alone?" she asked. "I don't want to be a wuss, but I don't relish the idea of being up there alone, looking out the window at zombies."

"We can do it together then," I said, "and don't forget we have the radio in case one of us has to be alone for a few minutes."

So that's where things stand today. It's already dark out, and we've come back downstairs. But for the next few days, I'm going to be uptight until I have more information. How many there are, whether they're armed . . . I need to know what I'm dealing with.

We played a few games of backgammon later, but my heart wasn't in it, so I went to bed early again.

November 28th

I got up a few minutes before seven o'clock as planned and turned on the radio. Michelle was still on the inflatable mattress, but she was awake and watched me in silence. We were disappointed when all we heard was the same repeating message we heard the day before. We decided to leave the radio turned on for a few hours in case I had the time mixed up. Or maybe the live broadcast got delayed.

We went through the motions of pretending it was just another day. Worked with the plants. Finally put Michelle's stuff away—some of it went in storage, her clothes went into an empty closet, some of her personal belongings she kept in an overnight bag. It would do for now.

We went up and watched the street. One of us would watch while the other person sat in a chair nearby. We made small talk. Got to know each other a little better. Neither of us did any flirting—personally I'm not in the mood to flirt, much less make an attempt at levity. My heart rate is up, as is my blood pressure, I imagine.

Michelle told me about her family, how they were strict church-goers throughout her childhood, and how much she loved her father. Women don't always say this about their dads, and it was touching. She didn't say much about her mom.

In turn, I told her about my family, my childhood memories of picking cherries in July and apples in October. I told her about Dad's garden that I didn't pay the least bit of attention to, and now wish I had. I'm sure I could have learned a lot from him. I told her about our vacations near the dunes. She's never seen Lake Michigan and wondered what the big deal is. I wanted to explain it to her . . . but I shrugged and told her she'd have to experience it herself. I offered to take her once we get out of this mess.

When it got dark, we went downstairs and had some dinner. She read while I fiddled with the shortwave. I heard one transmission, but it faded out before I could get a handle on what they were saying. It was in English—I don't know if this radio can pick up transmissions from very far away—being in the basement doesn't help. I'll need to figure out a way to rig a better antennae.

After a while, we called it a night and went our separate ways.

December 1st

The past few days have been a repeat of the entry above. Except we had our first snowfall. Only a couple of inches.

It's strange how in the midst of horror, we still find things to laugh about. After we'd done our chores (including harvesting some of the herbs and laying them out to dry), we went upstairs to take a look around.

When we exited the basement, I noticed there wasn't much light. Peeking out the window I saw an overcast sky and falling snow. It must not be very cold, because the snow isn't sticking to the road or the yard. Then I called Michelle over and asked her what she saw.

"I see the neighborhood, falling snow, and zombies," she replied.

"Take a closer look at the zombies."

Michelle stood looking for a moment, then said, "That's strange. The snow seems to be sticking to them. Why would it stick to them and not anything else?"

"I guess for the same reason a bridge will freeze before the road. The zombies cool down faster than the ground."

Michelle started laughing. "There should be signs posted, 'Caution: zombie freezes before road'!"

I laughed out loud. I thought it was hilarious. I was tempted to make a sign and go hang it around one of their necks, but decided against it. We chuckled for a few more minutes, then went back downstairs.

I don't think I've ever laughed—*really* laughed—with anyone more than I have with Michelle. Anyone since Tammy.

My earlier observation about the zombies moving slower in the cold was confirmed. I wonder what will happen when the temperatures drop to near zero, and we have a heavy snowfall? What would happen if we got hit by an ice storm? Would the zombies be rendered immobile? Are they like fish who freeze in the ice but are fine when the ice thaws? Maybe I'll find out soon.

December 3rd

It's incomprehensible what we saw.

After chores yesterday morning, we went upstairs to check the traffic, so to speak. It was my turn to watch, so I stood at the window, watching the street. The snow a few days ago didn't stick, but the sky was gray and overcast. Zombies milled about, slowly shuffling along. Things were uneventful for about ninety minutes until I saw movement with my peripheral vision.

I turned my head and couldn't believe my eyes: I saw the garage door opening on a house about half a block down the street. What looked like a modified delivery truck backed out. Steel panels had been welded onto the side, metal grating covered the windows, and a huge plow-like device (I think they used to call them *cowcatchers*) was mounted on front. I thought it was a snow plow until the truck headed our way.

Zombies were slowly congregating toward it, attracted to the noise and movement. The truck drove straight toward them, and the impact of the truck hitting the first zombie flung the creature onto the sidewalk, one dismembered leg flying into the grass beyond. Bone and tissue flew in all directions.

The zombies continued to move toward the truck, and it simply mowed them down. The truck was making no attempt to avoid them—in fact, it swerved to hit them.

Zombies with major head trauma quit moving. The rest would get knocked aside or run over and try to get back up. The ones unable to get to their feet began to crawl toward the truck.

The truck raced down the road past my house. The driver looked like he was enjoying himself. His window was open and he held a cigarette and bottle of beer. The passenger appeared to be laughing. Steering with one hand, the driver brought his left hand to his mouth to take a drag from his cigarette and a swig of beer, then tossed the bottle out the window. It hit a zombie in the shoulder then fell to the pavement and shattered.

When a zombie became snagged by the cowcatcher, the driver screeched to a stop, flinging the zombie onto the pavement ahead, then roared back into motion, running it over. Apparently the driver didn't think he'd done a good enough job, because he backed up and ran over it again. As the rear tire ran over the zombie's head, it exploded with a wet pop. They both thought it was hilarious.

Michelle was sitting on the carpet, leaning against the wall. She heard me gasp and rushed to the other window as the truck moved on down the street. Apparently there weren't as many zombies to have sport with further down, because the truck turned around and came roaring back down the street, mowing down more zombies. Zombies were still appearing, coming from around the sides of houses and sometimes from within houses whose front doors were open. The truck was honking its horn, too, which I couldn't understand—were they *trying* to attract the zombies? Did these guys have a death wish? Were they trying to draw a crowd? That's insane!

I was wrong when I said no one killed zombies for fun. I should have said *no normal person kills a zombie for fun.* Once the street was practically clogged with zombies, it happened. It makes me sick to even recall what I saw.

The truck screeched to a stop a few doors past us. After a brief pause, a roll up door on the back of the truck opened. Metal sheets were welded to the frame around the bottom half, blocking the zombies from reaching inside.

As the door rose, three men became visible. One guy, who was probably fifty years old and grossly overweight, may have been the driver. The other two were younger and skinnier—maybe in their late twenties. They all wore dirty jeans and soiled shirts. One had a garish tattoo on his left bicep, although I couldn't tell what it was. The third guy must have been in the back of the truck.

As we watched, the two skinny guys reached down to pick something up. It was a naked woman. Her head was covered with a pillowcase or cloth bag, stained with blood. Her hands and ankles were bound with duct tape. There were bruises across much of her body, as well as cuts and abrasions. Her entire back side—including her back, ass, and legs—had lateral bruise stripes. In several places were small scabbed over wounds.

She was limp as a dishrag and looked like she might be dead. A trail of smeared dried blood ran from her crotch down her left leg. She was gaunt and pale.

The men carried her to the edge of the door frame, causing the zombies to start their rasping sounds, mouths open, hands and arms scrabbling against the sheet metal as they tried to reach her. I heard Michelle gasp as the woman weakly struggled, apparently roused by the sound of the zombies. She desperately tried to get loose, squirming and twisting, but it was hopeless.

The big man reached over and pulled the sack off her head. One of her eyes was purple and nearly black, swollen shut. The look of panic on her beaten face when she saw the mass of zombies reaching for her, teeth gnashing, clawing at the metal plates, will haunt me all my days.

With the bag off her head, I could tell she was maybe thirty years old with bloodied and matted blond hair. Her struggling increased, but despite her desperation it was no use—between the duct tape and the guys' hold on her, she had no chance of escape.

The men held her out over the mass of zombies. She evidently lost control of her bowels. Liquid spewed over the zombies below her. The big guy spit a wad of phlegm onto her face. The zombies seemed to be getting more agitated. They were practically rioting. The throng pushed harder and harder at each other to get to her flesh. They began trying to climb over each other to get to the woman, trampling each other in the process.

As zombies fell, other zombies climbed on top of them, reaching for the woman. The two guys held her just out of reach, and when the mass of zombies grew too high, the fat man jumped back in the driver's seat and pulled forward about ten feet. The pile of zombies collapsed and then began to reconstitute at the back of the truck.

As Michelle and I watched in stunned silence, the fat man came back and ripped the duct tape off her mouth—taking some of the skin with it as she began screaming. Her lips and mouth started bleeding freely. The zombies went into a frenzy as the woman screamed wordlessly.

The two men heaved the woman into the horde.

With a tumult of rasping, the zombies swarmed her as her horrifying screams echoed through the neighborhood.

Michelle and I locked eyes. Hers were hard and dark, filled with terror, disbelief, and emptiness. Mine must have looked the same.

Michelle sank down on the carpet. I turned back to the window and saw the guy with the tattoo laughing. The other skinny guy watched with a smirk.

The screaming woman sank into the crowd of clawing, ripping, rasping creatures. A zombie party with a live human piñata.

As the woman's screams died out, the big guy unzipped his pants, pulled out his pecker, and began to piss into the crowd where the woman had landed. Steam rose from the swarm of feeding zombies.

While he was doing this, one of the other guys came up with two fresh bottles of beer, one of which he handed to the skinny guy while saying something that made them both laugh.

The zombies had swarmed the woman. I couldn't see her, thank god. All I saw was the occasional raised zombie head as it chewed a ripped and bloody piece of the woman's flesh, blood dripping off its chin.

When the man finished pissing, the three of them continued looking down into the fray, laughing and joking. The skinny guy chugged his beer and hurled the empty bottle into the crowd, then gave the zombies the finger. Now that the zombies were preoccupied with eating, the truck sped back to the house it had come from. The garage door opened and the truck pulled in. The garage door closed behind them.

The neighborhood no longer looked like the quiet street I have lived on for so many years. Sure, the houses were still there, complete with mailboxes lining the street. Cars were parked in a few driveways.

But there was a mass of rotting, broken flesh clotting the street, looking for all the world like a tumor. A writhing, bloody tumor, infecting the neighborhood with cancer. These creatures were no more human than maggots, or like vultures scrabbling over road kill.

Michelle and I were speechless, trying to come to grips with what we had witnessed. I felt nauseated and tasted bile in the back of my throat.

I crossed the room and held out my hand. She just looked at it blankly for a moment before reaching out. I pulled her to her feet, put my arm around her, and helped her downstairs and to the sofa. While she sat there, I found the bottle of Xanax and handed her a tablet. I swallowed one as well.

We sat in silence until I noticed she was shivering. I got a blanket, draped it over us, and began to talk to her, telling her not to worry, that we were safe, no one would find us, I'd take care of her, I'd protect her. I don't know if I believed my own words, but I repeated them over and over, and after a long time I felt her body—which had been utterly tense and stiff—start to relax. Her breathing got deeper, and as I looked down at her, I saw her eyes were closed. She had fallen asleep. I wanted to get up; my bladder was full and I wanted some bourbon. But I didn't want to wake her, so I sat there, feeling her warm body relax into mine. I started getting sleepy myself when Michelle's body started jerking and she began making whimpering sounds.

"Michelle, wake up! You're having a bad dream! It's okay, I'm right here!" I said to her. She looked around, eyes wide, and I could tell she was disoriented. She buried her face in my chest and began to cry. I put my arms around her and stroked her hair. She cried for probably ten minutes, then the sobs died down.

Her voice thick with emotion, she said "That woman! She . . . what kind of man would do that to another person? How could they be so horrible? How could they do that to her? They're worse than the zombies! They *know* what they're doing!" She looked at me with pleading eyes.

"I don't know. Those men were probably raiding houses and found her. They probably used her and tortured her until they got tired of her. Throwing her to the zombies was their form of entertainment. These are the same people who hate guys for being queer, or hate black people and call them *niggers*. Give them a chance and they'll act on their hate, as long as they can do it in secret. They're sick bastards. There's a defect in their character."

"That could have been *me!*" she choked, "If I had been in my house, they might have raped and beaten me and thrown *me* to the zombies! Kevin, how can we possibly protect ourselves from guys like that?"

"Michelle, listen to me. What *could* have happened doesn't matter. It didn't happen. You're safe. Even if they break into the house, they won't be able to find us. When I had this part of the basement renovated, I left the other part unfinished. There's a door in the kitchen leading down to that side of the basement. Anyone searching the house would go down there and find it empty. I'll show you next time we're up.

"Our trap door is hidden. No light escapes the basement. We'd have to be making a hell of a lot of noise for anyone to hear us. We have the radio upstairs. If they do break in, we'll hear them. If somehow they do find out we're here, by the time they break through the trap door we'll have escaped out the root cellar."

Michelle was still trembling, badly shaken by what she saw. Truthfully, so was I. I knew I was up against human monsters far worse than the zombies. It will be difficult to truly relax again, knowing they're out there.

After a few minutes, I lifted Michelle's chin toward mine, wiped the tears from her cheeks, and said, "Michelle, what we saw was horrible, more horrible than I can believe. But it didn't happen to us. We're still alive, we're hidden well, and we have each other. That's probably more than anyone else can say in these days and times."

I then bent down and kissed her softly on the cheek. "Let's keep doing things the way we have been, and let's continue getting to know each other. Like it or not, we're stuck with each other, so let's make the best of it.

"Let's resolve right now to watch out for each other. To protect each other. And to be smart. We're clever people. We can get through this as long as we're with each other. What was it you read in the Bible?

Two are better than one: if either of them falls down, the other can help them up. But pity anyone who falls and has no one to help them up,' I paraphrased.

She looked up at me, put her arm around my neck, and pulled me to her. She kissed me on the lips, then put her head back on my chest.

We sat in silence for a few minutes, and I started replaying the afternoon. I found myself getting tense and anxious again. I stood up and said, "Let's find something to do. We need to distract ourselves."

"What should we do?"

"I was thinking maybe we should paint the rest of the walls with my glow in the dark paint. When the grow lights go off, it's so dark in here it's almost freaky."

Michelle agreed. I went into the storeroom to get the paint and supplies. While I was in there, I poured myself a slug of bourbon and quaffed it.

When I came back into the living room, she was already pulling stuff out from the wall—the sofa, the book/cd shelves, the boxes of stuff I hadn't found a place for. I put everything down and went back for a drop cloth. We spread the drop cloth without saying much. Neither of us felt like talking.

I opened the can of paint and while stirring it with the paint stick I became aware of Michelle staring at me. I looked up and tried to smile, but it felt forced and she could probably tell. She continued to look at me, and I let myself look back at her. We held the gaze for probably ten or fifteen seconds. I don't know what she saw in my eyes, but in her eyes I saw a mixture of things: vulnerability, grief, fear. I could have sworn I also saw a hint of affection.

Looking into her eyes, I also became aware of *my* affection for *her*. It made me uncomfortable.

I realized I'd stopped stirring. I looked down at the paint, breaking the moment. We stayed silent for a few more minutes. Then she said "Kevin, about painting the walls . . . I don't do very well with paint fumes. I know they're not toxic, but they sometimes makes me sick to my stomach."

Without thinking it through, I offered to let her sleep upstairs.

"*I can sleep upstairs?!* Are you crazy? I mean, seriously, are you suggesting that I sleep upstairs, alone, after what I saw today? Those guys are still out there." She looked at me incredulously. Any hint of affection was gone.

"You're right, that was stupid. We could both sleep upstairs."

"Where would we sleep?"

Suddenly I felt like I was walking in a mine field. If I said *we could share the bed* she might think I was using our situation as a ruse to get in her pants. But if I said one of us could have the sofa, the other the bed, and she was hoping for something more, she might feel rejected. She might think I don't find her attractive—which is patently untrue. I thought for a moment and decided to take the safer of the two options.

"Since I sleep on the bed down here, I'll let you sleep in the bed upstairs. It'll be fine." I watched her closely to see her reaction. She didn't say anything but looked thoughtful for a minute. "I suppose everything's covered in dust, but I can't think of a way to fix that. We can't exactly put the sheets in the dryer, and we obviously can't go outside to shake them.

We can't shake them down here either. We'll swap out the bedding with fresh sets from the linen closet," I suggested.

"Why do you only have one bedroom?" she asked, "When you have room for three?"

"After five years or so of having no guests, I decided it was a waste of space, so I made one bedroom into an office and made the other into a TV/media room. I didn't spend much time downstairs, other than in the kitchen. Most of my time was spent upstairs."

The paint was stirred, everything was moved to the middle of the room, the drop cloth was spread out. We began to paint, first with two rollers, and then after about an hour we worked out a system. I used the rollers while she did the detail work. I had to admit to her that I'm lousy at doing the detail work.

Despite everything, I found myself enjoying watching her. Her back was to me most of the time, which gave me a good view of her ass. She was wearing jeans today, not too tight, not too loose.

Keeping busy was good for us. We started talking more, and I even made her laugh a few times. After about three hours, we were nearly finished. I was, anyway. I should have noticed the paint fumes, but it didn't cross my mind.

I offered to make us some dinner while she finished up, and made vegetarian shepherd's pie. It wasn't as good as the real thing, but I seriously did not want to eat meat, and doubted she did either. I didn't want to make anything with tomatoes either—I wanted nothing to remind us of blood or flesh.

I opened a bottle of grape juice and added some vodka. Michelle was wiping her hands on a towel, having just washed up. As I handed her the drink, I said "We used to call this a Purple Cow. Back when *I* was in school, this is what college boys used to get a girl in bed. Or tried to."

"Is that what you're doing, trying to get me in your bed?"

"It appears I don't need to, since you're already sleeping in my bed tonight."

She sipped the drink, then she smiled and said, *"I've never seen a purple cow I never hope to see one, but I can tell you this for sure, I'd rather see than be one."*

I smiled back. "The guy who wrote the 'Purple Cow' poem got so tired of people quoting it to him he wrote a sequel: *"Ah yes, I wrote the Purple Cow, I'm sorry now I wrote it. But I can tell you this for sure, I'll kill you if you quote it!"*

Michelle laughed and accused me of making it up, but I held up two fingers and said, "Scout's honor, you can look it up yourself." She asked if I was really a Boy Scout and I admitted I wasn't. Then she pointed out that she couldn't really look it up.

I opened a box of crackers to go along with the shepherd's pie. Usually I like some good crusty bread. Usually I like going to the store and buying what I need. Sigh.

As we grabbed our plates, I suggested we sit on my bed and eat. "Just don't get cracker crumbs in my bed!" I told her. The living room was in such disarray there was nowhere else to sit.

Heading into the bedroom, she said "You're going to kick me out of bed for leaving crumbs in the sheets? If you made your bed, that wouldn't be possible."

I placed my plate on the nightstand then quickly smoothed out the sheets and blanket. We sat down and began eating.

Michelle was looking around my bedroom. "Not much for decorating, are you?" she asked.

"I planned on doing more decorating, but things happened too fast and I wasn't able to," I said lamely. "Maybe we can do that sometime. You had some nice art in your house. You should hang some of it."

As we finished our dinner and drinks, Michelle said, "I hate to be a pain, but I'm getting a headache from the paint fumes. Can we go upstairs soon?"

I'd forgotten about the paint fumes. I told her of course we could, so we washed up and headed upstairs. Michelle brought along her pillow.

"I have more linens and pillows upstairs," I offered.

"And I'll bet they're as outdated as all your other décor and appliances," she teased, "but I don't mind stuff that's old, as long as it gets the job done."

"Is that right," I intoned. I'm pretty sure I saw her stifle a laugh.

We were particularly quiet as we made our way up the stairs and into the house. Once in the kitchen, we left the trap door open to help the basement air out.

It was nearly dark, but enough light remained for us to find our way around. I took Michelle's hand and led her into the master bedroom. She stripped the mattress while I found fresher linens and together we made the bed. I gave her a hug and retreated to the sofa in the TV room.

"Could you come and sit with me for a few minutes?" she softly called out.

I didn't mind in the least. I made my way into the bedroom and lay sideways across the foot of the bed, just like old times. I kicked off my shoes and they landed with a thump on the floor, a sound I'd heard countless times before.

After talking quietly for a few minutes, I started getting sleepy. I yawned and told her goodnight.

However, when I tried to get comfortable on the sofa, I became aware of a new problem. In the basement, the walls are underground and are essentially soundproof. But up here, in the house, it's a different story. I could hear the zombies outside, rasping, shuffling their feet. There were many more than usual outside our house, having been drawn by . . . I made myself stop thinking about it.

It's just the Michigan wind rustling the leaves, I tried to convince myself.

But I heard things, things I wasn't used to hearing. It was unnerving. It wasn't pleasant. It was downright awful. No matter what I did—pillow over my head, fingers stuck in my ears, deliberately trying not to hear—it didn't work. The sound was relentless. I tried some breathing exercises but wasn't having any luck. I sighed loudly.

Michelle must have heard me. "Kevin!" I heard her whisper, "Are you awake?" I got to my feet and made my way to the bedroom once again.

"Everything okay?" I whispered.

She sighed, then said louder, "I can't sleep. I keep hearing things, and keep thinking about that woman today. Those things . . . the noises they made . . . It's horrible and scares me, even though I know we're safe!"

I told her I felt exactly the same way.

"Is there any way you can sleep in here tonight? I'm sleeping in my clothes, just like you, so it's not like I'm trying to seduce you or anything," she volunteered.

I thought it over for a few seconds—not long—and said, "I wouldn't mind. The sofa isn't as comfortable as I remember. So yes, I'll sleep with you, but on one condition."

"Y-e-s-s-s?" She asked warily.

"I want to sleep on the side of the bed nearest the door. I've always slept on that side, even after Tammy died."

"Oh, is that all? No problem," she said, and I heard her sliding over and making room.

I quietly crawled into bed beside her, careful not to make contact. It was very strange. I hadn't had a woman in this bed since Tammy. It didn't feel wrong, but it felt . . . weird. I lay facing the ceiling, watching the shapeless, shifting patterns of light I see with my eyes closed. I could hear Michelle breathing next to me, and could tell she wasn't sleeping either.

"Thank you for taking care of me earlier," she very quietly said. "I felt like I was about to lose it. You helped me. Again." She reached over and touched my arm, then clasped my hand in hers. "I'm very grateful for all you've done for me and all you're doing, and I hope I'm not too much of a pain in the ass. I really am trying not to be an imposition."

"I'm glad to have the companionship," I replied. "I think if you weren't here, I'd have gotten very depressed. When I was getting all the work done on the house and basement, and buying all the food and stuff, I sometimes had to ask myself why I was doing it. Why did I care if I survived? It's not like my life has been one big happy party. I've wanted to give up many times, even before all hell broke loose."

"Why did you want to give up? What was going on to make you feel that way? Was this after Tammy died?"

"I was seriously depressed before Tammy got sick, stayed depressed while she was dying, and even more after she died. Before Tammy there was Jason."

"Who's Jason?"

I paused, bracing myself to go on. I hadn't spoken about this in a very long time, and saying the words was going to reopen a wound that will never completely heal.

"Jason was our son. Tammy got pregnant after we'd been married a few years. I've always wanted a son. Or a daughter. His birth was amazing. I cut his umbilical cord. I looked at my little baby boy and whispered, 'Happy Birthday, Jason!' I wasn't just a guy anymore, wasn't just a husband and a friend. I was also a father. I felt like it was a privilege to be his dad. I still feel that way. I paused again, and said more to myself than to her, "It *was* a privilege. I like to think he would have turned out to be a good man."

"Like his father," Michelle whispered, then waited for me to go on.

Our conversation now made things even more bizarre. I was lying in bed with a beautiful woman, in my own house, hearing zombies outside, and having a conversation with her that was many times more intimate than sex. Outside civilization has fallen apart, and I'm having a confessional about things that happened over a dozen years ago. I was talking about things I'd not talked about to anyone but Tammy. I felt naked bordering on ashamed.

"I loved being a dad, and I was great at it. I fed him. I changed him. I walked the floor with him when he wouldn't sleep. I remember one night when Tammy went out with some friends, I fell asleep right here in this bed with him sleeping on my chest. It was the best time of my life. Jason made me want to be a better man. I wanted him to be proud of his dad."

I paused to take a few breaths. These memories were precious, but they brought back feelings I'd denied for years. I felt a familiar and profound sense of loss. I felt my eyes grow moist, and my sudden emotions took me by surprise.

"When he was seven months old, Jason died. Sudden Infant Death Syndrome. I entered a very dark place and lived there for a long time. I was finally coming out of it when Tammy was diagnosed with cancer."

"Oh, Kevin, I am so, so sorry!" she whispered, squeezing my hand. She could have said more. She didn't need to.

"You know, I used to be religious. I used to believe that God answers our prayers. I used to believe in miracles. I can't believe those things anymore."

"I believe in God." she said, "I believe in Jesus. I go to church."

"I still believe in God," I said. "I still believe everything in the Apostle's

Creed. I believe Jesus was who he said he was. I believe God loves me. But I don't talk to him anymore. I'm mad at him. If he's really God, he understands why. During my darkest period, I started drinking. I wasn't a drunk—I never drank before work or during the day unless it was the weekend. But at night, I'd hit the bottle hard. I was self-medicating. I could tell Tammy was worried about me, but she was going through her own stages of grief, and we didn't have a lot of emotion left over for each other. She never brought it up and neither did I. We weren't talking much. We still loved each other, but where our hearts used to be there were nothing but smoldering cinders. I read once that many couples split up after the death of a child. At one point, I almost had an affair. There was this woman at the office and . . . well, you know how the story goes. We were attracted to each other and not only was she receptive, she was the aggressor. But even though I was tempted, and she was obviously willing, I couldn't go through with it. I'd even made arrangements to meet her at a hotel. But in the back of my mind, I still wanted to be the kind of man Jason would have been proud to call Dad. Cheating on his mom wasn't part of the picture. I drove to the hotel and sat there in the parking lot, wanting so bad to go inside and feel something, *anything* besides this empty ache. But I didn't go inside. I drove to the liquor store, bought some Jack Daniels and a cigar, went home and got drunk."

"I didn't know you smoked," she interrupted.

"I don't unless I'm desperately wanting to get drunk," I replied. "That night I felt the lowest I've ever felt. Looking back, I realize I'd already turned a corner. I'd chosen to do the right thing. I hoped God would reward me somehow. A month later, Tammy was diagnosed with cancer. Instead of being rewarded for making the right choice, God was punishing me for being tempted. That's how it felt. "Those first few weeks are nothing but a blur to me—I took a lot of time off from work under the guise of taking care of Tammy, but really I was drinking myself into a stupor. The rug had been ripped out from under me. I wasn't a father, I wasn't much of a husband, and I wasn't much of a friend. I wasn't much of a man. I was a black hole of self-loathing."

I could hear Michelle next to me, sniffling. She was quietly crying.

"After the biopsy, we learned it was stage three. I pulled myself together. Straightened up. I knew my job was to be her husband; her sober husband. I'd be worthless to her if I was drunk every night. I knew she needed me as her friend and husband, and she needed me sober. So I quit getting drunk. I still had a drink now and then, but seldom to excess. She fought hard. The cancer went into remission for a year. We thought she'd beat it. We were planning to go on a celebration cruise and maybe get pregnant again. But the cancer came back with a vengeance. We had no happy ending to our story."

Michelle was still holding my hand. Despite my struggle to hold myself together, I had quietly begun to cry. She wrapped her arms around me and drew me to her. I rested my head on her chest, still crying. This time it was her turn to comfort me.

"Shh, shh . . . it's okay. You got through it. Jason would have been so proud of his dad. You're a good man, Kevin, and I haven't met too many men I can say that about. I'm lucky to call you my friend."

I allowed myself the luxury of being comforted. It felt good. The memories were old, the emotions faded, but I knew the grief would never go away completely. Scars fade, but don't disappear.

Men aren't like women. Crying isn't cathartic for me. It's exhausting. I never feel better after crying, I just feel worn out with a headache. I struggled to rein in my emotions.

The creatures outside were quieter, but I could still hear them. As my tears dried and my muscles relaxed, I listened to her heartbeat and the sound of her breathing. As she stroked my hair, I drifted off to sleep.

When I awoke, we had shifted positions in the night, and at some point I had taken off my t-shirt. Now her head was resting on my chest and her arm was around me. I lay there, listening to her slow breathing. The sun had come up on an overcast day, and the room was dimly lit.

I looked around, taking in the contents of my former life. My closet still held most of my clothes. Some of my framed photos were hung on the wall. The dresser was cluttered with odds and ends—loose change, a watch I kept meaning to get repaired, wadded up receipts, a framed photo Tammy and me smiling into the camera.

Michelle stirred, sleep slowly leaving her. I kissed the top of her head.

"Good morning," I said, "ready to start the day?"

"Let me lie here jus' like this for another five minutes, 'kay? I'm so comfortable and you're so warm . . ." She still sounded sleepy. I liked the way it felt, her head on my chest, her body snuggled against mine. I pulled her a tiny bit closer and kissed the top of her head again. I could see the curve of her breast beneath the blanket.

I could feel myself start to get hard.

She began to lightly stroke her fingers through the hair on my chest. I felt myself get harder. She looked up at me, and I bent down to kiss her. She kissed me back. Her lips parted in response to mine, and tentatively our tongues began to touch and explore.

I stroked her shoulder, squeezing it, running my hand over her back. I realized I couldn't feel a strap. I have no idea when she took her bra off—probably when she first went to bed. I reached down and cupped her breast in my hand.

As we continued kissing, her hand continued to stroke the hair on my chest, and then she slowly moved it lower, taking her time, waiting to see how I responded. I could hear her breathing getting deeper, and I realized mine was getting deeper as well. I lifted my hand and began stroking her cheek, letting my fingers touch our kissing lips.

Somehow during the night a line had been crossed. There was an intimacy between us, and it wasn't because of the conversation we'd had. It was as if I had let down the barriers between us, as had she.

Her hands traveled over my navel, then around to my side, then back to the center again, this time lower. I had no reservations. No fear. I was aroused, willing, and able.

She broke our kiss, put her lips next to my ear, and whispered, "Kevin, please make love to me." Then she kissed me again. She rolled on top of me, her legs straddling mine, and reached down to grab the bottom hem of her sweatshirt. As I watched, she slowly drew it up, revealing first her tummy, then a bit higher, until I could see the swell of the underside of her breasts. I was breathing faster.

She continued her slow tease, raising her sweatshirt ever slowly higher until at last I could see her rosy pink areola, and then her hard nipples. I reached up and cupped them with both of my hands, as she finally pulled her sweatshirt over her head. She dropped the sweatshirt onto the bed and with her eyes closed allowed me to continue squeezing her breasts and lightly pinching her nipples. Her mouth was slightly open and her cheeks were flushed.

I felt her hand go to my belt buckle and begin to pull the belt loose. As she struggled momentarily with the button of my jeans, I lowered my hands from her breasts. I wanted to indulge myself in looking at her.

Her nipples jutted out from her areola, flushed deep red. Her breasts were full and large and round, womanly, and gorgeous. Her breasts could inspire paintings. Or poetry. Opening her eyes, she saw me watching her, and arched her back to push them out even further. She tilted her head back, and for the third time since I'd known her, she quietly asked, "What are you looking at, Kevin?"

"I'm looking at a beautiful woman who's straddling me, topless, her incredibly gorgeous breasts begging for my mouth," I said.

She smiled as she finally undid the button of my jeans and unzipped my zipper. Reaching inside my underwear, she grasped me and pulled freed me from the confines of my clothes. She stroked my hardness, her eyes closed, using my leaking fluid to lubricate my shaft. I felt like I was eighteen again, completely focused on my cock, immersed in a sexual ecstasy I hadn't known in many years. I couldn't help but gasp.

She rolled off me and began to undo her jeans.

"Please," I said, "let me do that." I reached over and unsnapped her pants, pulled down the zipper, and with both hands began to pull them down. She lifted her ass off the mattress to accommodate me. As her jeans traveled over her knees, she pulled one leg free, then the other.

I began to run my hand over her body, starting with her breasts. They were so large my open palm wouldn't even cover them. Then I let my hand wander down her side and onto her thighs. Her panties were dark maroon and lacy. I ran my hand over her mound, enjoying the feel of her sex. As I did this, she quietly sighed. I let my fingers take a tour of her genital landscape without making any direct contact. As I continued, I could feel her getting more excited. She responded with a quiet whimper.

I enjoyed the way she felt and the sounds she made.

She reached over and grasped my hardness again, and I struggled to maintain my composure. "No fair," she whispered, "I'm practically naked and you still have your pants on . . ."

I stood up and began to take off my jeans and underwear. When I turned around, naked, she looked me and said, "Mmmm!" As I lay back down, pushing the sheets to the foot of the bed, she said, "You look good enough to eat!"

Which is exactly what she did. She focused all her attention on me, taking pleasure from giving me pleasure. I was groaning and gasping, unable to control how loud I was. Reaching down and running my fingers through her hair, I said, "Michelle, if you keep that up, I won't be able to stop."

I was embarrassed. She'd only been using her mouth on me for a minute, and I was about to finish.

She moaned encouragingly.

"Are you sure this is what you want?" I gasped, knowing release was imminent.

"Mmm-*hmmmm!*" she hummed.

With renewed energy she began to focus on me. Unable to stop myself, I felt the physical and sexual tension mounting. As the pressure rose, so did my moaning, and within seconds I called out in passion, my voice raspy and uneven. The orgasm was not only the most intense I could remember, but also seemed to last forever.

For a split-second, my moaning reminded me of the zombies. I pushed the thought away.

Pulling her up to me, I said, "My god! I am undone!" I closed my eyes, satiated nearly beyond belief.

But another part of me was all riled up.

I was hungry, hungry to explore her sexuality and ready to express mine. "Now it's my turn!" I eagerly moved between her legs and began pulling off her panties. Then I lowered my face to her sex, luxuriating in the fragrance of an aroused woman I cared about. As I began to use my tongue on her, I lifted my eyes to take in her body. I could see her breasts and nipples, still hard, even more flushed than they had been a few minutes earlier. I felt like I was in heaven. For a few minutes I forgot everything and simply existed in a state of sexual bliss and satiation, using my tongue to give her pleasure.

After a few minutes she began to breathlessly plead with me, "Please . . . please . . . please don't stop . . ."

Suddenly she cried out, arched her back, jerked and pulled my head hard against her. I kept using my tongue until I felt her twinges subside. As I lifted my head from between her legs, she began to weep great heaving sobs. When I cradled her in my arms, I felt tears fall on my shoulder. She turned and kissed me deeply, her lips salty with tears and tasting faintly of my sex.

"Geez, was I really that bad?" I joked.

She laughed through her tears, and after several minutes, with a sweet voice weary with spent passion, she quietly said, "Thank god, Kevin, I was so afraid you were gay!"

I wasn't expecting this and laughed out loud. Hearing me laugh, she stopped crying completely and laughed along with me. We lay there, wrapped up in each other's arms.

Still chuckling, I asked her why in the world she'd thought I might be gay.

"Don't take this the wrong way," she sniffed, "but I figured either you don't take a hint or you weren't attracted to me."

"Um . . . what do you mean?"

"Well, geez Kevin, how much more obvious did I have to be? I tried my hardest to let you know I was interested. I gave you all kinds of chances to make a move on me. I flirted, I kissed you goodnight, I tried to dress sexy, I gave you compliments to let you know I was interested; hell, I even put your hand on my breast, remember? That night at my house when my heart was beating so fast?"

I reached over and cupped her breast in my hand.

"Do I remember? I'll never forget. Your heart really *was* beating fast. I remember standing there with my hand on your breast, wanting to slide it down and squeeze . . . but I was afraid I was misreading you."

Of course as I said this my hand slid down and squeezed.

"A single woman and a single man are standing close together in a dark room, and she puts his hand on her chest. How could that *possibly* be misunderstood?!"

"Michelle, I haven't gone on a date with a woman, kissed a woman, felt a woman's breast, or made love to a woman in ten years. I don't know how to recognize and interpret romantic clues anymore. I really liked you and was attracted to you, and was willing to settle for your friendship, as long as I still got to spend time with you."

She looked at me with tender astonishment. "That may be the sweetest thing anyone has ever said to me."

"Of course, it was made all the more difficult and overwhelming since I'd already seen you topless and your breasts began to preoccupy my thoughts. Even more than they already were!"

She stiffened slightly in my arms. "You saw my breasts? When?!"

"Back in early October. Before the Collapse," I said. "I was going through the house, turning off the lights and getting ready for bed. I had just turned the light off upstairs when in the corner of my eye I saw a light go on. I looked out the window, and there you were, taking off your sweatshirt. It was completely an accident," I said apologetically. "I wasn't being a Peeping Tom, I swear."

"And that's the only time you saw me without my shirt on?"

"Absolutely."

"Well, you missed plenty of other chances. I walked around my bedroom weasring just a sexy bra or topless with the blinds open plenty of times. I wanted you to see me," she confessed. "I noticed you glancing at my boobs a few times and I'll admit it—I wanted to give you a free show. I was alone, bored and feeling naughty. I guess I have a little exhibitionist in me."

"You did that on purpose? You slut!" I exclaimed with a smile, hoping she wouldn't take offense.

"I may be a slut, but you're getting hard again," she said, reaching down and giving me a light squeeze. "I wanted you to notice me, Kevin. I was feeling pretty low, and I wanted someone to appreciate me. The first few times we met, something in me clicked and I wanted to connect with you. Remember when you brought me the basil, and then went back and got me some lettuce? I thought it was so sweet! I haven't met a really,

really sweet guy in ages. You even helped me move in without my asking. Usually as soon as men see my boobs and get close to me, they turn foreign on me."

"Foreign?!"

"Yeah, you know . . . Roman hands and Russian fingers."

For the second time in just a few minutes, I laughed out loud. "I've never heard that one," I said.

Michelle continued. "I know I have big boobs. And I don't have to *catch* a guy looking to *know* he's looking. So I knew you liked what you saw, and yet every time we talked, you went out of your way to look me in the eyes and talk to *me*, not stare at my chest and talk to my mammaries. You treated me like a person, not like a walking pair of boobs. You have no idea how sweet that is."

"And you have no idea how much effort it took!" I admitted. "I even wrote about it in my journal. I'll show you sometime."

"Right now," she said, reaching down between us, "I'd rather you show me something else."

"I'd love to show you something else, but there's one problem."

"Oh?"

"I'm gay."

"Your mouth says you're gay, but other parts say you're straight."

"Actually, as you can tell, I'm really (cough) up for anything, but . . ." I hesitated, then said, "but I really think we should get downstairs. I can hear the zombies again outside, and if you and I end up being as loud as we were a few minutes ago, we might get their attention. We really don't want that—if I were a bad guy trying to find a home with people living in it, I'd look for a house surrounded by zombies."

"Well . . . okay. As long as we start up where we left off."

"And where exactly are we leaving off?"

"I believe you were getting ready to kiss me and make love to me."

"I like the sound of that. Let's get downstairs."

We scurried to get our clothes on. I put my jeans on, going commando, and she put on her sweatshirt, but left everything else off. We gathered our stuff and headed down to the first floor with Michelle leading the way. I thoroughly enjoyed watching her bare ass as it descended the stairs. I was obviously looking forward to the coming few hours.

Once we got to the first floor, I stopped by the window for a quick check of the street. It appeared the zombies had indeed heard us; many of them were milling around our house instead of wandering around on the street. I hoped if the despicable men were still down the street they wouldn't notice. Where the zombies had swarmed and killed the woman, nothing remained but a large dark stain and one small piece of tissue—maybe bone. I wondered where the rest of her went. I shuddered and turned away.

By the time I turned around, Michelle was already in the basement. Damn, I was wanting to watch her ass go down the stairs.

When I entered the living room, Michelle was in the bathroom, brushing her teeth. I could hear the shower in the background. She'd lit a couple of candles and the room glowed with their flickering warmth.

Glancing at me, she said, "It's about time! What took you so long?"

"I had to text my gay boyfriends and warn them not to come over for a few hours," I replied.

"Really. It's nice to know I have the power to cause you to change teams. I'm ready to play ball."

"I'll pitch if you catch," I said.

"I'm hoping you'll use your Louisville Slugger."

"Don't worry, I bring my balls and bat with me wherever I go," I said, appreciating the scenery as Michelle once again pulled her sweatshirt over her head.

She got into the shower, adjusted the temperature, then poked her head out the door and said, "Join me?"

"You bet. I was hoping to lather you up with my liquid soap."

"Is that what they call it these days? You already washed my mouth out with your soap . . . I can't wait to see what else you have up your sleeve."

"It's not what's up my sleeve you need to wonder about . . . it's what's up my pant leg. In case you already forgot what's there, I'll reintroduce you," I said as I pulled off my pants and joined her in the shower.

I stepped in behind her, admiring her wet and shining ass in the candlelight. I grabbed the soap and lathered up my hands, then ran them over her ass cheeks, making them even more slippery. I rinsed them off, then turned her around to face me. I leaned over and finally did something I'd been dreaming about for a couple of months; I took her left nipple in my mouth. As I was enjoying the taste of hot water and a hard, wet nipple, she took some soap and lathered up my manhood. "Mmmm," I growled, "I think we should finish up and take this into the bedroom."

"Too bad the air mattress isn't inflated. Your bed is so small," she said.

"It just means we'll have to snuggle."

"I plan on doing a lot more than snuggling," she said as she turned off the shower. We took time drying each other off, then I took her by the hand and led her out of the bathroom. We each picked up a candle on our way out.

When we got to the bedroom, we placed the candles on the nightstand and embraced on the bed. I took each nipple in my mouth in turn, and every now and then would lightly nip her with my teeth, causing her to jump as the pleasure took on a slightly painful edge.

I moved up so I could kiss her. As her mouth opened to receive my tongue, I slowly licked her lips all around, starting with the lower lip and traversing to her upper lip. She kept her mouth open, my tongue teasing and tickling her lips, until I finally felt her tongue join mine. I could hear her breathing getting deeper and faster I continued to kiss her, my tongue dancing with hers.

While I was doing this, I became fully firm, wanting attention. I placed myself at her entrance and with one slow forward thrust, I entered her. Michelle squirmed against me, moaning "Oh, god, you feel so *damn good!*"

Long before I wanted to, I could feel myself getting close and with a few more thrusts, I began to orgasm. The feel of my climax intensified her own orgasm, and with her eyes closed she nearly stopped breathing as her body was racked with spasms. We collapsed into a sweaty heap on the bed, breathing hard, spent. I felt my muscles trembling, especially my legs. They were quite unused to that particular exertion.

"I'm sorry I didn't last longer," I apologized.

"Mmm, you were wonderful! How long did you say it's been?"

"Ten years or so. I'm kind of rusty."

"You know what they say," she said as she reached down and gently squeezed me, "practice makes perfect!"

With a smile on my face, I pulled her to me and held her close. We fell asleep, spooning on my small bed.

When I awoke, Michelle was gone. I pulled on my jeans and a t-shirt, and went into the living room. She was on her knees, going through my CDs. A cup of hot coffee was beside her. She had put her sweatshirt back on, but wore nothing else. Her ass looked mighty fine.

"You realize having all these CDs ages you, right? No one buys CDs any more. They just download them from iTunes."

I walked over and kneeled next to her, pulling her close to me. "Oh they do, do they?" I inquired. She paused.

"Well, they used to. Maybe it's a good thing you do have these CDs. But I'll tell you what, do you mind if I pick out some music? I have a bunch of CDs next door, but I didn't bring any with me."

Well now, this will be interesting, I thought, *let's see what kind of music she picks out.* "Sure!" I said. You can tell a lot about someone by the type of music they choose.

Michelle continued looking through my collection for a few minutes, then picked one out. The first few notes sounded familiar, and it only took a moment for me to recognize the song: it was Billie Holiday, singing *Good Morning Heartache*. "This song used to be my theme song," she said. "I fell in love with it the morning after my boyfriend walked out on me. I got up in the morning, turned on Pandora, and this was the first song I heard. I've loved it ever since."

"What was his name?" I asked.

"His name was Wayne. For a while I thought it was the loveliest name in the English language. Now I can't stand it. I'm *so* glad your name isn't Wayne."

"Why did you two break up? I hope you don't mind my asking."

"Nah, it's ancient history. It stopped hurting a long time ago. Now it's just the ghost of a hurt. We were living together when he got a job offer in Chicago. When I told him how fun it would be to live in Chicago, he told me he intended on moving there alone. I don't know why. We got along well, had a decent sex life, and talked about a future together."

I had the strange feeling she wasn't telling me everything. I also felt something unfamiliar. I didn't like hearing about him. Especially about their sex life. It kind of made me mad. Or resentful. Or something. I guess it was jealousy. I did my best to ignore it.

Now that the walls were dry and the fumes gone, we re-arranged the furniture and took care of the usual chores. We skipped breakfast and I made lunch which in this case consisted of cream of chicken soup, canned green beans, instant mashed potatoes, and some canned pineapple. It was a lot, but making love had left me hungry, and besides, today felt like a celebration.

"Damn, I wish I had some of my wine," she said, thinking wistfully of the case she had left in her garage. "I'm hoping we can get it at some point."

Afterward we had a quiet night, this time playing backgammon, a game she brought with her. It's obvious she's been playing a long time—she won nearly every game. Of course, the fact that she never did put any panties or pants on, and kept deliberately flashing me when it was my turn had nothing to do with how well I did or didn't play.

After an hour or so of this—and we both had several of my beers—she nuzzled up to me and suggested we head for bed.

"Now you're talking," I said to her. "But you have to promise me you won't try to take advantage of me."

"Kevin, not only am I already taking advantage of you, but soon you'll be caught in my web like a helpless bug."

"Ah. The Black Widow. She mates, then she kills."

"I never said anything about mating. I only said you'd be caught in my web. But now that you mention it . . ." she said, reaching with her hand and stroking me.

"Seems to me you're caught in *my* web," I said with a smile.

"I must admit, your web is way nicer than mine," she replied. "But if we're going to do any sleeping tonight, is there any way we can use the blow-up mattress instead of your bed?"

What a great idea. Why hadn't I thought of it? We moved the

mattress into the bedroom and swapped my full for her queen.

Michelle offered to make the bed while I took a shower, and by the time I finished, the bed was made, something I hadn't done in quite a while. It looked very homey and inviting, but I hoped to have the sheets in disarray in short order.

I hadn't bothered to put any clothes on when I came out of the bathroom, and Michelle eyed my naked body with a look akin to hunger.

She then once again treated me to a quick strip show, slowly taking off her sweatshirt. Standing before me in the light of the LED lantern, she peeled it off, revealing her breasts and hardening nipples. Then she was standing in front of me, nude and blushing, allowing me to get an eyeful.

"There's no way you can know this," she said, "but it's actually very intimidating for me to stand in front of you, naked in the light."

I was taken aback. "What?! You're beautiful!"

"I don't really like my body. I'm not exactly the model type," she said, patting her rounded belly. "I know I have big boobs, and lots of guys really *like* a big rack, but I also have a big tummy and a big ass. I don't see how you can even like it."

"You're standing in front of a guy who's probably 30 pounds overweight, is mostly bald, and is out of shape. You're standing there naked, complaining about your body, while I get harder and harder by the minute," I said, reaching down and giving myself a quick squeeze. "If I wasn't attracted to your body, do you think I'd be getting hard?" I asked. "Many years ago, when I was younger and even more stupid than I am now, I might not have liked your body. But now, I see on TV all of these flat-bellied actresses and models with silicone boobs. They've had liposuction or lap bands or whatever else they do to make women skinny, have had their lips injected to make them fuller, have had Botox injections and labiaplasty, and you know what I think? I think they look like the perfect sex toy."

I paused. "But do you know what else I think? I think they don't look like women any more. They look fake and plastic and artificial. I don't like artificial women. I like a woman who looks real, complete with well-rounded curves and luscious breasts. Not too long before the Collapse, I quit watching broadcast TV entirely. The commercials started annoying me far beyond the ability of the programs to entertain me. I saw the commercials doing their best to manipulate my perception of beauty. All those flat-belly models and those guys with six pack abs. Real people don't look like that. I'd go hang out at the Jolly Pumpkin brewpub, and I'd see two things: I'd see how real people look—all different shapes and sizes, wearing glasses and having imperfect teeth . . . and I started to resent having some artificial definition of beauty shoved down my throat. The only people who look like that good are the ones who have lots of money to spend on reconstructive surgery and lots of free time to spend at the gym with a personal trainer. It's not normal, it's not natural, and I don't see them as being beautiful. They're like silk flowers—they look nice, but they're not real and they're not really alive. What's the point of artificial beauty?"

As I said this, I climbed on top of the mattress and patted the spot next to me.

"So you don't mind my being on the large side?"

"I prefer you being on the large side. Actually, I prefer you being on my left side," I said as she crawled onto the foot of the bed and inched her way forward ". . . or my top side," I said as she crawled toward me

Michelle moved forward, bending over and kissing my mouth. Our tongues played with each other.

"I'm not asking this to be insulting, but I'm curious: are you taking any 'male enhancement' pills or anything?" She moved to my side as she spoke.

"No, why do you ask?"

"Because we've already made love twice in the past twenty-four hours and here you are, ready to go again. I thought older guys had performance issues."

"My hand has been my date many, many times over the past ten years. But now I have a real, live, gorgeous and sexy woman who wants to make love with me. I don't need any pills." I was still squeezing and massaging her breast, rolling her nipple between my fingers and thumb. Her areola were a perfect shade of pink with a touch of brown, the color perfectly feminine. I bent down to take a nipple in my mouth. For nearly ten minutes I used my mouth and tongue on her breasts, driving her crazy. Eventually my hand travelled down between her legs. I couldn't believe how aroused she was. I could tell by her breathing and sighing how much she had enjoyed the attention to her nipples, but I wasn't expecting her to be quite this aroused. As I continued using my teeth and tongue on her nipple, I lightly began to stroke her with my fingers. Within thirty seconds she was once again caught in the midst of a massive orgasm. Once she calmed down, I was ready for some serious sex. We positioned ourselves so I was behind her and I took my time to enter her. She responded enthusiastically, moaning louder. Of course, the advantage to having had sex twice already was my stamina—which was confirmed when she came not once, not twice, but three times before me. Finally I couldn't hold back any more. The tension in my loins became unbearable and I had to let go. Every orgasm feels great, of course, but my third orgasm brought not just pleasure but a deeper sense of pride in coming multiple times in a fairly short period. It's a stroke to my ego and makes me feel like maybe I'm not so old.

"Oh my *god*, Kevin," she panted, "that was *sooo* good! You lasted forever!"

You done good, I mentally congratulated my package.

I was spent. All of me, not just my sex. My body, my mind, and my passion—all spent. Intimacy can be revitalizing, but also exhausting. As I lay down beside her, I felt myself slipping into a stupor.

As if reading my thoughts, Michelle murmured, "Damn, I'm going to sleep good tonight!" We crawled under the comforter and sheet. I put my left arm around her shoulders and brought her head to my chest. Within minutes we fell asleep.

I don't think we'll be sleeping separately anymore.

—Later—

I'm sitting in the living room now, writing down yesterday's events while Michelle sleeps. About an hour ago, I awoke from a puzzling dream. I rarely dream about Tammy any more, but tonight I dreamt we were walking along the shore of Lake Michigan, looking for Petoskey stones. We were holding hands and chatting as our bare feet were occasionally splashed by the calming surf. The sun was about to set; the day was fading into dusk; already the dusky eastern sky was fading into night with a few stars beginning to shine.

Tammy was dressed in a summery white dress. Some kind of gauzy material. It was lightweight and the sleeves fluttered in the Lake Michigan breeze. The colors of the sunset reflected off the material, and the folds and shadows picked up the blue of the darkening sky. With one hand she held the hem above her ankles, keeping the dress dry.

As the sun finally dipped below the horizon, we came upon a blanket near a beach fire. I recognized the blanket as being ours, and we sat down. Onto the foot of the blanket I spread my collection of beach treasures—a couple of decent Petoskeys, some Charlevoix stones, a piece of beach glass. From somewhere Tammy came up with a bottle of Merlot, which she handed to me along with a corkscrew. I pulled the cork from the bottle and filled our wine glasses. Gazing west out over the azure, darkening lake, which still reflected the waning glow of the day, we sipped our wine in silence.

I could vividly see the color of her hazel brown eyes as she turned toward me and toward the light of the fire. I could see the dancing highlights in her hair, reflecting the color of the flames. I noticed a mole on her left shoulder I had forgotten about. Her skin glowed in the firelight. She was healthy and alive. And beautiful.

I could smell smoke from our fire and, looking around, I could see perhaps a half-dozen more fires and could hear laughter of people nearby. I heard the murmur of adults talking as they watched fading colors of the sunset and welcomed the close of a splendid day. Slightly behind me and to the left, someone was artfully playing the guitar, singing *Waltzing Mathilda*. In the distance I could hear Blue, the resident German Shepherd, barking at seagulls. I felt the heat from the fire on my right side.

All around me, friends and families were gathered around beach fires. I heard an occasional squeal of laughter from the children. The high-school guys and girls were doing their obligatory flirting and showing off.

My observations contained details far beyond those of a typical dream; the sense of reality was profound. Even in the midst of it, I knew this was a vision.

We stayed there for hours, talking, sipping the wine (which never seemed to run out), watching a father and his little boy making S'mores. Soon we lay back, stargazing, exclaiming every time we saw a shooting star or a satellite.

A full moon had gradually moved to the west, and its light illuminated the landscape in varying shades of gray, blue, and black. Looking south, I saw the faint western face of the dunes, the forest around them nearly black. The coast of the Big Lake swept toward me, the shoulders of the dunes receding. Beach grass swayed in the light breeze. To the right of me, the dunes once again lifted their faces to the west. The lights of Frankfort glowed with the promise of activity while the beam of the Frankfort Lighthouse swept ever clockwise.

One by one, the other campfires were extinguished as families went back to their cabins; the college kids headed to town for excitement and alcohol, and couples strolled back to their rooms for privacy. Soon ours was the only fire left, and we had the beach to ourselves.

The moon was approaching the horizon now. The angel walk reflected various linear textures, silver against black, constantly changing as the moon dipped closer to the horizon. There was a feeling of worship in the air, of holiness. It was a sacred moment, begging my full attention.

Tammy turned to me, eyes gleaming, leaned into me and brushed her lips to mine. Into my ear she whispered, "I have to go now. But don't be unhappy. No one ever *really* goes away, you know. They just aren't where we remember them."

She turned back toward the lake, still smiling, still holding my hand. The surf was quiet as it sometimes is in late summer nights, the small waves chuckling as they hiss themselves into the swash. Savoring the moment, I leaned my head back and willed myself to absorb it all. With eyes closed, I heard Tammy say, "Give her the stars."

When I opened my eyes, I was awake in bed, Michelle sleeping quietly next to me. I felt a profound sense of loss, but also felt a lingering peace and joy from the dream. I quietly left the bed and came into the living room. The glow-in-the-dark paint made the walls faintly visible. I turned on a lantern and sat down. I sat still for a long time, trying to hold on to the dream even as I felt it slipping away. I opened my journal and chronicled the events of the day.

Michelle must have sensed I was gone, because she's now standing behind me, looking over my shoulder, reading as I write.

She's holding her hand out to me, beckoning me back to bed.

Thank you, Tammy, for your blessing. It took me a while to figure out what you meant, but now I think I understand.

Tomorrow I will give her the stars.

Outside/Inside

"He cried out, saying Father Abraham, have mercy on me, and send Lazarus, that he may dip the tip of his finger in water and cool my tongue; for I am tormented in this flame." Luke 16:24

Outside
The creatures murmur and moan
against the night
inside
we tumble and moan
against the sighing darkness

In the heart of hell
you offer to moisten my tongue
with cool drops of water.

I cannot resist.

I will not even try.

December 6th

In spite of all the events yesterday I woke up early and crept out of bed while Michelle still slept. In the kitchen I made a pot of coffee, then went to the laptop and booted up. I opened my astronomy program and changed the settings to Arcadia Michigan, June 21st, 2 a.m. The constellations were easily visible—the Big Dipper, the Little Dipper, Cassiopeia. I found a piece of paper, sketched the approximate measurements of the living room, then roughly penciled in the locations of the constellations. Knowing the room is on the north end of the basement, I made sure to align the drawing the same way.

I was still sketching the brighter stars when Michelle wandered out of the bedroom and went directly to the coffeemaker. Her hair was a mess, and it delighted me. Me, Kevin, watching a girl wearing nothing except one of my button down shirts—unbuttoned—fixing herself a cup of coffee. With bed hair. I couldn't believe my luck. She came into the living room and delicately folded one leg under her body as she carefully eased down onto the sofa. "How are you feeling?" I inquired.

"Mmmm . . ." she said, sipping her coffee. "It pleases me to no end to tell you I'm sore."

"Sore?" I asked, then immediately knew what she meant. "Oh. Gotcha. It was my pleasure, ma'am."

"*Mmm-mmm-mmm*, mine too," she responded. "What are you working on so early? I figured you'd sleep in."

"I feel like a new man," I said, "I woke up feeling creative. But you'll have to help. There's something I want to do."

"Well . . . okay, but remember, I'm sore!"

"I don't need that kind of help . . . yet. I could use some help painting."

"What are you going to paint? We already did the walls. Do they need a second coat?"

"No, this time I'm painting the ceiling," I said, "but not with a solid coat. I'm going to paint spots on it." She thought for a minute, then figured it out.

"Stars. You're going to paint stars on the ceiling."

"That's right. You said you really missed seeing the stars, so I'm going to give them to you."

She tossed back her head and laughed. "Are you kidding? You made me see stars several times yesterday!"

"That's right—first I *took* you to heaven, now I'm going to *give* you the heavens."

I explained to her how I'd like to mimic the true night sky at the height of summer, complete with constellations. I got the phosphorescent paint out, stirred for a few minutes, then told her I'd like to paint the constellations and she could paint background stars everywhere else. Standing on the stepstool (her) and a crate (me), we dabbed our small brushes in the paint and began. It took quite a while—we could only do a couple of feet at a time before having to step down, move the ladder or box, and step back up.

I went back and retraced my progress, giving the constellation stars a second coat to make them brighter. Then I helped her with the background stars. After we were finished, we used splatter brushes to add the myriad of far-distant stars seen on a good, cold, clear night. It was hard to tell, but I thought the Milky Way was going to look great.

It was early afternoon before we finished up. Michelle had started to anticipate how it would look, and wanted to turn the lights out to see. But I told her we had to wait until it was dark outside so it'd feel more natural. I really wanted to build up some anticipation.

We spent the remainder of the day doing our usual chores. One chore I hadn't thought through was the trash. Even though we were fairly self-sufficient, every time we opened a can of vegetables, or trimmed dead leaves, or opened a protein bar, we were creating trash. I knew I couldn't store trash down here—eventually it would either cause odor problems, or even worse, attract some kind of pest. We decided to take it upstairs.

I was nervous about being up there with those crazy bastards on the loose. But I knew it had to be done—and a couple other things to take care of while we were up there. I wanted to change the batteries in the radio and check on the number of zombies. If there were substantially less, it gave me hope they were dying off—if that's what you can call it—in the cold. Since their bodies are in various states of decay, I hoped they would eventually deteriorate to the point where they wouldn't be able to move anymore. Unless the disease prevented this.

I was also aware that I could be, ahem, dead wrong. Their being able to move at all made no sense. Maybe they won't ever decay. Maybe their tissue will just turn into some kind of organic polymer and they'll still be able to walk, move—and eat. But I wanted to check anyway.

We took two bags of trash upstairs, then debated where to keep it. My house didn't have a garage, only an open car-port, and I didn't think putting the trash outside was a good idea. Putting it outside could attract the zombies' attention—or anyone watching the house.

We decided to put the trash inside the dishwasher. It's self-contained, it seals, and you can't see inside it without opening the door. It should also help keep down the odors, although probably not for an extended period of time.

We removed the top and bottom dish racks, compressed the trash as much as we could and put the bag inside, closing and latching the door. We have to minimize how much trash we throw away. We can rinse cans out and keep them in the basement.

We made a circuit of the house, checking outside. What we saw was alarming. The number of zombies had not only increased—there were now close to a hundred milling about—but the air was full of smoke. Taking a look out the back window, we could see smoke from several fires burning in the distance. Should those fires spread, we would be in serious danger. I'm hoping they're on the other side of the river. I'm pessimistic about the chances should the house catch on fire.

I wasn't so much afraid of our getting trapped—with the root cellar escape hatch, we could get out of the house. But then what? Escape a burning house just to face a horde of zombies? No thanks. But what choice would we have? There is no fire department. Even if we saw the fire approaching, we wouldn't be able to do anything about it.

I presume if our house burns down, the whole neighborhood will be on fire as well, so we can't expect to escape. For now, though, I'm not going to let myself obsess over it.

For dinner tonight I tried to make some tuna and pasta, but it was terrible, so I splurged and made one of the chicken and dumpling boxed meals I stocked up on. I don't know why these don't make many of the survivalists' "foods to buy" lists. They're a bit expensive, but they come complete with meat, taste good, and I only had to add water. I wish I'd bought more of them.

It would have tasted fine eating it by myself. Eating it with Michelle made it delicious!

We did a little bit of laundry—we don't have a washing machine, which means washing by hand using buckets. We don't wash very often—it being winter, we're not going outside and soiling our clothes—but of course we have to wash our underclothes, and being sexually active I guess we'll have to wash our sheets now and then. *Or maybe every day,* I thought with an internal wink.

So we washed the few clothes and hung them to dry above the gas heater—it's the only way for things to dry out without going sour. I wish we could take them upstairs to dry, but that would be a sure sign to any intruder that the house was occupied.

The plant lights turn off automatically at midnight, so about 11:30 we began getting ready for the unveiling of the stars. I remembered to turn on the black light. Phosphorescent pigment responds quickly to black light, and even with the plant lights still on the stars were bright.

Michelle insisted we make an event out of it, so she popped some microwave popcorn, I made some drinks, and we brought my small mattress into the living room. I turned the black light off with just a couple minutes to spare.

Michelle started oohing and ahhing as soon as the lights switched off. The whole room was instantly transformed. Sure, it was kind of kitchsy but it was also somewhat artistic. We were both proud of it and pleased.

It looked *so* cool. The walls had a nice, soft glow, and the stars stood out brilliantly. It might not have been the real thing, but it looked great. I liked not seeing the stars with the lights on, it made it more natural somehow.

Knowing that I paid attention and responded to what she said she missed was quite touching for Michelle. We lay there for a while, holding hands, talking and looking at the stars. I pointed out the constellations I had painted.

What I hadn't expected was how romantic it would be. The walls slowly faded out like the night sky after sunset. At first all the stars seemed equally bright, but after twenty minutes the ones I had double painted stood out from the more faded ones. It looked pretty damn natural.

We started kissing, and soon we were both wound up. We had a kind of fun argument about who had to be on top—whomever it was wouldn't be able to see the stars. In the end I acquiesced and let Michelle be on the bottom. But before I climaxed (and after she had, thank god!), she wanted to be on top, so I got to enjoy the nightscape as well. I can't describe how *cool* it was. I couldn't see her at all, just her faint silhouette against the walls and stars as she straddled me. When we finished we lay panting in each other's arms for a few minutes.

She started yawning and was about to fall asleep, so I suggested she go on to bed. I turned on an LED lantern so she could see, and she made her way to bed.

That's the way things are now. She's in bed, softly snoring. It's taken me a long time to write this entry by light of the lantern, and I'm very sleepy, so I'm calling it a night.

December 9th

We have much to be thankful for today. Mainly for our lives.

We were still in bed this morning around seven o'clock (but we weren't sleeping, heh-heh!) when we heard a *thump!* from upstairs. Then another. We instantly stopped in our tracks and listened. I hurried out of bed and turned on the radio, which somehow had been turned off.

We heard another *thump!* come from above, and over the radio we heard breaking glass. Then we heard muffled voices.

We were both freaked out. Was it the guys who had tortured that poor woman? Sitting in silence, all we could do was listen.

Soon the voices got louder. Someone with a southern drawl said "I took a quick look around. The place looks empty."

"Help me pull the ladder in, damnit!" a second, gruffer voice hollered.

"Aah, shut your trap, you know those things can't climb ladders," a third voice replied.

We heard the familiar clanging sound of an extension ladder as it fell to the floor, but the sound only came over the radio, not through the ceiling. They must be on the second floor.

A few seconds later we heard "Seems deserted. Let's get this over with. I'm cold."

Our hearts were racing, but we were calm. There's no way they could know we're down here. We hoped. The voices were muffled as they took a quick glance around upstairs, then we heard voices in the kitchen and the sound of cabinet doors being opened and closed. I'd left a few things—mostly food I don't like and knew I wouldn't eat, like anchovies and some potted meat I got somewhere. There was also about a case of cheap beer I've had for a long time and never bothered to drink.

"Potted meat!" the southern guy exclaimed. *Figures*, I thought. *Nobody intelligent could possibly eat that stuff.*

"That ain't food," the gruff guy said, "unless you're a cat."

"Hell yeah!" the southern guy said, "A case of beer! Sure isn't much here otherwise. Looks like they bugged out a long time ago."

We heard the *snic!* of a can being opened, then the third voice said "Didn't find much in the medicine—hey, what's that?!"

That's when the trouble started.

Their voices got very loud and clear as they evidently picked up the radio. "Looks like some kind of toy radio."

"I know what it is! My ex had one when our kid was born. You put it in the baby's room so you can hear them if they wake up."

"You think someone is listening to—" the voice cut off in mid-sentence.

What an idiot I was. The radio's power light shone like a beacon in the dim light of the kitchen. By not thinking to put tape over the light, I had clued them in that someone was in the house and listening. They knew we were somewhere close.

We could hear their footsteps as they quickly walked around the first floor. It sounded like they were rooting through the house, trying to find us and/or more stuff. Then the footsteps receded—I suppose they went upstairs to look for us. We couldn't hear much at all for a while, then we heard them come back downstairs. We barely heard their muffled voices.

"What will we do if they find us?" Michelle whispered, her eyes wide with fear.

"We'll use the root cellar. And we have a gun. You keep it, you know how to shoot. I'll get something to hit them with," I whispered back. Michelle scurried to get the gun. She quietly checked to make sure it was loaded.

One of them found the door to the old basement, and we heard them start down the stairs. Realizing they might be able to hear the bubblers and fan in the plant room, I quickly and quietly turned the power off to the room.

"There ain't nothin' down here but junk," the southern guy said. The walls down here are pretty thin, so we could hear them.

"Well they got to be somewhere. There's no way that baby thing would still have power after four months."

"Would you guys shut up and let me think?" the gruff guy shouted. All was quiet for a minute or two.

"Someone must have put new batteries in it. And those things don't transmit far, so they must be close. Let's grab the shit we found and . . ." the voice trailed off as they started back upstairs. We heard their footsteps in the kitchen, then recede again as they went up to the second floor, presumably with their loot.

Without the radio we couldn't hear anything else. We didn't know if they were still in the house, hoping we'd come out from hiding, or if they'd climbed back down the ladder and run off.

"I don't know if they're still here or not," I whispered, "but just to be safe, let's stay as quiet as we can." I hated leaving the lights off in the plant room. Plants don't like it when their period of light is interrupted.

We crept around the house for about an hour when we were startled to hear the sound of someone quietly walking around the house. So someone *had* stayed behind, hoping to surprise us! Thank God we hadn't made any noise! We heard the footfalls quietly move into the kitchen and then a lengthy pause. Another ten minutes went by without a sound, then the familiar *thump!* sound again. We heard the footsteps—still in the kitchen—cross over to the staircase and then fade out.

"I think they're leaving," I whispered.

"Holy shit, Kevin! That scared the crap out of me!"

"Me too. I'm glad I disguised the trap door as well as I did, otherwise we'd have been toast."

As a few hours passed, so did our unease. Evidently they think we're no longer in the house, so we're safe for now.

I'm going to put a couple of liters of coke in the root cellar along with some booze. I wouldn't mind a couple of drinks tonight, and it's cold enough in there to chill them down quite a bit.

December 11th

Kevin asked me to write down what happened while the memory is still fresh. He's resting comfortably, but won't be able to write for a while.

I'm not as good at writing as he is, but I'll give it a shot.

We were in bed when we heard them start to smash open the trap door. Kevin said to run to the root cellar. I reached out in the dark and found the gun I'd placed on the nightstand. I guess Kevin picked up a piece of a two-by-four. We ran into the living room and he was reaching to open the root cellar when they broke through. We could see lights from a flashlight bouncing off the steps.

Kevin whispered fiercely to hide in the bedroom and then shoved me that direction.

They yelled for us to come on out. Kevin must have hit one guy in the legs as they came down the stairs. I heard the sound of his 2"x4" hit something, someone yelled, and then some scuffling.

Don't shoot, don't shoot! Kevin said.

The big guy shouted who else is in here with you. Kevin said why should I tell you anything, it's none of your business. Then I heard a pause and he said I live here alone, my wife died months ago.

I'm glad we didn't have any bras or panties hung up to dry over the heater.

Kevin asked what the guys wanted and told them to take it and get out. I heard another scuffle and I guess one of the guys punched him. Kevin was groaning. Then I heard them kick him. They grunted with each kick. One or two guys. I heard someone laughing and Kevin was gasping for breath.

Kevin groaned and tried to ask them again what they wanted. One guy said what do you got. Another guy said we want everything. Kevin said this is my stuff and my house and you don't have the right to take it. They all laughed. One guy said there's no such thing as rights only more. It's dog eat dog, and you just got ate. They all laughed again.

Kevin said nobody has to get hurt we could work something out. Someone said there wasn't anything to work out, they wanted our stuff and were taking it.

One guy told Kevin to show them where the food is. I don't know if Kevin pointed to the storage room or what. I was hiding on the far side of the bed with the gun in my hand.

I heard one guy go into the storeroom. Another guy shined his flashlight in the bedroom but not on me. Before he could look around much the guy in the storeroom started shouting for the other guys to come look. He said there's booze, food, drinks, everything. I heard a struggle in the living room as Kevin must have tried to get up to fight or something, but it sounded like he was punched again and he got quiet.

They started grabbing boxes and carrying them into the living area. I peeked over the bed to look.

One guy was bigger than the other two. These were the same guys who killed that poor woman. The big guy said hold on a minute, why should we move all this stuff, we should just move in.

The skinny guy took a big drink from one of our bottles of booze and they passed it around. He said what about this guy. The big guy said let's have some fun with him. I heard more fighting then I guess they had him by both arms.

The guy who wasn't skinny and wasn't fat said he wasn't going to have no fun with no guy. The big guy said his cock couldn't tell the difference between a girl's mouth and a guy's mouth. He asked Kevin if he'd ever swallowed a guy's come. Kevin said no. He said today was Kevin's lucky day. He told Kevin he had to suck his dick or have his head blown off. Kevin said no fucking way.

I heard them hit him a few more times and Kevin groaning. The big guy said grab him by the hair and make him kneel. I heard the sound of a zipper unzipping, but I couldn't really see anything with it being so dark. I guess it was the fat guy. He told Kevin to open his mouth nice and wide and get ready to swallow. Kevin said no again.

He got hit again, and then the guy stuck his gun right in Kevin's face and said you suck my cock or you die right now. Kevin didn't move. It looked like the guy stuck his dick in Kevin's face. There was a pause and I heard the guy say that's right bitch suck my cock. Then he yelled son of a bitch he bit me! Now you gonna die, motherfucker. He backed up and pointed his gun with one hand while he grabbed his bleeding crotch with the other. One of the guys was shining his flashlight on his bleeding cock. I could see blood dripping through his fingers.

I raised my gun and stepped out so I had a clear shot. I said hey. The big guy flinched right as his gun went off. Kevin fell over. But I didn't miss. I shot him in the forehead. The other two guys tried to get away. They ran up the stairs. I shot one before he got to the top but he kept going. I chased after them. They ran to the front door and ran out. The zombies had heard the three gunshots. There were a lot of them. I saw one guy get caught and disappear into the crowd of them. I don't know what happened to the other guy.

I rebolted the locks and went back downstairs. The fat man was now a dead fat man. There was blood all over the floor. He lay with his face in his own blood. But I didn't care about him.

Kevin had fallen on his side. His knees were bent. There was a pool of blood by his body but it was a small pool. He was breathing. His face was bruised from where they had punched him, but I wasn't worried about his bruises. I rolled him over and tore his shirt off. He had been hit in the shoulder. There was blood in front and back but no major artery was hit. It wasn't bleeding too bad. I got my med kit. I started cleaning up the wound. I knew the bullet had exited the body. I put antibiotics inside and outside. I hope the bullet stayed in one piece. I sewed him up front and back. While I was doing this he woke up. He was very weak. I told him he got shot and I told him he was a fucking asshole for scaring me again. He tried to laugh and said he loves it when I talk dirty. Then he passed out again. I finished putting in the stitches then bandaged him up. When I was done I made him wake up. I made him stand up even though I could tell it hurt. He had to get to our bed and not stay on the floor. I couldn't carry him. He made his way across the room and I helped him get on the bed. He was wincing.

I grabbed his arm and said this is going to hurt. Then I moved his shoulder around. I needed to know if any bones were broken. It seemed okay. While I was doing it he passed out.

I took his shirt and took off my bloody clothes and threw them in the wash bucket. I went and stared at the dead man. Trying to decide. How could I get him up the stairs? I didn't like having him there. But I didn't think I could move him. I tried but wasn't strong enough. I cleaned up all of his blood. It took a lot of towels.

I have a lot of washing to do.

I got a sheet and wrapped him in it. It was hard to do. Then I duct taped the sheet so it was tight on him. I found the bullet that hit Kevin embedded in the carpet. I pried it up and stuck it in my pocket. Then I took a shower and threw up.

Kevin started waking up. He was calling for Tammy. That was okay. I went to him. He asked me again what happened. I told him I killed the fat man and saw another one die but wasn't sure about one but he was gone. Kevin asked how bad he was hurt. I said I didn't know but he was going to be okay. I gave him some Versed I had and some antibiotics. He fell asleep.

I got the little mattress we don't use and dragged it into the bedroom. I made my bed. I lay in it but didn't sleep for a long time. I listened to Kevin breath in and out and it made me feel better.

The next morning Kevin woke up and he looked a lot better. He wasn't so pale. I made him take off his pants and underwear. I wished he wasn't hurt. I looked at his wound. It didn't look worse.

I asked Kevin to sit up. He did but I could tell it hurt. I told him the next day he was going to have to get up. I told him we had to move the body. He said okay. I told him to rest today or it would be worse tomorrow. When I turned around to leave he patted my ass. I knew he was going to be okay. I checked on him all day. He was bored and got tired of reading. I gave him the shortwave radio to play with. That made him happy. Men and their toys.

I took care of the plants and washed all of the bloody clothes and towels. It took a lot of water and they were stained. I miss my washing machine. I stared at the dead body a lot. And at Kevin. I realized I love him. Damn.

I fed him. I got him a bottle when he had to pee. He hated that. I told him he couldn't get up. I gave him another sleeping pill. I wanted to go look at the stars in the living room but didn't want to be near the body.

The next morning I made him stay in bed until late. I gave him a double dose of Oxycontin then helped him get up. He was stronger than I hoped. I helped him get dressed. We went out and looked at the body. He showed me where some rope was. We tied the rope around the dead guy's feet. I grabbed the gun and went upstairs. I looked around but no one was there. Kevin came to the top of the stairs and we started pulling on the rope to pull the body up the steps. We got the body most of the way there and had to stop. Kevin did all he could but I did most of the work. Kevin was pretty doped up, but I couldn't have done it without his help. I went out the trap door and tied off the rope then went back. Kevin was on the sofa. He was pale and kind of loopy. He told me he needed to rest. I let him. About four hours later we finished moving the body upstairs. Then Kevin went downstairs and slept until the next morning.

I puttered around and then went to sleep. When I woke up my arms and legs were sore. When he woke up he knew we needed to finish the job. The body couldn't stay in the house. We went upstairs and it was already starting to stink. We pulled the body to the side door. We checked the windows. It looked okay if we were fast. No zombies very close. We unbolted the door and started pushing and pulling the body outside. Some zombies saw us. They came toward us. We got the body outside. I jumped inside but a zombie nearly got me. It touched me. We bolted the doors.

Kevin sat in one of the upstairs kitchen chairs to rest. After a few minutes he was staring at the trap door. They had used crowbars to pry it up. The wood was ruined. I asked how they knew we were there. Kevin thought for a minute but then said look at the floor. Besides the spots of blood from the guy I shot I didn't see anything. But when I looked on the other parts of the floor I could see a lot of dust. At the edge of the hidden trap door, a path could be seen. Our tracks in the dust gave us away. Bastards. May they rot in hell.

Kevin said we will have to fix it. I said not today. He said okay. We went downstairs. He slept some more. I took care of everything. He didn't have to pee in a bottle anymore. I was glad because he didn't just pee. I told him he could take a shower and he did. I put fresh bandages on. I gave him more antibiotics. We tried to have sex but it hurt him too much with me on top. It hurt too much when he was on top too. So instead I used my mouth on him. We were both satisfied.

It's been about a week now and he's mostly better. The bruises on his face and body have mostly faded. I think it will take a while for his body to be completely healed. . But we are having sex again.

December 13th

I asked Michelle to write down what happened since most of the details are kind of fuzzy to me. Here are some of the few things I do remember.

Of course I remember them breaking in and beating me. I remember the big guy saying I had to give him a blow job. I remember being beaten again and him forcing his penis in my mouth. I remember I tried to bite it off, even though I knew he would kill me. I bit down as hard as I could and nearly tore it off before he hit me again. He said he was going to kill me and pointed his gun at me.

I heard Michelle shout something behind me, and I remember seeing the gun shift slightly in his hand as he looked up. I remember his gun going off, and I remember seeing a flash from his gun as it went off.

The last few days are pretty hazy. Michelle insists I helped her move the body upstairs, but all I remember is looking at the trap door and thinking what a pain in the ass it was going to be to fix.

I'm much better now. On my feet again. My first priority was the trap door. I realized it would be impossible to repair it convincingly, since I don't have any wood or the same stain, so I did the next best thing: I messed with it (mainly one-handed) until it worked, though not as good as it had. I glued a throw rug on top so the edges of the rug were just beyond the end of the boards. It disguises the damage, and I used a rug that used to lie in the same spot when Tammy was still here. It felt right to use that rug. Michelle was a little nervous about me working on it upstairs, but she didn't try to stop me. She did hover around me quite a bit.

I started listening to the shortwave radio when I couldn't do much but lay around. I've learned a lot, and most of it isn't good. Many of the broadcasts are the same looped recording from the Emergency Broadcast System, so I ignore them. I've heard a few survivors talking to each other but they don't answer me when I transmit. I guess the signal can't get out of the basement.

The only exception is an older doctor not too far from us, all things considered. He can pick up my signal most of the time. He's near Atlanta, Michigan, west of Alpena. He hasn't seen any zombies—his cabin is deep in the woods. I'm going to try and enhance the antennae so my transmissions go farther and I can talk to him more.

I was surprised at how excited I got to talk to another person. Other than Michelle and those assholes, I haven't seen or spoken to another living person. Now I know there are other survivors, perhaps a lot of survivors. But where are they and how can I trust them? It used to be a dog-eat-dog world out there; now it's a human-eat-human world; and watch out for bad guys.

When I think of how things might have turned out—the bullet might have killed me if he hadn't flinched when Michelle yelled out. Or he might have shot her. Or done worse—lord knows, from what we saw them do earlier, they would have had quite a good time torturing us and raping Michelle—or raping both of us, more likely.

Meanwhile, I've been enjoying making love with Michelle. She's very imaginative.

There's something different in her eyes, something that wasn't there before I got shot. There's still just as much lust, but it seems there's something deeper and warmer as well. Or, hell, maybe I'm seeing her differently, maybe my eyes are more wide-open.

When I bit down on that guy's pecker, I knew I was going to die. But when I looked down the barrel of his gun, I was not afraid. So when I woke up and realized I wasn't dead, I felt a change come over me. I was glad I wasn't dead. I wanted to live, and I wanted to be with Michelle.

Tammy told me to give Michelle the stars. Maybe she didn't mean for me to paint the ceiling. Maybe she meant for me to put little pinpricks of light in the darkness of these times. I'm no star in the heavens, but I believe I can help make her life easier. I can die knowing I made a difference in someone's life.

But I don't know with certainty if she feels the same about me. I'd hate to hear her say, *Gee, Kevin, I like you too, but we're just friends with benefits, okay?* That would . . . ugh. It would be devastating.

I wasn't sure of these feelings when I first woke up after I was shot. I knew I felt different, but it took a while for me to figure out how. Over the past few days, she's fussed over me and taken care of me. The more she does for me, the more she touches me and talks to me, the more affection I feel for her. And yet my fear remains. I'm afraid to fall in love. But is it too late?

The Wind in the Birch Trees

you save my life
one day at a time

when I find myself
swimming past the drop-off
I hear you mumble in your sleep and I am serene

when I find myself launching
into dark spaces of my psyche
you tether me with your bright laugh,
a carefree echo of song, a quick toss
of your auburn hair

you are the wind
in the mottled white bark of the birch trees,
the breeze sighing over the sun-dappled grass

your voice beckons and disrobes me
until I lie naked and aroused
upon the sandy ground

amazed at the sensation
of shadow and light upon my skin

December 15th

It's amazing the difference a couple of days make. There's no doubt anymore. I really do love her. It's not just lust and not friendship or gratitude. When I'm with her (which is almost all the time), I feel whole. I feel healed. She's wonderful, and although it's probably some kind of blasphemy to say, I'm glad the Collapse happened because it brought us together. I don't just want to be with her, don't just want to have sex with her, I love her. I love her and want to always be with her. I want her to be my wife.

I want to ask Michelle to marry me but don't want to just blurt it out. *Honey, can you hand me the pruning shears? Oh, and will you marry me?!* I want it to be romantic, something she'll always remember.

Okay, this is just an aside, but my rational side is demanding he be voiced. Here I am gushing on about my love for this woman I've only known a few months. Wanting to be together forever without even a clue as to what tomorrow holds. Things aren't looking up. I think most of humanity became infected. Survivors are few and survival is difficult. Some men have become evil. The long-term outlook is grim. And here I am excitedly pondering when best to propose to her. As if there's marriage anymore. As if there's anyone to marry us. As if it's a given she'll say yes.

December 21st is the solstice. That would be a cool day. We could look at the stars. Christmas Eve is romantic, and so is Christmas Day and New Year's Eve.

I'm still afraid she doesn't feel the same about me. But my fear is allayed by what I see in her eyes. And in her touch. When we're in bed, it's incredible. If I was having this kind of sex with Tammy, I don't remember it. Sometimes I almost hallucinate. It feels like her soul and my soul are merging. I feel something in me enlarge and expand beyond the room, beyond everything physical. I don't know how else to describe it. Sometimes, like I said, the experience is so intense it's hallucinogenic. Other time's it's more subtle, like an interesting note in a beautifully complicated chord.

But there's almost always a spiritual element to it I've never felt before—or felt but forgot. This is not just a biological function. This is not just an activity plugging into my pleasure receptors. This is something different. This can't just be an emotional/physical response to the release of our natural feel-good chemicals like oxytocin and phenethylamine.

Re-reading what I just wrote, I sound like a spaced-out granola wuss. I feel like I've gone off my nut. Maybe I have.

If I felt like this about someone before the collapse, I would have handled it differently. I might have backed off or kept her at arms length afraid of being hurt. I might have decided I didn't want to be in a relationship. It's so less complicated to be alone.

Michelle in almost all certainty is my one and only friend in the world. "I wouldn't sleep with you if you were the last man on earth!" suddenly takes on a whole new meaning.

December 17th

We went upstairs yesterday, something we haven't done in a while, but we had another small bag of trash. We exited the trap door around 3 p.m. and were surprised by how bright it was. It wasn't nearly as dim as I expected. Approaching the windows we saw it was a brilliant December day with freshly fallen snow on the ground, an emerald blue sky, and a dazzling yellow-white sun illuminating everything.

Looking outside we both started laughing. Five inches or so of snow covered everything. *Everything!* Including the zombies. It was like a sculpture park after a snow. Five inches of snow on their heads. Five inches of snow on their rotting shoulders. Their feet buried in snow. Big humps of snow were probably snow-covered bodies of zombies who had fallen in the snow and couldn't get up. It was eerie; even with the snow on them, they looked like people, not statues. But if these had been human beings, we would have seen the fog of their breath. There was no fog. There was no breath.

As soon as we started laughing, we stifled ourselves. We didn't want to be heard. Seeing how slowly they moved gave me an idea. I quickly went downstairs and got the gun off the nightstand. When I went back upstairs, Michelle asked what I was up to. I replied, "Some yard work."

I unbolted the side door and stepped outside. It was frigid. The thermometer on the outside wall near the door read five degrees below zero. The body of the big guy was still there, thankfully covered in snow. It reduced the stink. Thank god there are no maggots this time of year.

I quickly walked over to the nearest zombie and shot him in the head. His head exploded and he fell over. Bits of brain made a dry rattling sound as they hit the snow, as if the brain was completely frozen. And yet they move. How is that possible?

The closest zombie was slowly turning toward me when I got to him. I shot him in the head too. He fell over. One by one I walked around the yard, shooting zombies, reloading when I ran out of bullets, then shooting some more. I went through a whole box of ammunition.

I had one unpleasant surprise. As I approached a zombie, it looked somehow familiar. It was completely naked and used to be a woman. The neck had been eaten on both sides, both breasts were ragged and torn, and it had been nearly eviscerated. Shreds of its internal organs hung out grotesquely. Most of one arm was missing. One foot was also gone. Then I noticed lateral marks across the back of its legs and butt. Marks that looked like someone had beaten her while she was still alive.

It was the woman. The young blonde woman the men had thrown to the zombies. She had been mostly eaten, and had turned. I quickly walked up, placed the gun against its head and shot it. I turned away, a mixture of revulsion and pity seeping into my stomach. I decided not to say anything to Michelle.

As I rounded the corner of the house to go inside, I looked back. The beautiful, formerly virgin snow was now a scene I'd have never imagined. Scattered all over the snowfield were the remains of zombies. Bodies were everywhere. Frequently there were bits and pieces of zombie skulls and frozen zombie brains. It was all gray-ish black and puss yellow against brilliant virgin white.

If this was a horror movie, the scene would show crimson red against the white. But in reality, their blood had long since congealed and blackened. There were a hell of a lot of dead and decomposed bodies and body bits scattered across my lawn, Michelle's lawn, our driveways, and into the street. But no blood.

When I ran out of ammunition, I went back inside and was tempted to get another box, but my left shoulder was aching and Michelle could tell. I should have put a coat on when I went outside. She gave me a stern look and a lecture about not overdoing it. Then she gave me a pain pill. To my dismay and amusement, as I swallowed the pill she put on her coat, grabbed a box of ammunition, and climbed the stairs. Shortly after, I faintly heard a series of gunshots from the .22. They sounded kind of pleasant.

When I woke up, it was morning. I could detect the scent of a recent shower. And she had changed clothes. "Wake up, lazy bones, time to get to work."

"Get to work? Doing what?"

"We have a ton of cherry tomatoes we need to pick, probably enough for fresh pasta sauce. And with the herbs we have growing, it'll be great. Plus I have a surprise." That got my attention, but then again, I have a dirty mind and a wicked imagination. We picked a very large bowl of cherry tomatoes and some herbs, plus a few hot peppers had finally ripened. They sure take their time.

We pruned the lettuce and checked everything over for pests. I gave the few houseplants, like the spider plant, a fresh drink of water. Then we went into the kitchen. I mashed the tomatoes and put them in a pot on top of the natural gas stove we try not to use too much. I made sauce from the tomatoes and while it was cooking down I added some sausage flavored beef jerky. I chopped it into small pieces and added it to the sauce. As the sauce reduced, the jerky rehydrated. By the time it was done, the sauce tasted smoky and the sausage had the texture of real meat, not jerky. We boiled the noodles and I stirred the basil into the sauce just before serving it.

The whole time we were making dinner, I was half-erect wondering about her surprise. You wouldn't believe the scenarios running through my mind. When dinner was finally ready, she showed me the surprise. While I was asleep, she snuck over to her house to get a few things, including her case of wine and a bunch of CDs. I admit, it wasn't a bit of a letdown after the possibilities I had imagined. I was glad she had her wine and music, but the surprise I had hoped for was something a bit more . .

. tactile. Plus I didn't like her leaving the house without telling me. If something had happened to her, how would I have known? I swallowed my objections, however, and agreed to have a glass of wine. I've never been much on wine, but I must admit, the stuff she has is very nice. It made our Italian meal feel even more Italian. I can't recall the last time I had wine.

We had a huge salad, ate more spaghetti than I thought we could, then sat back and relaxed. She played some of her music—I'm glad her tastes run parallel to mine.

One song was called *Shagging the Night Away*. She was amused when I said the music was fun and playful even though they were singing about shagging. She laughed and told me it was beach music, and shagging is a kind of dance you do in the sand. I felt my face redden.

It reminded me of Fudgies asking what a pasty is—and pronouncing it 'pay-stee' instead of 'paah-stee'. Here in Michigan, you don't *wear* pasties, you eat them. I used to buy them from the Saline Downtown Diner, and I've been known to drive as far as Clarkston to drop in on Uncle Peter's Pasties.

I laughed along with her, feeling silly but happy. Maybe the wine is making me feel this way.

After we'd finished the bottle of wine, we brought out the small mattress and reclined on it as we played another game of backgammon. Each time it was my turn, she unbuttoned another button on her blouse. Within five minutes, her blouse was completely undone, and so was I.

I hate playing with a cheater. Then again, I love admiring her breasts. Losing a game of backgammon is quite worthwhile under those conditions. And indeed I did lose, but by then I was ready to devour her nipples. Which I did, among other things.

We fell asleep in each other's arms—again—under the stars. Not five feet from where just a few days ago, a dead man with a bullet in his brain had fallen to the floor. Right after he'd shoved his cock in my mouth. Bizarre.

Amazing

Which is more amazing:
dead bodies,
walking, eating, killing

or

this dead heart
living, loving, healing

December 19th

It's been a tough couple of days. The day after my last entry, I got up early, leaving Michelle sleeping. I made some coffee and went into the living room. We had left the CDs and cases out, kind of spread around, and I decided to tidy up. I put my CDs away first and then put hers away. After I put them away, I went through a few of her disks to see what kind of variety she had. In the process, I came across CDs with notes attached to them. Some had inscriptions written on the cases or on the inserts. They were love notes. From Wayne.

Wayne, telling Michelle how much he loved her, how she's his heart and soul, how passionate there love is. One case contained a folded over note; the outside said, "Michelle, any day is a good day to say three little words to you." On the inside it said, "Let's get naked."

I felt a stirring of darkness inside. A feeling I wasn't familiar with and didn't like. It was Shakespeare's green eyed monster. I was jealous of Wayne. I couldn't help myself—I went through all her CDs. I found seven of them with love notes, all from Wayne. By the time I finished going through them I was actually angry. I don't know why. I remember thinking, *So this is why she brought them over*!

The rational part of my mind recognized how absurd this was. How unfair and inappropriate my feelings were. It didn't matter; my emotions remained.

I put the CDs away and made myself get busy. All day I tried all day to reason myself out of my feelings. I couldn't do it. No matter what reasoning I used, I couldn't dismiss my anger. I made every effort in my interactions with Michelle to appear as if there was nothing wrong. We made small talk and joked with each other, but inwardly I felt stretched taut. Even as I write this I feel tight. I'm trying to act like things are okay, but they're not. I'm pretending.

Not long ago, we went to bed and made love. I remember a friend of mine, Brian, talking about a *grudge fuck,* where you're angry and you fuck like you're angry. I had no idea what he was talking about until tonight. I wouldn't say I fucked her with anger, but I would say I fucked her instead of making love to her. I was rougher than usual, but she didn't seem to mind. She fell asleep in my pretending-I'm-okay arms, and I lay awake, mentally chewing on this unaccustomed cud. Eventually I fell asleep despite my smoldering anger and questions.

This morning I woke up and stared at the ceiling, trying to figure out what was going on. Why did I feel so depressed and anxious? Michelle woke up and drowsily nestled her head on my chest with my arm draped over her back. I lay there listening to her breathing and she slowly stroked my chest. Once again I slipped into bizarre paranoia. I felt sure she was about to say, *Kevin, there's something I need to tell you.* She'd cry and confess and would say how sorry she was, but she couldn't help how she felt. I'd find out my suspicions were justified. I'd learn my life for the past few months had been a misguided illusion; a sham. At one point her hand travelled lower, between my legs, and even though I was already hard, I kissed the top of her head and said "Not this morning. Maybe later."

She moaned in disappointment and said "Okay, but later I'm going to ravage you!" Being ravaged didn't appeal to me. I'm a regular guy and I know I could have sex with her despite my bad feelings, but I didn't want to have sex with her. Except for last night I've never just had sex with her, it's never been mechanical. I've always celebrated her body and our feelings for each other. The other part of my once again was dismayed. *She wants to ravage you and you're not interested? What the* hell *is going on?!* I got up and again went through the motions of acting normal. She stayed in bed a few more minutes while I made coffee. I sat in the living room, glancing over at her CDs, remembering what the notes said. *She must have kept those notes and CDs because she's still in love with him and misses him* I concluded.

I sat and stewed for a half hour or so, occasionally sipping my now-cold and bitter coffee while she took a shower. My efforts to talk myself down from this emotional ledge were not working—in fact, my anger was building. I felt like I'd been blindsided. It felt as if I'd found a stash of pornographic photos of them.

As I was sat there stewing, Michelle came out of the bedroom and poured a cup of coffee. Carrying it into the living room she innocently asked "What are you doing?"

I tried not to say anything about the notes. "Just sitting here thinking." Then before I could stop myself, I quietly said, "Why didn't you tell me you were still in love with Wayne? Don't you think that's something I should know?"

"Kevin, you need to learn to hold off on trying to be funny until after my first cup of coffee. Or after we make love."

"I'm not joking. I want to know. I think I deserve to know what's going on."

She put the cup of coffee down. She'd barely sipped it. She looked me full in the eyes. "Kevin, I'm not in love with Wayne. That was a long time ago. Where is this coming from?"

"I'm not stupid. I came across his love notes with your CDs. About how much he loves you. About getting naked. You wouldn't have kept them if you didn't still love him." By now I was on my feet. I had begun to pace. I wasn't talking so quietly anymore. Even while it was happening, a part of me was thinking *Whoa! Slow down! You're overreacting!*

Michelle picked up her cup of coffee, took a sip, and then calmly put it back down. She looked at me again. "Kevin, listen to me. You're talking about Wayne in the present tense, like he's still around. But he's not. For all I know he's dead. I don't even know where he lives. So I still have the CDs he gave me. I like the music. So they still have love notes on them. You know I don't listen to CDs much, I listen to my MP3s. I didn't even remember the notes. I don't love him anymore! That's absurd!"

"How can you expect me to believe you?" I asked, my anger increasing. I was losing control, my emotions igniting like gasoline. "First you downplay how much you loved him, then you hide these CDs and love notes, and now you say you don't love him but the evidence says you do! How can I trust you when I know you're not being honest?" I moved toward her and got in her personal space. I could see the fear and anger on her face. At the moment, I thought she was mad because she'd been busted—because she'd been caught red handed. She backed up away from me.

"Kevin, what's wrong with you? I've never seen you like this! You're acting crazy! I didn't hide anything from you and I don't still love Wayne!"

"Oh, so now on top of everything else you're saying I'm crazy?!" I grabbed her coffee cup from the table and hurled it against the wall. Coffee went everywhere and the cup shattered. I guess that pushed her over the edge. She began shouting.

"All right, you're going to *stop this right now* and listen to me! I'm *not* in love with Wayne. I'm in love with *you*. Wayne is dead. Everyone I knew and loved is dead. How the *fuck* can you be jealous over a dead guy who *walked out on me when* . . ." She took a deep breath. "Yes, I loved him. Yes, he broke my heart. That was ages ago when we lived in a different world. My feelings for him . . ." She broke into tears.

See, there she goes, missing him and crying for him, my disturbed side commented. She covered her eyes for a moment, then looked up at me while wiping her teary eyes.

"This is no different than you having photos of Tammy around. And you still wear your wedding ring. Who knows what else I'd find if I snooped around? Do you see me getting all weirded out about that? Do you hear me accusing you of not being honest? No. But here you are, accusing me . . . She stopped closed her eyes, took a deep breath, and said "I can't talk to you right now. Please give me some space." She ran into the bedroom. I could hear her crying.

I felt such and odd mixture of thoughts and feelings. I felt like I was splitting into two parts of myself. My heart was saying, *I know what I saw. I know what I read. I don't care what she says. I know what I know.* My mind was telling me, *What the hell is wrong with you? You're acting like you caught her cheating on you. She says she doesn't love him. Has she ever lied to you? No. And even if she is still in love with him, so what? He's dead, either dead and buried or he's a zombie looking for someone to eat.*

Another part of me, a very small voice nearly unnoticed, said *And she said she's in love with you!*

But my heart wouldn't listen. Even writing it now, it feels absurd. I felt betrayed. I felt like I'd been kicked in the gut. Michelle, in love with another man. How could she do this to me? Here I trusted her, and once again, what did I learn? *Never, ever trust a woman. They'll lie to you, they'll abandon you, they'll stomp your heart in the ground with a hobnailed boot and then feed it to the zombies. Everyone goes away in the end.*

I stormed into the storeroom and got a bottle of booze. I poured a nice slug, slammed it, then poured another. It was barely 9:00. My hands were clammy and shaking and I felt crazy. I don't mean figuratively. I felt like I was losing my mind. Usually when I find myself overreacting to something I can talk myself down. But not this time. I wandered around, coming back time and again to the love notes from Wayne.

After about a half hour I grabbed the bottle of bourbon and headed upstairs. I deliberately made the trap door slam after I stepped into the kitchen. It was a cold, dark empty house. The house where I mourned the death of my son and the death of my wife. The house in which I made love to my wife. I walked around the rooms, muttering to myself, "I know what I know. I know what I saw." My mind was arguing with me the whole time, telling me to get a grip, I was being stupid and was about to mess up a good thing. I completely ignored it.

After wandering through different rooms, not really seeing anything, I ended up in our old bedroom. I had continued to drink the straight bourbon, and the alcohol started hitting me hard since I hadn't eaten anything. I don't remember much after that. I do remember staring at the photo of Tammy and me on our wedding day. Huge smiles. She was beautiful. She was dead and I was drunk. I'm going to let Michelle write what happened next, because frankly I don't recall.

So here I am, writing again. I hate writing. But Kevin asked me to. So here goes. After he flipped out on me, I ran into the bedroom. I heard Kevin open a bottle of booze. Then I heard the trap door slam so I knew he must have gone upstairs. I waited a few minutes to calm down. I didn't know why he was so mad. He was acting crazy. But I also loved him and was worried about him. I'd never had the slightest hint that he was unstable.

After giving him a half-hour or so to come to his senses, I went upstairs and heard him crying. I found him in his old bedroom. He was pretty drunk. He was talking incoherently to a photo of Tammy. I heard her name a few times and mine too. I don't think he even knew I was there. He was still holding the bottle of booze and was barely keeping his balance and the booze sloshed out of the bottle onto the floor. I heard a phrase or two I understood. He kept saying why did she do it, why did she do it. I didn't know if he was talking about Tammy or me. And a couple times I heard him say please don't go away.

Then he got sick. He turned toward me and his eyes were unfocused. I got out of his way. I don't know if he saw me or not—he didn't act like he saw me. He stumbled down the hall to the bathroom. He fell into the wall once. As he went into the bathroom he threw up. All over the floor. Then he was throwing up into the dry toilet. I went in and stood watching him. He didn't know I was there.

At first I felt like it served him right, being sick. Then I started feeling sorry for him. I found some washcloths in the closet and knelt down on the floor next to him. He had vomit all over his shirt. I tried to clean him up but it wasn't easy with him still throwing up. Eventually I got most of it off him. I cleaned up his face. He quit throwing up and I pulled him to me despite all the stink. I rested his head in my lap.

He was crying and mumbling but I couldn't tell what he was saying. He looked up at me with red eyes. His breath smelled like bourbon vomit. He was still crying. He looked right at me and said what did I do wrong? Then he started crying again. His whole body was shaking with his sobs. He started calling for Jason. He called his name over and over. My heart melted. He might pretend he's okay, and maybe sometimes he is okay, but there's also a broken part of him. These feelings have been bottled up inside him for years. They aren't because of me. They belong to Tammy and Jason. Maybe he never let himself grieve. I guess our intimacy brought those feelings to the surface. Opening his heart to me was reopening an old wound.

I sat on the floor. His head was in my lap. He was still crying but was probably about to pass out. The room stank. At one point he threw up on me. He didn't have much left in his system so it was okay.

I knew he probably needed to drink some water, and I really wanted to get downstairs. I told him let's go get in bed, but I had to say it loudly a couple of times before he responded. Then he seemed surprised to see me and started crying again, drunkenly wrapping his arms around me. He told me he loved me over and over. He'd never said that before. I told him again to come on downstairs and get in bed, and eventually helped him to his feet. He bumped his head on the sink in the process. He bumped it hard but was obviously feeling no pain. Literally. I had his arm around my shoulder and helped him downstairs. I was afraid we were going to fall down the stairs because he was so unsteady. He could barely walk. But eventually we made it and I half-carried him into the bedroom.

I made him drink some water. Then I put him to bed. He was pretty quiet by then. I went back and closed the trap door. I went into the bathroom and cleaned myself up. I hate puking, but even more, I hate someone puking on me. When I was finished I checked on him—he was passed out. Or sleeping. Whatever. I figured he was going to wake up with a bad hangover. He deserved it. The dope.

I went into the living room. I started going through the CDs. He was right about there being love notes on cases from Wayne. I hadn't thought about them in a long time. I gathered the notes and cases together and sat there reading them and thinking about Wayne. About how things ended. I cried some. I guess my heart never completely healed either. Then I put it all in a box. I was sorry Kevin saw them. I was also sorry I read them. They just made me feel bad. I don't love Wayne anymore. It's ancient history. I love Kevin. But Wayne was important to me for a while and thinking about it filled me with regret. When somebody you love hurts you it shouldn't cancel out all the good times you had and the memories you made with them.

I took a deep breath and made myself move. I took care of chores. I had to harvest the lettuce. I checked the water pH. I finally got a cup of coffee. Kevin doesn't make coffee as good as me. It's too weak. It was also a few hours old. I add a pinch of salt to the grounds before brewing. I checked again on Kevin. He was still asleep. His breathing was regular and deep. I went upstairs and looked out the window. A few zombies had shown up since we shot a bunch of them. They barely move in this cold weather. But they move a little now and then and sometimes slowly open their mouth and make that rasping sound I've come to hate.

It was a gray day. Kevin told me the solar panels don't work very well on overcast days. He said we need to limit how much power we use. Looking out the window made me very sad. I was sad for all the people I knew and loved who are gone. My parents. My friends. Musicians and writers I liked. Acquaintances. Even Wayne. He may have treated me bad at the end, but I used to love him and because of him I learned a lot about myself. For a while he was important to me. I feel like I should honor the memory of the people who are gone.

Then I started thinking about Kevin. Despite what happened today, he's been very good to me. He always tells me the truth, even if I might not like it. He takes care of me. He probably saved me from death. He's funny and smart and talented. Without his planning, I would have no food to eat or place to stay and I'd probably be out there walking with the rest of them.

I realized how much I love him, not because of what he can give me, but because of how he makes me feel about myself. Around him I don't feel fat. I don't feel I have anything to prove. He makes me feel like I really am the kind of woman I see in his eyes. I've started realizing that I am the woman I see in his eyes. It's not that he sees me unrealistically, it's that I've seen myself unrealistically. He looks at me like I'm beautiful and sexy and that makes me think maybe I am beautiful and sexy. Wayne overlooked my weight. He was okay with it. Kevin embraces it as a part of me he loves. He said he loves me. Even if he was drunk when he said it, I think he does love me.

I never want him to feel bad because of me. I want to make him feel as good as he makes me feel. I was still upset with him but part of me wanted to do something nice for him to show him I love him. Something to bring him back to me. I double-checked the zombies and when I knew it was safe I went to my house. I got some blouses I thought he'd like, low cut ones that showed some cleavage. Most of them I never had the nerve to wear in public, even though they were dressy. I picked out some of my prettiest bras. Then I picked out some lingerie I bought but never wear. I put the blouses inside a box, and the lingerie inside a smaller box. There's not much to the lingerie so the box was pretty small. I doubt Kevin will notice the box. That's how small it is.

I even grabbed a pretty dress, one with a plunging neckline. I know how much Kevin enjoys my cleavage. I've seen him staring at my boobs often enough. I also grabbed a couple of old photo albums. Then I went back home and went downstairs. Kevin was still sleeping. I was going through my photo album when I heard Kevin. He called my name. I went into the bedroom. He was breathing very fast and had a strange look on *his face. He asked me to come get on the bed. We lay there side by side. He started telling me how sorry he was we had a fight and he got jealous. He couldn't lie still. He was breathing fast and crying again. He was having a panic attack. He tried to tell me his thoughts but they didn't make sense. I held him and kept telling him it was okay. He kept apologizing and crying. He said he couldn't stop his thoughts and felt like he was going crazy. He said he was scared and didn't want to lose me. I thought that was very silly of him. What would I do, walk out on him? Go back to my house and starve or freeze?*

His panic attack lasted about forty minutes. He was a mess. He finally calmed down. After I gave him a Xanax. He was lying face down. His head was in his pillow. He put his arm across my chest. He started feeling my breasts. I really didn't feel like having sex but thought it might be good for him. But when we tried to, he couldn't get hard enough. I think it was all the booze, or maybe the Xanax, or maybe it was everything. I could tell he felt bad about that. Eventually he fell asleep.

I went out and looked at old photos again. Most were photos of my family. Some had Wayne in them. I removed those. I took them upstairs along with the cases and notes and put them with the trash in the dishwasher. The photos made me sad. All those faces, smiling and young. Now probably all but me are dead. Or worse. All of my former life in the photos is gone. The love, the friendship, the places. I can't even go visit the pre-zombie parts of my life. Some of those times were wonderful. Now not so much. But I do have Kevin, even if he was all whacked out today. I know it's a dangerous way to think, but he wouldn't have gotten so upset if he didn't love me. In some ways, I am all he has and he is all I have, except for my memories. Kevin makes me laugh. My memories don't.

It's evening, about ten hours after all that stuff happened. I've been drinking a lot of water and had a small salad—not much, as I have a terrible headache, which is no surprise. Michelle offered me some ibuprofen, but I said no. I feel like I've earned the headache. I don't recall being so drunk or hung-over since before Tammy died. When she was first diagnosed I freaked out and got stinking drunk one night.

I haven't read what Michelle wrote, and decided I don't need to. I don't really want to know what I said or did, because I know none of it was nice and none of it was pretty.

I do know she came looking for me. She didn't have to. And she took care of me when I got sick and when I was having my panic attack.

The panic attack was bizarre. I've never had a panic attack before, and hope I never have another one. I couldn't control my thoughts or my emotions. I felt out of control, and I don't like being out of control. I couldn't breathe. My heart was pounding. I couldn't stop crying.

The strangest part was the great divide between my rational thoughts and my feelings. My feelings were of anger, jealousy, and fear. I know it makes no sense, but I was emotionally convinced she was still in love with Wayne. I even convinced myself that when we're in bed, she's thinking of him. I was convinced she had betrayed me. How absurd.

My rational side told me those feelings were crazy. Wayne is most assuredly dead or a zombie. The idea of feeling threatened by him—it's absolutely ludicrous. But no matter how much I tried to talk myself out of those feelings, they wouldn't go away.

I felt sure it was only a matter of time before she left me. Having no place to go and no one to go to didn't matter. My feelings were completely irrational and I was off my rocker. The odd thing is, I still have some of those feelings. Even though I know they're crazy, I still feel . . . I don't know, threatened or at risk or like I can't compete with this dead guy who broke her heart a long time ago. Years ago.

I guess what it boils down to is this: I love Michelle. There, I said it. Or wrote it. I've never told her, but I have to admit it's true. That makes me vulnerable. For the first time in a decade, I have strong feelings for a woman. I didn't intend on it happening. I didn't try to make it happen. I don't even know when it *started* happening. But it's true; I'm in love with Michelle. And yet I can't bring myself to tell her. I know I should. But even the idea makes my palms get sweaty. Losing Jason and then Tammy, the two people I loved more than anyone, makes me so damned scared I can barely admit it to myself. To love someone is to set yourself up for heartache. It gives them enormous power to hurt you, to hurt you in a way from which you may never recover. Sometimes people quit loving you. Sometimes love isn't enough to make it work. Sometimes they leave or are taken from you. Sometimes—which I'm just now learning—your love can make you literally crazy, it can start a chain reaction which concludes with delusion and betrayal.

Michelle put some quiet music on and we sat side by side on the sofa reading. Or at least she did. I don't know if I even turned the page of my book. I pretended to read, but I was really thinking things over, and was appreciating how it felt to be sitting next to the woman I loved. I held her hand—I craved her touch. As the evening wore on, Michelle announced she was going to bed.

I asked her if she was okay with me sleeping with her. She acted surprised I'd even ask and said yes, of course I could. So after she got in bed, I lay down with her for a while. I wasn't sleepy, though, so I lay on top of the covers. We talked for a while, and at one point we were actually laughing out loud about something silly.

Somehow we got to talking about weird fetishes, and I wondered out loud why nobody has an armpit fetish. Lots of guys have an ass fetish, or a mouth or boob fetish, but no one ever seems interested in armpit sex. We both laughed, and Michelle surprised me by saying some people *do* have an armpit fetish, and it's called mashlagnia or something like that, and having sex with an armpit is called axillism. I asked her how in the world she knew so much about it and she said, "Believe me, you don't want to know. But you know the brand of deodorant called *Secret*?

"Sure. *Strong enough for a man but made for a woman.*"

"What's that mean?"

"It was an old ad slogan back in the day."

"Well, there's a reason why I quit using the Secret scent called *Body Splash*. Having *Body Splash* in my armpit brought to mind an experience best forgotten." We laughed about that, but I had to try not to picture it happening. Her and another guy. I handled it. It felt so good to lie there with my arm around her, laughing and talking. In a little while she fell asleep. I feel like I dodged a bullet. I was a crazy asshole, and yet there she lay, sleeping with forgiveness in her heart for me.

After she fell asleep, I poured myself some bourbon and quietly went upstairs. It was probably around 11:30 and I didn't have much time before all the plant lights clicked off, so I had to hurry. I spent some time in the living room writing Tammy a letter, then went up to the bedroom. I could smell my vomit on the rug and in the bathroom. That grossed me out, but I knew it didn't really matter.

I crept into the bedroom and felt my way to the dresser. I reached inside and took out a small box I keep there. I don't know why I kept it, as I never thought I'd use it, but there it was. I felt like the time to use it was approaching. I also found a small Petoskey stone I'd taken the time to polish. I always wanted to have it set as a pendant, like Lake Menekaunee friends wore. It's pretty enough—the clarity is great, and I polished it to a gleam. I used to carry it around in my pocket. After holding it in my hand and rubbing it with my thumb for a minute, I slipped it into my pocket. For just a moment I wondered if there were any zombies wearing Petoskey pendants. It was an unpleasant thought. Maybe Petoskey stones bring good luck; maybe they ward off evil. Maybe I should circle my house with them.

I went back down to the first floor and peaked outside. I couldn't really see much—it was very dark with no moon or stars. I stood there, holding the box in my hand, feeling the weight of my circumstance. Outside were zombies. Downstairs was Michelle, sleeping after a hard day dealing with a crazy man. As I stood there in the darkness, I felt the full weight of our situation. We have no idea if there are other people alive in Ann Arbor. We have no idea how many survivors there are, and how many of them have turned mercenary like those three guys. Are there any good people left? How are they surviving? Are there any groups of people who have banded together? This time of year, how are any survivors staying warm and what do they eat?

With a dawning awareness I realized we may have an important role among survivors. I know how to grow hydroponic food and a regular garden during the summer. Michelle has nursing experience and some medical supplies. Hell, if nothing else, I not only have booze in storage but brewing experience. If push comes to shove I know how to distill liquor and have the equipment to do it. And experience growing medicinal marijuana.

I stuck the box in my pocket and went downstairs. Michelle was still sleeping, of course. I'm glad she didn't wake up to find me gone. I lay beside her, gazing at her face in the fading light. Every part of her I saw, I loved. I loved her eyebrows. I loved her lips. I loved her ears. I loved every one of her wrinkles. I am hers, she is mine, we are what we are, with apologies to CSN.

It's been a long, exhausting day. I'm all done in.

December 20th
Dear Tammy,

After Michelle fell asleep tonight I poured myself a generous glass of bourbon and headed upstairs. It was nearly dark; I stood in the kitchen for a few minutes while my eyes adjusted and ended up going into the living room, sitting in an easy chair you had picked out at the furniture store. Diffused moonlight provided a little light, enough to see the basic shapes and shades of the living room. It was still decorated the way you left it; in the dim light I could see the art and pictures you hung, although really all I saw were dark rectangles of the art against a the lighter shade of slate gray walls. I could see the furniture you bought and the lamps. Even the old tube-TV was where you left it. I placed the laptop on the coffee table and started this letter.

After you died, I didn't come in this room much. I turned one of the bedrooms upstairs into a home theatre and the other into an office. I made my home upstairs and hardly even came in here. Back then, sitting alone in this empty room felt uncomfortable, the room where we'd had parties and watched movies and made love and talked about our day. Coming in here was dangerous. As dangerous as looking at old photos. This room was permeated with you, and I ached for you so badly I had to avoid this room. The bedroom was different; it felt empty of you, not haunted by you like the living room. Sitting in this room now I don't feel the same kind of ache; the hurt didn't go away, it just changed. In the beginning, if I can use sound as an analogy, the hurt was a shrill and shrieking violin; now it's a soft and quiet cello. It's joined forces with my old friend Andy Pression. They play the same melody, the same composition, just a different arrangement. Being in this room tonight makes me feel closer to you, and Tammy, I need to talk to a friend.

I can't reconcile my emotions and thoughts. My heart believes Michelle has betrayed me; my mind knows that's impossible. I try to reason it out. All I did was find some love notes from an old boyfriend, someone who broke her heart. I have love notes and other items from you; I treasure them. My having kept your love notes is no more a betrayal of Michelle than Michelle having kept Wayne's notes is a betrayal of me. And yet I feel betrayed.

The feelings of betrayal—they're only part of the problem. The other problem is how I'm responding to those feelings despite knowing they're poisonous, knowing they're the feelings of a lunatic. They're making me behave in a way I don't care for. By checking up on her, second guessing her behavior, not quite believing what she says—I'm being a person I don't want to be. I'm being a jealous, suspicious, unreasonable lover.

I analyze my strong emotional reaction. Michelle has never treated me badly, never had an occasion to lie to me, never betrayed me in any sense. I haven't known her very long, so I don't know everything about her, but she's always been genuine. I have no rational reason to believe she's been even emotionally unfaithful to me. How is it that my hot buttons are being pushed when I didn't even know I had hot buttons? I have no history of women cheating on me. So if this isn't old baggage, what is it?

I stopped writing for about a half hour just now and took another few swallows of bourbon while I thought it over. So here's what I think, Tammy; you weren't unfaithful to me, but I sure as hell felt betrayed when you died. Jason betrayed me by dying as well. The two people in my life I loved more than I thought possible betrayed me and left. It wounded me deeply. Had Jason lived and had you not died of cancer, I believe I would have become a different man, a better version of the man I am now. Keven version 2.0. More accomplished and fulfilled. A man who could look back on his life with satisfaction, a man with the resting assurance of having worked hard and made good choices. A man whose parents would be proud. Whose wife and children would love and respect him. He would be quietly satisfied with his accomplishments, including the accomplishment of having raised children of character. That does not describe my life over the past ten years. My life has either been a long series of misfortunes or an object lesson for what not to do.

In hydroponic gardening, it's inevitable you're going to screw up at some point. Maybe forget to check the pH. Maybe over-fertilize. At some point, you're going to do something wrong or neglectful and you'll see your plants suffer because of it. Many times the plants never completely recover. Maybe you'll still get some tomatoes, but not the huge bounty you were anticipating. Or maybe the plant will stay stunted and never really thrive. Or maybe you'll have a tomato plant that grows like crazy—big, bushy, green and blooming—but the fruit withers and dies on the vine. Anyone who has gardened long, hydroponic or soil, has likely seen it.

That's how my life has been, like a house plant that suffered some misfortune and never recovered. Sunscalding. Overwatering. Bitten by frost when left outside too late in the season. Nothing fatal, but enough to change how well it grew.

I've seen plants hit by frost that reacted as if they had been pruned. They came back stronger than ever. And I've seen plants get hit by frost and never recover. An agave plant of mine got bit by frost in October but wasn't completely dead until April. Indoors over the winter it died a slow death, first the outer leaves turning brown while the inner leaves stayed green, then finally the inner leaves browning and withering as well. Maybe I was doing that; slowly fading, turning dry and withered, a living ghost.

It's not like I crawled into a hole and never came out. I still had my job, still had friends I saw. But as time went on, I saw those friends less and less often, choosing to stay home instead of getting together with the SHIT (Sure Happy It's Thursday) gang for Mexican food and margaritas. I quit the bike club, stopped going to the homebrewing club meetings. I still brewed beer and spent many a night overindulging in my own ale. I quit caring much about work—I still showed up and did a good job, but I felt no pride or satisfaction. There were no new challenges, no accomplishments that won me accolades. My drive was gone. The days were slipping past, one after the other, changing from late summer to fall to early winter. An early winter evening, cloudy and gray.

Suddenly this fossilized winter of a heart felt the spring thaw. I met Michelle and liked what I saw. Then all hell broke loose with the Collapse, and circumstances forced us to spend time together. The seeds of companionship began sprouting and became a living, growing thing. I started to care. In all the years since you and Jason died, I've never let anyone get this close. It doesn't feel safe. My plans did not include letting Michelle or anybody else get this close. Apocalypse and zombies are notorious for interfering with plans.

I care deeply for her and believe she feels affection for me, which is like salve to my wounds. But it also feels like sticking my arm into the whirling propeller of a boat on Lake Michigan. I find myself in a situation I don't know how to deal with. Allowing myself to care about her feels like committing suicide. How can you be so stupid as to let this happen again?! a part of me asks. The past consequence of caring for someone were so severe I honestly don't know if I could survive it again. But what is my alternative? Hell, what are my choices? She lives with me. She sleeps in my bed. She needs me to survive, and I probably need her as well. I need to let go of my fear and anxiety, need to shut up the voices of alarm in my head, need to learn to accept and enjoy any smidgen of good that comes my way and revel in it. When the few good things about today are a thing of the past, I will ache for them. But only if I allow the good to happen in the first place.

And in the midst of all this reasoning, a very small part of me is near panic. When I focus on that part of me, when I give it a voice, it is completely irrational, and yet sings such a beautiful and tantalizingly horrific song I feel myself swayed. It is the sweet song of a siren, calling me to taste a little more of my addiction. My heart starts to pound and my breath quickens. I start picturing scenarios that could not possibly come true. I argue with myself. Yet for every rational argument against these crazy thoughts is a counter-argument.

She couldn't still be in love with Wayne, and even if she was, there's no way she could secretly be in contact with him. The odds are astronomical against his being alive, and even more astronomical that she somehow got in touch with him. But just because it's improbable doesn't mean it's impossible. If I were in her place I would figure out a way to make secret contact. I'm tenacious enough to find a way. If I'm capable of it, she's capable of it. She's a very bright girl. But in order for her to behave that way, I'd have to have completely misjudged her all these months. She would have to be deviously clever to have fooled me so completely. She's never given any inkling of being devious or beguiling. But just because I haven't caught her doesn't mean she isn't guilty. Now that's the thought of a crazy person, believing someone is guilty, they've just been too clever to leave evidence. But if I keep on my toes, I could catch her when she slips up. I'd have my proof. But to feel that way, I'd have to be emotionally unstable if not downright crazy. It's paranoia. But just because you're paranoid doesn't mean you're not right. Those are the thoughts endlessly circling me when I shallowly give in to the siren's song of suspicion. No rational thought can allay the suppositions of my paranoia. But eventually reason reasserts itself and I once again see through rational eyes. Yet deep inside, the siren song goes on, tempting me to come.

Are you listening, subconscious? My fear, my instinctive reaction to falling in love, is making my life worse. Loving and being loved is a good thing. Loving Michelle and being loved by her is a good thing. This insane reaction I've been having, this compulsion to see if she slips up and reveals some kind of deceit, it's only hurting us. I could be basking in warmth of truly devoted love, and instead I'm pouring cold water on the embers.

I'm scared, Tammy. I know I'll never have again what I had with you—you never step in the same river twice—but with Michelle I could have something just as good but different. I could have the kind of love that men and women alike long for. But I could also find myself at the mercy of love, desperately wanting to hold onto something even as it slips away. Opening my heart to the wonder of love is opening my heart to the possibility of devastating loss.

After ten years, I still miss you so much it hurts. I hate you for that.

Kevin
PS. I love you

Rescue

Every night
you rescue me

Half-thought accusations
and delusions of betrayal

are silenced
with the waterfall of your laughter
the feel of your shoulder
and the slope of your breasts

Until you
I never knew I could
feel a lover smile
in the dark.

In bed,
while your hand strokes
my graying chest hair
you quietly murmur expressions of love,
and, healed once again,

I abandon my insanity
and I believe,
I believe,

I believe.

December 21st

I woke up early again and made coffee. It's become a routine.

Thoughts from last night were still bouncing around inside my head. Thoughts about Michelle. Thoughts about other survivors. I powered up the shortwave and tried to find someone talking, but all I found were the same stations broadcasting a repeating loop. I wonder how they still have power. I made Michelle a cup of coffee and took it to her. I made it stronger than I usually do—she likes it dark. When I went into the bedroom she was already awake, staring at the ceiling.

"Good morning," I said. "You doing okay?"

"Yes, I'm fine. I'm just thinking about yesterday."

"Michelle, I'm so sorry. I don't know where—"

"Kevin, you don't need to apologize. I realized some things about you yesterday, and some things about us, and some things about me, too. I'll be honest, yesterday was tough. It scared me. But you've never acted like that before, so I figure there's a lot going on under the surface. I'm just sorry I triggered it."

"Please, Michelle, you don't have anything to be sorry for."

"I'm sorry you felt so bad. It makes me sad. But it also made me realize how much I love you. I want to be with you. I choose to be with you, even if you're a psycho nut case."

I reached out and took her hand. "Last night I went upstairs for awhile after you fell asleep. I sat in the living room and wrote Tammy a letter. I needed her help sorting things out. I admitted how much I care about you and how much I'm afraid I'll lose you somehow like I lost her. But in the end, I decided it was worth it. I know I might pay the price later, but for now I choose to let myself feel wonderful. To feel love. And to be loved." As my arm drew her to me, I leaned down to kiss her. Before now I never knew a kiss could heal.

As we continued to kiss I started getting aroused, and was going to ignore it, when she reached between my legs and gave me a light squeeze. Soon we were naked. I won't take the time to go into detail about what happened. But for the first time in my life, while having sex with a woman I felt a mix of shame, pride and relief. I felt privileged to have sex with her.

No, that's not right. I wasn't having sex with her. I was making love with her. Even though I hadn't overtly told her I love her.

When we were finished, I felt like a warm Ann Arbor spring day after an afternoon shower. Everything was new and fresh.

We lay there for a minute, then with a sigh she told me she was going to wash clothes. I got dressed, put my Petoskey stone in my pocket, then carried the hamper of clothes into the bathroom. For breakfast I made some powdered scrambled eggs. Usually they're kind of nasty, but today I liked them. We ate them with a comfortable silence between us. Or mostly comfortable. I'm still uncomfortable about what I saw. I have a niggle of paranoia and suspicion.

Then I took care of the plants. I feel like I've been neglecting them. I'm behind schedule on germinating seeds, and I'm worried about getting an aphid infestation, so I have to check them over very carefully. This is usually about the time I start seeing them. At the sight of the first aphid, I'll have to start aggressively spraying with Neem oil.

Several more of my hot peppers were ripe. I carefully harvested them, trying not to handle them too much. By the time I was finished adding water to the reservoirs, adding fertilizer, checking and adjusting the pH, getting rid of dead leaves, and moving some of the mature seedlings into the young plant section, it was time for lunch. Michelle had put a bunch of lettuce in the root cellar to crisp up, so I decided to make us both a salad. I took a knife and cut one of the Ghost peppers into tiny slivers and added a very few to my salad, then sliced up the lettuce. I should have realized that slicing the peppers first would get some capsaicin on the lettuce, but it never occurred to me. When I was done making the salad, I thoroughly washed my hands to make sure no pepper oil remained on them.

I called her to come join me, and she walked into the kitchen, wiping her hands and arms dry with a dishtowel.

"I picked some hot peppers for our salad," I said. "Want some?" I knew she'd say no. Which she did.

"Are you crazy? It's a wonder you have any taste buds left!" She added croutons, raisins, and dressing to her salad and began eating.

I took a big bite and was surprised at how hot it was. The ghost peppers were living up to their reputation! Youch! The heat was pushing the boundaries of my tolerance! I paused, considering whether to remove the rest of the peppers from my salad.

While eating, Michelle began suggesting we come up a better way to wash the clothes. In mid-chew her eyes opened wide. *"Kevin! You jerk! You put hot peppers on my salad!!"* She grabbed a glass of water, and I tried to warn her, but it was too late. Water only makes the heat worse. *"Aaagh! My mouth's on fire!"* she shrieked.

I know it was mean, but I couldn't help but laugh. I handed her some crackers and said, "Eat these. It works a lot better than water. You don't have to swallow them—just suck on them."

"That's the *only* thing I'll be sucking on!" she mumbled with her mouth full, shooting darts at me with her eyes. "That was *so* mean!"

"I wasn't trying to be mean. I just didn't think it through! I used the same knife to slice the lettuce that I used to slice my hot peppers," I said. "I'm really sorry, honest!" She might have accepted my apology if I hadn't been grinning.

"That was *not* nice. I'll never be able to trust you again," she said, still sucking on the crackers and taking long drinks of cool water.

"At least not with peppers, you mean." I got up and made her a new salad, tearing the lettuce instead of cutting it this time.

"Listen here, Mister, I'll tell you one thing: You ever try to go down on me after eating a hot pepper and the only action you'll get for a month will be with your own right hand!"

"Okay, okay!" I laughed. "I'll take that threat seriously! I'll be very careful from now on!"

"That's better," she said as she took a bite of her new salad. "Except my lips are numb! Maybe I should rub some peppers all over your hand and then have you stroke yourself. That'd teach you!"

I shuddered at the thought, remembering the one time I'd harvested hot peppers and forgotten to wash my hands before using the bathroom. I decided I'd have to watch her for a while. I wouldn't put it past her to seek revenge. We finished eating and I wandered upstairs again. I know I've been going up there too much, but I keep checking on the zombies and looking for more signs of trouble. I keep wondering about other survivors. I looked outside—it was snowing pretty heavily. There were a few zombies out there, not many, and again they looked ridiculous with snow covering their heads and shoulders. I didn't see anything besides them, no tire tracks, and no footprints. After a while I headed back downstairs, then rigged up a better antennae for the radio. I drilled a small hole through the ceiling in the northwest corner and ran the antennae through the hole and onto the ground floor. Then I repeated the process until I was upstairs, then finally into the attic where I secured the wires to the roof of the attic.

A few hours later, she helped me fix dinner. No type of meat this time, just beans and rice. Of course, I used a liberal amount of hot sauce on mine. Michelle eyed the bottle warily.

When nightfall finally came, I turned on the shortwave and hoped to hear from Doctor Steve, the guy from up north near Atlanta. We're already in the habit of calling him Doc at his request.

"W8D10C coming online. Anyone broadcasting tonight?"

"Hey, Doc. This is Kevin. Am I supposed to say some kind of numbers or call sign?" As I spoke, I was fingering the Petoskey stone buried in my pocket.

"Hi, Kevin. I guess I don't really need to use the call signs anymore, but old habits die hard. You're coming in loud and clear. How's Ann Arbor?"

Michelle had come into the living room and was listening in. She had on a button-down blouse with the top four buttons undone. I could see ample cleavage. I tried not to let it distract me.

"We're getting some snow, but things are quiet. How about you? Is everything still okay?" I asked.

"Oh, I'm fine, although it gets pretty lonely up here. I realized the other day that I haven't seen another human being in months. But I haven't seen any non-human beings either, if you get me. How about you? Are there any survivors in your area?

"The only survivors we've seen were some thugs who tried to break in and rob us. I'm here with my girlfriend." Michelle smiled, looking at me as she undid another button.

She wasn't wearing a bra.

"Did they get much or did you run them off?"

"One guy got a bullet through the head for his trouble, one of the other guys got eaten by zombies, and the third guy . . . we're not sure what happened to him. I took a bullet in the shoulder, but it's pretty much healed up now. Michelle has some nursing experience, so she was able to take care of me. Other than those guys, I haven't seen any signs of people. It's been pretty quiet."

"How about zombies? Are you having any trouble with them?"

"We've seen our share, but they move very slowly when it gets below freezing. We go outside and eliminate most of the ones we can find. Like shooting fish in a barrel."

"Is that right?" the Doc said. "I was wondering about the cold. What else have you learned?"

"They can't see much in the dark, but they can still hear. I have a camera with night vision, so I've been able to avoid them at night a few times."

"I guess that's good to know, although it doesn't help me much."

"Do you broadcast on a regular schedule? It's really good to hear another human voice." While I was talking, Michelle undid another button and slightly parted her blouse. I was getting aroused again. I tore my eyes away, trying to concentrate on the conversation.

"The radio has been a lifesaver. It helps when the loneliness starts to get to me. I've always been okay being alone, but this isn't the same. Knowing I'm one of the few breathing human beings left puts things in a whole different light." Doc sounded lonely to me.

"Have you had a lot of contact with people? My radio can't usually pick up long-distance signals," I said.

"No, not a lot. Maybe a couple of dozen world-wide. I figure not many people had shortwave radios, and of those, not a lot had backup generators. How are you able to broadcast?"

"I saw the end coming and had some solar panels installed. Even here in Michigan they provide enough power for me to get by."

"That's a great idea. I wish I'd done that. I have a generator and a five-thousand gallon fuel tank, but when it runs out, I'm S.O.L. I've used about a quarter of the tank already. I'm hoping to use less once we get through the winter."

"So you don't have anyone with you?"

"Nope, just me. I used to come up with my Irish Setter, Buddy, but he died a few years ago and I didn't have the heart to replace him. He was a good companion. So far, of all the people I've been in contact with, you're the closest. How far do you reckon it is from your place to mine? I'm north of Atlanta—do you know where Atlanta is? It's west of Alpena toward Gaylord."

"Let me check. Hold on." I booted the laptop and pulled up the map software. "Looks like you're two hundred or so miles from here," I said. "In the old days, it would have been about, what, three or four hours away? But now, with no gas stations, it would take weeks or months."

"You thinking about heading my way?" Doc asked.

"No, just thinking out loud. I figure eventually, we survivors will need to come together for our own common good."

"Bear in mind the highways are probably closed down. From what I heard before the bottom dropped out, people were leaving the cities in a panic and taking to the highways. Eventually there were pile-ups, and then the creatures discovered their own roadside buffet line. I wouldn't plan on using the highways. Maybe some of the back roads. But without a four-wheel drive to get around the major snarls, or major groups of creatures, it'd be mighty risky."

"You called them *creatures*" I said. "What do you think happened? What's your medical opinion? How did dead people start coming back and eating us?"

"I've thought long and hard about the subject. Before everything fell apart, I was trying to keep up with the reports posted on medical blogs, and was keeping up with other doctors and nurses. But the bottom line is, no one knows exactly what happened. This isn't a virus—if it was, our antiviral meds would have had an effect. It doesn't act like bacteria, either. It doesn't act like anything. If I was a spiritual man, I'd say God had finally lost patience with us. How else can you explain dead people with no organs, no real intelligence, no mind directing their actions, walking around and eating people?"

"We've seen some of them with injuries that would kill a normal person, completely ignoring their broken bones and missing organs. How can any creature with a broken leg keep walking around?"

"That's the thing, Kevin. This goes against everything I was taught in med school. I have no explanation. There were some theories being bandied about, but they were all quite a stretch. And now, with probably 99.9% of the population being dead, there's no one left to do the research to try and find a cure or make a vaccine. The best we can do is destroy them before they destroy us."

"But if you're right . . . if there are so few of us, and so many of them . . . what chance do we have?" I looked over at Michelle. Only one button was left. I had to end this conversation. "It won't be easy, I must admit. Numbers are on their side. But from what I heard over the radio, and what you just told me, they're slow, they're not intelligent, and they don't work together. I think we have a pretty good chance, especially during winter."

"But you have to remember, I've never even seen one of the creatures, I have no idea how many survivors there are, and I don't know of any organized group trying to destroy them. That's the good news."

"The good news? What's the bad news?" I was actually afraid to ask. While I asked, Michelle undid the last button and opened her shirt.

"The bad news is this: Zombies are not our greatest threat. People are. Those survivors who are willing to kill other humans in order to get something they want. Once again, we're our own worst enemy. And I have to tell you, when I think of it in those terms, who's worse? The creatures, acting on instinct with no morals, no thought processes, no humanity . . . or the survivors who steal and murder, knowing full well what they're doing?"

Michelle and I sat there in silence. I was listening to Doc but I was staring at her cleavage. Damn she looked good. She knew I was watching, too, and arched her back so they jutted out. She had a mischievous grin on her face.

"On the other hand, Kevin, there are people out there like you and me who are doing our best to keep our better natures alive. And, as you said, we need to band together at some point to re-institute structure and authority. And when we finally get some order restored, guess what we should do first?"

"Destroy all the zombies, of course."

"No, that's secondary. First we have to destroy our greatest threat. We have to destroy all the humans who used this catastrophe as an excuse to hurt, rape, and kill other people."

"Why not just lock them up?"

"Locking them up would involve capturing them, restraining them, and finding someplace to lock them up. Then we'd have to have someone watch them, someone cook for them, clean their waste . . . I can't imagine we'll have enough resources to do that for quite a while."

Michelle's blouse was now barely covering her breasts. "Bones, you've given us a lot to think about, but I have a couple of things here I need to take care of. When can we talk next?"

"'Bones'? Star Trek fan, are we?"

"I confess, I'm a Trekkie at heart, and this feels like a bad science fiction movie. I'm waiting for Roger Corman to yell '*Cut*!!' But right now I'm going to fix a drink, and I think Michelle has dinner ready." As I said this, she pointedly opened her blouse more, revealing her nipples.

"Ah, so you have alcohol? Tell me, do you have bourbon? I'm afraid I have a taste for bourbon, and I ran out quite a while back."

"A man after my own heart, and yes we do. Listen, thanks for the conversation. I'll try to catch you tomorrow night."

"Same bat-time, same bat-station. Give Michelle a hug for me. I haven't had a hug in a very long time. W8D10C signing off."

The radio went silent. Michelle looked at me, eyes lit up, a naughty smile on her face. I was about to ask if Doc's comments bothered her, but before I could say anything, she removed her blouse and tossed it to me. It landed on top of my head and covered my face. I took it off and threw it across the room.

Some of the things Doc said made me want to talk to her, but I decided we could talk later. Right now my fingers, tongue, and lips wanted to have a conversation with her nipples. I took her into my arms and she drove any questions right out of my head. A half hour later, we reclined in each other's arms.

"What do you think about what Doc said?" I asked. She thought for a minute before answering.

"Kevin, sometimes I forget how good we have it here. If what he said is true, the people who are out there trying to survive must have it very rough. Having to search for food and shelter in the dead of winter while they avoid zombies and fight other people who are desperate enough to kill them for their food . . ."

"Or their women," I interrupted.

". . . it must be brutal. Like the guys who broke in here. If they'd succeeded, they probably would have eaten our food, drank our booze, then trashed the place and moved on to take stuff from other innocent people. And who knows what they would have done to us—probably amused themselves with us like they did that woman. Sometimes I don't know if I want to live in a world like this."

The woman the men had tortured. They threw her to the zombies, and she became one of them. I suppressed a shudder, thinking about her body lying in the front yard. I wasn't even tempted to tell Michelle.

"I'm pretty sure I *don't* want to live in a world like this . . . without you," I said, absently stroking her hair. We sat there for a minute, just thinking and being. "Let's forget all about everything for the rest of the day," I said. "Let's take care of our chores, make some dinner, put in one of those, um, adult DVDs and have a few drinks. Let's pretend life is normal like it used to be."

"I can guarantee life with you was *not* normal even before all this happened," she replied. "I'll go along with your idea on one condition. You fix the drinks, and I get to pick the movie."

I agreed with her and headed into the storeroom. I felt like bourbon, but I knew she would probably want wine. To me, bourbon and porn go together better than wine and porn, but Michelle and porn go together even better than bourbon and porn, so if she wanted wine, I'd serve her wine.

I picked out a bottle called Arcturus Late Harvest Riesling, from Black Star Farms in Leelanau. After I uncorked it, I let it breathe for a few minutes while I poured my bourbon. Michelle was going through the DVDs.

"Find anything interesting?" I asked.

"That depends on what you're into," she said.

"I'm into you. Or I hope to be later."

"Ha. Play your cards right, maybe you'll get lucky."

"Just having you here makes me lucky."

She finally picked out a DVD called *2040*. It was supposed to be futuristic, with porn stars playing the part of robots who were 'pleasure models.' The plot was pretty thin, but it had high production values and the scenes were well filmed and well lit—it was a big cut above some of the really cheap stuff. There were scenes that went too far if you ask me, but it got us both in the mood.

Before the movie was even half over, I had my head buried between her legs. We'd finished the bottle of wine, and it definitely got her worked up.

"That's cause I want you inside me," she whispered. I took her hand, led her into the bedroom, and gave her what she wanted.

December 22nd

Yesterday was quiet. I didn't remember it was the winter solstice until just after 5 p.m., and the sun had already set. In the light of dusk I saw a few nearly stationary zombies that had begun filtering into the neighborhood. I put on my coat, grabbed my axe from the upstairs closet, and headed toward the front yard. The moon was barely rising in the east, but even so, a good six inches of snow had fallen, so I could see my way around with no problem even as the dusk faded. The darkness took on that shade of muted blue particular to snowy nights.

It was difficult to bring the creatures down. Not because they were moving, but because they were frozen. It was like trying to chop through a frozen and rotten side of beef. They'd fall over after I hit them the first time, but then it'd take a good two or three strokes before the axe would make it through their necks. Whatever is keeping them animated is also preventing them from freezing solid. Otherwise it would have been even tougher to eliminate them.

After brushing off the ice chips of frozen skin, clothes, tissue, and bone, I stood near the door, looking at the stars. While I had been taking care of zombies it had gotten completely dark and the night sky was magnificent. No light pollution, the moon just rising in the east, and the frigid air made for some magnificent viewing. Remembering something Michelle had said, I went downstairs and took a shower. Then I gathered some blankets and a couple of sleeping bags, grabbed a bottle of bourbon and a two-liter of coke, and told Michelle to get some warm clothes on and come upstairs with me.

"What in the world for?" she asked.

"Trust me. I have something to show you."

She shrugged and began to get dressed. Outside the temperature was hovering around zero, and I led her by the hand to the back yard. The dead zombies in the street yard were not exactly romantic viewing.

The whole world was dressed in white. It was very quiet, something I can't get used to. Except for the occasional tracks of a rabbit, squirrel, or bird, I could see no signs of life in the nearly pristine snow. Off in the distance, a mile or more away, I could hear a dog barking. Then it stopped.

For the first time since early summer we were outside without much risk. I'd taken care of the zombies, and they're so slow it wouldn't matter if I missed a few.

The clarity of the stars was simply amazing. We lay our blankets down, then put our sleeping bags on top of them, put the bourbon, coke, and two glasses in the snow, and lay down side by side, snuggled together.

"Wow . . ." She sighed with awe. "The stars. The real stars. And look how clear they are! I can't remember the sky ever being this clear!" she exclaimed. As we lay there, entranced by the vision, the Northern Lights began to put on a show. I'd never seen them so bright. They were like moving curtains of light.

Until you've seen the stars and Northern Lights with absolutely no light pollution, you haven't really seen them. I used to marvel at how clear they were on the beach at Lake Menekaunee. They were dim compared to what we were seeing tonight. Sweeping currents of greenish-blue undulating curtains of light with an occasional hint of red. It was mesmerizing.

Another difference was the horizon. I'm used to the horizon having a glow about it—faint when looking west, away from Detroit, but the eastern horizon was usually lit up with light pollution. Not anymore. The only way I could tell where the sky ended and the horizon began was the silhouette of snow covered trees and buildings.

Up until around the turn of last century, everybody saw the stars this clearly. Even in the cities, there couldn't have been much light pollution, with only oil lamps and gas lamps. The first city to get electric lights was Wabash, Indiana, back in 1880. Wabash is only a few hours from here. So even at the turn of the century, the night sky must have been magnificent. I was thinking what a waste it was to miss seeing a spectacular view like this, all so we could light our massive big box parking lots and freeways.

Of course, those thoughts came to a dead end when it dawned on me that those parking lots and freeways are now dark, and for the foreseeable future, there would be no light pollution.

I held Michelle's mittened hand in my gloved hand. We had no need to spoil things with our little words. Being able to see the stars with this incredible level of detail made the universe more real somehow. Before, the stars looked great—but their impact tonight was much greater. There's nothing like seeing cold infinity to help realize your own puny mortality, to get you in touch with the immensity and wonder of creation. In times past, when seeing nature in all its jaw-dropping splendor, I found it hard not to believe in a guiding power, a Maker, a being incomprehensible to my feeble mind. But tonight, lying in a dark and dead city, front yard littered with zombies, I saw chaos and the lack of Divine Intervention and thought, *If God is there, He has deserted us.* I pulled the bottles out of the snow and mixed us both a drink. Hers was heavy on the coke, mine was heavy on the bourbon. We sipped them in silence before Michelle started talking. She, too, was impacted by the beauty before us.

"You know, it makes me sad to think everyone might soon be dead, and all of this incredible beauty won't be seen or appreciated by anyone or anything. It would be like having a beautiful painting locked in a safe. All this useless beauty."

I didn't know what to say, so I said nothing.

After only about fifteen or twenty minutes, we were both cold, so we took our blankets and went back inside. The moon was higher in the east. I wasn't sure if it was waxing or waning, but I knew that a couple hours from now, the stars would not be nearly as impressive.

Not only was it amazing to look at the night sky and Northern Lights, but it was astounding to not feel like we were in imminent danger. I think winter is my new favorite season.

I've started craving a steak. A big, juicy ribeye, medium rare, hot off the grill from Knight's, with a baked potato on the side, along with a pint of Founder's Backwoods Bastard.

I wonder if I'll ever have another steak. I can't imagine anyone alive has a working freezer chock full of them. Chances are, all the ribeyes in the world have been eaten or gone rotten. Shit. My only hope is that not all cattle-ranchers became zombies. Maybe there's an Angus cattle rancher a just waiting for new customers.

December 23rd

Michelle decided to decorate for Christmas. I was at a loss. I haven't decorated for Christmas in years. Without Tammy around, I just didn't see the point. I tried decorating the year after she died, but it just made things worse. Cheery Christmas decorations with nobody in the house but me was depressing. I wasn't about to wrap presents for myself.

She had decorations at her house, so we trudged over there. She has a small tree, some lights and ornaments. We took everything home, assembled the tree and decorated it together. She even put on some Christmas music, which is something else I don't have. We heated up some wine and added some cinnamon and nutmeg, and soon sat back to enjoy the tree drinking our wassail.

I must admit, it made the place look festive. And the lights reflecting in Michelle's eyes—well, I was enchanted. I started nuzzling her neck, and my hand wandered between her legs. Before too long, we were both intoxicated from wassail, naked, making love under the tree. It was very romantic, a night I'll not forget soon.

The World is Just Us Two

How can I give her the stars
When I have no ladder tall
How can I hand her the moon
When I have no hands at all

How can I give her my heart
When my heart has crumbled away
How can I promise tomorrow
When I do not have today

How can I offer my soul
When my spirit died long past
How can I give her my kingdom
When destruction is all I've amassed?

    The stars are in my heart
    The moon is in her eyes
    My heart beats just for her
    Tomorrow is now's demise

    My soul she already owns
    My spirit she breathes anew
    My kingdom is simply her heart
    And the world is just us two.

December 24th

I slept in today. I don't think wine agrees with me. I had a headache in no way commensurate with how much wine I'd had. By the time I got up, the coffee was made.

Michelle makes a great cup of coffee, better than mine. I'm not sure what she does different. It's stronger. She was in the shower, so I went back into the bedroom to take care of something. Then I went upstairs.

A warm front had come through. No white Christmas for us. In fact, it had warmed enough for a whole new bunch of zombies to mill around, shuffling and scuffling about, going nowhere. I don't know where they come from, but they keep showing up. I looked all around from the windows of the house, but didn't see anything unusual. But something didn't feel right. After checking the windows one last time, I went to the door, checked the peep-hole, and quietly stepped outside.

I could see the zombies in the front of the house, shuffling around. But I couldn't hear any sounds coming from them. Usually we can hear them as soon as we leave the basement. Today I heard no rasping at all. It was strange. It reminded me of one of the scenes from Hitchcock's *The Birds*, where the birds are everywhere but not singing.

I knew a lot of zombies were in the front—more than I'd seen in a while—but why were they so quiet? It was downright peculiar. I didn't like seeing their behavior change. As I stood there, listening, one came shambling past the corner. It didn't notice me, so I quietly slipped back into the house and downstairs, absent mindedly humming *Silent Night*. I decided on a last cup of coffee.

Michelle had just gotten out of the shower but was still in the bathroom. When I took my cup into the living room, I noticed a wrapped present under the tree.

"What's that?" I asked.

"What's it look like, Bozo?" she quipped, drying her hair with a towel. With her hands running the towel through the air, her robe fell open. I could see her belly button, most of one breast (including the nipple) and the swell of the other. She looked great, and I couldn't help looking.

"I *said*, 'What's it look like, Bozo?'"

"It looks lovely but kind of lonely, I think it needs some attention."

She sighed but made no effort to close her robe. "Not my boob, you boob! You asked what was under the tree, so I'll repeat myself. What's it look like, Bozo?!" She tried to look irritated, but she was also trying not to smile. She still made no effort to close her robe, which had actually fallen open even more, showing both nipples now. Below her belly button I could see just a snatch of pubic hair.

I forced myself to tear my eyes away from her beautifully exposed body and looked back under the tree. "It looks kind of like a Christmas present. Who's it for?"

"I wrapped myself a present, what do you think?" she answered sarcastically, rolling her eyes with a smile.

"Can I open it?"

"No, you can't open it. It's not Christmas. You have to wait."

"That's not fair! I don't want to wait! Besides, we never said anything about exchanging presents! I didn't have any time to go Christmas shopping! The mall was closed! I left my wallet at home! They were out of your size! The dog ate my debit card!"

"Too bad. Deal with it," she said.

I turned on my heels and walked into the storeroom and brought out three presents. I had wrapped them while she was in the shower.

Her eyes opened wide. "Three presents? I have *three* presents?"

"I'm impressed, you *can* count! I don't know why everyone says you're so dumb!"

"Can I open them?"

"No. You have to wait till Christmas. Fair is fair."

"But I want to open them now! I don't want to have to wait!"

"Sorry, but you set the rules, now you have to live by them. We'll have to wait until Christmas."

I put the presents under the tree. Michelle closed her robe and immediately came over and examined the presents. She held them up, shook them, sniffed them, turned them over and around.

"Is it a new car?"

"No."

"A Cuisinart?"

"No."

"A hot tub?"

I moved behind her near the tree. "No. Quit asking. And don't let me catch you peeking under the wrapper," I said, slipping my hand inside her robe and exposing a breast. She slapped my hand away.

"Then you stop peeking under *my* wrapper!"

Then she got a pretend pout look on her face and set the presents back down. One box was very small and square, one fairly small but heavy, the other wide and flat. The box she had wrapped for me was fairly small, about the size of a shoebox. I couldn't imagine what it could be. I did the same thing she did—shook it around, tried to figure out how much it weighed . . . it wasn't heavy at all. Not a book. Not a CD. I couldn't figure it out. I put it back under the tree.

"I think you forgot to put anything in the box," I said.

"No I didn't."

"If it's a ribeye steak, it really should be refrigerated," I offered.

"You're way off. Or maybe it's one of the new kinds that doesn't need refrigeration. You'll find out. But don't let me catch *you* peaking either," she ordered, having to slap my hand away from her robe again.

Little does she know I am one of those people who doesn't like to peak. At breasts, yes, presents, no. It spoils the surprise. In fact, usually I don't *like* to get presents. Giving is better than receiving. Except with oral sex.

She stood up, still trying to look pouty but also with a sparkle in her eye. We took care of our usual chores, and I also cleaned the bathroom. Some soap scum had built up in the shower, and I figured it was best to take care of it before it got worse. It's not necessarily easy to clean a shower stall by the light of a candle, but I did my best. I sprayed some homemade shower cleaner (dish soap and dissolved baking soda) on the walls and left them to soak.

Later in the afternoon, after we finished our chores, I went back into the bathroom, took off my clothes and got in the shower to finish cleaning. I sprayed some vinegar on the walls and started wiping them down. The baking soda I'd sprayed earlier reacted to the vinegar, making the cleaning pretty easy.

I was startled when the shower door opened and there stood

Michelle, naked, her nipples hard.

"Got room in there for me?" she asked.

"Sure!" I answered. Part of me thought, *But it will have to be quick. There's not much sun these days, so the batteries don't have a full charge to heat the water!* But I didn't say anything. I made room and she stepped into the shower. We soaped each other up, rinsed each other off, kissed and groped each other for a few minutes, then got out and dried off.

"You know, I think we save water when we shower together," I suggested. "I think we should shower together all the time."

"Mmm-hmmm," she responded, reaching over and giving my erection a playful squeeze, "I think that's a great idea. Except when you're in there with me, the water chemistry changes. It turns into *hard* water . . ." That led to other playful squeezes, then some not so playful squeezes, and before long we were back in bed, doing our best to wear each other out.

We rested in bed a few minutes, smelling shower clean and like fresh sex. My favorite smell.

After a bit we started making a dinner of salad and canned veggies. I found a can of turkey Spam and we pretended it was a Christmas turkey. We don't eat meat every day, and even when we do, canned meat just isn't the same as an aged New York Strip, freshly seared on the grill, medium rare and so tender you barely need a knife!

I know I'm spoiled. I really am thankful for the food I have. Even so, I'll be glad if I ever get fresh meat and summer vegetables again.

After we cleaned up, I went through her DVDs and found a copy of *A Christmas Carol*, the black and white version with Alistair Sim. Michelle smiled brightly—she said she loved this version better than any other.

We watched it together, enraptured. *"You may be an undigested bit of beef, a blot of mustard, a crumb of cheese, a fragment of underdone potato. There's more gravy about you than grave."* What a great line.

When the movie was over, we realized it was 12:30.

"It's Christmas Day!" she exclaimed. "Can I open my presents?"

"Sure, why not," I replied. "But I want to get a little bourbon. The good stuff. Would you like some wine?" She said yes, so I made our drinks while she picked out some Christmas music. It almost felt normal. Finally we settled down by the tree. "You go first," I said. "Since you have three. You open one, I'll open mine, then you open the other two."

"Okay!" Michelle said. She reached under the tree and grabbed the small box first—the one I'd gotten out of the upstairs dresser.

"No, not that one, one of the other ones," I said. She put it back and got the longer, flatter box. She peeled off the wrapping paper and found a small notebook. In large letters were the words "Thawing Lake Michigan" underneath, in smaller print, was "Life with Michelle"

"What is this?" she whispered. She opened the notebook and read the dedication I'd written to her. "That is so sweet!" she said. Then she turned and read the first poem. Looking up at me with eyes shining she said, "Kevin! I had no idea you wrote poetry!"

"I was hoping you didn't," I said. "I wanted to surprise you."

She slowly read several pages, savoring the love poems I'd written her. I saw tears fall down her cheeks. Once she laughed out loud. After about ten minutes, she closed the book and fell into my open arms.

"That's the best present anyone's ever given me," she said. "No one's ever written me a love poem before."

"Well, now someone's written you a bunch," I said. "Sometimes I can write what I feel better than I can say what I feel. Aren't you going to read the rest?"

"Not right now. I want to save them. They're like this wine," she said, taking a sip. "You don't chug a bottle of good wine. You take little sips and make it last as long as you can." She tipped the glass back and chugged one last huge swallow before the glass was empty. Then she laughed out loud and leaned over to give me a very wine-tasting kiss.

I was happy with her reaction—it was everything I wanted. Some people don't like poetry. *She* might not like poetry. But she liked these.

"Now it's your turn!" she said. "I'm a little embarrassed, though. My gift can't compare with what you gave me."

"I'll be the judge of that," I said. She reached over and gave me the small box. I tore the wrapping off—I'm not one to carefully, gingerly remove the paper—and opened the box. What I found inside puzzled me at first—it was little scraps of material. In very female colors—pink. White. Light blue. Frilly and lacey. Then I held one up.

I whistled a cat-call. "What have we here?" I asked.

"It's lingerie. I thought you'd like it," she said.

"Oh, I do, I love them. But Hon, how did you know my size?!" I teased.

She hit me on the arm and said, "They're not for you to wear! They're for me to wear and for you to ogle them right before you rip them off!"

"Now we're cooking with gas!" I said. She giggled then asked me if I wanted her to model them. Of course, I enthusiastically said yes.

She grabbed the box and disappeared into the bedroom. A minute later she came out, wearing a see-through bra and matching panties. The bra was very sheer, very low cut. And very, very sexy. As usual, her nipples were hard.

"Wow! You look ravishing! I may have to ravish you!" I said.

"Not yet! You have to see the rest first!"

She then proceeded to model the rest of the lingerie. She was absolutely stunning. In some ways a scantily clad woman is sexier than a naked one. The last thing she came out wearing wasn't lingerie—it was a royal blue cocktail dress. Very low-cut. It displayed her ample cleavage at its best. "Wow! That's really, really sexy!" I said, standing up.

"You're tenting, dear." she said with a wicked grin. Looking down, I could see she was right. Big Kevin was at full attention.

"You bet I am," I said. Then she turned around showing off how well the dress framed her beautiful ass. She has an ample ass—she's not some skinny-cheeked faux-adolescent. I went over to her and took her into my arms, reaching behind her and cupping her ass. "You look wonderful! I can't wait to take you out on the town in this!"

She giggled again and then said, "Now, now, this is for special occasions, if we ever have any. I'm not going to wear this around the house while we fertilize the plants."

"Fertilize the plants, hell! I'll fertilize you after seeing how sexy you are in this dress!" I exclaimed.

She backed away from me and said, "Not yet you won't. I still have two more presents!" She grabbed me by my erection and pulled me back over to the Christmas tree. With a heavy sigh—and yet filled with anticipation—I knelt before the tree, then reached over and grabbed one of her presents. The heavier one. When I handed it to her, she said, "For a small box, this weighs a lot! I hope it's gold!"

"What good would gold do you?"

"Point taken," she said as she ripped the paper off the box. She then removed the lid and pulled out a half-dollar sized, polished Petoskey stone, nearly identical to mine.

"Kevin, it's beautiful! Did you find it?"

"Yep, found it and polished it. I wish I could have made it into a pendant, but I don't know how. Back in the day, I'd spend hours and hours looking for them, and would rejoice when I found a good one. They've always been kind of a good luck charm for me."

"So you found this on the beach? At Lake Minetonka?"

"Lake Menekaunee," I corrected. "Yes. I found that one on the dune called Old Baldy, about a hundred feet above the shore. It was a glorious mid-October day, and my friend Stan and I hiked from the resort through the woods, up to the top of the dunes and then back along the beach. This was the first Petoskey I'd found in over a year. Looking for it was like looking for a cool drink of water on a hot summer day. And when I found it, my heart was at ease, as if I'd recovered a lost treasure. Giving it to you feels . . . appropriate."

She was still turning it over in her hand, admiring the hexagonal pattern the fossil made on the stone.

She reached over and gave me a kiss.

"Thank you for the fossil," she said, "I'll keep it forever." Then she reached out for her last present, looked at me and said, "May I?!"

"Of course! I hope you . . . I mean, I wasn't sure if . . . I mean, if you don't . . . aw, hell, just open it."

She took her time taking off the wrapper. By now, I figure she knew what was inside—or had an inkling. She slowly opened the jewelry box and gasped.

"Oh, Kevin, it's *beautiful!*" she said as she pulled the diamond ring out of the box. Taking the ring, I knelt in front of her.

"Michelle, I know I haven't said it in so many words, but I love you. You're the best thing that's happened to me in a very long time. I want to always be with you. I want you to marry me. Will you? Will you marry me?"

She started crying, smiling, and nodding her head at the same time. "Yes! Yes yes yes yes yes!!" she said. I admit, I misted up myself. We hugged and kissed and just held each other for several minutes before breaking our clinch. Her eyes were still wet and shining. Mine probably were too. "I love you so much, Kevin. Thank you for making me feel beautiful and alive." Then she nestled up to me. We sat there, all wrapped up together, staring into each other's eyes, whispering words of love and comfort. Michelle noticed I was still tenting. She took me by the hand and led me into the bedroom. For the first time—but not the last time—I had the pleasure of unzipping her dress and watching the fabric cascade onto the floor.

Christmas Day was here. And Santa was about to come.

I was nearly asleep when she sat up and poked me. "Who says I'm dumb?!" We both laughed, then once again she nestled into my arms. She sleeps next to me now. I'm very happy. I don't know when I've liked a present as much as the present she gave me. She looks so beautiful in her lingerie and dress. I almost had an eye-gasm, lol.

And she liked my poetry.

And she said yes. What more could a man want?

Silent Night

Silent night, holy night.

They are silent
as if they sense the sanctity of this moment.
Standing by the bed, I listen

to the silence.

Underneath the blanket she dozes
nightmares forsworn.
The blanket covers all but the slope
of one breast

I watch it silently rise and fall
with her breath

just as my hopes rise and fall
hope for our love to last forever
fear that forever may be short

She moans in her sleep
then shifts slightly.
The blanket slips to reveal
the fullness of her breast,
culminating in one sweet blushing nipple

I disrobe
quietly join her under the blanket
and pray that, like her
tonight I shall

sleep in heavenly peace,
sleep in heavenly peace.

Christmas Day

It has been quite a lovely day. We spent much of our time in bed. I had her model all of the lingerie again. Then I had her take it all off again. The whole day, she kept glancing at her ring. A couple of times I caught her in the hydro room.

"Look how beautiful it sparkles under the LED lights!" she exclaimed. I took a look and she was right—the red and blue lights made the diamond practically glow.

We watched another movie, *A Christmas Story*, which Michelle said reminded her of her home town. We had a bit more to drink than usual, had a bit more sex than usual, and fell asleep a bit earlier than usual after one more dance between the sheets. It was the perfect end to a perfect day.

December 26th — St. Stephen's Day

The day awoke with a start. Michelle and I both heard something and bolted upright at the same time. "What was that?!!" she exclaimed.

I got up, threw on some clothes, and ran into the living room. The sound was coming from upstairs. I silently climbed the stairs in my bare feet. With my head close to the trap door, I could hear it—the sound of feet shuffling and scuffling on top of the trap door. There was snarling. And rasping. Zombies. '*Shit,*' I quietly mouthed. I silently went back downstairs. Michelle was waiting for me, a look of fear in her eyes. I held my finger up and pursed my lips to indicate *shhh!* Then I pulled her head close to mine.

"Kevin, what is it? More bad guys?!" she whispered. Her eyes looked frantic.

"No, it's worse," I whispered back. "Zombies. They're in the house."

She gasped. "In the house? How did they get in the house?!"

I stood there thinking. Reluctantly, I whispered, "On Christmas Eve I went upstairs. There were a whole bunch of zombies. But they were all very quiet. I thought it was weird, so I stepped outside for a minute. I must have forgotten to lock the door."

"So we're trapped down here?" she whispered, her voice betraying an edge of panic.

"No, we're not trapped. We have the root cellar exit. And there's no way they'll be able to get down here. But it means we have to be extra quiet until we figure out how to get them out of the house. The quieter we are, the fewer might come into the house."

I held her at arm's length, hands on both of her shoulders. "It's okay. We're still safe. We still have power. It's just a minor inconvenience," I told her. She didn't buy into it completely, but some of the panic faded from her eyes.

"We'll figure this out. We'll be okay." I leaned forward and gave her a quick kiss. "We're still together. We're safe. We're smart, a lot smarter than they are. It's just a problem waiting for a solution."

She dropped her eyes and said she supposed I was right. We spent the morning prowling around, afraid to make any noise. The whole time, we could hear the sound of them from upstairs. The sound of their feet on the floor above, the sounds of their rasping and snarling. It was quite unnerving.

While we took care of chores, I was problem solving, trying to figure out how to get them out of the house. What an idiot I was to leave the door unlocked. I'd been so careful up to now.

So they came in through the side door. I have no idea how many. I don't think they're quite smart enough to climb stairs, but I wasn't sure. I had one gun but not much else. Oh, and a plank of two-by-four. The axe was upstairs. If I used the gun, it would surely attract the attention of the zombies outside the house. And while I knew we were completely safe—there's no way they could find the trap door, much less figure out how to open it, it was still problematic. I knew for a fact that we couldn't stay down here forever. And heaven forbid if something went wrong with the solar power.

I'm also concerned about our water usage. As long as the weather stays below freezing, we don't get much water coming in. If we run out, I'll have to find a way to bring ice in to melt. No matter what, I'm going to have to go upstairs on occasion.

The only thing I can figure out is to use the root cellar exit. I've never tried it in the winter, with snow covering it, so I don't know how easy it will be. And I'll be operating blind. Should I open up the hatch and find myself in the middle of a crowd of zombies, things could get ugly fast. But it still seems a better option than trying to go upstairs through the trap door.

Michelle and I went into the bedroom and I quietly told her my thoughts. She didn't like the idea of me using the root cellar exit, but she also didn't like me trying to go upstairs. But she did have one excellent idea I hadn't thought of.

"You said it had warmed up outside," she said, "how warm was it?"

"It was in the mid-fifties."

"Is that normal weather?"

"No, usually the highs this time of year are in the mid-thirties, lows are in the teens or lower."

"What if we put a thermometer in the root cellar near the top of the ladder and checked the temperature. If in a few days the temps drop back to normal, the zombies will be much slower. It might not be completely safe, but it will be safer than it is now."

I nodded my head. She's a bright girl. The thought hadn't occurred to me. "That's a great idea! I knew I loved you for more than just your hot body," I said, "and if I exit during the night, using my camera, it will be a lot colder and they won't be able to see me."

"So once we're up there, what do we do? The gun makes too much noise, and we don't have any other weapons down here."

"Hold on just a minute," I protested, "what's this *we* business?"

"Come on Kevin. If we both go up, we can watch each other's backs. Remember the Bible verse?"

"It's not safe, and we can't watch each other when it's pitch black out. I only have one camera. Only one of us will be able to see."

"Maybe it's true indoors, but outside we'll be able to see by the moonlight. Don't you have a program to tell you how full the moon is? And you can figure out when it's rising."

I still didn't like the idea, but it was worth checking out. We continued to talk, making our plans. I pulled up my astronomy app and luck was on our side—the moon would be nearly full in three days, and would be rising about 4. Now we just had to hope the weather would cooperate.

Sure wish I could check the weather forecast.

After all the joy and romance we had yesterday, this was quite a buzz-kill. Back to reality.

December 27th

I've been talking with Doc every night. I told him our predicament and our plans. He made some good suggestions we're going to try to follow.

I mentioned in passing that our compost toilet was full. He suggested we take the compost with us when we go upstairs. That way, even if we accomplish nothing else, we'll have one less problem down here.

December 29th

Over the past few days we've been monitoring the temperature in the root cellar. The thermometer I have keeps track of the daily high and daily low. It's been getting steadily colder at night. Last night it got down to eighteen degrees. I'd like it to be even colder, but I guess it will have to do. The plan is to head out early tomorrow morning.

It's a pretty sobering plan. We know it could go completely wrong. Despite our plans, we could find ourselves trapped and fighting for our lives. Knowing the risk we're about to take, our time together has become more precious.

December 30th

Things could have gone better. Things could have gone worse.

I thought we'd covered all the bases. We had the compost to take with us. I made sure my night vision camera was charged. We went to bed early so we'd be well rested.

At 3:30 we awoke and got dressed. The air in the root cellar was very cold. The thermometer read sixteen degrees, so I knew it was probably in the single digits outside. We sat there for a minute, letting our eyes adjust to the darkness. I was hoping I wouldn't have to use the camera until we got into the house, since last time I used the camera the zombies saw the light emanating from the back of it.

Our plan was to climb out of the root cellar, eliminate any zombies in our immediate vicinity, then head into the house. Once there, I'd grab the axe out of the storage closet and we'd systematically clear out the house. Once the house was completely clear, we'd close and lock the door I'd stupidly left unsecured, then leave the clean-up work for tomorrow.

I reached over and found Michelle's hand and gave it a squeeze. "Let's get this over with," I said, "so life can get back to normal."

"Life with you will never be normal," Michelle said, holding on to the gun we'd brought in case we absolutely had to use it.

I climbed the ladder until my back was against the ceiling and my knees were bent, and pushed. It wouldn't budge. I tried again and felt it move an inch or so. I remember wondering how heavy it would be, but I hadn't taken into account the possibility of having several inches of snow or frozen ice weighing it down. I guess we'll have a white New Year's.

I braced myself and gave it one more try, this time climbing up a rung in order to get more leverage. Slowly the hatch started opening. I felt the grass roots over the seam give way. I climbed another rung, then wedged the two-by-four into the gap to keep it open. I climbed up and out and heard Michelle scramble up the ladder behind me. I heard a *thump* in the grass about ten feet away and concluded Michelle had tossed the compost, as planned.

It was completely dark. I hadn't planned on an overcast sky. I could see where the moon was, but it was just a faint glow behind the clouds and didn't provide enough light to see anything.

"Shit," I whispered. "I'm going to have to turn the camera on. Try not to look at the light. Grab my belt loop and stick with me." I felt her hand touch my back and then grope for my belt loop. Once she grabbed it, I turned the camera on.

Four feet away from me stood a tall zombie, slowly turning its head our way. One of its eye sockets was empty. It didn't have a bottom lip, and its rotting, frozen tongue hung down. It was missing its right forearm.

With an involuntary gasp, I instinctively stepped backwards and felt Michelle pulling hard on my belt loop. I had nearly pushed her back down into the root cellar. Only the edge of the hatch stopped her as she hit her head hard against it.

I quickly drove forward and to the right, pulling Michelle back from the brink of the hole. She was a brave girl—she hadn't made a sound.

I swung the camera back around and saw the zombie still slowly turning our direction. The one good arm was rising, the hand reaching out. It didn't pose an immediate threat. I had no weapons yet, so I couldn't eliminate it, but we could easily step around it.

I turned the camera off to avoid any undue attention, and realized a new problem. In looking at the view screen, I had completely shot my night vision. I didn't have time for my eyes to adjust, so now I was dependent on the camera for navigation.

I turned it back on and slowly panned around. There were three more zombies on this side of the house. I could see the door to the house, open as I suspected it would be.

I silently led Michelle toward the house. We could hear our feet scrunching on the snow. That was something else I hadn't counted on. I could see every zombie begin to turn their heads in our direction. I didn't say anything to Michelle, but one of the zombies was Mrs. Erickson. Her throat had been torn out and was now rotted away. I could see her spinal cord partially exposed. The bottom of her jaw was rotting out as well. I turned away, sickened by the sight and by the stench of the zombies.

We made our way to the house and through the camera I could see five or six zombies standing in the kitchen. One of them was blocking the storage closet. There was no way to get to the axe.

I leaned back to Michelle and whispered, "One of them is blocking the storage closet. I'm going to have to knock it over." We slowly and quietly made our way inside. I had to step around one zombie. Michelle stuck to me like glue, still not able to see anything. I reached out and pushed the zombie's shoulders as hard as I could. It was like pushing a statue. A statue with half-frozen rotting flesh and half-decayed clothes. This one was missing the bottom half of its face from what looked like a shotgun wound. A thought flashed through my mind, wondering if the person who held the gun had survived. I doubted it.

When I pushed, I expected the zombie to react. It barely did. It fell over just like the block of frozen flesh it was. On the way down, it grazed another zombie. This one tottered but did not fall, slowly swiveling its head as it teetered.

After the zombie fell, its legs continued to block the door. I grabbed the door knob and pulled as hard as I could. The door opened, but not enough for me to step inside. I reached my arm in as far as it could go and felt around. My fingers brushed up against the axe handle and I grappled with it, nearly knocking it over in the process. Finally I had it fully grasped in my hand and pulled it out.

Then I realized something else we hadn't thought of. I couldn't hold the camera, look through it, and wield the axe.

"Michelle! You're going to have to hold the camera!" I whispered. Even my whisper was enough to get their attention, as several began to make their rasping sound, causing the rest to join in. Being so close and hearing them in such a confined area was unnerving to say the least. With the camera still on, I held it in Michelle's direction until she took it.

"Which is closest?" I whispered. Michelle reached forward and held the camera in front of me so I could see the zombie. The light reflecting off my face got its attention, and it started slowly moving in my direction. Michelle pulled the camera back out of my way, and I tried to keep my bearings as I raised the axe in the air and brought it down on the zombie's head. Once again, it was like hitting a block of ice. The first blow must have glanced off its head. Michelle whispered, "A little more to the left."

I struck it again. This time, the axe penetrated about three inches, spraying frozen bone, hair, and brains throughout the kitchen. Michelle once again held the camera out so I could see. I raised the axe and slammed it down into the zombie's head, near where I'd struck it before, close enough for the axe to penetrate fully into the brain, destroying it. The zombie dropped to the floor with a thud.

Through the viewfinder, I could see the zombie I had first knocked over when I came in. It appeared to be moving a bit faster as it began to try and rise up. I brought the axe down onto its neck and felt the spine and tissues crunch as the axe shattered them.

"Kevin! To the right!" Michelle said. I swung the axe blindly until I felt it hit the zombie. I then shoved the axe as hard as I could, knocking it over as well. As I approached it in the dark, I felt its hand slowly try to grasp my foot. I wondered where Michelle was as I brought the axe down, first hitting it in the upper chest, then with a better aim I dispatched this one with a blow through the neck as well.

As I did this, I heard the outside door click closed. Michelle had enough sense to close the door and lock it. Thank god. The last thing I needed was to have more zombies slowly make their way inside.

I waited for Michelle to come to my side, and when she held the camera out, I could see there were two more zombies nearby. The closest one had turned its head in my direction. It couldn't see me. I swung the axe toward its legs, hoping to knock this one down too. But the axe struck at a glance and banged against my right shin. Ouch. I raised the axe and swung it at an angle, driving it hard into the neck. With a sickening snap, the axe severed the spinal cord. It fell, landing partially on top of the other fallen zombie.

One left. By now, my arms were tired. Trying to drive the axe through frozen flesh wasn't easy, as my muscles had obviously atrophied with the lack of exertion downstairs. I stood there, breathing hard, resting the axe on the floor. I could hear the remaining zombie slowly moving.

"Here, let me," Michelle said, taking the axe from me. There was enough ambient light from the camera screen reflecting off the walls for her to make out the shape of the zombie. With a huge grunt of exertion, she swung the axe with all her might, snapping its neck in two. The zombie fell with another thud. "Reminds me of chopping wood back home," she said smugly, "even though I never did." I felt like she had one-upped me but also glad she was able take care of zombies when needed. Zombies were now scattered all over the kitchen floor. I was tired. But I knew we were not finished. We made our way through the house but only found three more. None were upstairs, so obviously they can't climb stairs.

Michelle took care of two more zombies while I held the camera, and I took care of the last one. I was thankful there were none left, as I had some concern about whether I had enough strength to finish the job. That made the score five to three by my reckoning. Not that I was keeping score, like Legolas and Gimli.

The house was finally clear of zombies. But we weren't quite through. We made our way to the side door and opened it. None of the zombies outside had moved much—it was colder outside than inside so they moved more slowly. As Michelle stood in the doorway, I made my way to the root cellar door. As I approached it, the moon broke through a gap in the clouds. Suddenly the landscape was brightly lit.

There were scores of zombies. As many as we'd seen at once. And with all the noise we'd made, all heads were turned in our direction. I turned the camera toward Michelle. Her pupils were dark pools, absorbing the infrared light from the camera. Another difference between the living and the living dead—zombie eyes are all black in infrared, not just the pupils.

I rushed over to the open hatch, kicked the two by four back down into the hole, and heard it slam closed. Then I sprinted to the house, where Michelle was waiting inside. As I rushed in, she slammed the door closed behind me. Just before it closed, we heard a low rumble of sound as the outside zombies began their throaty, raspy vocalization. They were hungry, and we had escaped.

We stepped over the bodies, then pulled them off the rug over the trap door. I raised the rug until I could lift the edge of the trap door and raised it enough for us to scramble inside, where it was light and warm and safe. When we got to the bottom of the stairs, Michelle turned to me, smiling. "We did it!" She cheered. "We'd better get in the shower and rinse all this zombie crap off . . ." Suddenly Michelle's eyes grew wide. The blood drained from her face. "Kevin! You're hurt!!"

I looked down, and sure enough, blood was flowing freely through a gaping wound on my right shin. My immediate reaction was *I got bit!!* but then realized the axe had cut me when it bounced off the frozen zombie and hit my leg. At the time, I barely noticed it. It never occurred to me I was injured.

The implications hit me like a thunderclap. The axe head. We had used it to chop up zombies, and it had punctured my skin. We'd killed more zombies afterwards, spraying zombie tissue everywhere. It was likely I had gotten some rotting tissue in my wound. I stood there, dumbstruck, staring at the wound and the blood draining down my leg.

"Kevin! Snap out of it! Move your ass into the bathroom! *Move your ass!!*" she yelled. I finally got moving, following Michelle. She started the water running, adjusted the temperature, then turned to me. "Get in the shower! But don't take your pants off!" I stepped into the shower and paused. Michele stripped down to her t-shirt and panties, grabbed her medical kit and took out a pair of scissors and flashlight. Kneeling on she shower floor, she cut the bottom half of the pant leg off, nicking me in the process. Her hands were shaking.

"Ow!" I said.

"Shut up." she said matter of factly. I started to unbuckle my pants so I could take what was left of my jeans off. I didn't want to shower with pants on.

"Do. Not. Move." she commanded as she put a small LED flashlight she'd fished from her bag into her mouth and illuminated the wound. "This might sting."

"Geez, Michelle, if you wanted to get kinky, your lingerie would have worked just as well," I joked lamely, "but I thought I was the Dom! Where's the paddle?!"

"Shut up." she said again, her voice muffled by the flashlight. She grabbed some gauze, hastily poured hydrogen peroxide directly on gash, then started to clean it. She was right; it did sting. When she'd cleaned it, she gently pulled the skin back and examined it in the bluish light of the LEDs.

"It's a deep cut," she said, "but no major arteries were hit. That's what I was worried about." Without warning, she poured isopropyl alcohol into the wound.

"*Aaauugh!*" I hollered. "Damn, that *really hurts!*"

"Sorry, I don't have any saline to irrigate it with. But don't worry, the worst is yet to come," she said. "Get undressed." I quickly pulled off my sodden shoes and socks, the remainder of my soaking jeans, and my wet shirt.

"I didn't know we were having a wet t-shirt contest today," I said. "I think you're going to win." Despite everything, I couldn't help but notice her nipples and areola though her wet shirt. She didn't grace me with a response.

She grabbed some adhesive tape and taped the gauze on top of the wound. It was immediately soaked with blood. She ignored this and overlapped more strips of tape on top, effectively making it waterproof. Then she turned on the shower and told me to get busy washing.

"Use plenty of soap," she ordered as she turned to leave the bathroom. "And I mean *plenty* of soap."

"Where are you going?"

"To get you some bourbon and something to bite down on. This next part's going to be tough."

I washed my body from head to toe, seeing bits of decomposed flesh fall down onto the shower floor. It must have been lodged in my hair. It began to freak me out. I washed my hair over and over. When Michelle came back she had a highball of bourbon and several washcloths, one of them rolled up. I held the highball out of the water. She got in the shower, still wearing her wet underwear, and proceeded to roughly wash me all over with soap and the washcloth.

"I already did that," I protested. I expected her to tell me to shut up again, but she didn't say anything, she just kept on washing. After she'd thoroughly scrubbed me, she nodded to the glass of bourbon.

"Drink that." She said with a matter of fact tone of voice.

"Is this the good stuff or the cheap stuff?" I asked. She raised her head to glare at me.

I glanced away and drank the bourbon. It felt like fire in my stomach, and the warmth spread through my body. She took the tape and gauze off the wound. She handed me the rolled up washcloth and said, "Lean back against the wall and bite down on this."

"Wait!" I said. I reached down and pulled the Petosky stone out of my pants pocket which lay in a heap on the shower floor. I then put the washcloth in my mouth as I squeezed the Petoskey stone in my hand.

I leaned against the wall, all the weight on my left leg. She took the remaining wash cloth, poured alcohol onto it, pulled back the flap of skin, and began to scrub the wound. Now I knew why she gave me the wash cloth to bite down on. I'd never felt pain like this. Through squinting and watering eyes, I looked down and saw the floor of the shower turning pink with my blood. She kept scrubbing, continuing to add alcohol liberally. After about ten minutes, she sighed and said, "That's the best I can do."

She turned off the water and I stood there, dripping wet and tears still leaking out of my closed eyes. As soon as she stopped scrubbing, the respite from the pain was such a relief I couldn't even speak. I rested my head back against the shower wall, and willed my pain receptors to back off and my heart to slow down. My breathing became regular.

She got out of the shower and reached into her bag, pulling out a needle and thread. With tears in her eyes, she said, "I'm sorry, Kevin, I know this is going to hurt. But I have to." She held her free hand out to me and helped me to the toilet seat where I sat with my leg propped up. She proceeded to suture the wound. By now the bourbon had kicked in. It didn't help much, but it made the pain a little soft around the edges. Compared to the scrubbing, suturing the wound was actually tolerable. When she was finished bandaging my leg she put her arm around me and helped me hop to the bed. A bit ago she brought me my laptop. So here I am.

Damn, pain can be intense!

My leg has started to ache, and she says she's bringing me some Motrin later, then a Lortab to help me sleep. But first she wants to talk to Doc.

My hand hurts from squeezing the Petoskey stone so tight.

New Year's Eve

After I finished writing yesterday, she brought me the Motrin and ordered me to stay in bed. I got bored and asked her to bring me a book. I didn't even care what, just something to pass the time. She brought me the Bible. At least it was The Message, not the King James Version. I spent some time reading Ecclesiastes, getting a fresh take on the words *Much learning earns you much trouble. The more you know, the more you hurt.*

At 8:55, she came in with the shortwave radio and turned it on. Then we sat there waiting. Finally, we heard him give his call sign then say "Kevin, are you on tonight?"

I spoke into the mic "I'm here, for better or for worse."

"Oh? Something going on?"

I told him what had happened, and how I'd chopped my leg with the axe. He addressed some questions to Michelle. She described how she'd cleaned the wound and stitched it.

"You stitched his wound up? Ever done that before?"

"On occasion," she replied. "I was in nursing school for a couple of years. Plus my father was a doctor, and I helped him sew up the family pets when they got themselves torn up. I also stitched Kevin up after he'd been shot by the intruders we had."

"Good girl! What did you use for an anesthetic?"

"I gave him some bourbon when I was cleaning it out, which may have been a mistake, because then I couldn't give him anything else for a while except Motrin. So basically he didn't have any anesthetic."

"Kevin, how'd you do?"

"It hurt. But I behaved."

"Good man. I know it was tough."

"So Doc, here's the thing. Since the axe had zombie skin and tissue on it, we're afraid he may be infected."

"You mean, infected so he's going to become a zombie?"

"Yes, that's exactly what we mean."

Doc was silent for a moment. "Back when the web was still up, a lot of doctors were discussing this. The docs who worked in the city had the most experience. They claimed it was only through the bite of a zombie that someone could become infected. That didn't make sense to the rest of us, but they swore they saw it over and over. So, if they were right, I don't think Kevin's at much risk."

I was very relieved, and saw Michelle's eyes mist up.

"But let me reiterate: I don't think he's at *much* risk. Michelle, you're going to want to monitor him for the next 48 hours. It's possible the doctors were wrong, or the disease has mutated."

"Will do," she said.

"Meanwhile, if you have any antibiotic ointment, spread it on a couple times a day. Do you have any antibiotics by chance?"

"Yes, I have a full bottle of Amoxicillin."

"That's great. If you see any signs of infection—you know what to look for—start him on a one week regimen. And Kevin." he said, "stay off your feet as much as you can. You don't want to break those stitches."

"Fine." I said. By now, my leg was throbbing and I was getting grumpy.

"Michelle, why don't you and I have a little talk of our own? How about an hour from now?"

"I was thinking the same thing. I could use your advice."

"Wait a minute," I protested, "why do you two need to talk alone?"

"Kevin, he's a doctor. I need medical advice, and you probably don't want to hear the details. Besides, I think it's time to give you a Lortab and let you sleep."

"Fine, I said again. I didn't like being left out of the conversation.

"Doc, I'm going to go ahead and medicate him. Talk to you at 2200." Michelle said, slipping into nurse time. Doc wished us luck and signed off.

Inwardly, I was freaking out, although I did my best to hide it. I had just fallen in love, I wanted to live. I wanted to protect her, wanted a life together. I didn't want to be a zombie. I didn't want to eat her except in the Latin sense.

She brought me a Lortab a while ago. I was glad to get it, because my leg had started to ache. Now I'm getting sleepy. I don't think I'll be awake to see in the New Year.

January 3rd

A couple days have passed. Michelle has been hovering over me as much as I'll let her. I stayed off my feet for the first day, but for crying out loud, it's not a major wound. I only have a dozen or so stitches, and it's not likely I'll be ripping them out by over-exerting myself here in the basement.

I suspect Michelle and the doctor were discussing what to look for if I started to turn into a zombie. This is uncharted territory for all of us. But so far so good. Yesterday it started looking infected, but in a normal way—it was getting very red and hot. Michelle took my temperature and I had a low grade fever as well, so she broke out the Amoxicillin. We know we have to be very careful with the antibiotic—once it's gone, as far as we know we'll never have any more.

I could tell she was really worried about me turning. It seems like she checked on me every five minutes, and I caught her looking at me with a funny look in her eyes.

Would I be able to tell if I was turning, or would I feel fine one minute and the next minute start thinking, *Gee, her thigh smells good. I wonder what it would taste like?*

I finally had a talk with her. We were sitting together on the sofa, my leg propped up. "Look," I said, "we might as well talk about it. There's still a chance I could turn. I don't know if I'll be aware I'm turning—does it happen slowly, and you can feel it, or is it like falling asleep a man and waking up a zombie?"

"I don't know," Michelle admitted.

"But I think you would know if I was changing. I suspect you'd be able to tell the difference between me having an infection and me turning into a zombie. Michelle," I said, bringing my fingers to her chin and turning her face up to look at me. "If I start to turn, I'll have to be shot in the head. One of us will have to shoot me. You know I'm right."

She wouldn't meet my eyes.

"You might have to do it. You'll have to lure me upstairs and outside. And you'll have to shoot me in the head. It would be far more loving of you to shoot me in the head than to let me turn. I can't imagine how insanely horrible it would be for you to see me out there, shuffling along, making weird noises, knowing I'd attack you without hesitation and start eating you—"

"All right, Kevin, I get your point, you don't have to be melodramatic about it," Michelle said crossly.

"I hate to say it like this, but you'll do it if you love me. You won't let me turn. And I won't let you turn either." *Although if it was her, and I had to shoot her, I'd shoot myself too,* I thought. "The best and only way we could honor each other, and honor our love, would be for us to not let the other turn."

Michelle abruptly got up without so much as a glance in my direction and went upstairs, terminating our conversation.

What does the zombie get when he shows up late to the dinner party? The cold shoulder. That's what I got the rest of the night.

January 4th
Today my fever is gone and the wound looks a little better—more pink than red. She's still watching me pretty closely, but I actually made her laugh today. Tonight she put on her flannel pajamas again. If she doesn't *come* to bed naked, she probably won't be *getting* naked.

Even so, I'm going to finish this entry and see if I can get in her pants. They probably won't fit.

January 6th

It appears I won't live out my all-American boyhood dream of being a zombie. The Amoxicillin has knocked out the infection and the gash is healing nicely. It really wasn't such a big deal, I don't know why they overreacted like they did. Michelle and the doctor keep having these private conversations, and I must admit the crazy part of me keeps whispering in my ear, wondering what's up.

I finally did the smart thing and point blank asked her, "What is it you and Doc keep talking about?"

"You really wouldn't want to know, Kevin. It's a woman thing." That's the code women use for having plumbing issues and, truthfully, men really *don't* want to hear about it.

At one point in the past, I was the sole male in an office filled with females. I swore I'd never work with women again. They were constantly going on about cramps, and bloating, and how heavy the flow was, and getting a D&C (whatever that is!), boob jobs and labiaplasty. I can't tell you the number of times I left the room, embarrassed. So I suppose she's right, I don't want to know any more detail than she gave me.

Michelle mentioned something today I hadn't thought of. We'd left all those zombie bodies upstairs, and the ones we destroyed are still all over the lawn and in the street. I'd say there's at least forty of them.

The problem is, if we leave them there, it's going to really stink upstairs. I'd rather not have to put up with the smell of rotting zombies. And once it gets warm, we'll have flies and who knows what kind of rodents and disease.

But the real problem isn't inside, it's outside. We can't leave all those bodies just lying there. We have to get rid of them, and we'd better do it while they're still frozen. If for no other reason, having all those dead zombies in front of our house is a sure-fire way to let someone know the house is occupied.

She checked my wound and was visibly pleased. She said I could pretty much do anything I want, so I reached out and cupped her breasts in my hands. She slapped them away. "That's not what I meant." Can't blame a guy for trying!

Since there's no sign of infection, we agreed to go upstairs and take a look around. We looked at the bodies in the house and the bodies outside, then talked about where we should take them. The best place to get rid of them is in one of the ruins of a burned house. There are several on our block. Realistically, we can't take them much further, since we'll be hauling them by hand and they can be very heavy.

I'm glad it's as cold as it is—they were already smelling pretty bad. I can't imagine how they would smell come spring or summer. Having them frozen also helped keep the bodies intact. It would be gross to have one fall apart while we're hauling it, and then have to pick up the rotting pieces.

We got a couple of large cardboard boxes from Michelle's house and figured out how to rig them together so we could haul the zombies across the snow. It worked for the most part, but even so, it was quite a task to pull three hundred and fifty pounds (give or take) down the street, and find a place to dump them. We made six trips today and got rid of 13 bodies. This will take a number of days. It's disgusting work, so gross to have to dig them out of the snow.

When we were finished, my leg hurt. It still looked fine and I didn't let on I was in pain, but I could tell I'd done enough for one day. Tomorrow we'll do more. I figure it will take another three days minimum. My shoulder is aching as well. I suppose I should get used to these aches and pains.

One strange thing happened today that played right into my paranoia. We finished hauling for the day, and Michelle headed downstairs. I figured I'd check the dishwasher to see if we'd left any trash in there we should also haul off. When I opened it I found a bunch of photos of Wayne and Michelle along with the notes from the CDs, stacked neatly. I felt compelled to look at them all, and again they made me very uncomfortable. Half jealous, half mad. The paranoid part of me said, *She hid these up here so she could look at them without you noticing!* But the sane part of me said, *No, she put them up here because this is where the trash goes.* Honestly, I believe she threw them away, but I'm not completely able to silence the other voice.

I was still on edge when I went downstairs, so I grabbed a growler of beer and put it outside, right next to the door. In a little while I'll retrieve it, once it's cold. I drank one pint when it was still warm.

I haven't brewed any beer in a long time. Truth is, I'm still trying to finish off the last batch I made. It tasted great, but I just haven't been into alcohol as much as I was a few months back. That's probably a good sign, right?

Dear Tammy,

My friend Rich, when I was undergoing "cognitive therapy" with him, once advised me to write letters to people who had positively or negatively affected my life, and with all my confusing emotions right now, I figured maybe I should write to you.

First off, Tammy, I miss you. Last night I dreamt I was sitting comfortably in the upstairs living room when you came bursting through the door, weeping. You ran over to me, put your hands on either side of my face, and smothered me with kisses.

"I love you, I love you, I miss you so much!" you whispered, then jumped up and ran back out of the room, still weeping. When I tried to follow you I discovered the door was locked. It wouldn't open no matter how hard I tried.

When I woke up, my cheeks were wet.

I miss you so goddamn much.

Most things in the house are exactly as you left them. I never redecorated, got new furniture, or painted the walls. Every framed picture you hung is still in the same spot, even the Rothco print over the sofa. I never told you I don't like it, and yet there it hangs a decade later. Leaving things the way you left them feels like you're still here in a small way.

The Edna St. Vincent Millay sonnet comes to mind frequently, the one that begins "Time does not bring relief; you all have lied" and ends with

> And entering with relief some quiet place
> Where never fell his foot or shone his face
> I say, "There is no memory of him here!"
> And so stand stricken, so remembering him!

You're not the only woman I've loved in my life. There were a few before you, and now there's one after you, but you and I loved each other when we the strongest and healthiest we would ever be, and we had (we believed) the best parts of our life ahead of us. We had energy, we made time for sex, we were excited about the future. The times I loved women before you seemed even then like dress rehearsals.

Before you left me, we used to reminisce about our first dates and our wedding and honeymoon, and all the sexual escapades we had. Now I rarely let myself remember those times. If I were a better man, I'd find a way to salvage the good memories despite how things ended. But the bitterness of your leaving sometimes outweighs the sweetness we had. I wish I knew how to change that, because we had some wonderful times I hate to forget.

It's funny, the things I've already forgotten. I remember our first kiss—but not our second. I remember the first time we made love—but not the first time you had a climax. Was it during sex? Or during foreplay before we had sex?

I remember when you first told me you love me—but I don't remember the last time you told me.

Friends of mine—I guess I should say *late friends of mine*—used to tell me I could take solace in being reunited with you in heaven. And though I didn't argue with them, I don't believe it. I don't believe in grand reunions on the other side. If there is an other side, a beautiful paradise with no sorrow, why would we waste time waiting to welcome our friends and spouses and children and parents to show up? That would be hanging on to our former life, depriving us of the full joy of paradise. Paying attention to our former existence? It would be as if an adult dragonfly focused its attention on the life it lived as a larvae.

Maybe life as we know it is briefly center stage, but ultimately unimportant. Like an extra in a movie. To him, his scenes are the scenes of the movie, but to everybody else he's just part of the background visuals.

It would be quite comforting to believe one day I'll look into your eyes again, hold your hand again, kiss your lips again. But I'm afraid to believe it. It hurts too much to believe it's true, and it hurts more to believe it's not true.

There are times when I'm able to believe there truly is life after death, that you ascend to Paradise after death. Times when I picture you waking up in that new existence, or traveling down a tunnel toward the light of the new existence. I picture you waking up to a body made whole, a perfect body, with no flaws and no disease and no age. It's still one-hundred percent Tammy, but a Tammy with a perfect body. Perfect teeth, *perfect skin, perfect laugh. Quite unlike the last Tammy body I saw, a body eaten alive by cancer and decimated with chemo. And I imagine you discovering your new body, and how you'd respond. I picture you running and jumping and reveling in your strength and agility, delighted at what your body can do. I imagine you happy in that new life, freed from the diseased body you were shackled to, and my joy for you is so great it causes me to weep. I wouldn't want you to turn back and focus on me, living here in this existence you just graduated from. Stop looking at this dingy old life here and go live your new life with your new perfect body and shining sun and amber waves of grain. And then I spend fifteen minutes or so struggling not to cry, because I miss you so much and wish so badly we were together somehow, and usually end up reaching for the bottle of bourbon.*

The day of your funeral, before they closed the casket, I leaned over and kissed your lips. They were cold, they were lifeless, but they were your lips, never to touch my lips again, and so I kissed them one last time forever.

There's never a second chance to do the things we could and should have done. We only get one chance to be the person we want to be, to do the things we long to do, one chance to love someone the way they deserve, one chance to be worthy of their love in return. My chance with you is over. Any impact I had on your life is a thing of the past. Your impact lingers on, as you still make a difference in my life.

After you left, my wedding ring burned my finger like fire. I developed a rash. Eventually I took it off and put it in a small box in my dresser, under the photo of us on our wedding day. At some point I put it back on, but I don't remember when or why.

I know it's stupid, and I know it's wrong, but I'm royally pissed at you for leaving. I know it wasn't your fault. You didn't do anything to cause your sickness, you didn't give up. You fought hard. But you lost.

So even though it makes no sense, there have been nights, often but not always alcohol-induced, when I was so fucking angry with you I had to turn your framed photo face down. Seeing you looking at me, smiling so beautifully, so young and healthy . . . it angered me. I start to wish I'd never met you and so was never hurt by you. How I felt reminds me of part of a Carl Sandburg poem:

> I wish to God I never saw you, Mag.
> I wish you never quit your job and came along with me.
> I wish we never bought a license and a white dress

My love for you, my anger and pain at your leaving, is causing me problems now. I was thrown together with a woman named Michelle, and we hit it off and are now living together by circumstance and by choice. But I don't trust her to never leave me. I don't trust her to not hurt me. And I've started suspecting her of loving someone else, even though there is no one else alive. Intellectually I know she can't be in love with someone else, yet my heart remains unconvinced.

What would have happened if Jason hadn't died? Would you still have left? Did his dying make you sick? Or were you already a ticking time-bomb, and the cancer would have detonated inside you anyhow? If he hadn't died, would we have raised him together? Or would something bad have happened? Would we have stayed married or gotten divorced? Would one of us cheated on the other? Would we have gotten tired of each other?

In my heart, I believe we would have weathered any storm—and we would have had our share. Financial, physical, spiritual—there would have been rough patches, of course. There would have been dark days and high and mighty days. Days of wine and roses and days of stale bread and sour milk.

But even if Jason hadn't died, we might not have made it. We know, or rather we knew more couples who didn't make it than couples who did. You can love each other with a consuming love, and it might not be enough. The Beatles said "All You Need is Love" and then they broke up.

There have been a few nights steeped in bourbon when I agonized over what may have happened and why. Knowing we could have drifted apart even if you survived your cancer begged the question: what would have caused it? A weakness in my character? A flaw in yours? Which of us was more likely to struggle with fidelity? A few times I fell asleep filled with remorse, suspecting in our alternate universe I'd betrayed you, and equally hurt to think it may have been you who betrayed me. Those nights usually preceded mornings filled with a less emotional and more physical remorse at the amount of bourbon I'd consumed.

Despite what I said earlier about not believing in grand reunions, I believe in something probably just as—if not more—ludicrous. I choose to believe that somehow, somewhere there is a version of reality where Jason didn't die and you and I stayed in love until the day we died together of old age. My belief in such a universe comforts me. Somewhere you are still alive, Jason is now a happy grown man, and we're looking forward to retirement with each other and with nary a thought of cancer or the undead.

But in the meantime, what do I do about Michelle? Who can blame her for getting upset when I accuse her of something she didn't do, when I try to catch her doing things I know she isn't doing.

I love Michelle, I really do. But my love for her is not the same as my love for you. There's no innocence, no faith in the future, no complete and utter willingness to face whatever happens. I'm just too scared, Tammy. I don't have it in me.

I wonder what you would tell me if you were aware of my problems. I had a dream a few months ago where you told me to give her the stars. At first I thought you wanted me to paint stars on the ceiling, but later I thought perhaps the stars were more like actions I could do to create pinpricks of light in the darkness of her trials, allowing light to stream in like god-rays. In his song Lovers in a Dangerous Time *Bruce Cockburn sang "gotta kick at the darkness 'till it bleeds daylight." Maybe you meant for me to break up her dark times with little spots of light. Lord knows these are dark and dangerous times. Lord knows she's been a light for me.*

You know I don't believe in time travel. If time travel ever became possible, we'd know it now because we'd have time-traveling tourists from the future coming to watch important historical events. Having no visitors from the future proves time travel will never happen. But if time travel did exist, if we could revisit our younger selves, I would travel back in time to give you one more kiss, hold your hand one more time, spend another hour with you, or another day, or week, or year. Just to lay my eyes on you one more time, to hear your laugh, to hear you cry, to hear your sighs of passion. And when our kiss, our hour, was over I think I'd choose to end everything. I've heard the secret to a long life is knowing when it's time to go. Maybe I should have left when you did.

So there you have it, Tammy. I know you're never coming back. I know I'll never hear your laugh, or feel your hand in mine, never even get the chance to irritate you by leaving all the cabinet doors open after I've been cooking. You're never coming back, and I can't bring myself to spend time remembering the time we had together. It just hurts too damn much.

I miss you so much. I think it's time I got drunk. Or drunker.

All my love forever,
Kevin

January 9th

Last night I couldn't sleep. Sometimes wine messes up my sleep and gives me strange dreams. I dreamt about Tammy. Again. When I woke up, I couldn't go back to sleep. I got out of bed, fixed a glass of bourbon, and wrote her a letter.

When I was finished, I was pretty upset. So I refilled my glass of bourbon and went upstairs. I peeked out the window. It was a gorgeous night. Several inches of fresh snow had fallen, and there was a full moon. I checked the thermometer and saw it was about twenty-five degrees—cold enough to slow the zombies down, but not cold enough to render them harmless.

I hadn't bothered to put any clothes on, and it probably wasn't the brightest thing to do (I blame the bourbon), but I decided to go outside. I put on a pair of shoes I keep by the side door, checked the peep hole, threw back the bolt and stepped outside.

As I looked to my right, toward the road, I saw five deer ghosting through the neighbor's yard across the street. The light reflected off their flanks, and their shadows were cast to the east. I must have made a little bit of noise, because suddenly they all looked at me, ears up, and then bolted away, between houses and out of sight. I walked through the crunchy snow to the corner of the house by the back yard.

The landscape was silvery and luminous. The half-moon was already in the west, and shadows were cast on the virginal snow. There was no wind, no noise, no lights. Despite the moon, I could clearly see stars, especially in the north and east. The moon itself was so brilliant it almost hurt my eyes. I heard a couple of owls hooting somewhere in the near distance. In the snow I could see tracks of animals—deer, rabbits, mice, birds. A mile or so away I heard the high call of a coyote.

The snow softened the shapes of everything, making the landscape look like a Christmas card. Only the footprints of small animals and deer broke the surface of the virginal snow. I haven't seen any bear tracks yet, but I'll bet I will in time.

I stood there, naked, my willy shrinking up, caught up in my emotions and the mystery of the moment. My left hand held the glass of bourbon; my right hand migrated to my willy and covered it for warmth.

The trees in the neighbor's back yard had a layer of snow on the branches. The roof of Michelle's house across from me practically glowed. The fence between our houses also had several inches of snow on top, and the fence cast a blue-black shadow on the ground.

Because of my dream, my thoughts at first were still about Tammy, but soon I began thinking about the snow, and how in a few months it will all be gone. I thought about the transient nature of things, and I began to think how things would never be like this again.

At some point in the future, I will die, or Michelle will die, and the other one will be left to carry on. I can't imagine how I would live without Michelle. She's my lifeline, my sanity, my only friend (except for Doc). I can't imagine leaving her alone to fend for herself.

I thought, too, about life after we're gone. Once I'm gone, there will be no one left to remember Jason. It will be as if he never existed. And once Michelle's gone, there will be no one to remember me. The story of my life will be unwritten.

I thought about my grandparents, and their grandparents before them. I don't even know what my great grandparents' names were. They are gone forever, even their names forgotten. In this world we live in, I suppose nearly every former living person is now forgotten forever. Whatever dastardly deeds they did in their lifetime, no matter what heroic feats were accomplished during the Collapse—all of it is forgotten.

I took another sip of bourbon, and then watched, fascinated, as a great horned owl flew over my head and landed in the neighbor's tree. It didn't make a sound, the flight completely silent. I saw a small cascade of snow silently fall from the branch on which it landed. With the moonlight shining on it, it sparkled like star dust as it floated down.

After a few minutes it took flight. Without even a breath of sound it lifted off and flew over to the fence between our houses. I stood still, admiring its shape in the moonlight. It was perhaps twenty feet from me. The moon in the west highlighted its wings. It perched there, head swiveling around, as it surveyed the yard and probably looked for a meal. At one point it looked right at me, watching.

After a few minutes, it moved on, north and out of sight. I stood there, shivering, again thinking about the temporal nature of things. When I die, there will be no one to remember the owl. And one day Michelle will be without me, or I will be without her. My eyes began to tear up, and I chided myself for it.

I've never experienced a love like this. It's vital to me now. My love with Tammy was just as intense, but it was completely different; they're different people and these are different times. How could I manage to go on if Michelle died? Even the thought make me sad. I don't know if I could survive such a loss again.

From somewhere to the east, I heard the owl hoo-h'*hoo*-hoo-hoo, and then heard the mate answer from farther away.

We may very well look back on this time as the best years of our lives post-Collapse. I resolve to live more in the moment, to notice more about Michelle, to express my love to her more, to do what I can to make her life better. When I make her my focal point, all is right with the world. When I start to think about me, and whether she's making the same amount of effort to love me—in other words, when I become self-concerned—that's when things deteriorate. Suddenly it's not unconditional love.

I want to die knowing I loved her with all my heart, strength, and mind, whether she goes first or I do.

I thought, *This time will soon pass away, and I'll wish with all my might for just one more day with her, like I do with Tammy. But my wish will not be granted.* The very thought filled me with melancholy.

But as I lifted the glass to my lips and sipped the last of the bourbon, I heard the owls call again. And I thought, *Yeah, it will happen. But right now, the woman you love sleeps peacefully no more than thirty or forty feet from where you stand.* I turned to my right and took a quick piss, watching the steam rise from the darkening snow.

With a sense of urgent joy overflowing my heart, I crunched my way back to the side door, went back downstairs and opened the laptop to write down these thoughts. Soon I will slip into bed beside her. And though I'd like to press my body against hers, to feel her skin, to nuzzle her neck, after having been outside, my cold hands and feet would awaken her. So I imagine I will lay there, listening to her breathe slowly in and out, and just like the calls of the owls outside, my breath will soon began to answer hers as I drift to sleep.

February 1st

Not much to report over the past few weeks. We've gotten into a groove and a pretty good routine. We actually have a schedule.

Monday: Spend time on the plants (check the pH, replenish the water, add fertilizer, harvest, replant, check for pests, clean up). Germinate seeds. Check in with Doc.

Tuesday: Seek and destroy (eliminate any new zombies who have wandered into the neighborhood). Haul off a couple bodies.

Wednesday: Check neighborhood houses for zombies/survivors. Destroy zombies. Haul a few more bodies. Rescue survivors (if we ever find any). Check in with Doc.

Thursday: Return to cleared houses, gather any needed supplies (food, alcohol, weapons, booze, prescription drugs).

Friday: Laundry, cleaning, plant seeds, move sprouts to hydroponic raft, harvest anything ready, check pH and water levels. Haul bodies (if any left). Check in with Doc.

Saturday: Breakfast in bed (pancakes, coffee, and each other). Scout out neighborhood for any signs of zombies or intruders.

Sunday: Lounge around naked. Enjoy each other. Watch DVD or listen to music. Read. Dance in bed.

One thing I always look for when we're scavenging through houses are spices. I don't want to run out. Once the spices are gone, I may never (for example) taste cinnamon or cumin again.

Michelle's the one who checks for drugs, since she's most likely to know what they're good for. I wouldn't know them by their generic names.

We're always looking for antibiotics, pain meds, and ADD meds for those days when we'll need an extra boost. We haven't found a whole lot of useable meds yet (most are long expired), but at one point Michelle jauntily entered the kitchen (where I was packing up some canned goods) holding up a medicine bottle and shaking it so I could hear pills rattling.

"Lookie what I found!" she chimed, "a bottle of tadalafil!!" She had a gleam in her eye I found curious.

"What's tadalafil?" I asked.

"Generic Cialis!" she replied rather gleefully. I've never used it, but even so, it sounds like fun. Not that I *need* it. But hey.

We also retrieve any liquor and beer we find. We stockpile alcohol in the crawlspace under Michelle's house. No point in leaving anything out in the open.

We come across dead bodies in some of the houses. When possible, we haul them away with the zombies. Sometimes it's not possible (if they're too large to haul up flights of stairs, for example), so we close the door to those rooms and leave them.

Yesterday we came upon several disturbing scenes while scavenging houses in the neighborhood. One house was pretty trashed inside, with empty beer bottles, cigarette butts, and liquor bottles scattered everywhere. We heard rustling upstairs—it sounded like small animals—and went to check it out. We've seen plenty of rats in these houses, along with a few raccoons, opossums, some feral cats and even a wild dog. They all run when they become aware of us.

So we weren't surprised when we went upstairs and saw a half-dozen or so rats scurry into holes they'd chewed through the walls. We could smell something decomposing, and in the master bedroom we found the remains of a dead man lying in bed. His hands and feet were duct taped to the bed frame and his head showed signs of trauma. The mattress had a lot of blood stains.

It was hard to tell what happened to him. The rats had been feeding off the remains.

Michelle is the one who pointed out the blood on the mattress. Bodies don't bleed after they're dead, so the rats couldn't have caused the blood we saw. His head trauma could not have come from himself or the rats—they must have come after the fact. He couldn't have taped himself to the frame. It appears someone did this to him.

Michelle went into the master bathroom to look for pharmaceuticals. I headed downstairs where I found more bloodstains on and around a coffee table. Looking closer, I saw duct tape stuck to the legs. While I was puzzling over this, I realized this was the house where the bad guys pulled their truck into the garage. She must have lived here and been captured by them. The body on the bed must have been her husband or boyfriend.

The blood was on the coffee table and carpet must have been hers. They must have taped her down so they could have their fun. There was a broken broom handle, which they probably used on her too. I can still picture the nasty lateral bruises on her legs and back as they heaved her into the horde. I'd hate to think what else they might have used the broom handle for. Sick bastards. May they rot in hell. I can just see the fat man grinning and having a drink as they tortured her.

I decided to see if the truck was still in the garage.

I opened the door into the garage and flinched when I saw another bunch of rats—maybe a dozen—swarm away from me and disappear. The stink of dead flesh was pretty strong there, too.

Sure enough, the truck was there. The day they broke into our house they must have left it here so we wouldn't hear them approach our house. I heard a slight scrabbling sound coming from behind the truck.

Instantly I recalled that Michelle killed the guy whose pecker I bit, saw the other guy get eaten by zombies, but didn't know what happened to the third guy. Was he still here, alive after all this time? If so, what would I do?

I raised my gun (I no longer carry it like I'm a TV actor) and quietly followed the trail of blood to where the sound was coming from. It led behind the truck. Dim light filtered in through the narrow windows at the top of the garage door.

Peering around the corner of the truck, I found a strange sight.

Three rats were gnawing at two decomposing bodies lying in a pool of blood and tissue. One was a few feet from the other, the back of its head blown off, presumably by the gun still grasped in other body's right hand. Bits of dried bone and flesh were splattered onto the tailgate.

The body holding the gun was collapsed against the garage door, its neck and shoulder ripped out. The back of its head was blown off, a gory spray pattern of brains coating the garage door. Ample amounts of blood stained his filthy shirt. A pool of dried blood spread around the body and underneath the truck. There was no blood around the other body.

"*Scat!*" I shouted at the rats. They quickly ran under the truck and disappeared, I assume into another hole in the wall. I suppose the house is completely infested.

Michelle must have heard me, because shortly afterward I heard her call my name. "Kevin? Are you okay? Where are you?"

"In the garage," I called. She found me staring behind the truck. She couldn't see the body from her doorway vantage point.

That was the moment I noticed something that gave me a great deal of perverse satisfaction.

"Michelle, come look!" She warily came over, holding a cloth to her nose. When she came to stand by my side, she flinched and jumped back.

"Ugh, two more. We should open the door and haul them away."

"No, wait, look closely. See how the one leaning against the garage door had his neck and shoulder torn out? See all the blood on his shirt and the floor? He was attacked. The other body must be the zombie who attacked him. He must have been bitten and then killed the zombie before killing himself."

"So? We've seen worse. It's disgusting. Why do you want me to look?"

"Do you see anything familiar about the body?" I asked her, pointing to the one in the pool of blood. She glanced at me with a look of impatience before looking back at the body, the cloth still held to her nose.

"I don't—" she started, then stopped. The hand holding the cloth slowly dropped to her side. I knew she was a very observant girl.

"His arm. That tattoo. It's him."

His right arm, the one holding the gun, had a garish tattoo—the tattoo we'd seen on one of the guys. Now that we were closer, I could see that it was a Dixie flag. The skin was shrunken and shriveled, but it was clear. This was the third guy, the one who'd gotten away.

"When he ran off he must have made his way back to get the truck and was attacked and bitten by the zombie. During the scuffle he must have shot it in the head, and then as he bled out he must have killed himself so he wouldn't turn."

Michelle and I looked at each other for a long minute. Searching her eyes, I could see a lot of what she saw in mine as well. A sense of satisfaction and relief mixed with disgust.

Michelle turned away.

"I didn't find anything," she said, "those guys must have taken everything worthwhile. Let's get out of here. I want to go home."

I turned away, and on impulse looked into the cab of the truck. Besides empty beer cans littering the floor along with empty cigarette packs, the only thing usable was a roll of duct tape—which I decided to leave. There were blood smears on it.

We headed home for a quiet night. Seeing that guy, seeing his tattoo—it rattled us both.

We decided to leave both bodies where they were. That sick bastard didn't even deserve a zombie burial. Let the rats eat him.

February 4th

We finally finished hauling away all the bodies. There were no major problems, although we were both glad to be done with it. We dumped them in the basement of one of the burned-out houses.

Every day after we hauled we were compelled to take a shower (I was equally compelled to shower *with* her). Handling the zombies also had an effect on my appetite. Usually, hard physical labor will make me hungry, but when it comes to hauling half-rotten bodies . . . well, let's just say I won't be eating any canned meat for a while. Michelle, however, seemed fine. If anything, she seems to be eating more. The nurses training she had must have eliminated her squeamishness.

She continues to act a little strange around me. And she's moody. I know a lot of women have PMS, but I've never noticed it in her before. A couple of times I caught her crying, and when I asked what was wrong, she said "Everything." I wondered if it meant she wasn't happy with me, but an hour later she was dragging me to the bedroom, desperate to get a taste of Big Kevin. I don't get it. Was she mourning her friends and family who are gone? Mourning the loss of our world? Or, hell, was she upset because she's gained a few pounds? I haven't said anything about her weight—I'm not a complete idiot *all* the time.

A few times I noticed her staring at me. Not in a loving or lustful way—hell, I *like* those stares—but in a way that made me uneasy. What's she thinking?

PMS. Geez, what a number it does on women! I've known women who had it so bad, I didn't dare go near them. What's the difference between a zombie and a woman with PMS? You're allowed to shoot the zombie.

I wonder why Michelle is getting it so bad now? Is it the environment, the lack of sunlight? Seasonal Affective Disorder? Some missing vitamin or nutrient? Is there something in the air? Or is it just the level of stress we're under?

When she looks at her ring, she's usually smiling, although once I caught her crying. I asked her again what was wrong, and this time she said, "My ring is so pretty and I'm so happy to be with you." Seems an odd thing to cry about, but I never claimed to understand women. My not being able to understand her merely confirms that she is, indeed, a woman.

She had another talk with the doctor tonight. Maybe she's having plumbing problems. Women are usually reluctant to talk about that stuff with their man, and men are usually reluctant to hear it anyhow. I can't imagine what else it could be, unless I've turned into a zombie but am unaware of it. I'm not craving her thigh, as far as I know, only what's between her thighs.

A good ribeye, on the other hand . . . that, I'm craving. Damn, I miss

Knight's. I still remember how it smelled when you walked through the door on a cold winter day—grilled steak mainly, but undertones of alcohol, baked bread and fried food. My mouth's watering just thinking about it.

And the way the plate smelled when the server first put it down in front of me, the seared steak still slightly sizzling as the juices began to pool on the plate near the melted butter from the baked potato. Drops of condensation beginning to form on the pint glass of Founder's.

Sigh. I need to stop with the food porn.

February 7th
Yesterday was kind of odd, not having to haul bodies like we've been doing nearly every day for weeks. It was nice to just putter around the house. We actually watched a movie, too. Between scavenging, hauling bodies, taking care of the plants, cooking and cleaning up, we haven't had as much leisure time lately.

Michelle used the down time to jump my bones a couple of times. I think her PMS has affected her libido, as she seems to want it more than ever. Not that I'm complaining. But I'll be glad when she finally has her period and gets over her PMS! When she's not horny, she's moody. She's like a pendulum, swinging from emotion to emotion. I never know what to expect.

Never trust women. I should get it tattooed on my forehead. Or chest. Or maybe a lower body part.

So today started out great. We'd had a nice day. Nothing unusual, unless you consider being in love, barricaded in a basement surrounded by zombies and growing plants under lights unusual. We'd had a nice dinner, I had some beer I'd cooled in the root cellar, Michelle had a glass or two of wine.

She didn't know it, but I also took one of the Cialis pills. Just to see.

I was sitting on the sofa when she came and sat next to me. I put my arm around her, and she leaned over and kissed me. I kissed her back, one thing led to another, and before too long we were laying naked on the bed. She had stroked me until I was hard, then said, "I'll be right back."

"Where are you going?" I asked.

"To get some lube." she replied. Lube? Since when did she need lube?

She disappeared for a minute and came back with a bottle of lube. I noticed she had rubber gloves on.

"Why the rubber gloves?" I asked as she lay back down and poured some lube onto her hands.

"Sometimes I react to the glycerin," she said, then reached over and started stroking me again. It felt very nice. "Besides, it's kind of kinky."

That sounds interesting. I've never been into latex, but it might be a novel experience, I thought. Little did I know.

She asked me, "Hon, what's that Klingon Proverb they used in one of the Star Trek movies? Something about revenge?"

"'Revenge is a dish best served cold.' It was in the second Star Trek movie, *The Wrath of Khan*. Why are you asking?"

"I don't know, it just popped into my head. I don't think I agree. I think revenge is a dish best served hot."

"Is that right?" I asked. It was hard to concentrate on what she was saying, as her hands (both of them) felt so great stroking me. I don't think she'd ever given me a hand job before, and I liked it! Her hands felt so warm and slippery. The latex added an interesting texture. I was wondering if the lube she used was some of the warming lube, because it started really warming up and feeling nice. But within thirty seconds, it was warmer than any warming lube I ever used. And being alone for ten years, I had plenty of time on my hands (so to speak) to try different kinds.

"What kind of lube is that?" I asked. It was starting to get a little *too* warm. "Is it some kind of warming lube? I might be having a reaction to it."

"No, it's just regular lube. Speaking of warming though, remember when you sliced my lettuce with the same knife you sliced hot peppers with? Wasn't that funny?!"

"Sure, I thought it was funny."

The lube was starting to get *too* hot.

"Well, before I came back, I cut open a hot pepper and rubbed a little on my hands."

By now the heat was definitely on the uncomfortable side. It wasn't horrible, but it sure wasn't pleasant. I jumped out of bed and started fanning my penis as it bobbed up and down like a hyperactive kid on a pogo stick.

Now mind you, it wasn't excruciating. But when I realized she was seeking revenge, I decided to overreact. Then perhaps her need for retribution would be satisfied.

"Ow! This hurts! I can't believe you did this!!" Fanning didn't seem to help. I ran into the bathroom and turned on the shower, no hot water, just cold, and jumped in. I gasped as the water hit me. Michigan water in February is *very* cold.

I grabbed the soap and started washing myself—I knew my only hope was to wash off the capsaicin. The cold water helped, but I couldn't tell if the soap was doing any good.

I could hear Michelle, the snake, laughing in the bedroom. *"You're a horrible person! You're not getting any for a month!!"* I yelled, hoping she couldn't hear my smile. I kept washing with soap, rinsing, washing with soap. Lather. Rinse. Repeat. Michelle's laughter disappeared for a minute, then she rushed in carrying a big handful of snow.

Trying to look apologetic (but her grin was counterproductive), she said, "Here, maybe this will help." She packed the snow around my erection, which cooled the burning just a tad.

"That's better! Get more snow!!" I cried. *"No, forget it!"* I jumped out of the shower without drying off, dashed through the living room and up the stairs, then straight out the door and into the snow. Michelle followed me.

I think under most circumstances, I would have gone flaccid by now, but the Cialis seemed to be living up to its reputation. Sticking straight out, as I ran into the yard it wagged around like a dog's tail, except this dog was *not* happy.

With the moon shining bright, I turned around, dropped to my knees and started shoveling snow onto my crotch. Even in the dim light, I could see how red I was. Michelle was laughing so hard she couldn't even stand up. She fell back against the wall of the house. Pointing at my woodie, she gasped "You have a cherry dicksickle," and collapsed in laughter.

I, however, was doing a good job of not laughing. The look of my fully-engorged bright pink cock in the pure white snow under the blue light of the moon was perhaps the most surreal thing I've ever seen.

Had there been zombies close by, my penis and testicles would have made a spicy meal for them. Spicy Kevin nuggets.

I continued shoveling snow onto my crotch until the burn subsided a bit. I assume my body released endorphins in response to the pain. The rest of my body was freezing—literally. It's not a good idea to go straight from the shower into the winter air in Michigan.

I finally stood up. Michelle was still grinning like the Cheshire cat. I threw a snowball and hit her right in the forehead. She just started laughing again.

"Snowballs," she gasped, "you have snowballs!!" and she fell down again, laughing. I marched past her and locked the door behind me. She started pounding on the door.

"Kevin, let me in! I'm cold! There are zombies out here! And coyotes! And women selling Amway!" I ignored her and marched straight downstairs.

Within minutes, the endorphins had kicked in completely. I was feeling an endorphin high chile-heads only dream about. I lay on the bed, still standing at attention, and just let the waves of bliss wash over me. I was going to give Michelle another minute before letting her back in.

Just then, she walked into the bedroom. "How the hell did you get in?" I asked.

"I have a key, remember? I hid it outside."

Damn. I'd forgotten. She sat down on the bed. If not for the endorphins, I would have despised the grin she had.

"Feeling better?"

"It's waning. But that was incredibly mean of you. I'll never trust you again."

"Revenge is a dish best served hot," she replied, still grinning. "My stomach hurts from laughing so much!"

"I ought to throw you down on the bed and stick this inside you," I said, grabbing myself and shaking it at her.

"There probably isn't even any hot stuff left on it," she said, then got a wicked gleam in her eyes. "One way to find out."

She leaned over and engulfed me with her mouth. "Mmm, still a tad spicy," she murmured when her mouth wasn't full. She pulled back to admire my manhood. "Now there's a hot pepper!" she said, "or should I say *hot pecker?!*"

"I don't care what you call it, just don't stop!" I begged. Then her mouth gave me her full attention.

Between the endorphins, the Cialis, and the oral sex, it was the best damn orgasm I've ever had. I saw stars. Molecules. Universes. Gluons. I meant to ask her if my personal sauce was spicier than usual, but drifted off to sleep before I remembered.

February 11th

We've been talking more to Doc. I think he's lonely. Practically every night we're on the radio with him. He likes to tell stories about his exploits as a doctor, and I think Michelle sees him as a surrogate father figure, since her own father was a doctor. She enjoys his stories and relays some of her father's adventures.

She may be talking to someone else too. Yesterday when I went upstairs to check on the house and neighborhood, I came back earlier than I expected to and thought I heard her softly talking, but when I got downstairs I found her in the bedroom lying on the bed, reading a book—coincidentally close to the radio I'd left on the nightstand.

Am I inventing this in my head? Did I really hear her talking to someone, or was she just clearing her throat? Who could she be talking to besides Doc, and why would she hide it from me? She said she'd marry me but the way she's acting now I'm not sure where things are going. Could it be she's found another survivor and hasn't told me? Is there any way in hell it could be Wayne? If it's neither of those, why is she being secretive? There's no reason to talk to Doc behind my back, unless she thinks there's something wrong with me but doesn't want me to know. Have I changed since the axe bit me? Have I turned into a zombie and don't know it? As far as I know I'm acting normal; I eat the same food, drink the same bourbon, have the same libido. To the best of my knowledge, we're both doing well—healthy and free of sickness.

Other times she seems almost manic, and absolutely crazy about me.

The past three days she's had to have me seven times. Her shifting moods keep me constantly guessing what's going on with her. So I try to surreptitiously watch her, guage her emotions, check her body language. I'm observing her.

    I hate to keep my eye on her. I hate to check up on her. I hate to doubt her. But what can I do when she's acting so odd? I've known her for five months and have never seen her like this. There has to be a reason for her change in behavior. Unless I managed to fall in love with someone who has cyclic mood changes, and she's entering a dark phase. If that's true, I can deal with it. I just want to know how to prepare myself.

    These thoughts are akin to the feelings I had when I freaked out about Wayne, and they're putting me in a bad mood—which puts her in a bad mood. We're not exactly fighting, but we're not quite the bosom buddies we were not so long ago. We still have sex with wonderful frequency, but it's always at night, she doesn't seem to be interested during the day. In fact, she's rarely allowed me to see her naked for the past few days. She keeps her top on during sex unless it's completely dark. Is she going back to being ashamed of her body? Doesn't she know I love her the way she is? She keeps saying her nipples are super sensitive and doesn't want me to touch her breasts. For a guy like me, that's very frustrating. Why are they so sensitive? It's not from me playing with them! Is she using nipple sensitivity as an excuse to hide her body from me? So she's gained a few pounds. We're stuck in a basement during winter with very little exercise. It doesn't bother me. If that's not it, what is it? Once again I wonder if somehow there's a real or imaginary guy she's thinking about and bothered by. I'm paranoid that when she's in bed with me, she's thinking of him—whomever 'him' could be. Maybe she's saving her breasts for him.

    In the old days I could have followed her, or checked her cell phone records, or rigged up a key logger. Now I can't do anything but suspect, and suspicion makes my stomach hurt. Which puts me in a bad mood. Which puts her in a bad mood. Which makes me wonder why she's in a bad mood. Sigh.

February 18th

When I went to bed last night, it was raining. Overnight the temperatures dropped to just below freezing, and I awoke to a full-fledged ice storm. A layer of ice about a quarter inch thick covered everything. The trees, bushes, mailboxes, cars . . . and zombies. A few had wandered near during the recent warm spell and we hadn't gotten around to clearing them.

One was particularly close, just at the end of the driveway. It used to be a man, somewhere between thirty and seventy. Its skin is so sallow it's hard to tell the age; much of his hair is missing, especially on one side. What hair remained was matted down, stiff with ice and wet with the continuing drizzle. Ice had encased the eyes in their sockets. Icicles had formed and were dripping off its nose, chin and ears. Just like all the other zombies, its body was completely encased in ice. The mouth gaped open obscenely, but even it was iced over, the glazed and frozen tongue protruding from one side of the jaw.

Being incased in ice made them look more like statues than ever. And it appeared to stop them from moving, as they stood stock still for hours. Occasionally one would manage to move slightly, and the ice encasing it would fall off and shatter as it hit the ground, the shards scattering across the surface of the snow for many feet. It made an odd rattling sound every time it happened. I saw two of them move slightly and then fall over as the ice on one side fell off, leaving them unbalanced.

I took advantage of the situation to eliminate as many as I could. Between the physical exertion, the cold, and the rain, I was exhausted when I finished. It's harder to chop their necks or heads through the layer of ice. When I was finished, I stood by the door, breathing hard, looking up and down the street. There were no more standing. But the rain was mixed with snow as the temperatures began a slow decline, and over the next couple of hours the rain slowly transitioned completely to snow. One of those heavy snows where nearby Blue Spruce trees, obscured by falling snow, turn the very lightest shade of bluish-gray against a slightly lighter shade of gray.

There was very little wind, so the snow fell nearly straight down. By dusk, I'd say three inches had fallen, enough to cover everything completely, including fallen zombies. Then the snowstorm blew past us to the east and the western sky cleared to a brilliant blue just after sunset. The waning colors of dusk bathed the land in shades of blue and salmon against the white of the snow. All the while, snowflakes were still falling from the cloudbank to the east. I headed downstairs and talked Michelle into joining me outside. When we exited the house and turned to look at the surrounding landscape, Michelle gasped. It was impossibly beautiful. It looked like a Thomas Kinkaid painting. All the world was covered in a three-inch blanket of snow reflecting the colors of the sky. It looked pure, clean, virginal. It felt innocent. Beneath the white of the snow, occasional sparkles were seen from the ice just underneath. As we stood looking, a tree branch across the street ripped free of the trunk and went crashing to the ground in a muffled *thump!*

Looking at Michelle, seeing all the colors of the landscape reflected in her eyes while her auburn hair became flecked with snowflakes, caused me to be momentarily free of my paranoia, and the unfamiliar freedom brought a rushing euphoric release of emotion. With a laugh I abruptly ran and jumped into the yard. I jumped through the layer of snow and onto the ice where I promptly fell over. It was nearly impossible to walk, and when I slipped and fell the second time, I learned the crusty layer of snow just above the ice is *sharp!* I broke my fall with my right hand, which of course went through the snow and then through the layer of crusty ice, getting bloodied in the process. Nothing serious, of course, but I never enjoy seeing crimson red against virginal white. Not when it's my blood.

I made my way back to her and together we stood near the door for a few minutes, looking at the trees dripping icicles and covered with snow. For the first time in quite a while, we could hear noise in the distance—in this case, the sound of trees falling over and branches breaking under the weight of the ice and snow. There would be a snap and then a rumble as the heavy branches thumped to the ground. I packed some snow around my hand to slow or stop the bleeding.

Michelle looked lovely, in a way I never thought I'd describe someone: beatific. She was stunning. It wasn't her clothes or the way she'd fixed her hair or her make-up. It was her face. Her cheeks were all rosy from the chill February air. Her skin was relaxed and healthy. Seeing her in that context, another cliché I'd never actually applied to someone: peaches and cream. I couldn't stop looking at her. Her beauty surpassed that of the gorgeous sunset. A thought occurred to me; I turned to her and said "Stay still." Then I proceeded to unzip her coat and remove it before I unbuttoned her blouse, starting with the top button. She rarely wears a bra these days, so when I opened her blouse I was treated to the lovely sight of her breasts and hardening nipples.

"Kevin, what are you *doing*?!" she asked me with a slight edge in her voice.

"Making art," I replied, "stay here for a minute. Please."

She sighed and said okay, so I rushed down stairs to get my camera. When I came back outside, I snapped a few shots of her upper torso, white flakes of snow landing on her open dark blue blouse. The snow landing on her breasts melted, droplets forming in their place. I took a few photos of the flakes of snow, then reached over and took her blouse off entirely. Maybe it was the snow, maybe my state of arousal, maybe the time of month—but her breasts looked larger than I remembered. I didn't mind that at all! "Kevin! It's *freezing* out here!" she complained.

"It's just for a minute," I begged, then circled her, snapping as many photos as I could. The snow in the background, now barely hued as dusk fell, brought out the warm color of her flesh, and made her dark areola stand out even more. I took a few shots highlighting her face, but my favorite shots were the few I captured of her nipples just as flakes landed on them. The close-ups look spectacular. I don't believe I've ever seen a photo of nipples with snowflakes on them, and the ephemeral nature of the images made the photos even more wonderful.

I took a few dozen quick shots before Michelle said, "Okay, mister, enough's enough. I'm *freezing!*" She grabbed her clothes and headed back into the house. Naturally, I followed the beautiful topless woman like a puppy with his tail wagging. Watching her tail wagging. Once we got back downstairs, I showed her some of the photos and she had to admit she liked them too. Looking at the photos together was arousing for both of us. We spent the next hour in bed, although she wouldn't let me touch her breasts much, saying they're too sore.

Snowflakes on Nipples

The snow falls
in the cold December air
I open her blouse
to reveal her breasts

her nipples harden
unmolested
until
a flake
and another,
and then again
lands on her breast

hesitates

then melts into a small
droplet
resting on her areola.

They say
no two are alike

February 25th
We were snuggling on the sofa, in the midst of post-oral sex bliss. Or at least I was, since I was the sole recipient this time. I was very content, in a half-stoned, half-energized bliss only Michelle has ever evoked in me simply through the use of her mouth.

She was topless—I prefer her topless when she goes down on me, it makes it even more exciting—and she leaned her head against my chest. I had a shirt on, but it was unbuttoned and she was running her fingers through my chest hair. I'm glad she likes my chest hair—if she was one of those girls who only liked men whose chests were bald it'd be a pain.

My leg was propped up on a pillow. Every now and then it aches, especially if I've been outside in the cold too long. I try to keep it elevated when I'm not on my feet.

I thought Michelle was also in a state of bliss until I felt something warm and wet drip onto my chest. About the same time, I heard her sniffle. In my ignorance, or bliss, or whatever, I thought, *She's so happy, she's crying!* This illusion was shattered when I put my hand under her chin and pulled it up to look in her eyes. What I saw in her eyes was far from bliss.

"What are you crying about?" I asked, feeling the stirring of alarm.

She looked away from my eyes. Hmm.

"I'm kind of afraid to tell you," she replied after a minute.

My paranoia kicked in big time. *Here it comes,* I thought, *she's going to admit she's been talking with Wayne and thinks about him all the time. That's why she hid his photos upstairs. Or she's going to tell me she found someone else via the radio.*

Despite the instant ache in my heart and the painful way my stomach lurched, I managed to calmly say, "C'mon, Hon, you know you can tell me anything. No secrets, right?"

She sighed and said, "It's not like I could keep this from you anyway." She sat up on the couch with a resigned look on her face.

My paranoid heart said, *See, what'd I tell you. Here it comes.*

"Keep what from me?" I managed to say. And, being the knucklehead I am, I blundered forward, straight into yet another quagmire caused by my own insecurities or scars or well-earned lessons in abandonment.

"Are you going to tell me why you hid the photos of Wayne upstairs?"

She sat up straight and said, "What?"

"The photos. The ones of you and Wayne. I found them upstairs. You didn't hide them very well."

Michelle moved back on the sofa, away from me.

"Kevin, please. I really don't need this right now. You're not making it any easier."

Oh, so I'm supposed to make it easier for her to tell me she loves someone else? I thought. I was cognitively aware I was slipping once again into behavior that was bound to cause problems, but I wasn't able to control it. So I did the next best thing; I kept my fool mouth shut. After a few minutes, I said, "I'm sorry, please tell me what you're crying about."

Michelle looked away from me again and said, "I'm so afraid to tell you. I mean, you get jealous of stupid stuff, like those photos of me and Wayne. I didn't hide them from you. That was an ugly accusation. I put them in the dishwasher because that's where we put trash."

My paranoid delusion had no response. It was true. The sane part of me just said, *See?*

"I'm afraid to tell you because I don't know how you're going to react. The last time I had this talk, things didn't exactly work out."

"What didn't work out?"

"Do you remember when I told you about Wayne getting a job offer and walking out on me? That was true, but it wasn't the whole truth. I was afraid to tell you everything."

"What are you talking about?" I asked. Now I was confused and concerned. Part of me was completely flummoxed, the other part was preparing for the worst. She was about to change everything.

"He did walk out on me. But it wasn't because of the job offer. He walked out on me because he didn't want to be a father."

"Why would he walk out on you because of that? I don't understand."

She was crying a lot now, wiping her nose with the back of her hand, sniffling, and while giving the appearance of control she still wouldn't look at me. When she spoke, there was a slight edge of anger or exasperation in her voice. "Sometimes men are such blockheads. He walked out on me because *he didn't want to be a father*. And I had just told him he was going to be one."

She was right. Sometimes men are blockheads. I was still confused, still didn't get it. What was her point? "So what are you saying? That you and Wayne had a baby? That you're a mom? Or what?"

She looked at me, and with absolutely no humor in her red-rimmed eyes, she said, "You can really be such a dope. If I didn't love you so much, I'd run away. If there was someplace to go. No, I didn't have his baby." She looked down. Her eyes had dark circles under them, and her face was flushed and swollen from crying. Her hands were in her lap, and they were fidgeting with each other. "I'm afraid to tell you because I'm afraid you'll react like Wayne did. And I don't know what I'd do."

Suddenly I figured it out. It was like a blindfold being taken off.

"Michelle, are you trying to tell me . . . that . . ."

Tears streaming down her cheeks, with a look of stress, fear, and angst she glanced into my eyes and blurted out, "Wayne walked out on me because I told him I was pregnant. He tried to talk me into an abortion, but I said no. I wanted the baby, and I wanted Wayne to want it too, but he didn't. We fought about it and he left. He didn't come home that night."

"I was upset, and ended up driving to my folks' house the next day. They weren't expecting me, and even though they could tell something was up, they didn't ask. I spent most of a week with them. My dad seemed especially worried about me, and made sure to keep me company most of the time. But I wasn't able to talk about it for a few days. They finally sat me down and made me talk. I told them everything. They didn't know I was living with Wayne, so I had to tell them. Then I told them I was pregnant and he walked out on me. They hugged me and we all cried and for a few hours things felt better. But then after I went to bed, I heard them arguing. My mom was very upset and Dad was trying to reason with her."

Michelle went on, a leaden look in her eyes. "My mom was saying some pretty ugly things about me. I couldn't take it. The things she was saying—some were outright lies! She told my dad I'd been pregnant before and had an abortion! Kevin, that's an absolute a lie!" She now had a pleading look in her eyes.

"Kevin, you have to believe me! I never got pregnant before! I never had an abortion! Why would she say that? It's like she was trying to turn my dad against me!" She sighed, soft and long. "It wasn't the first time she'd been cruel. Dad never knew how things were when he wasn't around, and being a doctor meant he wasn't around plenty. When he wasn't there, Mom used to hit me. When I was old enough, and stronger than her, she went to hit me but I grabbed her wrist and twisted it, hard, and said "You will *never* hit me again!" And she didn't. She just changed her tactics, and became manipulative. She had me convinced I was worthless, would never amount to anything, and should leave all the thinking to her. I usually did—it was easier than fighting. And losing."

"A smart girl like you? Why would she—"

"Please let me finish," she begged, "let me get it over with!" She paused and then continued. "But even though she'd been mean, I'd never known her to try to turn someone against me. I just thought she didn't like me. Hearing her words, I felt betrayed. I thought back on my childhood. We were a close family. We used to go on vacation to incredible places. We used to go skiing in Colorado, we went to Hawaii once . . . but when I stood up to my mom, things changed. She turned on me. I'd caught a few glimpses of it in the past, but this was full-on distortion. So when I heard her saying such terrible lies about me, I packed up my things in the middle of the night and left without saying goodbye. I drove back to our apartment. Dad tried to call me a few times over the next week, but I wouldn't answer. I never heard from my mom. During the week I was gone, Wayne came back and moved out. He really did get a job offer in Chicago, and he really did walk out on me. I didn't lie to you. I've never lied to you."

I was awash in conflicting thoughts and emotions. Part of me was processing the awful story she was telling me, feeling very badly for what she had gone through. I couldn't imagine my parents turning against me, and I couldn't imagine *any* mother lying about her daughter to turn her own family against her! For Wayne to walk out on her at the same time, *while* she was pregnant with his child . . . geez. That could really mess someone up.

The other part of me was thinking *Is she trying to tell me she's pregnant? How do I feel if she is?*

I knew it was hard for her to tell me these things. No wonder she hadn't told me before. It was emotionally wrenching for her to even remember what happened. *(is she pregnant?)*

"I was lucky, I had some very supportive friends from church. One of them moved in with me. None of them knew I was pregnant, they just thought Wayne had moved out and I was heartbroken. A few of my friends had gotten abortions, and I didn't want them to try to talk me into having one, so I kept my pregnancy a secret. I started going to the clinic, started taking pre-natal vitamins, the whole bit. I was still mourning about Wayne, but I was excited about the baby. I hadn't deliberately chosen to be in my situation, but was going to make the best of it."

She paused for a long minute. I was watching her eyes, seeing her pupils dilate and then contract. Her memories were being played out in her mind's eye.

"Then one weekend when I was about six weeks along, while my roommate was out of town I started spotting. And I had a few mild cramps. I don't know why. I woke up in the middle of the night cramping badly. I had started bleeding but didn't know it. By the time I realized what was happening, it was too late. I lost the baby. I should have gone to the hospital, but I didn't really have anyone to take me. I still felt like it was this big secret I had to hide. In the morning, I stopped cramping and stopped bleeding. I made it to the clinic and they made me spend the night. I was anemic. They told me the baby was gone."

Damn. *(is she pregnant?)*

"So I lost my boyfriend, my parents, and my baby, all in about a month. When I ran into friends, they acted surprised to see me. Mom had started telling people I'd gotten into drugs and was pregnant by a man who abused and controlled me. She said they tried to talk sense into me but I wouldn't listen and refused to have anything to do with them. I told them I had no idea why she was saying those things. I told them I lived in an apartment with a girlfriend, that I wasn't pregnant and wasn't even dating anyone. They could sense I was telling the truth, which left them not knowing what to think. I went home and thought about it. My mom was telling people lies about me. She made it sound like she was a loving mother who was grieving over her lost daughter. She made it all my fault. My own mother, trying to turn people against me."

"That's awful, Michelle!" I reached out and took her hand. It was clammy. "What did you do?" I asked. *(is she pregnant?)*

"Remember the movie *Sleepless in Seattle?* There's a scene in there where the Tom Hanks character says something like, *I made myself get out of bed in the morning. I reminded myself to breathe in and out. After a while I didn't have to remind myself to breathe. After a while I didn't have to force myself to get out of bed.* That's what I did. Eventually I stopped fixating on how I'd screwed up so badly. I started trying to pull myself together, and after about a year of licking my wounds, I started nursing school. I moved here to do my clinicals at St. Joseph."

I was trying to think of something to say—something like, 'I'm glad you did,' or 'Thank God!' or something, but it all sounded trite and trivial. Before I could figure anything out, she looked at me with fear in her eyes and whispered,

"Kevin, I'm pregnant."

I sat there, staring at her. I felt like my brain was rebooting. Or maybe it wasn't—maybe it was stuck at a DOS prompt. Or maybe I'd just experienced a mental BSOD. My mouth was probably hanging open.

That's when my doubts disappeared. I knew how I felt. "You're pregnant. With my baby." Her eyes instantly took on a hard light. I saw a fire in them that stopped me in my tracks. I realized she thought I was questioning whether or not it was mine. I may have periods of paranoid delusional jealousy, but I'm not that far gone. Of course it was mine. Duh. I inched my way across the sofa and put my arms around her. At first she struggled, as if trying to protect herself. But when I started trying to kiss her, she stopped fighting. "Michelle, I'm so sorry all the bad stuff happened to you. I'm sorry your mom betrayed you. I'm sorry Wayne walked out on you. Well, no, I guess I'm not sorry about that, but I'm sorry he hurt you so bad. But *sweetheart*," I whispered, bringing my lips up to her ears, "I'm not Wayne. I'm not going to walk out on you. I'm not upset you're pregnant. In fact, I'm *thrilled!*" I leaned back away from her, grabbing her hands with mine in the process. I wanted her to see the look in my eyes. "Meeting and falling in love with you is the best thing that ever happened to me. Your being pregnant is a close second." As I said this, my face lit up in a smile. "I can't believe you're pregnant! This is great news! Here, feel my heart!" I placed her hand on my chest, much as she had done to me oh-so-long ago. "Feel how fast it's beating? That's because I'm very, very happy. I'm thrilled you're pregnant! I never thought I'd hear . . ." Now it was my turn to get choked up. My eyes were brimming. I leaned in to hug her and felt her arms encircle me. "I thought you were going to tell me something bad, like you had a disease, or you didn't love me, or you wanted me to sell Amway. I never even considered you might be pregnant! But, my God! I'm going to be a daddy! With our baby! I love you so much!"

The paranoid delusional, suspicious, neurotic part of me packed up its bags and walked out. He knew it was game over. I practically heard the door slam shut behind him.

Still half-crying, she said, "So you're not upset?"

"Yes, I'm upset! In a good way! The idea of you and me making a baby . . . it's wonderful news! Oh, my God, this means . . . January, December, November, October . . . you're going to have the baby in October!"

"Or maybe September, I'm not completely sure. Are you really happy about this?"

I got to my feet, ignoring the ache in my leg.

"Let's have a toast! Can you drink? Will it hurt the baby? Or, let's go have sex! Or, let's tell someone! Who is there to tell? Let's tell Doc! . . . Oh my *god*, I think I may just explode! Let's dance!!" I think that's what I said. I don't even know if I was making sense.

But she saw the absolute joy on my face and stood up, a smile breaking across her face like the warm sun breaking through clouds on a cool Michigan spring day after a recent shower.

"So you're really happy? You're not just pretending?"

I gave her a huge hug. "I'm very, very happy," I whispered in her ear.

She finally accepted the fact that not only was I not going to leave her, but I was happy with the news. She started laughing. And crying.

"I was so afraid you'd be upset," she said, "I didn't know what I'd do." She smothered my face with kisses. "I'm so relieved and happy! Yes, I'm going to have your baby! I love you so much, and I wanted to be happy, but I was afraid! Oh, Kevin, thank you for not being upset. Thank you for being happy! Thank you so very much for not being gay!" She reached out and grabbed my hand and then pulled me down onto the sofa with her. Then she immediately stood back up. "I'm going to have your baby! I'm going to have our baby! I'm going to have a *baby*! I'm going to be a mother!!" Suddenly she sat back down and her face grew pale. "Oh my God. I'm going to be a mother. What if start acting like my mother? What if Kevin Junior or Michelle Junior hates me?!"

I pulled her back up into my arms and said, "Now whose turn is it to be a knucklehead? You're a wonderful person, you're going to be a wonderful mother! When did you find out?"

"I started to suspect about a month ago. I was late, but I didn't have any way to find out. I don't exactly carry around pregnancy tests in my bag. I told Doc about it and he told me what I already knew—missing one period doesn't mean you're pregnant. But I've missed two now, and my body feels different. My breasts are getting bigger. See?" She unbuttoned her dark blue blouse and slowly took it off. God, I love it when she does that. It was especially nice since she'd been hiding them from me for a while. She wasn't wearing a bra (why bother?), so I was instantly treated to the sight of her full breasts. She was right, I could tell they were bigger, just as I noticed last week when I was taking the topless photos of her in the falling snow.

"Do you really think they're bigger? I can't really tell by looking," I lied. "I'd better have a hands-on check." I reached out and cupped both breasts in my hands, feeling the full weight of them. There was no doubt—what used to be a large handful was now *more* than a handful."

"Careful!" she warned, "they're very tender!"

"Do your nipples feel the same?" I said, lightly pinching them between my fingers and thumb.

"Ouch! I told you, they're sensitive! But I'll bet if you're gentle your mouth and tongue would feel nice," she said with a twinkle in her eye.

I leaned over and did exactly what she suggested—I used my mouth on her nipples. And on her kitty. And even though I'd just come a half hour earlier, I was already getting hard. Then we got naked, she straddled me and we had glorious sex.

When we were back to snuggling—the second time today—she started talking again. She told me she had been having conversations with Doc about it. He asked her a lot of questions and told her not to worry so much.

So that was who she was talking to. And that's what they were talking about. No wonder she's been acting strange and moody. She suspected she was pregnant and thought I'd toss her out. Good grief.

I leaned back on the sofa in the dim light, my mind racing. A lot of the pieces of the puzzle about her fell into place. Why she was single. Why she didn't talk about her parents much. Why she moved here—it was partially to escape, to start over. Then something occurred to me. "Michelle, you nut, why in the world did you give me a blow job right before you told me this?"

She blushed. "I thought it might put you in a good mood. But that's not the only reason. For some reason, I've been horny ever since I got pregnant. And tonight I really wanted to have you in my mouth. I wanted to have one last moment of intimacy before I told you, in case you threw me out. But then after you finished, I got sad, wondering if that was the last time I'd get to do have you in my mouth."

I started laughing. "A pregnant woman gave me a blow job this afternoon. I can't wait to put *that* in my journal!"

A pregnant woman gave me a blow job this afternoon.

Michelle is pregnant. With my baby. I can't get over it. I feel love and happiness and a twinge of fear. She won't have any medical care. No doctor or tests to run or sonogram. But women had babies long before there were sonograms or blood tests. We just have to be careful and smart.

Now she sleeps next to me. It's been a long day. Between the oral sex, the intense conversations, the paranoia, the revelation that I'm going to be a father, and the magnificent sex afterwards, I'm all done in. Not to mention the time it's taken me to write these thoughts down. I think I'll go crawl into bed with Michelle. Pregnant Michelle.

At Last She Sleeps

After hours of weeping
At last she sleeps

for the people she loved
and her family she weeps

halting and tearful
her despairing recollection

Of the places they went
Before their heartless disaffection

Back when they loved her
Back when they spoke

Back when they lived
Back when she hoped

March 19th

It's been just over a month since I wrote last. We've been busy, converting part of the storeroom into a nursery, raiding the houses in the neighborhood for diapers and baby food. I even found a copy of *What to Expect When You're Expecting.*

We're in the middle of a cold snap now, so we don't have to worry much about zombies attacking us when we're outside foraging. But we're always on our guard, looking for other people. When possible, we travel through back yards to avoid the street.

I worry about entering a home and being attacked by a survivor who thinks I'm a bad guy. So when I enter a house, first I gauge the temperature. If it's completely unheated, then obviously no one is living there. So far, every house has been pretty icy. Some of the houses' windows have broken, from zombies or survivors or bad weather, so the elements have had free access and so have the varmints. I have to be on my guard—one moment of distraction and Michelle would somehow have to survive her pregnancy and birth without my help.

The houses all seem to fall into one of three categories. Actually, four categories, but one category is finding survivors, which hasn't happened, so I've only come across three categories.

One: the house is empty. The owners bugged out.

Two: the occupants are in the house, dead at their own hand. I've come across some horrific scenes—in one house, just two streets over, I found a family of five, huddled together in bed. I saw no signs of struggle, no blood. I'm glad it's been so many months since they died, because I'm sure the stench must have been fierce back in the fall. As it was, the house still smelled bad, but it was tolerable.

The mother and father were probably in their early forties. They held what appeared to be a baby and two kids. The kids looked to be under the age of ten. It was difficult to tell, since most of their flesh had rotted away, and it looks like some kind of varmint got to them at one point. At least there weren't rats like in some houses.

After making sure the house was safe, I started looking for supplies and discovered the gas stove was open and the gas had been left on. The parents—one or both—must have planned it. They asphyxiated peacefully, as a family. At least the house didn't blow up.

Which might explain why some of the houses *did* explode or catch fire. I suppose some people may have turned the gas on, forgetting to turn off the pilot light.

But I found a treasure trove of goods in the house with the gruesome family scene. A crib, a baby bed, formula, baby food, even a lot of powdered milk and diapers. When I went back on my second trip, I even rounded up some stuffed animals and toys.

I have a lot of things to accomplish these days. Not much time for writing.

March 30th

Michelle is suffering with morning sickness. I know it's normal and usually wears off, but Doc says it sometimes lasts all nine months. I feel sorry for Michelle, but I also feel sorry for me—for whatever reason, the smell of hot coffee makes her puke. I've broken the coffee habit, but when I feel desperate I go upstairs and make coffee with the French-press. I drink the coffee while peeking out the windows, then dump the grounds into one of the pots filled with dead houseplants.

When I go back downstairs, I have to brush my teeth right away. We learned by experience that even coffee on my breath is enough to send Michelle racing for a bucket to throw up in.

Pregnancy has done wonders for her. Her breasts are getting bigger (yay!), and her areolas have doubled in size. It's very sexy, as is her baby bump. She's let me take a lot of photos. Sometimes after she falls asleep I get up and look at the photos. Her pregnant body is an unexpected turn on! Unfortunately, her sex drive has waned. Initially, she couldn't get enough, but now we only have sex three or four times a week. That's okay, I can deal with it. In fact, it's hard to feel sorry for myself when I recall friends complaining about their wives only wanting sex three or four times a year. Plus, when she's in the mood she still enjoys using her mouth on me. She's an oral artist.

Michelle's calling. I'd better run. She might need me to empty her barf bucket.

Life's a dream.

April 7th

Michelle is starting to show. She has a cute little baby bump. She still has morning sickness, too—I was hoping it would wear off. Strangely enough, she's gotten over her nausea from coffee. Now she drinks half a cup along with me, although we're trying to limit how much caffeine she gets.

I've been revisiting houses in the neighborhood, emptying them of anything we can use. Tools, weapons, even some art objects I liked. Plus diapers and formula. In one house I found a shoebox of Petoskey stones. I felt like I'd hit the jackpot.

I'm worried about Doc. I haven't heard from him for a few days. That's not like him. I keep the radio turned on all the time, hoping he'll call, but he hasn't. A lot of scenarios run through my head. Zombies, of course, but he could have been hurt in some kind of accident, or he could have gotten the flu, or maybe somebody broke in and attacked him. The problem is, something may have happened and I'll never know.

Michelle doesn't seem as worried about it as me. She says he probably went on a hunting trip or something. I sure hope he's okay. He's my only friend besides Michelle.

April 11th

Still haven't heard from Doc. Could he still be hunting? Do people hunt in March? What would they hunt for? I know most hunting seasons are in the fall—or were in the fall, but now I suppose it doesn't matter. Or maybe he's fishing. Maybe he loaded a canoe with camping gear and fishing equipment and is having a good time. Or, hell, maybe his radio broke somehow, or he ran out of fuel and has no power.

I had a frightening encounter today while scavenging. I go alone now, I don't let Michelle go with me. The further I get from our house, the more zombies I see. I avoid most of them.

I have to do everything I can to be ready for the baby. I need diapers—not just newborn diapers, but diapers to last until the baby's potty trained. That's two years or more! Geez, I have one hell of a lot of diapers to stock up on.

Which brings up another point: What on earth will we do with the dirty diapers? During warm weather I can bury them, but what about during the winter? Stack them up in a frozen mound outside? That's not very appealing. I guess I can toss them into the zombie dump.

We've had a warm spell for the past week. Highs in the 40s, lows in the 20s. The zombies are moving a bit faster. I don't believe it's an early spring—it's way too early. I recall plenty of snowstorms in May.

When I go scavenging, I take along a small glass cutter left from my feeble attempt to create stained glass windows years ago. I use the glass cutter to make a small hole in a window, just large enough for me to reach my hand in and unlock the window (or door, if it's a storm door or sliding glass door). There's no point in causing any more damage than I have to, plus it's much quieter than smashing a window or forcing a door.

Earlier today I was on my bike, towing a small wagon I use to haul stuff. I crossed over into Dicken, a neighborhood nearby. I'd say the houses sold in the $200,000 range and up. They're fancier, the lots are larger, and hopefully their pantries are larger.

I was being as stealthy as I could. That's not easy—obviously the streets haven't been cleaned, so they're filled with dead leaves, small branches, and acorns under oak trees. No matter how careful I am, I can't help but make noise. When zombies hear me they start moving in my direction, but they're slow enough to avoid as long as I don't stay in one spot too long.

I pulled down a side street and went around the back of the first house. It was a two story brick house, nicely maintained. When I got to the back door, I saw it had been forced open, perhaps recently. It looked like someone used a crow bar. I entered cautiously—whoever had broken in could still be here. I stood still just inside the door, listening, looking, sniffing. I couldn't smell the stench of zombie. I couldn't see anything amiss. I didn't hear any sound. It was very cold in the house—probably in the mid-30s, which confirmed no survivors lived there. The door I entered led into the kitchen. There were a few dishes on the counter and in the sink. A bouquet of dead flowers was on the kitchen table, along with some mail and a newspaper, the Sunday edition of the Ann Arbor news. The headline read: *DISEASE CONFIRMED IN ANN ARBOR*. It was from mid-

September, about the time I rode my bike out past Dexter.

The cabinet doors were open and most cabinets were empty. Checking around, I found nothing I could use. No food, no drugs, no alcohol or weapons. Usually I can find *something* I can use, but this time I struck out. Someone beat me to the punch.

This bothered me for several reasons. One, it indicated there were other scavengers. Two, if they were going house to house like I was, they would eventually get to our neighborhood. And to our house. That could be serious bad news. Three, by beating me to the punch, they are taking things I need.

According to my way of thinking, canned goods, dry goods, alcohol—once they're gone, there will be no more. Maybe ever. What's easy pickings now will end up being impossible to find later.

Not knowing if the person or people were still around, and feeling nervous about it, I decided to head back home. I was walking the bike back to the front when I noticed movement out of the corner of my eye.

I immediately flattened myself against the wall. Peering around the corner, I could see a man across the street a couple doors down, loading a bunch of cans into a grocery cart near the front door. He had a German Shepherd with him. When he finished loading the cans, he went back in the house and a few minutes later came back with more stuff.

I noticed he had a pistol tucked into his jeans. I decided it would be best to avoid him.

I grabbed my bike and quietly began to move toward the back yard. I had only taken a few feet when I stepped on a stick that broke with a loud *snap!*

Immediately the dog started barking, and it sounded like it was running my way. At the rear of the yard was a chain link fence—I ran toward it, threw my bike and my wagon over, then vaulted over. Of course, the bike and wagon crashing to the ground made even more noise.

I left the wagon where it landed, but grabbed my bike and ran behind a tool shed. Just as I rounded it, I heard the dog come racing into the yard, barking and growling.

As it continued barking, I heard a male voice say, "Sic 'em, Matey!"

The dog bounded over to the fence and continued barking. Thank god there was a fence between us, because his bark alone scared the shit out of me. The dog kept barking, racing along the side of the fence. I stood pressed against the shed, wondering what the man was doing. I felt like I stood there for a half hour. I tried to breathe as quietly as possible, and my heart pounded in my chest.

"Matey, come," I finally heard him say. The dog gave a few last barks, then retreated, following his master back toward the front. At least I hoped so.

I didn't dare move until I was sure the man and dog were gone. After about five minutes of silence, I dropped to the ground and inched my way along the shed to peer around the corner.

No sign of man or beast. Thank god. I was about to get my butt home as fast as I could—this was the first survivor I'd seen, and it unnerved me—but then started reconsidering.

What if this man wasn't a bad guy? What if he was like me? Maybe we could help each other.

How was he surviving? Were there others with him?

Was he a threat?

Plus, knowing he could come scavenging in our neighborhood—it didn't sit well with me. I decided I had to at least *try* to find out something about him. I left the wagon and bike and jumped a few side fences until I was a half-block or so away. Then I cautiously made my way between two houses and crawled along some bushes in front of one of the homes. From there I watched the man make a couple more trips into the house and load the shopping cart.

He began to wheel the cart down the street, the dog warily following along. When they got a decent distance in front of me, I skirted to the next house, then the next, following them discreetly.

He took a few side streets, and after about a half mile I saw him approach a large building. As I got closer, I could tell it was a school. He opened one of the side doors with a key, then the man, dog, and cart all disappeared. The door closed with a *clang!*

I took a look at the grounds and saw a playground and basketball goals. An elementary school. As I thought about it, I realized it was a pretty smart place to hunker down. Schools have a lot of security features. The doors were solid metal, the classroom windows were very small and barred, and there was a lot of open space around the buildings. Good for surveillance. Looking closer, I could see security cameras. I wondered if he had electricity.

The school would be equipped with a large kitchen, limited medical supplies, showers, and probably with a large pantry filled with enough food to feed hundreds of kids.

He had a good setup. I didn't begrudge him. I still didn't know if he was alone or not—for all I knew, there could be hundreds of people inside. Or there could be just one man. And a dog. Keeping all this in mind, I headed back to my bike. I decided it was time to get home. Being outside like this made me suddenly feel very vulnerable.

I also realized it would be as easy for someone to follow me as it had been for me to follow him. So I took a circuitous route, at first deliberately heading the wrong direction, took a bunch of side streets, dodging zombies in the street, and when I felt safe, I rode as fast as I could without upsetting the wagon, hoping to shake anyone who might still be trailing me.

Just because you're paranoid doesn't mean you're wrong.

April 13th

Today started out a fairly typical day. We tended the plants and harvested some spinach and some herbs and tomatoes. The tomato plants are starting to play out. We added fertilizer, adjusted the pH, etc.

We've had a cold snap (lows in the single digits, highs in the 20's) and another light snow, so we took advantage of our current relative safety to get rid of the trash we'd accumulated during the warm spell. There was a time when I would have complained about the smell, but compared to rotting zombies, stinky trash is almost pleasant.

We also emptied out the water we couldn't recycle—the water from boiling noodles and vegetables, the water I drained from the hydroponic reservoirs when the TDS meter showed a significant salt buildup, urine, etc.

I started a lot of tomato and pepper plants. A month from now I'll be putting my garden in. And this time, it won't be just for the delight of fresh vegetables; now I need the food to survive. I usually buy my garden plants at the nursery, but those days are long gone, like most of the things I took for granted.

After I hauled the trash outside, I loaded it onto a large piece of cardboard we use for hauling over the snow, and headed for our current trash dump. I also wanted to check for more zombies in the neighborhood and to check the zombie bodies in the burned-out house. It doesn't look like the zombies' bodies have been disturbed. Apparently, even coyotes don't like dead zombies.

I dumped the trash, then began scouting the maze of streets, sort of on patrol. My own neighborhood watch. I was looking for any sign of survivors, and also trying to figure out which houses I hadn't explored yet.

I had crossed back over into Dicken, the neighborhood close by. As soon as I got beyond the area we'd cleared, I found a lot more zombies. They were slow with the cold. I had my axe with me, so I chopped the heads off a dozen. A dozen is about all I can handle when they're frozen, then my shoulder starts aching again.

I finally decided to head home. When I crossed the side street where I'd seen the man and his dog, I saw footprints in the snow. My heart started beating faster. The trail led from north to south. I looked around, uncertain. I was sure I hadn't gone down that street, but the trail seemed to be leading from the direction of the house. That's when it hit me: I hadn't made those prints. Which meant only one thing!

I started running back to the house. Running through snow while carrying an axe isn't easy. I let go of the cardboard and kept running. I tripped over hidden stuff under the snow a couple of times and bloodied up my left hand. I was mentally castigating myself, cursing my stupidity with every step. What an idiot I had been! Every time I went outside in the snow, I'd left a trail leading right to our house! Any bad guy, any thief, any rapist or murderer could easily find us.

When I finally opened the door to our house, I could hear a man's voice. My worst fear realized! Maybe it was the guy I saw with the dog. Maybe he'd followed me. I took the steps three at a time. I could smell freshly brewed coffee. I heard Johnny Cash singing *I'll Take You Home*

Again, Kathleen. Time slowed down. I felt a burst of adrenalin energy. I rushed into the living room, my axe at the ready, anxious to dispatch whoever was threatening Michelle. Then I stopped cold in my tracks.

Michelle was there. So was a man I'd never seen. He had a pistol strapped to his chest. It wasn't the man with the dog.

The crazy, paranoid part of me briefly reared his ugly head, and I thought *Is that Wayne?* Michelle's eyes grew wide as I burst into the room. I must have looked like a complete lunatic.

"Leave us the hell alone!" I shouted, raising the axe up to my shoulders. "I've gotten pretty good at cutting off heads!"

The man approached me, smiling, empty hands out to his side. "Easy there, Kevin. You don't want to put an axe through the head of a friend."

"Kevin! No!!" Michelle cried out.

The man continued approaching me, and at the last minute stuck out his hand. "I'm Steve. Doctor Steve. Doc."

Epilogue

It was a simple ceremony.

Michelle and I had talked to Doc, and asked if he would officiate, even though he's not an ordained minister. You can imagine our surprise when he told us we were wrong.

"I became a legally ordained minister about fifteen years ago," he explained, "mainly to piss off my ex. I was an early user of MySpace, and I posted a scan of my ordination certificate because I knew she secretly visited my page."

I asked him if he went to seminary, and he laughed. "No, not me. I used one of those internet sites that ordains you for free with no requirements. It is a legally binding ordination, there just isn't any religious affiliation, education, or training involved."

So we had a bride, a groom, and a minister.

That morning, Michelle made me go upstairs while she got dressed. I thought she was being silly, but I'm no fool—on a woman's wedding day, you don't argue with her. Besides, I had to go upstairs to get my dust-covered tuxedo.

Doc went back and forth between us, playing gopher, and generally amusing himself with our nervousness. When Michelle was finally ready (a full forty-five minutes after our agreed upon ceremony time), Doc had me come downstairs and go into the bathroom with the door closed, while Michelle went up the stairs. Our stairwell is the closest thing we have to an aisle, and Doc insisted on a grand entrance for the beautiful bride.

We didn't have a copy of Chopin's *Wedding March*, so instead we played *Spring* from Vivaldi's *Four Seasons*. I was standing in the living room with Doc standing next to me.

When Michelle descended the staircase, I couldn't take my eyes off her. She was wearing a beautiful dark blue dress she'd retrieved from her house, and had even made some kind of veil. Her baby bump was adorable. In her arms she held a bouquet of flowers. Her face was radiant as she came forward to join me—the smile on her face practically lit up the room. I must have been standing there with my jaw agape, because she giggled and put her hand under my chin to raise it, forcing my mouth closed. That made me blush a little, and Doc laughed.

Doc's ceremony was short and sweet. He told us we were gathered here before God and each other to join our lives together, then turned to me and said, "Kevin, do you take Michelle to be your wife, to love, protect and nurture, til death do you part?"

"I do."

He turned to Michelle. "Michelle, do you take Kevin to be your husband, to love, protect and nurture til death do you part?"

"I do."

He turned back to me. "Kevin, do you have a ring signifying your love for Michelle? If so, please place it on her finger."

I dug the ring out of my pocket and laughed nervously when I saw my hands shaking while putting the ring on her finger.

He turned to Michelle. "Michelle, do you have a ring signifying your love for Kevin? If so, please place it on his finger." Michelle cradled the bouquet in the crook of her arm while she reached over and pulled the ring off her right hand where she'd kept it, then placed it on my finger. Our eyes met, and we were both smiling—and yet we were tearing up at the same time.

"I do charge you by oath to faithfully terminate the life of your beloved should he or she become infected by a zombie, as a sure sign of your love and loyalty to each other, and ask you to signify your fealty to this oath by saying 'I do'."

"I do," we replied in unison.

"By the power vested in me by the Universal Life Church and the state of Michigan, I now pronounce you husband and wife. Kevin, you may kiss your bride."

I pulled her to me and gave her what started out to be a tender kiss, but soon blossomed into a longer, passionate kiss.

"Easy now, kids, save it for later when I'm not around," Doc said with a grin.

For dinner we splurged on canned ham, fresh salad (which isn't very special for Michelle and me anymore), some very nice Old Mission Peninsula wine, and Michelle had baked a cake mix she scavenged. It wasn't a white cake, just a yellow one, but the chocolate icing made it pretty tasty. Doc had his fair share of bourbon.

I asked about the flowers—that was Doc's doing. He'd scoured the neighborhood, looking for early daffodills and vernal witch hazel. God bless him!

After dinner we sat around, drinking more wine (except Doc—he stuck with bourbon), laughing and talking and listening to some of Doc's tall tales of life as a doctor. But about 10:30, Doc announced he was calling it a night, and gave us a surprise wedding gift: He'd changed the bedding upstairs and was sleeping up there, giving us the basement alone for the night.

"Don't think I'm doing it for your sake," he said, "I'd like to get some sleep tonight. This is your honeymoon, after all, and you young lovers have a tendency to get loud." Michelle and I both blushed, but Doc laughed it off. "Enjoy yourselves. I'm very happy for you and very jealous." After filling a highball glass with bourbon, he grabbed his sleeping bag and headed up the stairs, closing the trap door behind him.

"We have the place to ourselves!" I marveled, as I heard the trap door close.

"We don't have to be quiet . . . !" Michelle sighed.

"We can walk around naked."

We raced for the bedroom, fingers already unbuttoning our clothes, while visions of sugarplums—or something even better—danced in our heads.

ABOUT THE AUTHOR

James is a graphic designer by profession who spends much of his time engaged in his favorite hobbies; writing, photography, singing in a variety of choirs and a barbershop quartet, hydroponic gardening, brewing and drinking beer, and perfecting his Zombie Blood hot sauce *("Reanimate Your Taste Buds")*. He lives in Athens, Georgia with his wife, Gretchen, while dreaming of northern Michigan. This is his first novel.

Follow the author on www.myzombiehoneymoon.com for the continuing saga of Life in the Age of Zombies, including information about the soon to be published sequel, *Zombies In Paradise*.

Made in the USA
Middletown, DE
04 August 2015